SEKRET MACHINES

BOOK 1

CHASING SHADOWS

SEKRET MACHINES

From the
imagination of

TOM DELONGE

with *New York Times*
bestselling author
Foreword by
Jim Semivan,
FMR Senior CIA Officer

A.J. HARTLEY

BOOK 1

CHASING SHADOWS

Sekret Machines Book 1: Chasing Shadows
Copyright © 2016 by Tom DeLonge

To The Stars, Inc.
1051 S. Coast Hwy 101 Suite B, Encinitas, CA 92024
ToTheStars.Media
To The Stars… and Sekret Machines is a trademark of To the Stars, Inc.

Cover Design by Jesse Reed
Book Design by Lamp Post
Managing Editor: Kari DeLonge

Manufactured in the United States of America

ISBN 978-1-943272-15-0 (Hard Cover trade)
ISBN 978-1-943272-16-7 (eBook)
ISBN 978-1-943272-17-4 (Hard Cover Limited Edition)
ISBN 978-1-943272-29-7 (Trade Paperback)

Distributed worldwide by Simon & Schuster

*This book is dedicated
to my children, Ava and Jonas,
as we are all trying to build
a better world for
the next generation.*

TOM'S ACKNOWLEDGMENTS:

I WOULD NOT BE HERE PRESENTING THIS HUGE WORK OF art if it wasn't for my beautiful wife Jennifer supporting me and believing in my infinite madness—

To our adventure together and beyond.

A.J.'S ACKNOWLEDGMENTS AND THANKS

THOUGH THIS IS A WORK OF FICTION IT IS GROUNDED AS much as possible in real places and events. As a result, a tremendous amount of research had to go into writing the book and I couldn't have done it without a lot of expert opinion from the armed services and intelligence community, some of which, for obvious reasons, must remain anonymous. I can thank Marine pilots Janine Spendlove and "Timmy" Hurst; Gray Rinehart on spaceflight engineering; Chris Hartley on satellites and other orbiting tech; and Peter Levenda on Operation Paperclip and Nazi research. Any errors of fact or judgment in the book are entirely mine. My thanks always to the team at To The Stars, to my editor Peter Nelson, to David Wilk, to my agent, Stacey Glick, and to my family who indulge my work beyond all reasonable expectations. I am deeply grateful to you all and to those whose names I can't reveal here. Lastly, a special thanks to Tom DeLonge without whom this book would not have been written, and whose creative vision and yearning for answers was the origin of this novel.

FOREWORD

In early April 2016, a good friend of mine, a former senior intelligence officer with a strong interest in Unidentified Aerial Phenomena (UAP), called me and asked if I had ever heard of Tom DeLonge from the punk rock band, Blink-182. I had not, as my musical tastes ceased growing somewhere between Motown and classic rock. Aware of my own lifelong interest in UAP and what is now commonly referred to as the Phenomenon, my friend suggested that I listen to a recent interview Tom had done on *Coast to Coast* radio about his new book, *Sekret Machines: Chasing Shadows*, and remarks on his coterie of former and current U.S. Government advisors who were offering him guidance on what they purportedly knew about the Phenomenon, or at least offering helpful hints on how Tom and his company, To The Stars, Inc., could approach the subject matter in books and films with a degree of veracity. The interview was illuminating, primarily due to Tom's desire to research and disseminate information on the Phenomenon in a more balanced and scientifically rigorous fashion than is currently being done in some of the popular literature on the subject. To me, this sounded like a highly innovative and worthwhile endeavor. And as a career civil servant, I found that Tom's intent to portray the U.S. Government in a more positive light was an added plus. Within a few weeks, Tom and I managed to synchronize our schedules and get together for some very long and animated discussions that culminated in an agreement to work together, through Tom's company, To The Stars, Inc., on advancing credible research on the Phenomenon and reporting this research to the general public. I readily agreed to work with Tom because I found him to be a highly innovative, creative artist with a very serious mission to get the message out on this most perplexing, complex and intriguing subject. In his own parlance, he is gnarly.

My own fascination with the Phenomenon started in earnest while I was an undergraduate and later a graduate student majoring in English literature and American Romanticism. Reading the visionary and mystical poetry of William Blake and the transcendental musings of the American Romantics fueled my interest in the "other." It was only a short leap for me to the works of the seventeenth-century Swedish mystic Emanuel Swedenborg (who knew Emerson had so many of Swedenborg's works in his library?), Christian Mysticism, Mystery Schools, and then onward to the vast library of metaphysical literature. Those on the journey recognize the path. As for my formal introduction to the Phenomenon, as we know it in today's context, it came suddenly and unexpectedly. I will not attempt to go into the experience here, but I will say that it was one of life's game changers for both my wife and me. The experience was simultaneously frightening, perplexing, frustrating and absurd. It was also both physical and emotional, although I am undecided as to whether there was any spiritual addendum. Almost thirty years later, I am still not sure what to make of the experience. What I do know, however, is that this event changed my view of what constitutes our collective version of reality.

I joined the Central Intelligence Agency in 1983 and had a wonderful twenty-five-year career there, working briefly for the Directorate of Science and Technology and then later transferring to the Directorate of Operations, the clandestine service, for the bulk of my career where I served as an operations officer. I was later promoted into the ranks of CIA's Senior Intelligence Service. I bring this up for two reasons: full disclosure, and as background on how I approach the peculiar nature of the Phenomenon. As an intelligence officer, I was taught that my primary job was to collect information—intelligence—for the president. And that the information I collected had to be well sourced and vetted thoroughly and properly. In other words, the information had to be as accurate and truthful as humanly possible. And this is the same approach I use when discussing the Phenomenon. Speculation is fine in and of itself, and when dealing with something as complex and extraordinary like the Phenomenon, speculation is more often than not all we have to work with. But we must always label speculation as such and not muck up further what is already a vast and murky body of literature on the subject, much of which is barely intelligible. And I am convinced that this is how Tom also wants to approach research on the Phenomenon. Having said the above, however, I am very much aware, particularly in regard to the Phenomenon, that this measured and linear approach is arguably laughable. How do you make sense of any of it when there does not appear to be any apparent "there" there? The Phenomenon seems to work on another level (consciousness, dimensions?) unknown to our science. A friend once remarked to me that it perhaps the Phenomenon seems to exist at the nexus of quantum mechanics and consciousness. If that is so, and I personally believe this may be a viable way forward, then our science needs to expand its horizons to include things beyond the quantifiable and replicable.

If you work in the Intelligence Community (IC) and follow the Phenomenon, then you are aware that there is no readily identifiable place in the IC that houses a department or unit that works exclusively on UFOs or UAPs or any other type of paranormal phenomena. (Read John B. Alexander's wonderful book, *UFOs: Myths, Conspiracies, and Realities*, for a look at how the inner workings of our military and intelligence communities deal—or do not deal openly—with this issue.) I have worked across the CIA and various elements of the IC throughout my career, and I can state that I have never happened upon a place that looks at this topic, exclusively or otherwise. Does that mean the U.S. Government does not investigate UFOs, UAPs, or other paranormal phenomena? In my opinion, they probably do. And I also believe what John Alexander has said in his book, that "disclosure has already happened, it is confirmation that we are after."

UAPs are real. The Phenomenon is real. There is no way to deny or refute all the evidence accumulated over just the last few decades alone. But what is the Phenomenon, exactly? What intruded, uninvited, into my life almost thirty years ago? Well, that is the quest Tom and To The Stars, Inc., are pursuing, pulling together a strong team of scientists, researchers and adventurers willing to venture into the unknowable for answers. We may stumble upon something that we should not have disturbed; then again, we may just fall headlong into a new realm of existence that has been hidden from us and has always been our birthright.

If you are interested in the Phenomenon, get started by reading the many wonderful and informative books by Jacques Vallée and Hal Puthoff on the Phenomenon and its many tributaries.

I hope you will love reading *Sekret Machines: Chasing Shadows* as much as I did. It is a well-written and thoroughly enjoyable work of science fiction with engaging characters, a thrilling plot line and enough real science to spark the imagination. Fare forward.

Jim Semivan
Alexandria, VA
November 2016

INTRODUCTION

FOR AS LONG AS I CAN REMEMBER, I HAVE SOUGHT ANSWERS. That search led me to the escape of music, expressing thoughts through my lyrics, voice, and guitar. But it was only one thread of the search. Time saw other paths emerging as family and businesses and hobbies. But I found no challenge for that which was understood—I had a need to find answers to the unexplainable, knowing that the odds of success were even less than that of a kid becoming a rock star. We humans are creation engines, both in thought and physical objects. When my thoughts are challenged by consistent unknowns, I need answers to allow me to see the effects of those unknowns, hoping one day to stumble upon a clue as to their source.

UFOs became one of those journeys. UFOs—a vision consistent in mankind's journey from past to present while evading explanation. We have pondered, *"What are those things in the night sky whose movements defy gravity and explanation?"* Combine that with the physical world of mankind's amazing creations—harnessing science and technology to advance health, productivity, comfort, convenience, and security—to make answers that fall short of complete. And then there are the others that complicate the question—fame hounds, lunatics, and intellectuals polluting the search with distractions. I knew, and know, there has to be an answer. And it will be a simple answer once we hear it. But right now, that answer evades our understanding. It is like trying to understand the description of a color we have never seen.

As my search grew, opportunities arose—some as a result of that search, but others by fortunate circumstance. And so, it was an unusual summer morning in 2015 when I got the call from an old friend who worked at one of the largest and most elite defense contractors in United States. Even though he had recently retired, he told me for the first time his company was having an Open House: a day when relatives of employees can come and celebrate with their significant others (husbands, wives, mothers, fathers) in what they do on any given day under the guise of absolute secrecy. He asked me if I would be willing to introduce their "Lead Executive," the head of their advanced programs division ("The BossMan," as I call him to people who don't need to know the details of his identity) to the crowd. I instantly said yes, but said only if I can sit with him for a few minutes. I wasn't sure why I said that, I just knew that was an opportunity I needed to take advantage of.

When the meeting came, I took the bull by the horns, and I pitched him an idea, mostly about a benign idea I had for a project that could help the youth lose their cynical views of the Government and the Department of Defense. In many ways *Sekret Machines* was just that . . . and a few other things as well.

The meeting went well to say the least, and he said I could come up and give him more details at a second meeting.

That next meeting was the time I entered four layers of security; Guns, electronic code entry systems, hallways with speakers lining nondescript ceilings (playing "white noise" so nobody could hear each other's conversations), and a series of solid doors flanking my view, each with rotary locks and not a single window in sight. Maybe because all that was out there was . . . *nothing* . . . and that *nothing* was surrounding many miles of secret airspace directly above.

By the time I got into the half-assed pitch, I had way more than I bargained for, including two top engineering executives of the company, and another who, unfortunately, had done quite a bit of research on me. I talked about a lot of things, but I did NOT talk about UFOs. I was smarter than that. The issue was, that Exec knew that I was quite into that taboo subject. So she asked me point-blank: "What *are* your intentions with the . . . *conspiracy stuff?*"

I tried to dodge the question (knowing I'd just been caught long before ever leaving the damn runway), and by the grace of God I was saved by someone new walking in. The BossMan decided to attend. I thanked him for coming, he looked to the side, then back to my *fish-out-of-water eyes* and said, "We cannot be involved in any type of project whatsoever that has this topic associated with it, specifically because there's never been any evidence whatsoever that this stuff even exists." I thought: *Holy shit, I'm in trouble.* Were they monitoring my stress level? Did they know I was shitting my pants? I hadn't even pleaded my case yet.

The only thing I could think to say at that exact moment was this: "If Edgar Allan Mitchell—the sixth man to walk on the moon—is out telling every kid in the world that this topic is real, then we have a problem. But that's okay, we don't need to talk about this subject, or include this information, we just need to address these credibility issues at some point. But give me your time, please, to hear me out."

And then I went for a Hail Mary. "Sir, can I speak to you alone for five minutes?"

Everybody looked around at each other, baffled. Then, he said: "Sure."

Now, I cannot tell you what I said to this man in that meeting, and I cannot tell you about the hour-long conversation I had with the other two executives right afterward. But I *can* say that over the next few months things started to go light-speed for this project. I was no longer alone to offer a vision, an inspiration, a piece of *art* to provoke one's mind with possibilities. After all, are these not the gifts of literature and film?

I am here to tell you that an entire history of an unexplained and infamous myth—a *Legend*—IT'S ALL TRUE.

It started to get very serious when I got an email by The BossMan a few weeks later to meet next to the Pentagon at a certain day, at a certain time. He was going to introduce me to somebody who was "connected." You see, I grew some balls and sent him the prologue that Peter Levenda and I were working on for a series of nonfiction books, a thesis on certain elements within this project. And it seemed to have made quite the impression, because now I was on my way to meet "others."

I was scared when I entered the dark room; I had no idea whatsoever what I was walking into. I had no reason to be doing these types of things, anyway. But I was ignited by a passion within that it was time to put myself out there a bit and accomplish something I believe is hugely important. I spoke for about forty-five minutes straight as a man stared across at me from a wooden table with squinty, learned eyes. He had a beard, a suit tired from a full day's work, and a hand gripping his adjacent wrist: a posture that seemed full of confidence. He really did look straight out of a spy movie, if you've ever seen one.

After my speech, he watched me for a few seconds, then told me something I will never forget:

"Things like this do not happen at the White House, they do not happen on The Hill. They happen at places like this, at tables like this, where a few men get together and decide to push the ball down the field." Meeting was over. Jesus Christ, my heart was beating again. How fucking cool. Cool, but real. I must remember to not lose sight of that.

You see, I pitched a massive entertainment franchise that involved novels, feature films, nonfiction books, documentaries, and everything else that goes along with a story that's been told over decades and teaches people the truth about something that is almost too big to handle. I knew more than most that this phenomenon was scary, and everything that we did over the past sixty years was based on the enormity of the unbelievable task at hand. We had to rethink religion, history, national security, secrecy, physics, defense, space exploration, cosmology, *humanity*. But the generations of civilians who followed this matter felt left out, lied to, and disrespected.

And truthfully, after I jumped into this project and learned what I have, I realized we were rightfully treated the way we were. We *all* would've done the exact same thing if instead we were chosen to deal with the extraordinary. But we weren't, other brave men and women who came before us were, and they had to face the difficult consequences of such a reality. A reality demanding some type of strategy to "*comprehend ... and outwit*" (not my words, but those of one of my advisors).

I've had meetings in mysterious rooms far out in the desert. I've had meetings at the highest levels of NASA. I have had conversations at research centers, think tanks, and even on the phone connected to secret facilities. I've been introduced to a man whom I call "the Scientist," and another whom I call "the General." And there are many more of whom I cannot say much about, but some have become true friends, and all have become close counselors.

Each of these men has all held, or currently holds, the highest offices of the military and scientific elite.

The point is, I have done it. I have assembled a team of men and women "in the know." And they all believe I am doing something of value, something worth their time and yours.

All along I was never just another "conspiracy theorist." So don't be naive, and become one yourself. Don't regurgitate the same old alien tale. I was never immature about the matter, nor should you be. I respect the fact that it is a matter of national security, and I thoughtfully commiserate with the men and women dealing with what we could easily call the most important discoveries in mankind's brief history.

I MET A.J. HARTLEY ON THE PHONE FIRST, BUT IN PERSON many more times over the past year. We had a lot to go over. I had to start from ground zero with him; he knew very little about the phenomenon. He was a distinguished Shakespeare professor, a *New York Times* best-selling author, British through and through, but most importantly, an open-minded skeptic. At the end of the day he took in my madness with open arms and together we created an architecture to level the playing field once and for all. We have opened a door for you all to experience these topics in a way as if you were there yourself, which would, in all truth, be a frustratingly mind-blowing existence if you're not given the entirety of facts in one dose. A Shakespeare scholar and a rock star join forces. *Who would've thought?*

This first novel sets up many things: important events that had their genesis as far back as World War II and continue today. The events, locations, and moments of wonder are all true. We weaved them together in a way that echoes what really happened to those who stumbled across something spectacular, wondrous, and a bit frightful. The glue is fiction. The building blocks are not.

As earlier scientists, engineers, and leaders had to learn day by day, we will do the same with you, page by page. Once again, you will be given important information to live through as though you were there yourself. And by design, we are not answering all the questions that may be posed. A lot of these answers will come in later books, over time.

This subject is full of questions we've not been able to answer right away. Each event was studied closely, and sometimes it was painfully misunderstood and confusing at the time. There is just a lot more to the story than you and I could imagine. So we consciously tried to reflect that throughout the narrative, to give you time to digest and time to think back as to *what may be what.*

So to all my passengers taking a ride into the land of *Sekret Machines*, I have been granted the opportunity to tell you a story over a series of novels about the important events that happened over the past sixty years. These moments shaped our world in more ways than one. I know it seems unbelievable, but it's true.

And this all started because on a whim I asked The BossMan if he could speak to me alone for five minutes. Remember, he said: "Sure."

Well, this adventure may finish somewhere even more exciting.

I recently asked another important individual if there is a possibility to get support from The White House itself for the truth to be expanded upon, and communicated further within my project.

And that man said: "Sure."

—Tom DeLonge, 2016

SEKRET MACHINES

BOOK 1
CHASING SHADOWS

ALAN
Safid Kuh, Central Afghanistan, September 2014.

MAJOR ALAN YOUNG CHECKED THE HARRIER II PLUS' Heads-Up Display, put a few ounces of pressure on the throttle with his left hand and adjusted the trim with his right thumb. Far below the Harrier, the arid mountains of Afghanistan's Hindu Kush range rose and fell away, invisible in the darkness as the plane banked to starboard.

Deep in those mountains, a MARSOC team was already on the ground, working to secure an asset from a remote rebel base. Alan knew what he needed to know to complete his mission and was not interested in knowing more. It hadn't always been so, but he had learned the

1

discipline of incuriosity, a gift, his old flight instructor had been fond of saying, that kept on giving.

You don't need to understand the nail to be the hammer.

How many times had Alan heard that? A hundred? A thousand? And he heard it now, felt it in his bones with the hard, cold certainty of truth beyond faith. He had his mission, which, God willing, would be uneventful, a routine patrol in support of ground operations. If it became anything more than routine—and when you're pulling four hundred knots at altitude, nothing is truly routine—then something had gone wrong.

Alan had been flying AV-8Bs—Harriers—for eight years, three of them in Iraq and the last two in Afghanistan, the culmination of his twelve years as a Marine. He'd flown dozens of sorties and never seen a bogey, but that was hardly surprising. The enemies he'd faced had no air power to speak of. It was their GBAD systems and shoulder-fired SAM missiles you had to watch for.

And over-confidence.

But Alan had that under control. He'd let it out again once he'd returned to base, but until he was RTB, but there was no place for that *Top Gun* swagger up here. In ancient Rome, he'd once read, a legionary who put the lives of his comrades in jeopardy through cowardice, stupidity or some other disciplinary failure would be beaten to death in front of his unit. That seemed about right. Unquestioning loyalty to your superiors and to your comrades and the discipline to act upon it regardless of the circumstances was the frame, the purpose of your skills, your life. Alan Young happened to fly a $30 million airplane, but in his heart, he was simply a Marine.

The lead Forward Air Controller on the ground was Sgt. Barry Regis, a great bull of a man who had once—long ago and a world away—been the heart of an offensive line which had protected Alan when he had played quarterback for Monroe High back in North Carolina. Go Redhawks! It was a long and deep friendship that crossed lines of class, color, rank, and branch of service. Regis was also a pilot but, like other FACs, he was serving a ground tour and seemed to have found his calling. He joked that he'd done so because he was too big to fit into the cockpit of all but the most luxuriant of aircraft.

"The Air Force wanted me," he once told Alan, "but they woulda had to slather me up with butter and jimmy me into the F-16s." He made squelching, oily sounds with his mouth and made a show of running his huge, dark hands over his body.

There would be no jokes tonight, not until they were back at Camp Leatherneck.

With Regis was a twelve man Marines Special Ops team with three objectives: infiltrate the enemy base and eliminate all resistance by capturing or killing its leader; locate and recover a pair of computer hard drives; and, most challenging of all, locate and extract a captured US operative—alive. Even with all his emotions iced for flight, that last task left a knot in Alan's gut.

It was hard enough getting a team into a secure facil-ity, but to do so undetected, before some zealous insurgent

3

could run back to a holding cell and put a bullet in the head of his captive, was next to impossible. The team had HALOed in shortly after moonset and had spent the last three hours making their approach on foot and in silence. The closer they got, the more dangerous it was. If they were detected even thirty seconds before they were in position, all that planning and preparation would be for nothing.

Alan circled twenty kilometers from the LZ ready to throttle up at the first sign of trouble, but otherwise content to patrol the night sky, where the roar of his engines wouldn't alert enemy sentries, until Barry Regis called him in. In the Air Force, he might have flown strike missions—fly out, drop your ordinance and fly back on schedule—but that was not how the Marines worked. Alan was flying tactical Close Air Support, like the "taxi rank" Typhoons and Tempests called in to deal with stubborn Nazi armor at the end of World War II. You got close to the combat zone, and waited for the call. It made Alan feel a little like one of the black buzzards back home, in the sky above the woods of North Carolina, drifting aimlessly until the scent of death brought it swooping down . . .

Regis' voice came in over the radio. "Black Eagle, you there?"

"Copy that, Rattlesnake," said Alan. "What's your status?"

"Five hundred meters southwest of the facility. Still undetected. Insertion teams are performing final weapons checks. Closing in two mikes."

"Roger that, Rattlesnake," said Alan. "Be right there."

So saying, he tipped the Harrier hard to the port and squeezed the throttle, feeling the pressure on his head and chest as the plane leapt forward. As he reentered level flight, Alan flicked on his fire control station and scrolled through the available munitions. The Harrier Mark II, as well as being unique in the Marine air force in its short takeoff and vertical landing capacity, could be armed with bombs, missiles and guns suited for a variety of targets in the air, on the ground, or in water, and could rain down all manner of hurt on anyone unfortunate enough to find themselves in the pilot's sights. But you didn't carry bombs if you were going into a dogfight, and you didn't carry air-to-air missiles when there was no possibility of running into enemy air power. Civilians thought the Harrier, also capable of vertical takeoff, could also hover, hanging in place like a helicopter gunship over the battlefield, but it couldn't. You got in, high and at speed, and then you got out.

Alan checked his navigation display. It was a moonless night. He was flying entirely on instruments, so that though he could sense the motion of the plane, it was weirdly directionless, something like being in an elevator. Intellectually, you know what's going on, and your body knows *something* is happening, but a part of you is still very slightly surprised when the doors open and you're on a different floor. Sometimes pilots flying in dense cloud cover or darkness emerged upside down, their senses baffled by the strange combination of solitude and sensory deprivation.

Which is why you don't rely on your eyes when you have state-of-the-art computer systems to tell you when you're upside down.

Old pilots romanticized the glory days of propellers and non-fly-by-wire mechanical controls and peering around to see if anything was about to blow you out of the sky, but Alan would take his APG-65 radar, his forward-looking infrared sensors and his AN/AAQ-28(V) LITENING targeting pod, thanks very much.

He doubted he would need them tonight. When the MARSOC team was done, they were to be reclaimed—with their recovered human and technological assets—by four Night Hawks, two of which were MH-60L DAP models packing the fire power of a battleship. The rebel position—base was too grand a term—was a huddle of cinderblock and mud brick buildings nestled on a mountain slope so steep it was nearly a cliff face. There was a warren of tunnels and caves beneath the buildings, a perfect place to hold prisoners and engage in secret meetings. It was too rugged and too remote to reach with serious armor, which meant the insurgents would have to rely on whatever weapons they could carry. There was a small tabletop plateau, about a hundred meters from the compound, which would serve as an LZ for the Night Hawks. The enemy would be looking to make landing difficult, and that was where Alan came in.

Dropping fast from fifteen thousand feet, the Harrier rode the night air like a dragon, all fire and peril. He was cruising at three hundred knots and keeping the angle of bank to a minimum, but the Harrier was a notoriously finicky bird to fly, those wings requiring a firm hand and constant concentration even when you weren't trying to direct the multi-nozzled exhaust ports. All jet fighters were fast, but the Harrier was easier than most to lose track of, and if you "got behind" the aircraft, as the pilots said, you were lost.

Alan mentally checked off the plane's available munitions—Paveway laser guided bombs, a couple of AGM-65 Maverick air-to-ground missiles, two heat-seeking Sidewinders, and a 25mm cannon in a pod below the fuselage. It was a formidable arsenal. If he stopped to consider it, Alan might find a moment to pity those he was about to target, but it would not stay his trigger finger for even a fraction of a second. He had his orders. There were men on the ground who needed his support.

He'd learned at his preflight briefing that the asset's name was Morat, a deep cover operative who'd been captured with classified information and technology on his person. He was being held, according to signals intelligence, at this remote location by an enemy who would soon spirit him away to a new location, where they would torture him for what he knew, then execute him. The strike team had been assembled hurriedly, in hope of getting Morat out before the enemy realized what they had stumbled upon. Both SIGINT and HUMINT indicated these were not goatherds turned half-assed freedom fighters but seasoned Mujahedeen. It would be a mistake to assume they didn't know what they were doing. Even goatherds had cell phones and computers, and access to information and communication systems unimaginable only a few years ago. The billions of dollars of tech that kept his Harrier in the air didn't protect him from the terrible knowledge base which was the Internet.

"Black Eagle, this is Rattlesnake," said the radio. "Sentries eliminated. Team positioned to enter facility. No indication we've been detected. Lighting up LZ GBAD targets now."

"Roger that, Rattlesnake," said Alan. "Black Eagle on course to engage. Stay clear of target."

Alan dropped his heavy NVGs over his eyes and saw, ahead in the darkness, two infrared lasers, invisible to the naked human eye. He swung the Harrier hard to port—performing the hiccupping breathing pattern as he felt the aircraft pulling Gs—then began his bombing run.

Ten nautical miles to target.

Alan shifted fractionally, squeezing out some of the tension that was building in his back and performed a final systems check. Directly ahead, washed by the pale glow of starlight, he could just make out the cliffs of the rebel hide out. There were three points of non-infrared light on the ground.

Fires.

It had started.

"Black Eagle, this is Rattlesnake. Enemy engaged. You are good to go."

Distantly, hollowly, Alan could hear the flat rattle and crack of gunfire over the radio.

"Roger that, Rattlesnake."

The Falcon view from drone intel had shown a single sandbagged machine gun nest overlooking the LZ. It was quite possible that whatever troops were manning it had RPGs or shoulder-mounted rocket launchers, either SAMs or US-made Stingers captured from Afghan allied troops. As Forward Combat Controller, Sgt. Regis—Rattlesnake—was Alan's eyes on the ground, targeting the emplacement with pinpoint accuracy. Alan came roaring in from the south, releasing his laser-guided bombs from two clicks out.

"Ordnance away, Rattlesnake. Keep your head down."

The explosions lit the night like a massive flare, but Alan paid no attention, lining up the Harrier for another run, waiting for word over the radio and checking his FLIR for signs of movement in the combat zone.

Nothing.

The flash of the bomb had illuminated the sharp lines of the terrain, the cliffs with their warren of caves and the surface buildings showing bright green geometric shapes through the night vision goggles, but moments later it was all lost in fire and smoke and darkness. Alan waited, listening, feeling the pressure of his G suit as he pulled the plane around.

The radio crackled at last.

"Nice hit, Black Eagle," said Regis' voice. "Target destroyed. That's an all clear for the recovery team."

Alan permitted himself a sigh of relief.

"Black Eagle to Rattlesnake and Dragonfly 6," he said. "Your LZ is secure. Repeat. LZ is secure."

"Roger that, Black Eagle," said the lead helicopter pilot. "Helo 1, ETA in twelve."

Alan began to trace a lazy arc over the combat zone. Barring surprises, his work was done, though he couldn't relax until he was back at Camp Leatherneck. For the next two minutes, all was quiet below, then the radio came back to life.

"Yeah, this is Rattlesnake," said Regis, and Alan could hear the smile in his voice. "We have the human asset. He's ready for a beer but is otherwise in good shape. Enemy resistance has been reduced to nil. Still searching for technical asset."

"Good work, Rattlesnake," said Central Command.

"I'll watch your six until Dragonfly 6 gets his ass over here," Alan added.

"Thanks for that, Black Eagle," said the helicopter pilot. "We are on schedule. MARSOC finished early. Not our fault if some people are a bit over-efficient. Nine minutes out."

"Beers are on you, Dragonfly 6," said Alan. "All good here."

But as soon as he said it the radio spat again.

CentCom again.

"Black Eagle, we have bogeys incoming from the northwest. Three helos."

From the northwest?

"Come again, CentCom," said Alan with steely calm, thumbing his radar to air-to-air mode. "Helos from the northwest?"

"Confirmed," said CentCom. "Ten clicks away. Look like MI-35s. Could use your attention ASAP."

Alan could see them on his screen now. As CentCom ordered the helos to prepare to engage, his mind raced.

The MI-35 was a variant of the Russian MI-24 attack helicopter, an updated version of an older aircraft used by a host of international powers, though where they'd come from, Alan couldn't imagine. More troubling was how they had approached unseen. AWACs should have picked them up ages ago.

"Roger that," said Alan, pulling the Harrier around onto an attack vector. "Coming in hard. Dragonfly 6—hold your position until we've cleared the LZ of hostiles. Any chance of getting those MH-60L DAPs in fast?"

"Still six minutes away," said the Night Hawk leader.

Which was at least four minutes too long.

"Understood," said Alan. "Preparing to engage."

The hesitation was only fractional but it spoke volumes.

"Roger that, Black Eagle," said the Night Hawk leader over the radio. "Show 'em who's boss."

He had maybe seventy seconds to determine who they were and what they were doing there. He checked his FLIR, but the blips that had been there only moments before had gone.

"CentCom, this is Black Eagle. Bogeys no longer registering on air-to-air systems. Please advise."

Another momentary pause.

"Copy that, Black Eagle," said the voice over the radio. It was carefully neutral but Alan thought he heard a note of confusion. Even alarm. "Estimated time to intercept last known coordinates?"

"Fifty seconds at current speed."

"Roger that, Black Eagle. Maintain course."

"You have them on radar, right?" he pressed.

A fractional hesitation. "Negative, Black Eagle. We've lost them, too."

Which meant what? Some kind of stealth tech they hadn't anticipated?

Back at Central Command, there would be shouting, earnest phone calls, analysts huddling around monitors. Alan ran through his weapon systems checklists but he couldn't keep his mind entirely on the *how* of what would happen next. He hadn't expected this. No one had. The Taliban had no air power. ISIS had some captured Russian and Chinese and American equipment, but no training on how to use any of it, and last he'd checked, ISIS was in Afghanistan in token numbers. Alan scrolled through his munitions, thinking fast.

And now the unidentified helicopters below him were back on Alan's FLIR, three of them, exhaust ports belching heat. The one upside was that since the Night Hawks weren't on hand, he could use his Sidewinders, assuming there was enough heat coming off those enemy choppers for the missiles to grab onto.

The radio crackled with static, the channel opened for a second, then closed again. The Harrier hurtled through the Afghan night.

Intercept in thirty seconds.

The radio came back to life.

"Black Eagle this is CentCom. Green to engage. Repeat, engage all bogeys in LZ. Clear the area."

"Roger that, CentCom," said Alan.

He banked the Harrier hard to the port side, selecting a Sidewinder missile, targeting the closest helicopter, thumb over the release button.

There was a brilliant flash of light, hot at the center and cooler at the edges, but no sound of any explosion. Stranger still, the light did not dissipate. For a second, Alan was blind. He flipped his NVGs up, unsure if he'd fired without meaning to, or if he'd been fired upon. As his eyes grew accustomed to the glare, he saw that the light hung motionless, like a midday sun, perhaps one nautical mile to starboard.

All three helicopters were suddenly, terribly visible in the light of . . . whatever it was. As he circled, Alan could see them all clearly, hovering like great mosquitoes, suspended in the unnatural glow.

Without another thought, he pressed the trigger button to release the first Sidewinder. Nothing happened.

What the hell?

Alan pressed the trigger again, without result. He tried retargeting the system, but the missile wouldn't lock. He engaged the 25mm cannon and pointed the Harrier at the target, but when he pressed the trigger, there was silence.

He stared in horror.

"Complete weapons systems failure," he said. "I cannot engage the helos. There's something out here, jamming my electronics. Repeat, I cannot engage bogeys. Rattlesnake.

You have to get your men into cover. Dragonfly 6, LZ is not secure. Hold your position."

"Copy that, Black Eagle," said the Night Hawk leader, "but we can be there in three minutes."

Too late.

"Negative," said Alan.

"Can you repeat that?" said the helicopter pilot. "Not sure I copy."

"I don't think your weapons will work any better than mine. There's something . . ." Alan began, shielding his eyes from the orange white glare of the sphere suspended to his right. "None of my weapons systems are functioning. I have an unidentified bogey in visual range. CentCom—are you seeing this? Configuration unknown. I think . . . I don't know," he managed. His hand had developed a tremor, and he felt the unfamiliar tingle of panic. "I think it's disrupting my weapons systems."

And then the unidentified helicopters swung away from him, angling to face the huddle of buildings that now cast hard shadows in the strange fiery light of the sphere.

"Bogeys locking on your position!" Alan said. "Rattlesnake, get your people out!"

"Black Eagle, engage!" said the voice of Central Command. "Fire all weapons immediately!"

"Unable to comply," said Alan, overwhelmed with dull horror. "Systems down. I'm sorry . . . I just can't . . ."

And then the missiles began raining down from the three enemy helicopters, and in the strange terrible light that hung like an unholy star in the black Afghan sky, Alan saw it all.

JENNIFER
Luve, Swaziland, Present Day

Jennifer Quinn stared at the American woman in outraged disbelief.

"You can't do that," Jennifer said. "You are not allowed."

"I have spoken to the school principal, and he feels that it would be confusing to the girls," said Mavis. She wore a prim smile that Jennifer wanted to slap off her face.

"Confusing?" she echoed, gripping the table edge until her knuckles went white. "What is confusing about condoms?"

She slammed a foil packet onto the table between them. Mavis averted her eyes but spoke in a maddeningly even tone.

"You are attempting to politicize this event," she said.

"AIDS *is* political," Jennifer shot back. "Rape is political. Pressuring girls into marriage is political."

"It is not the place of Peace in Action to interfere with local custom and beliefs."

Jennifer gave a hollow laugh.

"This isn't abut local customs. This is about your own prudishness!" she shot back. She was losing it, she knew, and it would only make things worse, but she could not hold back the anger that had been building over the six weeks she had spent in Swaziland. "This is about sex, Mavis. I know you don't want it to be, but it is, and refusing to talk about it is not helping anything. Hell, even the government knows it! When you cross the border from South Africa, there are boxes of free condoms at the customs and immigration checkpoints!"

"This event is supposed to be about female empowerment," Mavis returned, still placid, still secure.

"Exactly!" Jennifer shot back. "And that's not something you get with a few posters or *girl power* sing-a-longs. And it sure as hell isn't something you get, reciting poems about 'Our Lord and Savior.' Peace in Action is not a religious organization, and you need to stop using social activism as an excuse to preach your damn beliefs."

Mavis' composure buckled. "You may think you are better than us, Miss Quinn, but I will not tolerate that kind of language in my office."

"That kind of language?" exclaimed Jennifer. "We're trying to build a culture where girls don't get beaten into prostitution or die of every known STD on the planet, and you're offended by my language? You know what, Mavis? Fuck you and your holier-than-thou attitude. I don't think I'm better than anyone, but I am paying for this event, and we will not only give out condoms—we will demonstrate their correct use. So I suggest you go down the market and buy a box of cucumbers. Hell, you can even eat one."

She knew, as soon as she said it, that something wasn't right, and not just because she'd finally called the poisonous old bitch on her sanctimony. Mavis smiled, not her usual serene and beatific smile, mimicking the smile on the plaster saint that looked down on her desk, but a smile expressing something smaller and harder: a bitter satisfaction, that was almost amusement.

"Well, there's the thing," she said, sitting back.

Jennifer waited, but, when Mavis said no more, prompted her. "What's the thing?"

"You say you are paying for this event," said Mavis, "but that's not strictly true, is it? Your father in England is paying for the event."

"Same difference," she said.

"As it turns out," said Mavis, enjoying herself, "not so much."

"Why? What do you mean?"

Mavis' smile widened until she looked like one of the crocodiles sunning on the riverbank not half a mile from where they now sat. She fished a note pad from her drawer and made a point of consulting it.

"Your father has terminated all fiscal support for this project," she said. "I spoke to him personally, warning him that this might jeopardize your position here since it has been, as I am sure you are aware, somewhat vexed."

"And?" Jennifer prompted again, keen to get this over.

"Apparently," said Mavis, "and believe me when I say that I really can't imagine why, he wants you to come home."

JENNIFER MARCHED AWAY FROM THE THATCHED HUT AND stopped, breathless, under a devil thorn in the gathering dusk, and released the tie around her chestnut ponytail so that it broke in a ragged wave around her shoulders. She was wearing khaki shorts that left her long, tanned legs bare from thigh to calf, her feet encased in sturdy boots. She thumbed open another button of her sky blue safari shirt and wafted the fabric, sweat running down her chest. Overhead, a flight of royal ibises rehearsed their raucous calls, and somewhere, she heard, first, the roar of an automobile engine, and then the call of a hippo. Further down the road, she could see the children in their uniforms making their way home after school, chattering in Siswati, some of them laughing and jumping about with the kind of childish delight she rarely saw in England these days. Her rage faltered, and she was struck with a sudden sadness that felt like failure. She snatched her cell phone from her pocket, then remembered she would have no signal out here. She would have to drive to Mbabane, just to talk to her meddling father. The thought of the drive on narrow, uneven roads in twilight, pausing for cattle and warthogs in the road, and then his smooth, patronizing tones when she finally reached him, made her anger spike anew.

This is so like him . . .

She cursed loudly, a stream of furious invective that made some of the kids down the road strain to hear what the funny white woman was shouting about. When she felt suitably chastened, she took a long breath, restored the ponytail to keep her hair out of her face, and climbed into the Jeep.

EDWARD
Hampshire, England, Present Day

EDWARD QUINN PLACED THE PHONE ON THE EDGE OF his polished mahogany desk and considered it. She wouldn't call. Not yet, at least. Possibly not at all. He rubbed his face, feeling the jowly flesh move. He had put on weight over the years. He didn't know when exactly. It had just happened, like a slow poisoning, all those years sitting in boardrooms, eating foie gras and drinking port. He avoided mirrors now, not so much disgusted by his own swelling bulk as disappointed with the loss of who he once was.

That was why Jennifer wouldn't call back. She could pontificate about the evils of capitalism, but he sensed in her, lately, less moral outrage and more of something simpler, a disappointment in him for not being the father she had once believed in. It used to make him angry, but now, slowing with age and afflicted by all the persistent little ailments that came with it, he felt only loss. And sadness.

It was time to do something about it.

She had no right to be indignant, he reminded himself, lighting a cigar. She had been raised wanting for nothing and had been sent to the best possible schools, where she had flourished. He had given her everything. Too much, perhaps. It had all come so easily for her, and now, almost a decade clear of her Oxford graduation, she was still drifting from one save-the-world project to another, without focus or any larger sense of purpose. Certainly she was smart, and strong, and clever. She worked tirelessly. He couldn't deny her that, pouring every ounce of her heart and soul into whatever she was doing, as if nothing on the planet was more important, but then she would read about a new endangered species, or a virulent disease, something that needed saving or preventing, and she would walk out and get on the next plane to South America or Africa. She could do so because he made sure she could, providing her with a constant stream of funds from the various businesses he owned, money she so despised. He had never thought her a hypocrite, but he would be lying if he didn't say that there were times when he thought that she had also disappointed him. She had so much talent. So much energy and resourcefulness. Scattered like crumbs before pigeons.

But dwelling on it would avail him nothing.

Quinn turned to his desktop computer and accessed his protected files with a series of complex passcodes. "Protected," the hackers he had hired to break in had remarked. That was an understatement. He had employed a deep encryption system based on lattice reduction and other forms of asymmetrical algorithms, linked in chains and separately coded by independent operators, none of whom knew what the rest were doing. It was, he was confident, more secure than the Bank of England, the British government and MI-5 combined, which was just as well, because leaking the contents of his hard drive to the press would bring all three down at a stroke.

He scanned his accounts: hundreds of millions of pounds, billions. His investments were solid, like continents, great sprawling rafts of money spreading from one side of the earth to the other, sustaining much of what lived on the surface. But from time to time the entire mass would buckle in a great tectonic shift, erupting and reforming in ways that changed the world.

Today would be one of those days.

Continents moved at their own pace, according to their own rules. Money, for all its chaotic energy, could, with a firm hand, be made to do what you told it.

Edward Quinn had such a hand and could, with a few keystrokes, alter the fate of the entire planet.

This had been true for a long time. He had known what his money was capable of doing for twenty years or more without it unsettling him unduly. But then Anne—his wife, his one true love, his confidante in all he could safely share—had started losing weight and suffering from inexplicable fevers. Non-Hodgkin's Lymphoma, the doctors had told him. He hadn't known what the words meant, a fact that shocked him almost as badly as the diagnosis itself. So he had learned everything there was to learn about non-Hodgkin's Lymphoma, because that was how Edward Quinn met adversity: with knowledge, and expertise, and, of course, with money. He'd learned to speak fluently about B-cells and to nod with understanding when his consultants used words like "immunoblastic" or "lymphoplasmacytic," and he'd written checks that would have paid off the national debt of small nations.

None of it helped. After a struggle lasting two years, the girl he had first met half a century ago collecting shells on Brighton Beach, his sweet, beautiful, perfect Annie, was gone. Edward was left with a rambling mansion full of servants whose names he didn't know and a daughter who never called, except to ask for money for some new cause. There was more, of course. More stuff. More things. More money. None of it seemed to matter much.

There was his work, of course. Not the corporations on whose boards he sat, the companies who listed him on their mastheads. His real work. But lately, even that had started to trouble him. He lay awake most nights now, thinking, remembering, regretting.

Something had to change. The Board wouldn't like it, and it was going to be the hardest battle he had ever fought—which was saying more than most people would ever know—but it had to be done. It was time.

Jennifer would help. Maybe not consciously or deliberately. He might not be able to tell her everything until the worst of it was over, but her presence at his side would make all the difference. That, too, would be a battle, but if Edward Quinn couldn't wrangle his own daughter, it really was time for him to . . . what did the Americans say? *Hang it up*? Something like that.

She would understand, eventually. He was almost sure of that. After all, the work had been good once. They had lost control of it, allowed it to turn into other things, but it had been good at the start. He still believed that. Sometimes it was the only thing keeping him going.

There had been that one day, when she was small, when she had come into this very room and found him studying what he thought of simply as "The Project." There had been a chart on the wall that she should not have seen. She had stood in the doorway, a little girl of nine or ten, staring, her head cocked to one side, trying to make sense of what she was looking at before he whisked it away. He wondered if she remembered. Perhaps. It was time to show her the rest.

The intercom buzzed.

"Yes?" he said.

"Your helicopter is approaching, sir," said Deacon, Quinn's private secretary-cum-butler. Quinn checked his Roger Dubuis watch—a spectacularly expensive piece he liked because he could see all the inner workings through its silicon casing—and sighed. It was a thirty-seven minute flight to the office in central London.

"I'll be right there," he said.

He looked at the framed photograph of Annie and Jennifer on the corner of the desk, the two of them in shorts and T-shirts after some mother/daughter 10K, both holding their medals and beaming. He had only put it there last week, after a lifetime keeping work and home as far apart as was possible. Too late, perhaps. Certainly for Annie, though he felt in his bones that she would approve of what he was about to do.

Quinn logged off and shut down his computer. He had just shut his briefcase when he heard the door snap closed behind him. He hadn't heard it open. Quinn was surprised when he turned.

The figure in the doorway was pointing a long-barreled pistol at him. "You?" he gasped.

"Hello, Edward."

"How did you get in?"

"I'm good at getting into places people don't want me to. You ought to know that."

"And you like to keep things between friends," said Quinn. "Though the gun doesn't look especially friendly."

"I wasn't planning to use it."

"Then why do you have it?" said Quinn.

"If it becomes necessary, I'll use it, but I thought you jumping out the window would be more poetic."

Quinn glanced to where the smoked, bulletpro French windows opened onto the balcony. It was or four-story drop, but it would achieve the results his seemed to want.

"And what makes you think I would do that?

The visitor moved to the desk and, eyes still on Quinn, turned the pistol onto the photograph of Jennifer and Anne.

Quinn's composure evaporated. He was dead, he knew, but he would not give up his daughter.

"If you touch Jennifer . . ." he began.

"You'll what?" asked the visitor.

"Why would you hurt her?" Quinn asked, hating the crack of desperation that snuck into his voice. "This has nothing to do with her."

"Exactly. And I'd like to keep it that way. And if you sign this little note I have prepared for you, and then step off your very fine balcony, that's how things will stay."

The visitor placed a single sheet of paper, a suicide note written in flowing blue-black ink. Quinn glanced at it, admiring how it was meticulously forged, with what looked like his own Cartier fountain pen, in his own hand. They were always so careful.

"What assurance do I have that if I do as you say, you won't kill her anyway?"

"Why would I? As you say, this has nothing to do with her. She's merely a bargaining chip. Something that gives me an edge in negotiating. You, of all people, should respect that."

Quinn let go of the attaché case and considered the window. In the same moment, the intercom came back to life.

"The helicopter is here, sir," said Deacon.

The visitor raised the pistol to shoulder height and was sighting down the barrel into Quinn's face. Edward gave a ctional nod.

26

"I'll be right down," he said.

He signed the letter. As he sat back again, he knocked over the little wooden lion Jennifer had given him for Christmas when she was ten. He considered it for a moment, then put it carefully down. Pausing only to pick up the photograph of his wife and daughter, which he clutched to his heart with a surge of sadness, he stepped toward the window.

He opened the French windows and stepped out into the English air, damp and cool, gazing down at the mansion's gravel forecourt below, wreathed in a mist that was almost rain. He did not look back toward the visitor with the pistol, or down to where his broken body would soon be found by a shrieking maid, but instead gazed out into the gray air, seeing nothing. His hands gripped the photograph, and as he stepped up onto the ornamental balustrade, he whispered to them.

"Sorry. I tried. Too late, I'm afraid. But I tried."

TIMIKA
New York, Present Day

I T WAS TYPICAL. OF COURSE TRAFFIC WOULD BE BUMPER to bumper on a morning when she had a Skype interview from the office, first thing. Timika eyed her fuel gauge uneasily.

"Don't give up on me now," she warned Dion's moldering Corolla. The car had taken to burning oil at twice the usual rate, blowing out great clouds of blue, acrid smoke behind her.

"You've gotta get that POS fixed," she had told Dion the night before. "It's gonna die and leave me freezing by the curb."

"If it's such a piece of shit car," Dion shot back, "why not take the subway like everybody else?"

"Yeah, God forbid you should break out your wallet for anything you can't stick in your PlayStation," Timika had shot back, staring her boyfriend down until he wilted and his eyes slid back to the TV. "That's what I figured."

They were supposed to be going to Atlantic City for the weekend. Her idea. She'd pick him up after work and they'd be on the road by six, assuming that the car survived the day. If it didn't, or something else happened to screw up their trip, and if she got the message that Dion was relieved, things were gonna go down hill in their Mt. Kisco apartment faster than the crappy little car was ever likely to manage.

The Corolla sputtered, stalling. She gave it a little more gas, watching in the rear view mirror as another cloud of black smog plumed out behind her.

"Jesus, lady," said the cab driver who was sitting alongside through his window. "What are you burning in there—napalm?"

"That's hilarious," she spat back. "You should be on stage."

He made a face, and Timika urged the Corolla forward a few feet so she wouldn't have to look at him. On the west side of Union Square, she saw blue lights flashing. In front of a café, the sidewalk had been partly cordoned off with yellow crime scene tape. A pair of uniformed police officers were standing around doing nothing, as far as she could see. The traffic slowed to a crawl so that drivers could rubberneck, but there was nothing to see.

She leaned across to the passenger side, brandishing the ID in her wallet.

"What's going on here?" she called to the closest cop as she crawled by.

He stooped to look into the car and rolled his eyes.

"Figured it would be you, Mars," he said. "At the precinct, they call you the Question Girl. I can't think why."

"Well, thinking never was your strong suit," she replied.

His name was Officer James Brown, and boy hadn't she given him a hard time for that in high school. His phone number was still on her contact list from when she'd organized their tenth reunion.

Hey Jimmy boy, you feel good? Like you knew you would? Still funny.

"Old guy got mugged," said Brown. "Your crackpot website got a crime beat now?"

"Just a concerned citizen," she said. "He okay?"

"You'll have to ask St. Peter," said the cop. Another comedian.

"Here? At this time of day?"

"Another beautiful day in the Big Apple. You wanna move up? You're holding up traffic."

"Yeah, I'm the one holding up traffic," Timika returned. "You wanna get these cars moving? Some of us have to get to work."

The cop just rolled his eyes and shrugged. *What am I supposed to do about it?*

"Yeah," Timika growled back. "That's what I figured."

She drove to the parking garage on East Sixteenth Street and swung by an ATM to pick up the five hundred bucks that was her share of the rent. Five minutes later, she was tearing up the stairs to her office, shedding her jacket as she ran up the stairs. The office was a couple of tiny rooms above a vegetarian restaurant, next to the classical façade of the New York Film Academy on Seventeenth Street. It was cheap and functional, an address that hinted at prosperity, seriousness and class. It also meant that she was able to include, on her website, a shot of the Union Square subway entrance, with a shallow dome and hat-brim ring that made it look like a classic flying saucer.

Timika bypassed the coffee pot with an effort of will and settled in front of the computer monitor in the one corner of the office that looked like an office, as opposed to one of those crazy lady apartments where no one throws anything away and the cops only go in when the corpse smell alerts the neighbors. It was the professional corner. The Skype corner.

She checked her appearance on her webcam—she was wearing her brassiest wig for maximum effect, a mop of glossy ringlets flecked preposterously with gold.

Her business card read "Timika Mars—Freelance Investigative Journalist and Blogger." She was also the host of Debunktion.com, a podcast and website dedicated to exposing (and ridiculing) urban myths, pseudo-science, conspiracy theories of all kinds, and what Timika grouped together as "mainstream superstition." She had pages on everything from the Loch Ness monster and the JFK assassination to miraculous statues of the Virgin Mary in Mexico. Though she wasn't getting rich off it, the site was one of the most visited of its kind, and the advertising revenue was steady. *The Huffington Post* interview she was about to do would surely boost her visibility. Her staff was a part-time tech support guy called Marvin whose brilliance with computers was matched only by the amount of weed he smoked, and Audrey Stanhope, who Timika likened to both a bloodhound and a pit bull when it came to sniffing out and chasing down stories. The metaphor worked, Timika thought, because she could also be a royal bitch when it came to negotiating with advertisers.

"Goddamn it," she muttered. The wig looked fabulously outrageous, but she had a coffee stain on her sweater. She was already two minutes late for the interview and didn't have time to rinse it out. She pulled the detachable fur collar off her scarlet coat and arranged it around her neck, trying to decide if it worked as some kind of quirky fashion statement. It looked like a pair of weasels were mating on her shoulders, but it covered the stain. "Oh, what the hell."

She logged into her Skype account and waited for the call to come through, scanning her e-mail on a second computer for links to various news stories, one featuring blurry pictures of Bigfoot, another showing some suspiciously two-dimensional English fairies, and a brace of other idiotic stories too obviously faked to merit *debunktion*. That was what she called it. A ludicrous, bombastic and eye-catching word that had become her trademarked website title, something sure to come up in the imminent Huff Po interview.

The interview began well. The host, a perky but shrewd-looking blond woman named Nicole, lofted softball questions and Timika knocked them out of the park: "How long have you been running the site? What was the first case you wrote about? Tell us about some of the more elaborate hoaxes you've uncovered? Why do you think people are so quick to believe implausible things?"

Timika was calm and confident:

"Two and a half years."

"The Essex crop circles, which turned out to be the work of two drunk teenaged boys using a tractor and some towable farm gear."

"Well, there was the time the bankrupt owner of a Virginia lighthouse wanted to draw tourists by inventing a series of ghostly apparitions. I'm telling you, Nicole, this thing read like the script for a *Scooby Doo* episode. And he would have gotten away with it too, if it weren't for us meddling kids . . ."

It was only the last question, why people want to believe in things that obviously aren't real, that gave her pause. Timika trotted out some familiar ideas about why people who live boring lives are drawn to mystery and conspiracy, and then Nicole, hinting at a bitterness she hadn't shown thus far, asked how Timika felt about spending her life destroying other people's harmless fantasies.

Timika paused for just a fraction of a second, adjusting to the unexpected jab, then answered. She said she felt fine about it, thank you, Nicole. She added that some of the things people believed in weren't harmless at all, and some were quite possibly dangerous, and that even harmless delusions were manifestations of a larger culture that had reduced science and objectivity to a kind of he said/she said debate in which no one person's authority or credibility was valued above anyone else's. The opinion of an eminent physician, archaeologist or environmental scientist was worth no more than that of anyone with access to a twitter account, and sometimes the opinions of accomplished scientists carried less weight than those of people who were famous models or athletes or actors on a sitcom.

Nicole seemed satisfied with Timika's answer. In hindsight, Timika felt the woman was attempting to goad her into saying more, because it made for better footage, not because she disagreed with her. Even so, she was rattled at the end, and when the interviewer wrapped things up with "And can I just say that I love your hair and that fur drape! So fun!" Timika wasn't sure if she was being mocked.

Guess we'll see when it goes live, she thought. *Welcome to life in the spotlight.*

Well, if it brought in some more revenue, it was worth it. She didn't need the *Huffington Post*'s endorsement to know she was doing good, necessary work. She was glad they'd asked her, *Why do you do this?* It forced her to answer it for herself, something she hadn't really done before.

She approached the day's work with a new buoyancy that even Audrey's whining about her sorry personal life and how the people at Fox News got paid more than she did could not dampen.

"What's that thing around your neck?"

Marvin had finally shown up and was peering at her, leaning with one hand on her desk like he wasn't sure of his balance.

Timika snatched the fur off and tossed it onto her jacket.

"Nothing," she said. "I was covering a stain."

"Right," said Marvin, nodding with greater seriousness than the remark justified. "Got it."

Timika wrinkled her nose. "You stoned, man? Because I told you about coming to work like that."

"No, no," said Marvin, dropping into a bizarre half crouch and putting his hands up in a half-assed surrender pose as he always did when he felt threatened. "Swear to God. It's just, you know, passive."

"Passive?"

"Yeah—my roommate had the bong going this morning, and I may have caught some of the collateral vibe, you know?"

Timika gave him a dubious frown. "You up to installing the new firewall?" she asked.

"Totally," said Marvin. "Well within my powers. I'll have it done before you can say 'firewall.'" He paused, reflecting upon this. "But you might wanna not say it for, like, two hours."

"Deal," Timika said.

"Oh, and there's a package for you," he added, producing something about the size of a shoe box, wrapped in brown paper and tied with thin twine. "The Doorman just handed it to me. He said an old guy came by before you got in."

He placed the parcel on Timika's desk. Her name was written in unsteady block capitals in magic marker. There was no return address or sign that it had been through the post.

Not everyone was a fan of what the office produced. She usually received belligerent explanations in the mail, rather than actual hate mail, but she'd had her share of death threats from people angry because she'd picked apart or ridiculed the assumptions they considered true or even sacred. She held the package gingerly, weighing it.

Too light for a bomb, she thought. *But not for anthrax or ricin or—more likely—talcum powder, which would shut the office down until they could get an all clear from the health department.*

"I'm gonna open this outside," she said, fishing scissors and rubber gloves from her desk drawer.

"You want me to come with?" Marvin asked. Audrey, Timika noted, was making no such offer and eyed the parcel warily.

"Nah, I'm good," she answered. "If I'm not back in five minutes, call in the hazmat team."

Marvin looked unsure. "Is the number in your Rolodex thingy?" he asked.

"I was kidding, Marvin," said Timika, picking up the package and stalking out of the room with a pointed look at Audrey.

"Hey," said the reporter with a better version of Marvin's hands-up defensive gesture. "I just work here. You don't pay me enough to get blown up."

"Yeah," muttered Timika as she pushed through the door and into the stairwell, drawing her scarlet raincoat tight to her body. "That's what I figured."

She didn't really believe the package was dangerous, but she crossed to the square across the street and chose a bench away from two old people who were exercising their dogs. She opened the parcel carefully, donning the rubber gloves and slitting the paper, then turning the box upside down at arms' length. No telltale white powder trickled out. When she lifted the lid, she found only a notebook. It was blue, hardbound, with a cloth cover stained with age and use. Inside the cover was an envelope, thick with heavy stationery covered in spidery script.

"Dear Miss Mars," the letter began. "I hope to be talking you through the contents of this book in person since there is much to be explained, but in case I am not able to, I wanted you to understand something. The contents of this book are extremely important. I am confident that it will change your life and your sense of many things. It is also extremely dangerous. There are people who would kill me to prevent you from reading it and may attempt to kill you for doing so. For that I apologize. I will trust your judgment as to whether you will take that risk, though I am confident in my regard for your sense of ethical responsibility. Read. Investigate all I have to say. Check it. Subject it to your most rigorous 'debunktion,' then call me. My time is short, even if no one tries to make it shorter. Until then, I am sincerely yours, Jerzy Aaron Stern."

His name was followed by a phone number.

Timika wasn't sure what to make of it. It screamed conspiracy theory nonsense—especially the paranoid hinting about lives in danger, which was one of the major hallmarks of the genre—but the writing itself gave her pause. It was an old man's writing, unsteady, but sophisticated, as was the phrasing. Most of what she received was a train wreck of small and capital letters, third-grade spelling and text-message punctuation. This felt . . . different.

She opened the notebook, carefully, feeling its age and startled to find that it contained more of the same longhand script, though the penmanship looked younger, more confident than the letter she'd just read. There were pages and pages of it, occasionally broken by little sketches and diagrams. It was clearly a journal, all entries carefully dated. She flipped to the front and caught her breath. The first entry, laid out in blue ink, the desiccated pages stained and smeared with dirt or even old blood, was labeled Kraków, Poland, 1939.

No way.

"You okay there, Timika?"

She looked up to find Marvin standing over her.

"You look kind of spooked. You need me to call those hazmat guys or something?"

She hesitated, staring at the first entry. "You know what, Marvin?" she said at last. "I'm really not sure."

JERZY
Kraków, Poland, September 1939

THAT DATE MARKS WHERE IT STARTED. I AM WRITING this entry a decade later, in America and, as you can see, in English. I will write more from here as it happens, but my story begins before what I think of as the present so I am going back to my childhood in Poland. That, as I say, was when things started, though I did not know it at the time.

I WAS TEN YEARS OLD WHEN THE NAZIS CAME. SOME OF MY family had already fled, but most did not go far enough. They went to other parts of Europe, and the war eventually overtook them. I was told I had an uncle who made it to

England, and a cousin who set out for America, though I do not know if she made it all the way. I lost touch with them as I lost touch with all my family. As far as I know, I am the only one who survived.

I remember the first days of the war only vaguely, and my memories are confused by things I read or saw later. I know that the day before the fighting started, I sat with a Polish soldier, a little man who smiled at me and ruffled my hair. He was the driver of a kind of little tank. It had a machine gun, and it seemed to me that it was the greatest, most terrible weapon imaginable. I do not know what happened to the man and his machine, but I think they were probably both destroyed within a day or two of our conversation. The Germans came fast and strong. There were stories of our soldiers armed with lances, riding against the German tanks on horseback. I do not think the stories were true, but I know that after a week, the war was largely over for us, or rather the fighting was over. The war went on much longer. Parts of me are still fighting it.

The Russians came from the north and east, and the Nazis from the west. I lived in a village close to the Czech border, surrounded by green forests. Some of the men from our area—including soldiers who had not been killed in the initial onslaught—were taken to work in the Škoda factories in Pilsen, but Jews like us were considered incapable of such work. At first, it was just strange, and for a few days, it seemed that Mama, Papa, Ishmael and I were the only people still living in the village, watched over by hundreds of German soldiers. I am sure my parents were very frightened, but they hid it as best they could. My brother and I were more confused than we were scared. Children, I think, are tougher than adults realize. Children adjust. In our case, we lived for—days? Weeks? I'm not sure. We had mainly hunger and isolation to complain of. Things changed when we had to leave the house we had lived in all our lives, but even as we were packed onto the train to Kraków, Papa managed to make it feel like an adventure, a kind of holiday.

It wasn't, of course. It was a version of hell. Poverty and want are one thing in the country, but they are something entirely different in a city, particularly when you are packed into a few square blocks with thousands of others, many of whom were in worse condition than we were. I was still under twelve years of age then, so I did not have to wear the armband, and I remember feeling a peculiarly childish and conflicted form of shame at this. I was embarrassed for my parents and brother, who wore the yellow star, and relieved that I did not have to wear it, but I also carried a deeper, more insidious self-loathing because I was not standing with them. These feelings only deepened when my brother and I were taken away.

Ishmael was three years older than I, a strong and solid boy who knew more than he confessed to me about what was happening in our corner of the world. He had black hair and high cheekbones in a pale face, with eyes as dark as pools at night. I idolized him, and he, for his part, protected me.

"This will be over soon, little Jerzy," he told me every night. "You see if it won't. And when the Germans run screaming from the British bombers, you and me, we'll chase 'em out, laughing at the tops of our lungs."

But the British didn't come. The war went on, and though the Russians changed sides, nothing changed in Poland. It became impossible to remember things had ever been different, or imagine that the world would ever go back to what it had been. I saw it in my mama's eyes, in her drawn, haggard face, and in my father's slow watchfulness when he looked at us. His life had been ambushed, redirected, and it would never get back to what it should be. My parents worked long hours in a munitions factory, coming home exhausted, their hands red from the chemicals.

We had been in the Kraków ghetto almost a year when the trucks came. They arrived early one morning in March. It was bitter cold, but everyone crowded into the square to see what was going on, in case there was food or other supplies. But the trucks were empty except for the guards. They were there to make selections for labor camps, packing eight men into the back of each truck.

My family hid, but when they came the next day, and the day after that, we began to wonder if the camps could be worse than where we were living, huddled with another family in what had once been a tool shed in someone's garden. The walls were a single plank thick, and even with every blanket and coat we owned, the nights were unendurably cold. There was no toilet, no running water, and precious little food. One night, after a tiny meal of potatoes and pig fat, shared with two other families, our stomachs achingly hollow, my brother decided he had had enough.

"At least in the labor camps, they'll feed us," Ishmael urged that night, speaking to me in a hoarse whisper as we lay huddled for warmth. "I can't stay here any longer. I'll go mad. I'll go work, and get fed. Then I'll come back. I'm not afraid of work. It has to be better than here."

It did not occur to him—or to me—that we would not be brought back to our families. I often wonder if my father overheard us. He said so little those days that it wasn't always easy to tell when he was awake or when he was asleep.

The following day when the trucks came, Ishmael pushed to the front. He was, as I said, a big boy for his age, almost a man, and one of the officers spotted him immediately.

"My brother too," he insisted, pulling me forward through the throng.

The officer looked me over disparagingly, but shrugged. He didn't care who they took. I remember looking across the square, sorting through the anxious, drawn faces for my mother or father, but couldn't see them.

I never saw them again.

Within months, the ghetto was purged. Many were killed in the streets. Others were herded onto trains and packed off on their one-way journey to Auschwitz.

We knew none of this. The full scale of it didn't register for years. The horror of the so-called Final Solution was unimaginable to us. Even now, when I read about it, I find myself wrestling to visualize the enormity of the thing, even

though I lived through it. Everyone knows the big number—
six million dead—but that is not a figure the mind grasps
easily. I suspect that for some, when placed in the context
of the war, and the length of time it all took, and the sheer
geography of it all, six million dead seems somehow . . .
I don't know. Ordinary? Understandable? Certainly, it is a
kind of abstract knowledge, a fact without faces. But the
terrible mathematics get worse when you think small. At
Bełżek, at its busiest, Jews were unloaded from train cars
at a fake railway station building, where they were stripped
and their belongings confiscated, before being escorted
into buildings for showers. Two hundred at a time. They
were then gassed with carbon monoxide or Zyclon B. The
process took about thirty minutes. Afterwards, dentists
removed any gold teeth from the corpses with hammers,
collecting as much as two cupfuls for melting. The bodies
were buried in shallow graves, but the smell was said to
carry for ten miles, so cremation became the order of the
day. At Auschwitz, the ovens burned constantly, consum-
ing a thousand bodies a day.

Somewhere among all those corpses were my parents.
I didn't know it for certain for another two and a half
years, but the sense of something lost hung over Ishmael
and me the very first night we were away from them. The
trucks carrying my brother and me had left the city behind
and rumbled on into the mountains, heading southwest
towards the Czech border, familiar ground for us, so that
in spite of our exhaustion, our hunger, and our uncertainty,
we felt the thrill of returning to land we had known as

children before the war. We looked at each other, grinning madly for the first time in months as we peered through the window slits in the truck walls and saw hills and church towers we knew. It was only when the sun began to set that we realized how far we had come, and how unlikely it was that we would be going back to Kraków and our parents any time soon.

I asked the guard, speaking in my faltering German—the one talent I had been able to use for my family—when we would go back, and he just sighed, almost as miserable to be there as we were.

"*Wenn der krieg vorbei ist*," he said. "When the war is over."

We slept in bunks in canvas tents. It was cold, but no worse than it had been in the ghetto. Ishmael was wrong about the food. That first night, we were given a small piece of black bread and a fragment of cheese and told it was to last us until lunchtime the following day. Ishmael was first incredulous and then furious at how stupid we had been to volunteer for something so awful. He shouted at a guard and said that we wanted to go back to Warsaw. The soldier struck him on the side of his head with the butt of his rifle, and Ishmael fell heavily to the ground, unconscious.

As I knelt over him, weeping, a spider-thin man, a fellow Jew, crouched beside me and put his hand over the swelling bruise on my brother's temple.

"That was a stupid thing to do," he remarked. "If you want to survive for any length of time here, you and your idiot brother will learn to keep your mouths shut."

"Will he be all right?" I asked.

"He'll have a hell of a headache when he comes around, but yes, I think so. Unless he does it again. You don't get second chances here. And to make the point so that you both remember it, I'm going to eat his cheese."

He did so, sourly and without relish, but I was too drained by our predicament to muster any real outrage.

"Where are we?" I managed.

"They call it the Wenceslas mine," he said.

"What will we do here?"

"It's a mine," he said, bitterly. "We dig."

But that, as we learned over the next few awful days, weeks, and months, was only partly true. We dug and tunneled, but we also built, pouring concrete and pushing wheelbarrows of rubble out until our hands bled and we couldn't stand. We toiled beneath the earth like moles, constructing we knew not what, and sometimes we wept for those we had lost, and for what we had become.

That there was more to come, stranger and more hideous than anything we had seen so far, we could not have imagined.

ALAN
Camp Leatherneck Marine, Helmund Province, Afghanistan

H E HAD DEBRIEFED AFTER MISSIONS A HUNDRED TIMES. He knew the drill, and usually, nothing fazed him. This time was different. This time, he felt the weight of shame and confusion and with them came the long tail of dread. Major Alan Young was a Marine pilot, to the very marrow of his bones. That identity was encoded in his DNA. It was who he was.

And he felt it ending, and there was nothing he could do to stop that from happening. The damage was done.

He had filed his report the moment he landed at Leatherneck, thankful for the armed escort that had carried him away from Barry's towering rage at the landing strip. The MARSOC team had lost three men in the barrage from the helicopters. Four survivors had to be stretchered out, and two of them were in surgery with shrapnel wounds.

Alan's fault.

It wasn't, of course. He knew that with his head, but in his gut, his failure burned like hot metal. Almost as bad was knowing that the more he tried to explain what had happened, the more he would jeopardize his position. Mechanical failure was one thing, but coming under the influence of an unidentifiable object? That would blow his career in a heartbeat and land him in the psych ward. He had already decided to say nothing about it, to make it sound like he'd just had a weapons malfunction due, perhaps, to a software glitch, one which—of course—was now fixed and undetectable.

Alan chewed his lower lip, his one nervous tick.

The moment the bogeys had opened fire, the strange glowing sphere had vanished, streaking upwards at unimaginable speed and vanishing into darkness. Their work done, the enemy helos had vanished over the hills, winking in and out of radar like ghosts before the Night Hawks could engage them. If anyone had seen the strange object in the sky, they weren't saying.

The debriefing building a Sensitive Compartmentalized Information Facility—SCIF for short—was a low cluster of offices plastered in desert yellow. The operations command team was familiar—two lieutenants and a captain who Alan had seen routinely for months, though today they were stiff, formal, and reluctant to make eye contact. He felt like he'd been called to the principal's office, something he hadn't felt since his first days at MCAS Cherry Point. Under other circumstances, it might have been funny.

But it wasn't. He'd filed his report immediately following the mission. The duty officers had sent him back to his quarters to rest while they reviewed the details, ordering him to return at oh nine hundred. He'd slept badly, playing and replaying the events of the night in his head, looking for something that might plausibly explain what had happened that night over the mountains. In his report, he'd said that the weapon systems had failed, and that he'd been temporarily blinded by a bright light. Perhaps it had been some kind of flare launched by one of the enemy helicopters, or some new kind of drone designed to illuminate the target area, there simply to light the position, and his problems in the Harrier were unrelated.

If it was equipment failure, he would know soon enough, because the ground crew was going over his bird to determine what went wrong. They would have a preliminary report by morning, maybe sooner. Alan considered this as he shaved. His blue-green eyes were bloodshot with tiredness, the sockets shadowed, his always lean face looking more than usually drawn and hollow.

"You look like hell, Major," he observed.

He ran his hands through his short brown hair, noting the way it was graying at the temples, then hurried to the SCIF, hoping to God he didn't meet anyone who might ask how things had gone.

But everyone would know. You didn't lose three of your own without the whole base knowing.

"Please be seated, Major Young, sir," said the intel officer, closing the door behind him. "I'm Captain Thwaite. We've met before."

About a hundred times, thought Alan.

"Captain," he said.

"And this is Lieutenant Jonah," the Captain continued, nodding to the woman sitting next to him, who did not look up, "and Lieutenant Simmons." The burly officer by the door. No one was smiling.

Alan nodded and took the proffered seat.

The Captain's formality bothered him. The intel guys were always careful, but this was different. There was an air of caution that suggested everyone was covering their ass.

Alan's heart sank. He could be reliving last night's fiasco for months, possibly even years, in depositions and reports and interviews.

Captain Thwaite opened a manila folder, rotated it and pushed it across the table towards him.

"This is your account of the events last night," he said. "Before we start, I just want to be clear; we're looking for a clear picture of what happened, putting your account together with the data gathered from drones, AWACs, satellite surveillance and other witness accounts. No one is accusing you of anything and your record, which is exemplary, is duly noted. Is there anything you would like to add to the report you've already made? Or change?"

The hesitation between those last two sentences had been only a fraction of a second, but it was loaded with meaning.

"No, Captain," he said.

Another pause, icy despite the still mounting heat of the day.

"Nothing at all? Are you sure about that, Major Young?" asked the Lieutenant opposite him.

He considered her question for a half second. Alan had seen her, a week ago, at an off base restaurant frequented by a British regiment. She had looked—as much as possible in her multicam utility uniform—glamorous, sexy even, in make up that pushed the limits of what was considered acceptable. She had seemed light-hearted, even a little flirty, then. There was no trace of that playfulness now, though she had the decency to avoid his gaze when he said, "No, Lieutenant. I stand by my report."

The Captain produced another document, slightly dog-eared. He considered it thoughtfully, and edged it towards Alan, moving as if in slow motion.

"This is the preliminary report on your aircraft, from an examination conducted in the early hours of this morning," he said. "A test pilot will take the plane up later today to do further live tests on its weapons systems, but as you can see, the first pass engineering report says that all systems seem to be operating normally. The flight data recorders show no record of any attempt on your part to engage said systems during the mission last night. Can you offer an explanation for that?"

"No, Captain, I cannot," said Alan. "Though the loss of power to the systems, which I outlined, would explain why there's no record of the attempt to deploy. It was off-line."

"That would be the Sidewinder you say you attempted to launch at the enemy helicopter?" said the Captain.

"Yes. The LGBs worked perfectly. The systems only went down when the helicopters appeared."

"You think they were somehow jamming you?"

"I don't know, Captain, but I think that possibility should be thoroughly examined," said Alan, opting for the same formal professionalism as his interrogators. "I doubt my launch systems failing at the exact time the 35s showed up is a coincidence."

"Yes," said the Captain, levelly. "I would agree. Though I'm unsure of any system that could affect your weapon systems but not your flight controls."

Alan shifted in his chair. He could feel the heat rising in his face. They said they weren't accusing him of anything, but there was more than confusion in the room. There was skepticism.

The Lieutenant silently moved another sheet of paper in front of the Captain. They did not look at each other, but Alan felt that the action had been discussed, planned. Something was about to happen.

"Do you recall what you said over the radio last night, Major?" said the Captain, looking up.

"Not word for word . . ." Alan began, but the Captain waved the rest away.

"Of course not, Major," he cut in. "But do you recall saying, and I quote, 'I have an unidentified bogey in visual range. Configuration unknown. I think it's disrupting my weapons systems . . .' Do you recall saying that?"

Alan stiffened.

"I think what I meant was . . ." he began, but again, the Captain interjected.

"Do you recall saying that, sir?"

"Not precisely."

"Are you doubting the accuracy of the cockpit voice recorder?" the Lieutenant chimed in.

"No," Alan said quickly. "I just don't recall using those exact words."

"Well," said the Captain, managing a mirthless smile, "I can assure you, Major, that you did, and I'm wondering what you meant by them."

"Well, as I said," Alan began, "I was wondering if maybe something on the helicopters . . ."

"But you don't say *helicopter*," the Captain pressed. "You say *unidentified bogey. Configuration unknown*. Singular. So it seems you weren't referring to the three helicopters."

He let the sentence hang in the air. Alan said nothing.

"Did you see another aircraft last night, Major? Other than the three helicopters you failed to engage when requested to do so by your ground team?"

Alan felt cornered, and he had to fight down the urge to come out fighting. There was nothing he could say that wouldn't make the situation worse.

"I feel like I need legal counsel or something," he said.

"This is a routine debriefing, not a court of law, Major," said the Lieutenant.

Alan's lip buckled into a derisive smile. There was nothing routine about what was happening this morning. But then there had been nothing routine about last night either. He considered. It wasn't their fault that they had to probe him to get a sense of what really happened. If another pilot had told him the same story, would he have believed it?

Probably not.

He would have guessed that this was some trumped up horseshit to cover some more shameful failure. Panic. Incompetence. Even cowardice. These were the words floating in his interviewers' heads. Ugly words which, if they found their way out of their heads and into any formal account of last night's debacle, would cost him his career at very least.

"I did everything I could," he said. It was true but it sounded lame and desperate. In that instant Alan knew he had made a mistake. He should tell them everything, let the chips fall where they may. Maybe the AWACs had picked up some anomalous signal which they'd examine more closely if he said exactly what he thought he had seen. His silence was making his situation worse . . .

"Why don't we take a break and reconvene this afternoon?" said the Lieutenant. "You can think things over, we can talk to the survivors from the ground force, get the test flight completed, and then we can talk later. See if we can't connect these dots better."

The survivors . . .

Alan nodded.

"For the record, Major," said the Captain, "Flight Command has asked that you remain grounded until our investigation is concluded. Until tomorrow then. Major—would you wait here, please?"

His debriefers left the room and, for a moment, Alan just sat there wondering what the hell he had been thinking. Maybe if he went after them, told them he wanted to change his story, this might all start making some kind of sense. He got to his feet, but before he could get to the door, it opened and a man came in.

He was middle aged, lean and fit-looking wearing a trim, charcoal-colored suit in spite of the desert heat. "My name is Special Agent Martin Hatcher," he said, opening a folding wallet and slapping it onto the table so that the three letters printed on the card inside could be read: CIA. "I'll be taking over this interrogation."

"This is a Marine corps matter," Alan said. "You have no authority . . ."

But Martin Hatcher was unflappable.

"NCIS are aware of my presence," he said. "I can wait if you'd like to call your superiors," he remarked, moving around the table until he faced Alan, sitting in the Captain's former seat. "But that will only waste everybody's time and you'll still find that I have all the authority I need."

His tone was conversational, his manner professional but pleasant, as if what he was doing was ordinary, today's business a minor shift from normal operations. Alan stared at him, saying nothing.

"Major Young," he went on, taking an envelope from his briefcase. "I have something requiring your immediate signature."

He opened the envelope and offered Alan a single sheet of paper, a neatly typed letter, addressed to Alan's commanding officer. The first sentence read, "I, Major Alan Young, do hereby resign my commission in the Marine Corps, effective immediately . . ."

Alan looked up.

The CIA officer gave him a level stare, then plucked a ballpoint pen from his shirt pocket and held it across the table.

"Now, please, Major," he said.

JENNIFER
London

I T TOOK JENNIFER THREE DAYS TO GET BACK TO LONDON. She had to bribe two different sets of South African traffic cops en route to Johannesburg airport. They could spot a rental a mile off and tailed you until they saw something they could claim as an infraction, usually someone straying over the solid line dividing the highway. Normally, she was painstakingly careful and alert to police presence, but she was driving in a furious fog that seemed to thicken with each mile the more she considered her father's typically high-handed bullshit.

It was so like him, meddling, subverting what she did, what she worked for, what she believed in. She had called once, leaving an angry voice mail that said she was on her way but refused to say when she'd arrive. The call completed, she had turned off her phone and stowed it deep in her luggage so that she couldn't be tempted to try to reach him again. What she had to say would wait until she was standing in front of him, and she had spent most of the journey crafting in her head precisely what those words would be.

On the outskirts of the Johannesburg, skirting a black township edged with rusty corrugated iron and shelters made of oil barrels and polythene sheeting, she moved into the center lane to avoid herds of wandering cattle and goats, and still had to brake hard when a baboon ran across the road through heavy traffic. She was in sight of the city's metropolitan sprawl, but it still felt like what her father considered "third world."

And people like him made it so.

She didn't hate her father. She was sure of that, but of late, it had become harder to distinguish the man from his work, and there was no question that she had hated his work for a long time. Edward Quinn was a financier. That was how he introduced himself, saying it with a modest twinkle that implied he could, with a click of his mouse, bring half a dozen small nations to the brink of bankruptcy, but it wasn't a big deal. If money made the world turn, then it was people like her father who controlled how fast it turned, and while she could live with the sickening profits he reaped in the process, she'd learned, as a child, to loathe the idea that channeling money to one place meant taking it from somewhere else. The tasteful excess she had grown up with—the sprawling Hampstead mansion, the Tuscan villa, the scattering of elegantly appointed apartments and hotel suites in every corner of the world, the Jaguars and BMWs, her father's Saville Row suits, which cost more than most people in Swaziland made in a year—it had all become emblematic of everything that was wrong with the world.

For years now, she had vacillated between her moral outrage at the source of her father's wealth and the idea that she could put some of it to good use, despite the harm his corporate cronies had done to the world, but she was off balance now. His meddling in her work couldn't go on. She would sit him down, look him in the eye, and tell him.

She was tired of being held hostage. She wanted no more of his money. Ever.

The irony that she had used her father's credit card to buy an airline ticket, first class, was not lost on her. Life was about to get very difficult. It would be some time before she could get back to the kind of work she saw as her calling, her cosmic duty to balance the damage her father had done to the world.

People managed, she told herself, as she boarded the British Airways flight to Heathrow. She was educated, accomplished. She would be able to find work, good benevolent work that paid enough that she could cut her ties to her father and still put enough bread on the table to get by. It would be an adjustment, but she could do it. If it meant losing her fiscal safety net, it also meant she would gain her independence.

She extended her pod-like recliner all the way back, reveling in its luxurious privacy, comfortable knowing this was the last time she would do so. From here on, Jennifer Quinn would fly coach, and rarely.

She landed shortly after dawn, on a typically cold, damp English morning. She felt strange, returning to her past, considering all that she had gained and lost since she was last home. Maybe she would go for a run in the rain after she got home. Clear her head. She normally ran every other day without fail and the cramped confinement had left her body feeling like a compressed spring.

She had not left her flight details on his voice mail so he wouldn't be able to send a car to get her. Her plan was to take a series of trains and busses like an ordinary person. So she was surprised to see Reg Deacon, her father's personal assistant, waiting for her just beyond customs and immigration.

For a second, she watched the man her father called "his old retainer" as he scanned the faces of passengers emerging from customs and immigration with something like contempt. Then her surprise at his being there at all deepened and grew more complicated. Deacon was a chief of staff, and his duties spanned a range of responsibilities, both domestic and professional. They did not, however, include chauffeuring.

Deacon was in his early sixties, a tough, unreadable man who had ghosted Jennifer's entire life but who gave little away. As a girl, she had liked him, but she had distanced herself from him more and more over the years, seeing him as another cog in her father's great machine. This morning, he looked tired, drawn, and there was something in his face she had never seen before.

Then the man's eyes found her and locked on. A flash of recognition was immediately replaced with a kind of sigh as his body sagged, his face hollowing, his eyes full of sadness and apprehension.

Something had happened. Something bad.

For a moment they just stared at each other, oblivious to the milling travelers, and something passed between them. Jennifer's anger evaporated in the sudden absolute certain realization that her father was dead, and then the world went away, and she was not aware of herself enough to be amazed by her own tears.

DEACON HAD BOUGHT HER A CHEESE AND ONION PASTY for breakfast, because she had loved them when she was a kid. Sitting in the car parked outside Heathrow's terminal 3, she took a half-hearted bite, and then, though it tasted of nothing, devoured it hungrily, washing it down with a bottle of orange juice.

"Now, before we go home," said Deacon carefully, floating that last word uncertainly, as if he didn't know if it would comfort or distress her, "I wanted to ask how you would like to handle some legal matters."

She gave him a blank look, as if he were speaking Siswati or Zulu and she had to grope around for a mental dictionary.

"Legal matters?"

"Though we could not reach you, your father's unfortunate demise . . ."

"Suicide," she interrupted, trying the word out to see if it sounded more plausible when she said it. It didn't.

"Quite," said Deacon with studied caution. He was treating her like a bomb that might go off at any moment. "It has . . . set things in motion. Which is to say . . ." he hesitated. "When ordinary people die, the world goes on, and those who knew the deceased are given time to grieve. But your father was anything but ordinary. A great deal of important business depended upon him. His absence—particularly since it was so sudden and unexpected—has left many matters in need of resolution . . ."

"I don't care about any of that," she said, flatly, watching the rain, which had begun to streak the car's tinted windows.

"Which is understandable," Deacon said, "but a lot of other people do. I don't need to remind you of the scale of your father's business involvements."

"I said . . ."

"You don't care, I know," Deacon pressed. "But wheels are already in motion to resolve those matters left in limbo by your father's absence."

She looked at him.

"His death," Deacon conceded.

"So?" she said. "What does this have to do with me?"

It was a stupid remark. She had always avoided thinking about what she would do when her father's money one day became hers, and she had always assumed that was about defiance, a refusal to be interested in what he had worked so hard to accumulate. Suddenly she wondered if she had avoided the subject because it meant acknowledging that he would die and she would be alone.

"You are his sole surviving heir," said Deacon. "Though I'm sure your father's business dealings are of little interest to you, you must be present at the opening of the will, which is going to explicate those dealings. As well as more personal matters. The lawyers are already assembled at Steadings. I am happy to send them away for today, but matters must be dealt with in a reasonably prompt . . ."

"It's fine," said Jennifer quickly.

"Fine?"

"I'll do it today. As soon as we get home."

Deacon considered her gravely.

"Are you sure?"

"Yes," she said, forcing a smile, which almost buckled into something else before she could turn her face to the window. "Best to get it over."

But reading the will got nothing over. Quite the contrary.

Jennifer sat in the drawing room at Steadings, the Hampshire mansion, its French windows looking out over formal gardens and a ring of trees, which shrouded the house from prying eyes, avoiding the eyes of the formally dressed lawyers and the watchful businessmen who had been assembled to hear what Edward Quinn had thought fit to do with his numerous, weighty assets. Some of the men were known to her. Two or three had been shadowy features of her life from as long ago as she could remember, but they had all become part of the world on which she had turned her back and she met their murmurs of condolence with chill politeness.

She was the youngest person in the room by a good two decades and the only woman. They were all, of course, white. Herman Saltzburg, who she remembered hiding from as a kid because his almost skeletal face and hands had given her nightmares, was eying her with vague surprise as if he had forgotten her existence entirely. He was still hollow-cheeked and lean to the point of cadaverousness, and when he offered her a hand to shake it was dry as paper and she could feel every bone and sinew, so that for a moment she was eight years old again and desperate to run back to her room and close the door. At the opposite end of the spectrum was Ronald Harrington-Smythe, a man so large he seemed to fill an entire corner of the drawing room all by himself. He was bald and his bullet-shaped head emerged from the collar of his massive shirt like the tip of a great cone.

There were plenty others she didn't know, including one who came in just as proceedings were about to begin, younger than the rest, with raven black hair which—at least by the standards of the room—was positively disheveled and gave his finely cut suit a rakish look. His eyes flashed around the room, lingered on her for a fraction of a second, then moved to where Deacon, flanked by lawyers, had begun to speak.

"We are here today," he began, sounding like a minister, "to consider the last will and testament of our friend, colleague, and—to Jennifer—father, Edward Quinn, a special proviso of which is the deceased's request that you all be here, whether or not you stand to benefit directly."

Jennifer caught an elderly man stealing a glance in her direction. She ignored it.

Let's just get this over with, she thought for the fiftieth time that morning, *and we can all go our separate ways . . .*

Deacon continued with the formalities. To her right a man with diamond-studded cufflinks shifted in his seat, and then one of the lawyers was unsealing a large envelope and reading in a thin, wavering voice.

"Edward Quinn's will, spelling out all of his holdings, is a long and complex document because his interests were numerous," the executor said, "but at its core, it is remarkably simple because Mr. Quinn made a substantial codicil to amend it, three days before he died."

There was a subtle change in the room, as if the air had been charged with electricity. Brows furrowed, spines stiffened, pens, which had been scribbling on paper, stilled, and all eyes locked onto the lawyer. They had not expected this, and Jennifer, to her surprise, found herself interested, even amused. It seemed the old man had one last trick up his sleeve.

"We will go through the details in a moment," said the lawyer, "and I'm sure you will have a lot of questions, but the core change is summed up in the introductory sentence to the codicil, witnessed by myself and one other, which reads thus. *I, Edward Quinn, being of sound mind and body, as attested by competent authorities and witnesses, do hereby bequeath, excepting those few gifts made to my staff and in particular to Reginald Deacon, all my possessions, all capital, stocks, shares and properties, all assets, partnerships and business interests under my ownership, including those seats on executive boards which are mine to control, and retaining to them the full executive power I have wielded in life, to my daughter, Jennifer."*

TIMIKA
New York

MARVIN LED TIMIKA BACK TOWARD THE OFFICE WITH his usual, bobbing gait, jiving vaguely to some private soundtrack only he could hear. They were met on the sidewalk outside the door by Audrey Stanhope, Debunktion's pit-bull reporter. She looked excited.

"Bomb scare," she announced, delighted. "We're supposed to clear out for the day until the premises are rendered secure . . . and yeah, that's a quote."

"From who?" Timika demanded. She adjusted her crimson coat, feeling conspicuous. It made her feel like a stop sign.

"Hunky bomb squad guy," said Audrey. "Didn't give me his name. Yet."

She fluffed her blond hair hopefully.

"Bomb scare?" Marvin whined. "Oh, man. Harsh. We really can't go in?"

"Really," said Audrey. "But they want to talk to us before we leave."

"They?" Marvin echoed. "You mean . . . *cops*? Oh, man."

Like a lot of stoners, Marvin had a deep-seated paranoia about the police.

"I'm going nowhere," said Timika. "I've got work to do."

"Don't tell me—tell him," said Audrey, nodding to a clean-cut young man emerging from the building. He was wearing a navy blue sweater, matching slacks, and a heavily padded jacket, which looked like it covered body armor, marked "Police HSI." Audrey snapped on her most radiant smile and gave him an absurd wave that made her look like a distressed starlet from a fifties screwball comedy.

"You gonna shout 'yoo hoo!?'" Timika asked. "Complete the picture."

Audrey stuck her tongue out at her, but recovered the smile as the hunk swaggered into earshot.

"The boss," said Audrey by way of introduction. "Timika Mars. I don't think I caught your name."

"Miss Mars," said the young man, apparently immune to Audrey's charms. "I'm Agent Cook with Homeland Security Investigations' Special Response Team. Mind if I ask you a few questions?" He was addressing the three of them.

"Here?" asked Timika, considering his badge.

"We can sit in the park if you like," said the policeman. "It may be some time before the building has been cleared. The team is already in."

Timika glanced up and down the street. Mrs. Singh, at the nail salon next door, was arranging a special offer display in the window.

"Sure," she said. "What do you need?"

Marvin's face was pale, and he was breathing shallowly.

"Have you had any threats lately?" asked the cop. "I believe you run a controversial website."

Timika gave her principal reporter a look. Controversial was an Audrey word, designed to make the journalism sound edgy.

"No more than usual," she answered. "Nothing serious."

"Any unexpected deliveries?"

The agent had plucked out a notepad and chose this moment to look down at it. It was probably nothing, but for a split second, Timika felt sure he had avoided her eyes.

She shook her head, feeling the weight of the strange notebook in her coat pocket. Marvin opened his mouth, his face a comic mask of confusion, but said nothing. "Nothing yesterday," she said. "Bills and junk. The usual."

"And today?"

"It's ten o'clock in the morning, man," she said. "Mail doesn't arrive until two."

"Right," said the cop. "And no hand deliveries?"

"Hand deliveries?" asked Timika with more hauteur than she felt. "What you think I'm running here—a trading post?"

"No ma'am," said the agent, offering her a card. "My number, if anything occurs to you. We should have you in again in two or three hours."

"Two or three hours!" Timika said. "What am I supposed to do until then? Can I at least get my laptop?"

"What does it look like?"

"Like a laptop," she said, marching toward the door. "Come on. I'll show you."

"Can I get a card too?" Audrey cooed. "In case anything occurs to me?"

"Yes, ma'am," said the cop, fishing in his jacket pocket as Timika opened the door and made for the stairs. As she walked, she stared straight ahead, saying nothing, but thinking furiously.

Timika was used to sniffing out BS on a daily basis, and Dion said she was naturally suspicious, untrusting. But it had to be more than that. Everything about this felt wrong.

Letting a civilian back into a building that was being searched for a bomb? Not closing down the street? Not leading the people in the vegetarian restaurant, or the optician's, or the nail salon to safety behind a perimeter of brightly colored police tape? Two guys performing the inspection with no support team, no vehicles, no protective gear? Either they didn't really expect to find a bomb—in which case she was being messed around for no good reason—or something else was going on entirely.

Whatever it was, she sure as hell wasn't about to leave her computer behind.

She entered the office without apology, hearing Cook clattering up the stairs behind her. Another uniformed man, broad-shouldered and sporting a crew cut, stood up quickly behind Audrey's desk, eyes lasering in on her, his right hand moving to the holstered pistol at his hip. He froze when she saw him, not relaxing until agent Cook said, "She works here. Just getting her laptop." His voice was careful, as if he were saying more than the words alone suggested. Timika suddenly felt uncomfortable with him behind her.

What the hell was this?

For a moment she felt panic encroaching at the edges of her consciousness. She half turned and gave him a smile, as if nothing could be more normal. She made a show of folding the laptop closed and slipping it into its case, like a magician showing his audience he has nothing up his sleeve. The handwritten notebook that had been dropped that morning—that was what they were looking for. She was sure of it. Why, God knew, but this was no bomb squad.

"When can we get back in?" she asked, as perky as she could muster. "I've got a ton of stuff to get through."

"We'll be done by noon," said Cook. "Hopefully sooner, so stay close."

"Great," she said, holding up the laptop like a shield as she made for the door. "I'll wait for you outside."

"Hold it," said the man by Audrey's desk.

She felt the urge to run, but stifled it and turned.

"Your coworkers need to get any of their stuff too?" asked the second man.

Timika breathed. "No, and they aren't my coworkers," she said, finding a little swagger as she marched out. "This ain't no damn commune. They work for me."

Marvin and Audrey were waiting for her on the pavement outside, watching the building warily, as if half-expecting it to erupt into flames any minute.

"Is it me," said Audrey, "or did that feel really weird?"

"It's not you," said Timika, cinching her long red coat a little tighter. "Let's take a walk."

It was early spring but still cold, the trees were bare and stark, as if all color had been drained from the square. At least there was no snow on the ground.

"So what do we think?" Marvin asked, scared out of his stoner glaze. "Not cops, right?"

"Right," said Timika, flicking the absurd wig out of her face. She wished she hadn't worn it. It had been a private joke with Dion. That seemed like a very long time ago now.

"*Daily News? The Post?*" Audrey suggested.

Timika scowled but said nothing. It wouldn't be the first time a tabloid had tried to poach a story from her, but she knew most of their reporters personally, and these two were new to her. She pictured the way the one with the crew cut had watched her from behind her desk, the way his hand had strayed to his gun when she walked in. No. She didn't know who they were, but she was prepared to bet her last dollar that these guys weren't reporters.

She was also prepared to bet she knew what they were looking for.

Though she complained about them from time to time, Timika trusted Marvin and Audrey completely.

"They want this," she said. "I don't know why, but I'm not going back until I've read it. See what might be worth a stunt this crazy."

Audrey nodded.

"First things first," Timika said. "Let's find a copy shop. If someone's going to try to steal it, we could use a backup. And since I work best with caramel macchiato inside me, I suggest East Side Copy on thirteenth, and then Joe's."

"Sounds like a plan," said Audrey.

A flock of pigeons ballooned into the air on their left, wings clapping. Timika, who disliked birds, winced and shielded her face, turning back the way they had come.

And that was how she saw them, Cook and the other man in their HSI uniforms, moving purposefully towards her, watching her, then breaking into a run as soon as they realized they'd been spotted.

"They're coming," Timika gasped. The one with the crew cut was reaching for his weapon.

"Go," said Marvin, with none of his usual flapping indecisiveness. "Run!"

She met Audrey's eyes, saw the fractional nod of agreement, and broke into a plunging dash along the path toward the subway station. Behind her, someone shouted, though she couldn't catch the words. In front of her, a bicycle courier swerved and spilled onto the grass as she barged through. A woman with a baby carriage cursed her, and businessmen stared as if they'd never seen the like before, and then there was a pop and an almost instantaneous answering bang from a mailbox yards in front of her, a neat hole punching through the steel.

They were shooting at her.

A cry went up behind her, a rising wail of panicked horror. As she turned, she saw the path behind her clearing as people flung themselves to the ground.

For a second, she saw the gunman clearly. He was perhaps a hundred yards behind her, weapon raised and sighted. She saw the muzzle flash before she heard the report, heard the zip of the bullet through the air beside her head, and then saw the gunman crumple under Marvin's inexpert sideswiping tackle.

The two men went down together. Timika started back towards them.

God! she thought. *God!* But then she saw Audrey screaming at her to go, and she began to run again, though now her legs felt like they were made of iron and concrete.

Oh God. Marvin.

The subway was behind her. She glanced back, heading south on University past the fancy furniture store, and when she could no longer see behind her, turned quickly onto Eleventh Street, forcing herself into a steady trot. She was wearing the wrong heels for running. Turn her ankle and she may as well go back and hand them the book . . .

Pace yourself.

Marvin wouldn't be able to handle himself in a fight. The crowd would think he was attacking a policeman.

Keep going.

She should have just given them the damn book. What was it, anyway? Some crackpot's scrapbook of made up history, designed to get his idiot name into the twitterverse. It was absurd.

There were no alleys to duck into. Desperation mounting, she risked a look back. The man who had called himself Cook had stopped and was looking her way, talking into a radio attached to the shoulder of his jacket. It meant there were more of them.

Timika scanned the street corner, fishing her phone from her pocket and unsteadily thumbing on her GPS. She was looking for a cop, but stopped herself. Any uniform in the area might be working with Cook. By now, back in the park, someone would have called 911. Legitimate police were surely on their way. Ironically, that meant the safest place to be might be back where she'd come from, if she could elude the impostors pursuing her. There was also her car, but it felt like it was parked a hundred miles away.

She made a hard right and stepped into the first store she saw. She thought it was a dry-cleaners, judging by the hanging, plastic-covered garments, but then she saw dressmaker's manikins, a long counter with a built in yard stick, and racks holding bolts of fabric. An elderly Asian lady looked up from her sewing machine expectantly.

"You got a rear exit?" Timika asked.

The woman's face tightened.

"You gonna buy something?"

"Kind of in a rush," said Timika, checking the door behind her.

"What I look like?" asked the old woman grumpily. "Trying to make living here."

Timika pulled her wallet from her coat without breaking stride, tore out a five and flung it on the counter as she sped by.

"To the back," said the woman, eying the bill. "Right, then green door on left."

Timika shouldered her way through the heaps of material and made it to the back just as the front door opened.

Cook.

She ducked around the corner and found the green door. It was bolted shut. Half cursing, half sobbing, she worked the rusty bolts back and dragged the door open. He would be on her in seconds.

"Hey!" called the old woman's muffled voice from the front of the shop. "You buying something or what?"

Timika pushed out into a dim alley full of sour smelling trashcans. She reached for a fractured wooden crate and tried to jam it under the door handle like she'd seen people do in movies. She doubted it would delay her pursuer.

Pursuers. Plural. She had no idea where crew cut was, and there could be others.

As she started to run again, she told herself she should spend more time in the gym and less time eating pizza. The thought needled her, but it was the kind of needling that took her attention away from what might happen, and that was all to the good.

Knew you'd be running for your life today, did you? she demanded of herself. *Saw this one coming? Yeah, that's what I figured.*

She took a few more staggering strides, gasping for air, and thought of Marvin, who had thrown his incompetent self at the gunman back in the park. A pulse of sadness coursed up through her chest, tightening around her heart. She couldn't run much longer.

She heard the back door of the tailoring shop open behind her.

Timika made a left at the end of the alley, breathing hard. She didn't know this block at all. She was scared, struck with the certainty that she couldn't stay ahead of him much longer. He was strong, fast, and ruthless. She was none of those things. In the movie version of this moment, she would be waiting and ready, her concentration channeling unexpected combat skills gleaned from years of recreational Tae Kwan Do or some such shit, and she would dance her way out of danger with a quip and a grin.

But this was reality, and she was almost out of time.

JERZY
Wenceslas, Poland, December 1944

THE REGIMEN AT THE WENCESLAS MINE DID NOT change. We got up before dawn, straightened the straw of our beds for fear of beatings or the loss of our meager daily meal, and stood silent and motionless for an hour or more—whatever the weather—in front of the barracks. There, we were inspected and given our instructions for the day before being marched to our work sites. We worked until nightfall without breaks, without food, getting only a bowl of thin soup and a crust of bread before bed. You lost track of time, not just minutes or hours, but weeks, months.

Around us, workers dropped—Jews like us, but also Poles, Czechs and Russians. Sometimes they were still there the next day, frozen in the snow until we were allowed to bury them. But even as we fell, the great complex of tunnels and structures we built formed around and below us. Much of it was in use already. I saw great vaulted concrete hallways buzzing with white-coated scientists and civilian inspectors. The complex was like a great beast that needed constant feeding as it sprawled and expanded.

Ishmael and I lived in constant fear of being separated, and though our records showed we were brothers, we were careful not to talk where people might see us. Families were divided for spite and, I came to think later, to create a sense of isolation. People in a state of true despair are easier to control. I suspect many of the guards simply liked to see us reduced to the unthinking beasts they believed us to be. We worked hard, so that they would have no reason to separate us.

No one knew what we were building. Some said the mine was a test facility for great ballistic rockets and the jet aircraft the Nazis thought might yet turn the tide of the war. The secrecy under which we worked was fierce and uncompromising. Once, when a party of five men took a wrong turn in the warren of tunnels, an officer had them all shot on the spot because they had seen something they should not have seen. That was enough. The corpse recovery detail sent in to take out the bodies took twice as long as usual because they were blindfolded and led by a kapo and guards who pulled them along using ropes.

But we heard stories. Strange vats of chemicals were trucked in. At times, the mine seemed to hum with a peculiar, throbbing energy. Workers in some parts of the facility spoke of a glowing violet light pulsing through the cracks in doorframes, and those who saw it complained of sudden, inexplicable nausea. Ben Aizinberg, a burly man who had once run his own slaughterhouse in Kraków, said that he saw two scientists arguing with a guard about returning to a particular chamber. His German wasn't good, but he understood enough to learn the source of their terror.

"*Die Glocke*," he said, in a hushed voice.

The Bell.

What this might be, we had no idea. A weapon, perhaps, or some new torture device. Just being near it made people sick. The German soldiers had learned they could not take their guard dogs close to the site, because the dogs would whine and cringe away, and lie huddled and whimpering for hours after. Some said it was a power source, others that it did not exist, and that it was just another story to keep us scared.

But we learned, at great expense, that it was not just a story. I will relate this part of my narrative carefully, but it is hard. Even now, my hand trembles as I try to recall precisely what happened that terrible day.

Ishmael and I were digging trenches for a concrete pouring when an officer came to speak to the guards. He was young and blond, like many of the SS who ran the camp, but I had not seen him before. The insignia on his collar had three pips and two strokes, so it looked a little like a domino. Our kapo that day was a man called Boritz, a mean, self-interested Pole who delighted in brutally lashing out at prisoners when his Nazi masters were watching. Though he was Jewish like us, he was well-fed and well-clothed, wearing, as a badge of pride, the green triangle insignia that identified him as a *befristeten Vorbeugungshäftling kapo*. Ishmael and I watched as he saluted the young officer and engaged him in conversation while the guards looked on. Then they started scrutinizing the workers, so we lowered our eyes to what we were doing and held our breath. It was never good to be noticed.

But noticed, we were. Ishmael and I were chosen, with five other men who were older than us but whose bodies had not yet yielded to the starvation diet and brutal work-load. Without explanation, we were escorted by two guards with submachine guns and marched behind the blond offi-cer, up through the main hall and then down a series of the great V-shaped tunnels we had spent the last few months casting. We did not speak, and at first, I could barely see for fear. It was not uncommon for prisoners to be publicly executed, merely to send a message to the rest, but the fur-ther we walked, the clearer it became that we were moving into areas of the mine we had not been before, areas where few prisoners were permitted to go. After we had been walk-ing for a few minutes, the noise of the workforce fell away behind us, and our own footsteps echoed strangely in the concrete passageway. Twice, we saw officers and men in laboratory coats, but no more prisoners, and my fear soon mixed with something else, a strange and dreadful curiosity.

We passed through a series of guarded doors where the officer leading us showed papers. The duty soldiers looked us over carefully before blindfolding us and pushing us inside. The blindfolds were old, and the fabric of mine was almost rubbed through, such that although I was careful to fumble about and move at half speed, like the rest, I could see fairly well with one eye. I did not flinch when the guard waved his hands in front of my face. Once inside, I was careful not to turn my head to look around.

We were in a vast, concrete hangar. At one end, huddled around a console of some sort, were a pair of armed guards and men in lab coats, all under the watchful eye of a middle-aged man in a suit. He had a slanted smile of ironic amusement on his face. He wore a coat draped over his shoulders, and the collar of the coat was studded with SS insignia. I had never seen the rank badges before, and though he gave off the air of an office worker, the others kept a respectful distance. When his eyes fell on the blond officer, the latter clicked his heels together and saluted. Whoever this man was, he was important.

I heard the blond officer introduced as *Hauptsturmführer* Ungerleider. It was a name I would come to loathe.

The perimeter of the vast chamber was girded with access gantries and ductwork. At ground level, I saw glass-fronted offices facing the center, where I saw a strange metallic structure the size of a small shed but with a dome-shaped top and walls that flared out at the bottom. I recognized it at once from Aizinberg's stories.

The Bell.

Pipes and tubing and cables laced it to the offices and to various tanks, or to bottles and vats placed on the floor, all cluttered with what looked like steam valves and electronic controls, but also coiled up into the great gray ceiling. I did not dare raise my eyes. We were led to a metal staircase and urged up.

I smelled fresh air. We were going above the surface. When we were all up and the steel trap door to the stairway clanged shut behind us, our blindfolds were removed and tucked into our waistbands. For a long moment, we stood bemused, blinking at the cold, pale sky and the strange concrete structure that loomed over us.

It was a great concrete ring, standing on eleven cement pillars, perhaps thirty-feet high, all painted turquoise and strung with heavy cable. I had never seen its like before, but it reminded me of pictures I had seen in a schoolbook of an ancient monument in England called Stonehenge. The barren earth beneath our feet was strangely charred in parts, bleached in others, and there was no trace of the weeds or the lichen that clung to all the other buildings at Wenceslas. Around the perimeter was a high fence topped with barbed wire and four watchtowers sprouting machine guns, the big 42s. Beyond the fence—and this was almost as strange—were only dense pine forests. No roads, no checkpoints or buildings of any kind. If there was a protective wall, it was far out of sight.

Drainage holes in the earth at the base of each pillar seemed to communicate with the chamber below. From each hole, a heavy cable emerged, its end marked with a pronged electrical connector. The kapo got his orders from the SS officer, and we were told to scale the columns, using ladders, and plug the cables into metal fittings that ran around the circle of concrete at the top.

It was grueling work. It took all seven of us to haul the first cable up from the chamber below—twelve meters of it, wrapped with wire and canvas tape like some monstrous tentacle. When we had it out, we lay sweating and panting in the snow until the kapo said we were taking too long and had to get on with the next one. We got back to our feet, formed a line and pulled the next cable up and out, huddled against each other's bent shoulders so that we inhaled the stench of soiled clothes and unwashed bodies, straining to get each length out and extended, one after another.

Even with the menacing of the kapo and the guards, it took us two hours to get all eleven cables pulled through, and all the while, Ungerleider, the blond officer, watched, his face impassive. The next task was to position ladders and crawl up to the concrete rim of the henge, the cables looped around our shoulders. This was harder still, because only three of us would fit on the ladder, and the highest one had to manipulate the plug into the socket, which meant he could bear none of the cable's weight. As the smallest, that job was given to me, but exhaustion and months of doing jobs designed for bigger, stronger men, finally took its toll. I was fitting the third cable into place when I lost my footing and fell from the ladder. If Ishmael had not broken my fall, I would have surely died on the concrete, but my brother caught me awkwardly and we both hit the ground together.

He took my full weight on his left arm. I heard it break distinctly. His left ankle crumpled beneath him and he winced, jaws clenched, tears in his eyes as we sprawled together, but to my garbled apologies, he said only, "Shh little brother. Say nothing. I will be fine."

He wouldn't, but we both knew there was no place in the camp for a Jew who could not work. When the guards came over to get us roughly to our feet, he shrugged them off with a gesture that said he needed no assistance, but when he stumbled and I couldn't keep him up, we were ordered to sit in the corner with the tools. We were blindfolded again and waited while the others finished the work.

I could still see through the worn and ragged scarf, and I was able to watch, without moving my head, as the rest of the team plugged in the final cable and climbed back down the ladder.

"I'm sorry, Ishmael," I whispered. "I was just so tired. How is your arm?"

"Shhh . . ." my brother answered, "they'll hear. Don't worry about it. You think I'd let you fall? You looked like a wingless goose dropping out of the sky."

I grinned at that, though I was worried about his arm. Then I realized that the others were being blindfolded. As the scarves were tied in place, Ungerleider spoke to the guards and moved away. The guards moved too, heading for the hatch leading down into the mine. The prisoners were left standing in the center, alone. Waiting.

"Ishmael," I said. "Something is happening. Stand up."

"I can't. My ankle is swollen . . ."

"Get up! I can see . . ."

I hesitated, trying to make sense of the images. Ungerleider stood at the mouth of the great pipe-like access passage, watching as some of the soldiers went down, and then he was looking up to the machine gun towers. He nodded once, and then climbed into the shaft, dragging the hatch closed behind him.

I tore the blindfold from my head, threw it down and snatched at Ishmael's.

"What are you doing?" he gasped. "They'll kill us!"

But they were going to kill us anyway. The men in the towers were readying their weapons, training them down onto the circle below. We had, it seemed, seen too much.

But Ishmael resisted. For a second he glared at me, his eyes full of fear and exasperation, and then the strange quiet of the place registered, and he looked around to where the other prisoners, including the kapo now, also blindfolded, shifted uneasily, the six of them looking so small under the great, strange ring and pillars of concrete, like blind priests at some ancient temple.

Or sacrificial offerings.

I saw the tools, scattered on the concrete close by, and my heart skipped back into life: wire cutters. I snatched them up and turned to face the fence and the woods beyond, so close but still so far away.

"What's happening?" asked Ishmael as if he were on the brink of sleep.

For a moment there was an eerie stillness under the concrete henge, and then with a thunderous roar, the great guns opened up, raining down from all four watchtowers at the perimeter.

I didn't wait to watch them fall. I loped the few yards to the fence, expecting to feel the bullets tearing into my back, threw myself down and set to work with the wire cutters.

"Ishmael!" I called over my shoulder. "Ishmael!"

I didn't dare look around. Any second, the guns would find us too. I sheared away and pulled at the wire. As I did, I saw a bit of exposed metal on the ground on the other side, half covered by snow and pine straw.

Mines.

But to remain inside the fence was certain death. I would take my chances in the minefield. I snipped again, bending the wire back. The ground around me suddenly kicked up dirt as the gunners homed in on me. The hole in the fence was, perhaps, big enough.

"Ishmael!" I called, turning back, extending a hand to him.

But Ishmael was lying on his belly, facing me. He was fading. Blood pooled beneath him where he'd been hit.

"No!" I shouted. But when I moved towards him, his face changed, focused.

"Go, little brother!" he said.

And then the machine gun rounds were flashing around us, thudding into his prone, broken body, and he was gone.

ANDY
Kofu, Japan 1989

ANDY BICYCLED THROUGH THE THICK JUNE EVENING, wishing—not for the first time that day—that he could stop and shower. A Northern Englishman, only a year out of university, whose world traveling had been limited to Greek and Italian beach holidays, he was unprepared for the hot, humid summers in Japan. A few weeks into his stay, he'd awoken to the sound of something moving in the kitchen and found, to his horror, a three-inch-long black cockroach scuttling around in the stainless steel sink. Insects big enough that you could hear them from the next room were not a feature of the Lancashire life he'd known.

The roaches weren't the only problem. The loud cicadas in the trees, the giant locusts in the grass, the stag beetles in the pet shops, even the sweet and salty crickets served in place of nuts in the bars, all gave him the willies. Bicycling at night was particularly awful because you were moving too fast to see what might fly into your face. Two nights ago, he'd hit a moth so big he thought it was a bird, and almost lost control of the bike in his panic.

Still, bicycling was how he got around, when he wasn't taking the train. The Japanese driving test was famously—some said deliberately—punishing on foreigners, containing a lengthy written section that demanded language skills no one could achieve with only a year or two of college Japanese. Not that Andy had even that. He'd been an English major, and had landed a position with the fledgling JET program, which placed native English speakers in Japanese high schools, largely because so few people from the UK had any real experience with Japanese. Andy had known next to nothing about Japan when he arrived. As a result, the whole experience had been a bit of a trial by ordeal, and one that concerned more than just bugs.

He had one foreign friend, a Mexican-American named Jesús, the son of migrant field laborers now settled in northern California. Jesús was a big, thoughtful guy Andy's age, a skilled visual artist, a thinker and a wit. Andy suspected he might also be gay, but they didn't talk about that.

The community of foreigners in the little town of Kofu, a little over a hundred kilometers west of Tokyo, was almost entirely comprised of JET employees, a few Mormon missionaries who kept to themselves, and a few other Americans who taught classes at the YMCA. Andy had met an older Canadian man who had settled in Kofu years ago, married a Japanese woman and had a pair of teenaged daughters, but the others were here for no more than a year or two. The word was that the JET program was going to send its Australian members home at the end of their contract, whether they wanted to renew or not, because of tax treaty issues, so the pool of English speakers would get smaller still.

Circumstances had thrown people together, united by the fact that they all spoke English and were all a long way from home, in a place that was alien and strange, and though Andy liked most of them well enough, Jesús was the only one he could see being friends with elsewhere. The Japanese were generally welcoming, and some of them seemed to idolize every foreigner they saw, but they were also different, and for all their apparent friendliness, tended to keep their distance. When you were separated by language from even the TV and the billboards, Japan could be a very lonely place. Andy had never been especially social in university, but he couldn't get enough of it now, both the gatherings at the local bars with their red paper lanterns, and the quiet evenings with Jesús, where they would sit and chat and drink until they were comfortable enough to just be quiet and think their own thoughts.

Andy lived up on the Kofu bypass, which arrowed along the northern rim of the town, while Jesús lived down in the basin, separated from the urban center by one of the craggy mountainous outcrops that typified the area this side of Mt. Fuji. By Japanese standards, Kofu was a smallish city, a couple of hundred thousand people clustered together in one of the country's only land-locked prefectures, two hours from Tokyo. Parts of it felt ancient and strange, elegant tiled rooftops and tiny, immaculate gardens, while other parts were clean and modern, but distinctly Japanese in ways that made them a bit unreal.

Andy pedaled on, bracing himself for the long tunnel through the mountainside. It was generally hot and poorly ventilated inside, the air bitter with exhaust fumes that made him feel lightheaded. There were never any pedestrians on the elevated sidewalk. Andy pedaled hard, keen to get through and out. Even so, it took several minutes to reach the end, and he emerged into the warm night air coughing, his head thick with poisonous smog.

The other side of the tunnel, where the red neon letters of the TDK building marked the only significant structure, was an entirely different world. The road down into the basin was steep and narrow, a series of hard switchbacks that zigzagged down to the quiet suburbs of the town, marked by vineyards and ancient Buddhist temples sprouting unexpectedly from the crisscrossed interlacing of little streets lined with tidy houses. In daylight, you might see uniformed schoolchildren or grannies bent over double, their backs loaded with bales of rice straw, as if the town couldn't figure out which century it was in.

As Andy came round the corner, riding his brakes and not needing to pedal, he looked up and saw an object in the sky. He stopped, amazed. It was long and roughly cigar shaped, and dark, with no lights at all, and if it hadn't been silhouetted against a moon that was nearly full, he wouldn't have seen it.

It hung motionless in the sky, slightly tilted up at what Andy took to be the nose, though the shape was feature-less, and both ends looked the same. It was stationary, slimmer and more rigid-looking than a blimp or those old dirigibles he'd seen in pictures, the R101 or the Hindenburg. He marveled at how those names came back to him.

He got off his bike and stood watching it. In daylight, he would have had with him his camera, a Canon T70, his pride and joy, which he took everywhere, knowing that in Japan, every day was a photo opportunity. But he didn't have it with him now.

He waited for ten minutes, hoping someone would come by to corroborate what he was seeing, but the road was deserted. The object did not move, nor did its appear-ance change. After a while, as the strangeness wore off, he grew frustrated and decided to ride down to Jesús' place as fast as he could. His friend would have his camera. He would confirm what he was looking at.

Andy set off, watching the sky for anything that might suggest how big the object was, or at what altitude. He could not get an accurate sense of proportion. If he had to guess, he'd say it was the size of a small commercial air-liner, and no more than a few thousand feet up. But as he cycled, the road cutting back and forth as it angled down into the basin, the object's position in relation to the moon changed, and he lost sight of it. By the time he reached Jesús' apartment, there was no sign of it.

They went looking for it, camera in hand, but it was a hard slog back up to the Heiwa Dori, and they didn't see anything unusual in the sky.

The following day, he shared his story with his fellow teachers at school. Everyone nodded and smiled and said no, there had been no reports of anything on the television news or in the paper. One teacher told him that Kofu was well known for its UFO sighting. Others just shrugged and smiled, and said it was perhaps some kind of balloon, though why such a thing would be up there at night, no one could say.

Andy lived in Japan for another year. During that time, he saw nothing like the strange cigar-shaped object. He returned to the UK, then moved on to graduate school and work in the US, first in Boston, then in Atlanta. He married. He built a career for himself. In all that time, he never saw anything like the object he had watched in the sky over Kofu.

Andy also stayed in touch with Jesús, at first by letters, then by phone calls, and then through social media, though they saw each other rarely and never discussed that particular night. There was, after all, nothing to talk about. Andy had seen something strange, something he couldn't explain, but it had been an undramatic occurrence without a climax or obvious significance. It had no narrative arc. He had seen it, and then he had lost it. He hadn't even witnessed it moving away. As such, it was both event and non-event, something he never forgot, but didn't know what to do with.

He supposed that was the way it was for most people who see strange things in the sky. They carry the memory with them, and a residual uncertainty about the nature of the universe, which they keep private for fear of looking foolish, hoping that someday there will be some simple, ordinary explanation that will, once understood, render the whole thing ordinary. But until that happens, he thought, you have to keep a door open to the possibility that something strange had occurred, something that could turn reality on its head and make the world foreign, even alien.

ALAN
Camp Leatherneck Marine, Helmund Province, Afghanistan,
September 2014

U S FORCES IN AFGHANISTAN, UNLIKE SOME COALITION
troops, were not permitted access to alcohol for fear
of disciplinary issues resulting from drunkenness.
Alcohol also diminished an individual's capacity for good
judgment and restraint. Alan understood the rule and
agreed with it, particularly after a murderous attack on
local civilians by a drunken sergeant, several years prior.
Even if he hadn't agreed with it, Major Alan Young did not
break such rules, though on this Afghan night, after hours
of grueling interrogation and the resultant sense of paranoia and failure, he might have made an exception.

He was still a Major in the Marine Corps, though the clock was ticking.

Hatcher, the CIA man, in response to Alan's reluctance to sign away his career, had given him the night to think it over, though there really wasn't a choice to be made. Either he resigned voluntarily, or he was dishonorably discharged, and while the loss of pension and benefits would certainly cause all manner of hardships, it was the dishonorable part that really stung. He had taken the matter to his commanding officer, asked as formally as he could how it was possible that the CIA could interfere in a Marines matter like this, and though he could sense his CO's fury at being thus pushed around by another government agency, there was apparently nothing he could do to stop it. Whatever happened next, Alan had flown his last mission as a Marine pilot. Life as he had known it, as he had built it, brick by careful brick, was over.

The base was no place for privacy. The place teemed with US, NATO and local personnel at all hours of the day and night, in spite of President Obama's much-touted draw down, particularly since the extension of the runway they shared with the Brits at Camp Bastion. Would he miss it? Thirty-six hours ago, he would have laughed at the idea, but now . . . If only he'd kept his mouth shut and never mentioned the bogey—if he'd just claimed an unexplained system malfunction, he might have talked his way out of it.

He walked the streets and hangars of the airport complex, avoiding people's eyes, showing his ID when necessary, trying to think of nothing, trying to just wear out his body so that he might get a few hours of unbroken sleep.

Things had changed a lot over the last few months as the troops had gradually been pulled out of combat operations. There was a sense that everyone was killing time, waiting to go home. As personnel redeployed stateside, some of the features of what had been a small city were vanishing. It had never been like Kandahar, with its TGI Fridays and KFCs, but Leatherneck had a decent PX, the base chow hall had been expanded, and there were now four gyms. But none of them were to stay in the Marines' control. In the course of the next month they would all be withdrawn and the base handed over to the Afghan army.

Alan didn't mind. It had always felt odd to him, this curious, insulated sense of American normalcy in a war zone, separated from the indigenous population by concrete and wire, so that the only Afghans some of the soldiers ever saw were the ones bussed in daily to operate the Hadji shops.

There was still the rec center, with its gym and video games, and the Green Bean coffee shop ("Honor first, coffee second") where they compensated for the base's lack of alcohol with massive doses of caffeine, and there were soldiers, shopping and wandering around the tents and shipping containers in regulation T-shirts and combat fatigues, but it wouldn't go on much longer. If he had lasted another thirty days or so, Alan would have gone home with the rest of his squadron, his reputation—and his career—intact.

Alan passed through the gap between a tan communications building and a concrete shelter and was waiting for a pair of white vans and a sand-colored Humvee to pass when he saw four men coming round a massive pallet of plastic water bottles. One of them, the one with the bull's shoulders, was Master Sgt. Barry Regis, code named Rattlesnake, Alan's hometown friend and former high school football teammate who had, the last time he had seen him, looked almost ready to kill him. Alan had a hunch his companions were members of the MARSOC team. Alan's step faltered, but it was too late. They had seen him. Regis lowered his head, his face dark and tense with suppressed emotion as he came purposefully on.

Alan waited for him, hands by his side, ready for Regis, and for his steam hammer punch, should he decide to toss his career away in the fury of the moment. The base bristled with security. Any serious altercation would be broken up quickly and with serious consequences. He stood there because a part of him felt if the big man laid him out, it was no more than what he deserved.

"Taking a stroll, Major?" Regis asked. It wasn't just a challenge. It was heavy with feeling. "Thought you'd be in detention."

Alan nodded. "They want my resignation first," he said.

"You get a choice?" Regis replied. "Well, that's nice. My team didn't get a choice."

The two men flanking him were staring him down, and for a second Alan thought one of them might kill him. The idea did not distress him much. His life, as he had just been reflecting, was already over.

"I tried," he said, not to calm them but because he had to say it. They had to at least hear him say that he was no traitor. "My weapons wouldn't fire."

"Yeah," said Regis. "You said. I guess things malfunction sometimes."

It was a kind of concession earned by years of friendship, and something of Regis' anger seemed to wilt so that he looked merely sad, but when Alan made a move to extend his hand, the big man flinched and looked away. A dozen troops bound for the PX circled around them, oblivious. Alan shook his head and tried again.

"Didn't you see something up there with me?" he asked, trying to keep the pleading out of his tone. "Apart from the helicopters, I mean."

"Apart from the helicopters?" Regis echoed, his face hardening again. "The ones that shot up my unit, you mean?"

"There was something in the sky," Alan said, his voice lowering a fraction. "It might have looked like a flare from the ground."

"We were busy dodging missiles, sir," said one of the others, evidently a member of the MARSOC team.

Alan started to raise his hands in some gesture of surrender, or apology.

"I saw a flare," said a dark-haired man. "Hanging in the sky like a beacon. Right?" His voice was smooth, strangely neutral, and though Alan doubted he was from the States, he couldn't identify the foreign accent.

Alan nodded.

"I'm sure our intel people will sort it out," said the dark-haired man. "I am sorry that the mission proved so costly. I've been trying to show the team here my gratitude. My name is CIA Senior Officer Jean-Christophe Morat."

The asset the team was sent to recover. And he was CIA, which explained why Alan's case was no longer in the hands of the Marines.

"Would you be prepared to testify to what you saw?" asked Alan. It was the slimmest of hopes, but it was worth pursuing.

"If necessary," said Morat.

Alan nodded.

"I'm sorry too," he said, looking at Morat but speaking to the others. "If there was anything I could have done . . ."

"Sometimes," said Morat in a voice loaded with resignation and a touch of sadness, "there is nothing that can be done. We find ourselves at the end of a sequence of events set in motion long ago. We can only do our best and live with the consequences."

Alan stared at him, almost entranced, then nodded once more. There was a scent in the dry air, a hint of spice, mixed with gasoline. The fire had gone out of Regis' face. The second man's rigid posture had softened and relaxed.

"Perhaps you and I could discuss it in private?" Morat concluded, his tone conversational now.

"Not tonight," Alan said. "Another time."

He looked at Sgt. Regis one more time, nodded a farewell, and turned on his heel.

BACK IN HIS QUARTERS, ALAN LAY ON HIS BED, HIS MEAGER personal effects racked up on shelves and plastic crates beside him, and stared at the ceiling of the prefabricated hut. He had just gotten comfortable when there was a knock at the door. For a moment, his eyes flashed to the 9mm Beretta on the nightstand.

It was Hatcher, the CIA man who had taken charge of his case. His life.

He had let himself in before Alan was off the bed.

"Please, Major," he said, almost casually. "Don't get up. I thought we might have a little chat, off the Marine Corps Records. Okay with you?"

Alan sat up and swung his feet down to the floor as Hatcher sat in the folding chair.

"Does it make a difference what I think?" he asked.

"Of course," said Hatcher, drawing the resignation letter from his pocket and laying it carefully on the foot of the bed as if it were fragile. "Though I think you should sign this before I leave."

"Last chance?" asked Alan with a bleak smile.

"Something like that," said Hatcher. "I'll be on the first transport out of here in the morning, and I'd like you sitting beside me."

Alan blinked. "Are you offering me a job?" he asked, incredulous.

"More than that," Hatcher replied, "but if it helps to think in those terms, yes, I'm offering you a job. One you can't take without resigning your commission."

"I appreciate the offer, Special Agent, but I don't think I'm interested," said Alan. "I'm a Marine pilot."

"Not anymore. You know that. You can go out honorably and move into a . . . *stimulating* new career, or you can crash and burn. Go down as a failure, in disgrace, possibly even a traitor."

"You know I'm not," said Alan, suddenly sure it was true.

"Your commanders don't. All they know is that you failed to fire on enemy helicopters, jeopardizing the lives of your comrades on the ground. And that your excuse is some malarkey about UFOs."

"I never used that word," Alan cut in.

"No, you didn't," said Hatcher. "Which is interesting, wouldn't you say?"

"Not really. I don't believe in stuff like that."

"You didn't," said Hatcher. "Not until a couple of nights ago. Now, you're not so sure, and that terrifies you. But it's all right, Major. I bring tidings of great joy. That thing you saw—it wasn't a flare. It wasn't marsh gas, or a weather balloon, but it wasn't flown by little green men either."

Alan's mouth was dry, and he felt like the room was spinning, like when he'd drunk too much in college and couldn't get to sleep. He said nothing. Hatcher continued.

"You said it was like a ball of light, yes?" he said.

Alan licked his lips.

"I don't recall precisely."

"Ah, the Reagan strategy," said Hatcher. "Very original. And I'm guessing you don't recall the flight characteristics of the vessel in question, either?"

Alan listened to the wind on the tent roof, and then the words came out.

"It was unlike anything I'd ever seen," he said. "Like nothing on earth."

Hatcher nodded, smiling less with encouragement than with satisfaction that Alan had conceded a point.

"I understand," Hatcher said. "But you're wrong. Pilots have been recording encounters like the one you had for a long time. Did you know that, Major? Bomber crews in World War II called them Foo Fighters—like the band. A corruption of the French word *feu*, meaning 'fire.' They appeared as burning spheres, moving contrary to any known flight dynamics, shooting off at impossible speeds and angles. You've heard of this, right?"

Alan gave a grudging nod.

"They aren't actually spherical. That's an illusion created by their energy signature."

Alan gaped at him, trying to make sense of what he was being told.

"Why are you telling me this?" he asked.

"They are remarkable things," Hatcher concluded, and for a moment there was something else in his voice, something like wonder. His eyes seemed to glaze, as if he were picturing things on the very edge of imagination. He came back to himself with a smile, picked up the letter and thrust it towards Alan's chest.

"Sign this," he said, "and I'll show you."

12

JENNIFER
Steadings, Hampshire

SHE'D EXPECTED TO GET SOMETHING. SHE HAD NOT expected to get everything. The stunned silence, which had greeted the announcement that Jennifer would be taking over all her father's business interests, lasted no more than a second. It collapsed into gasps of astonishment and the kind of plummy-voiced outrage that recalled a particularly bitter parliamentary session, in which Deacon and the lawyers played the roles of both the besieged Prime Minister and Black Rod, the sergeant-at-arms, responsible for keeping order. Her father's business cronies were aghast that "some bit of a girl," was now involved in matters she could not possibly understand. It was too much for her reeling mind to process.

She got up and moved towards the door, avoiding the hostile stares of the elderly men around her. Only one met her gaze with something like understanding: the young man with the raven black hair. He looked sympathetic, and his fractional nod toward her was understanding, even encouraging.

She fled to her room and locked the door.

Alone, surrounded by the remnants of her childhood and adolescence, the resentment she'd long felt towards her father's high handedness returned tenfold. What the hell did he think he was doing, dropping her into his world like this, a world he knew she despised? It was so utterly typical. And outrageous. She had neither interest nor competence in high finance. The idea that she could sit at a conference table with all those ancient, suited men her father did business with was absurd.

Well, she wouldn't do it. It was as simple as that. She would not let him bully her from the grave.

Jennifer sank onto the bed she had slept in for the first eighteen years of her life, absently clutching Mrs. Winterburn, a plush rabbit, now so patched and worn that the stuffing poked out around the throat. The toy had been her constant companion, and when she got too old for stuffed animals, she hid it from visiting friends and from her father, lest they think her childish. She considered it now, its dull glass eyes, its lumpy, shapeless body, and then she set it carefully down beside her half-unpacked luggage.

It was time for her to leave Steadings for good. She would turn aside her father's final attempt to transform her into him, and that meant walking away from all he had been.

Jennifer drew in a long, shuddering breath, blinking back tears of exhaustion and loss. But she was certain of her decision. She glanced around the room, suddenly wanting a picture of her father, so that she could talk to him as if he were there. She needed to explain, and defy, but there were no photographs of him among the childish knickknacks and posters of The Cure and Depeche Mode. She had to go to his study.

Her father's study—his inner sanctum, to which she had rarely been admitted—was on the top floor overlooking the grounds at the front of the house, as if he'd wanted to survey the world he'd built as he worked.

She closed the door quietly behind her and moved through the hallways to the staircase. She hesitated at his study door, and it took an effort of will to open it without knocking.

The room was big, for an office, decorated in a slightly fussy Victorian style, in over-stuffed chairs, dark wood paneling, smoky landscapes in heavy frames, and a desk the size of a battleship. She stepped inside, moving slowly, her feet silent on the familiar Persian rug, and set her luggage down. She'd stood there quietly many times before, waiting for him to look up from his book or—in later years—his computer, tasting the tang of his pipe smoke in the gunmetal air. There was an old carriage clock on the mantelpiece, and its ticking filled the room like memory.

This is why you have to leave, she told herself. All this. It's just too much.

She remembered once coming here as a child, disturbing him when he was working on . . . something, she couldn't recall what. But he had been furious, and she'd fled, weeping.

Something about the half-memory bothered her, a nagging sense that she was missing a vital detail that gave the whole thing meaning, but it wouldn't come. She pushed the thought aside. She hadn't come to think about the past.

There was a photograph of her father on the wall behind the desk. He was smiling, wearing academic robes and a ridiculous tam. It had been taken at some awards ceremony where he'd received an honorary degree from the London School of Economics for services to British industry, or something like that. She thought Prince Charles might have been involved, and then remembered that her father had been angry with her for not showing up in support. The thought confounded her for a moment, and the speech she'd been mentally rehearsing as she'd walked through the empty house stalled on her lips.

She looked back to the desk and the leather wing chair, in which he would never again sit, and she saw the wooden lion. It was facing the door she had come through. Instinctively, she reached for it, but her hand froze in mid-air and she frowned.

This was where he had died, Deacon had told her. Through those windows and down, holding a picture of his dead wife and estranged daughter. Jennifer stepped around the desk and looked out to the damp grounds below.

Not so very far below, but enough, apparently, to kill him—but only just, which was, she thought, curious. It was hardly a sure-fire way to commit suicide. He might have escaped with some bad breaks, spending his remaining years in a chair, perhaps, paralyzed . . .

Not Dad's style.

She'd forced herself to think of him as "her father" rather than "Dad" because that made it easier to rage at him in life, but now that she entertained the more familiar word, the strangeness of it all landed. Deacon had expressed surprise that he had taken his own life, and said no one could offer any explanation. No one had glimpsed any change in his recent mood, though something seemed to have been weighing on his mind.

Edward Quinn had been a man who made definitive choices and stuck to them, a man—at least in business terms—of action. He had been strong, deliberate, frequently ruthless and dispassionate. Jennifer could count on the fingers of one hand the number of times she'd ever seen him sad. Self-pity was beyond him, and if he'd been prone to depression or even despair, she knew nothing of it, or what, in this instance, might have precipitated such a mood.

Was this a man who would kill himself?

Jennifer sat in the leather wing chair for the first time in her life, surveying the desk as her father would have done, and as her gaze fell back on the little wooden lion, she felt a rising tide of doubt.

She was still sitting there when Deacon came in, half an hour later, curling her chestnut hair absently round her finger. He stopped short upon seeing her.

"I'm so sorry," he said. "I did not know you were here."

"It's fine," she said. "Are they gone?"

"Most of them," said Deacon. "A few are still poring over the relevant documents."

"Looking for an escape clause?"

Deacon framed a wry smile. "They do seem to be paying a good deal of attention to details which would normally be considered formalities," he conceded.

"Who are they more pissed off at? Him or me?"

Deacon coughed politely. "Opinion seems divided," he said, his gaze taking in her luggage. She was fleeing the scene, as she had so many times as an adolescent after screaming at her intractable father.

"This is where he died," she said after a moment. "Through these windows."

Deacon hesitated, as if unsure whether he was being asked a question, then nodded.

"You were home at the time?" she asked.

"Yes. Mr. Quinn was scheduled to take a helicopter into the city for a meeting."

"And he gave you no indication that his plans . . ." she faltered. "That he wouldn't be going?"

"None whatsoever," Deacon said. "Is there something on your mind, Miss Jennifer?"

She shook her head, but she could not say it.

"You found him?"

"Yes."

"And he had just . . . it was right after he jumped?"

"It could not have been more than ten minutes," said Deacon, carefully. "When he didn't go down to the heli-pad, I came looking for him and found the windows open. I saw his . . . I saw him, from up here, then went downstairs and outside, but it was too late."

"Did you tidy up in here at all?" Jennifer asked.

Deacon cocked his head slightly.

"Miss?"

"Did you rearrange any of his things? On the desk, for example."

Deacon frowned and shook his head. "No, Miss. I did not return to this room until the police came, and I touched nothing. Your father was very particular about the state of his desk. I have not been in again since. Is something missing?"

Jenifer's eyes fell on the wooden lion. Deacon took a step closer to the desk.

"Did you move this?" he asked.

"Haven't touched it," she said. "The police?"

"I do not believe so. But . . ." He paused. "Mr. Quinn always faced the lion towards him. Your lion, he called it. A gift from when . . ." Deacon caught himself and stopped, flushing.

"You can say it," said Jennifer.

"From when you loved him," he said. "I'm sorry. It was what he said. He kept it close to him and facing him always."

"Why would he turn it away from him before going out of those windows?" Jennifer asked.

"So that he wouldn't feel you looking at him?" Deacon tried.

"But he took the photograph. The one of mum and me, that sat right there," said Jennifer nodding to the space on the desk. "He was holding it when he jumped, you said."

Deacon nodded. "It's downstairs," he said. "The frame needs mending."

Jennifer's eyes wandered back to the photograph of her father at the event she'd missed, all those years ago.

"Do you think," she said, not taking her eyes off the face in the picture, "that my father was the type of man who would commit suicide?"

For a long moment, Deacon said nothing. She turned to look at him, and found him standing rigid, his hands up to his face, fingers steepled against the bridge of his nose.

"No," he said at last. "I didn't believe it until the police said there was no other explanation. A part of me still doesn't believe it."

Jennifer stared at the wooden lion again, imagined her father's pale fingers turning it carefully, deliberately to face the door.

"I think," she said, "that my father was in trouble. Though what could scare a man like him, I really can't imagine. He called me back. He made that absurd will, designed to drop me in the middle of it. And then . . ." she stopped, reached for the wooden lion, turned it to face her and considered its clumsily childish paint job. "I don't know," she concluded, lamely. "Something happened."

Deacon seemed to wait for her to say more, but when she didn't, his eyes fell once more on the luggage at her feet.

"Should I call you a car, Miss?" he asked.

Jennifer thought, doubt hardening into resolve like setting concrete.

"No," she said. "I'll take them back to my room."

"You're staying?" Deacon asked, and there was an unmistakable twinkle of pleasure or amusement in his eyes.

"Seems that way," she said.

"And following through on your father's wishes, will you be taking his seats on the various boards, managing his interests and so forth?"

"You don't think I can do it?" she said, giving him a frank look.

"I think, as your father also thought, that you can do anything to which you put your mind," he replied.

Jennifer smiled. "I doubt his business associates will agree," she said.

"No, Miss," Deacon agreed. "I think they will find the next few days most stimulating."

13

TIMIKA
New York

SHE TRIED TO FIND THE BUSIEST STREETS, BUT THE unseasonable cold was keeping everyone inside. She zigzagged her way south to Eighth Street, but the man who called himself Cook kept her in sight the whole way. In fact, he was gaining on her. She couldn't outrun him. She couldn't outfight him. That meant she was going to have to outthink him if she was going to survive.

How hard could that be? That bomb scare ruse had been seriously lame . . .

He hadn't made his move or taken a shot, which meant he was biding his time, tracking her. He was dressed as a cop, which meant that no one would give her the benefit of the doubt if she got into any kind of altercation with him. Furthermore, he wasn't alone, and they, whoever they were, had already showed they were ready to shoot her in broad daylight. They weren't worried about witnesses looking out of their windows. Even so, she needed to stay where people could see her. If a van pulled over and two men, dressed as cops, bundled her inside, it was possible no one would raise a finger to help her, but it was also possible someone might at least take out their phone and shoot a video of it.

She needed a plan, and quickly. Something bold and simple. Something that played to her strengths.

Which were what, exactly?

The Huff Po lady thought I was fun, she thought, bleakly. *Maybe I could just sass and smile my way out of being killed for a book I didn't ask for and haven't read . . .*

But from inside the snark, an idea emerged. Sass and fun might actually help. Both were enshrined in her bold scarlet coat and that ridiculous glossy and ringleted wig. Cook, or whatever his real name was, had never seen her without them . . .

She checked behind her, then scanned the street, looking for a department store. She could have kicked herself for coming so far downtown. If she'd gone straight up Fifth Avenue, she would have had plenty of options, but down here . . . She spotted an Army-Navy store, next to a burger joint. It would have to do.

She crossed the street at a staggering jog, feigning exhaustion, looking anxiously over her shoulder. Cook was following, eyes locked on, talking into his radio again, his manner calm, deliberate. Unhurried. He probably figured he had her. She stumbled, playing up her all too real panic and uncertainty, dragging one foot as if she had twisted her ankle. As she did so, she discreetly unfastened her conspicuous red coat. She tried to see as much of the Army-Navy store's interior through its plate glass windows as she could. Once inside, she was going to have to move fast.

She labored with the heavy door, like she was a hundred-years old, but as soon as she was inside, she bolted like a rabbit for the back, squeezing book and purse under her sweater as she shed her coat and snatched the ridiculous wig from her head, putting both on a manikin in the women's section, its back to the main doors. Noting that the clerk was busy with another customer, she pulled a long Navy Officer's coat—black wool with brass buttons—off a rack and shrugged into it. Without pausing, she returned to the front door, past a counter covered with folding knives and defused hand grenades, where she snatched a pair of cheap shades off a rack, her body language transforming as she pressed her phone against her ear. She'd been cowed and desperate when she came in, limping and scared, but now she was upright and purposeful, barking commands to an imaginary assistant over the phone in the thick New Jersey accent she'd long ago learned to turn off. Timika Mars stepped back out into the street another person entirely. It took all her strength not to look at him as she brushed against Cook in the doorway.

He looked right past her.

Then she was out, walking briskly, as if late for a meeting, looking up and down the street for a cab. Cook would be scanning the store for a woman with lustrous ringleted hair and a scarlet coat. She had bought herself a few seconds—a minute at most—but if he came looking for her now, she was just another sleek-headed black woman on the sidewalk, unrecognizable unless he looked her in the face.

She strode off, still barking into the phone.

"I told you I couldn't make no four o'clock sales meeting, so you'd better unarrange it," she said, improvising. "You hear what I'm saying? And if DeMarco doesn't like it, he can kiss my shapely . . ."

And the Academy Award goes to . . .

A cab rounded the corner onto Macdougal, its roof light on. She stuck her arm out like she'd ordered the cab an hour ago, then slid into the back seat. She didn't look back to the army surplus store doors until they were pulling away.

Timika had the cab circle the block where the Debunktion office sat, twice. As best she could tell, the coast was clear. Her new bridge officer's coat looked pretty sharp too, she decided. When this was all over, she'd go back and pay for it. Maybe tomorrow. Or the next day. A part of her feared that was wishful thinking, but she was elated at her escape and pushed the thought away.

She paid and got out at the parking garage where she'd left Dion's car. Nothing suggested anyone had been snooping around it. She doubted Cook and his buddies even knew which car was hers. The more she thought about it, the more she thought that while these men were serious and efficient, their search of her office and their attempt to recover the book from her—assuming that was indeed their mission—had been improvised. It felt unplanned, hasty. Clumsy, even. They may be building a file on her right now, but she might still have the advantage of them.

Once safely inside the Corolla and heading down Broadway, she called Marvin and he picked up on the first ring, sounding jittery. She asked if he and Audrey were okay and, satisfied on that score, told him to go to the coffee shop where they had intended to kill part of the morning. Then she called Dion and got his voice mail.

"Listen hon," she said. "Can't make Atlantic City after all. Something has come up at work and I'm gonna have to go out of town for a couple of days. I'll try to look after the car."

She hesitated, then hung up without saying anything more. The less he knew, the safer he would be. Then she scrolled through the phone and dialed a different number.

"Officer Brown," said the voice at the other end.

"Hey, James, this is Timika Mars."

"Mars?" he said. He sounded surprised. "To what do I owe the pleasure?"

"That case you were working when I saw you this morning," she said. "You got a name for the victim?"

"Not yet. Whoever shot him took his wallet. Why?"

"Try Jerzy Aaron Stern," she said, her eyes on the passenger seat where the battered book sat.

"Yeah?" he replied. "Why?"

"Just a hunch."

"The city has eight and a half million people," he said. "That's quite a hunch."

"Yeah," she said, her voice edged with something like sadness. "He wasn't from around here. I'll check in, James."

She turned the phone off and took the battery out. When she spotted a Radio Shack, she parked illegally, ducked inside and bought two burner phones with a hundred dollars on each. One, she pocketed. After she recorded the number for the second phone, she brandished it in her hand as she flagged down a cab. She moved alongside the driver's window.

"Are you getting in or what?" said the turbaned driver.

She handed him the burner.

"You know Joe's on Thirteenth?"

"This is a cab, not a courier service," said the cabbie.

"And this is a fifty dollar bill," she returned. It was turning into an expensive day. "Ask for Marvin or Audrey. No one else."

The taxi pulled away and she returned to Dion's vehicle. It was time to hit the road.

But the road to where?

She didn't know, but it would be a good start if she put some distance between herself and the city. She took Canal Street to the Holland Tunnel and Interstate 78, heading west, her hands firm on the wheel her mind turning events over and over like a spade in dark earth. Jerzy Stern's journey—and it had been a long and strange one—was over. Hers was just beginning.

14

JERZY
Poland, 1944

WITH ISHMAEL GONE AND THE MACHINE GUNS around the perimeter firing at me, it took no great courage to crawl through the fence and sprint blindly across the minefield. I went around the first mine I saw and leapt over another, but I barely cared. Inside, I was already dead. That I made it to the tree line was, I suppose, a matter of extraordinary good luck, but I felt no relief or satisfaction. My brother, my dearest companion, my sole friend in all the world, the final remnant of my family and last piece of what my life had been, was dead, and I could feel nothing but grief and rage and loss.

They came after me, but the woods were dense and the ground too hard for tracks. Once, I heard dogs, but for whatever reason, they did not pick up my scent, and after the first day, I never heard them again. Perhaps the strange experiments in the mine had confused the hounds' senses, as old Aizinberg had said.

I escaped. A bleak triumph it was. I had nothing to wear but the clothes I'd woken up in, inadequate for a Polish winter. The best thing that could be said about my meager rations is that I was used to going hungry. For the first two days, I kept walking in what I thought was a straight line, just trying to get away from the camp. From time to time, I could hear the sounds of a train, but knew that trying to stowaway onboard would surely get me caught, and even if the trains didn't go back to the camps, where was I to go? It was not as if I could take a locomotive to Switzerland. I was safer alone in the woods.

I slept in a hollow tree beside a frozen stream, that first night, and woke so weak for lack of food that I determined to find the village I had heard the guards talk of: Ludwikowice. I dared not talk to anyone, since no one could be trusted not to turn me over to the Nazis merely for an increase of their butter rations, but I hoped to find larders or fields from which I might steal, or smokehouses I could plunder after dark. I walked for hours, disoriented by grief, hunger, and the strange uniformity of the forest. Eventually I realized that I had traced a broad circle, arriving back almost where I had begun. Demoralized to the point of despair, I lay down again and would have slept, were it not for a pair of rabbits not twenty yards away.

I had not eaten meat in over a year, and the thought of trapping and eating them gave me the energy to get up and stay awake. Looking back, I think those rabbits may have saved my life, though I had neither the skill nor the tools to catch them. I was succumbing to cold, hunger and exhaustion, and had I gone to sleep then, I think I would never have awoken. Instead, I ate some snow and ice, then followed the loping rabbits through the snow and came to a spot where I could smell wood smoke. A hundred yards ahead, the trees seemed to thin, and though I was almost crawling by then, I found myself looking down on the houses of a village.

One of them had a shed in the small field at the back. I was able to make my way down, fairly sure that I had not been seen. The door to the shed was unlocked, and I slipped inside, glad to get out of the wind.

Inside were rusty farm implements, old tools, bags of seeds and, to my astonishment and joy, a sack of potatoes. I rubbed the dirt off their skins and ate four uncooked, filling my belly as it had not been for years, then washed it down with bitter rainwater from a barrel and curled up on the shed's wooden floor.

I don't know how long I slept. When I awoke, it was dark, and there was an apple beside my head. For a long moment, I lay there looking at it, marveling not that I had food, but that someone had seen me and not killed me or turned me over to those who would. It was a gift from

God, and it fed my bruised and broken soul. When I found a knife in one of the tool crates, I cut the apple in half, then in quarters. I ate one quarter, put two in my pockets, and left the fourth exactly where the apple had been, then crept out into the cold night, running bent over into the blackness of the forest.

For an hour, I wandered the woods, always keeping a sense of how close I was to the village, listening to the soft hoot of the big gray owls that haunted the forest. Then I found a hollow stick, and used the knife I had borrowed from the shed to peel off the bark. I whittled one end and made a few small holes, so that when you blew in one end, the pipe made a low, reedy note not unlike the owls. I ate what was left of my apple and then, when the moon sank and dawn was near, returned to the garden shed on the edge of the village. I left the pipe I'd made outside the door in payment for my lodging, then crept inside and went to sleep.

For ten days, this was how I lived, hiding out in the woods at night, sleeping in the shed during the day, leaving whatever meager tokens I could find or fashion in the forest, in the desperate hope that whoever owned the shed would not turn me in. Each day, I woke to some small gift of food, sometimes a piece of bread, sometimes a hunk of cheese, once a leg of cold goat meat, which was the most delicious thing I had ever tasted. They never brought pork, and though I had peeled the yellow star off my jacket, its shape was still visible. Twice I considered lying awake to see who my secret benefactor was, but decided against it. I was in a fairy story, and spying would only break the spell. I had had enough reality for a lifetime.

One day, I woke to find a piece of candied fruit wrapped with a ribbon, and with it, a candle and matches. Hanukkah had passed uncelebrated. The memory of all I had lost was like a great weight on my chest, but I wept tears of gratitude for the candy and the candle, and the fact that someone wanted me to be happy.

Soon after that, as we crossed into the New Year, I started to hear the rumble of what I first thought was thunder, but which turned out to be guns. The Russians were coming. I didn't know it yet, but much of Eastern Poland had already fallen before them, and though lower Silesia would fight on for another month or so, the Germans were pulling out of the Wenceslas mine. In spite of the harrying by allied bombers, the trains seemed to be running constantly. One day, as I wandered the edge of the woods, not so very far from the minefield and the fenced henge where Ishmael had died, I came across a work detail clearing an old airstrip of weeds. I kept my distance, fighting the urge to sprint headlong into the trees and never look back, and watched them work until a pair of trucks and a half-track came to collect them. Before they left, they inspected the strip, and when the officer in charge turned and squinted down the pale concrete, I saw his face and knew him.

It was Ungerleider, the handsome, blond captain who had ordered the guns to fire upon us when we had finished rigging the cables above the chamber with the bell. It was the man who killed my brother.

I got to my feet, trembling with a rage that left me incapable of thought. I stepped out of the trees, just as he turned away and clambered into the half-track. Shouting at him, I began to run blindly, stupidly toward him. The engines drowned out my cries, thank God, and by the time I had come to my senses, they were driving away, their wheels spitting snow. I stood staring after them, tears running down my cheeks.

Gradually, I realized how cold I was, and went back into the woods. I now knew its paths and hollows as well as any house I'd ever lived in, but as I walked back toward the village and the shed that had become my home, my outrage turned to grim determination. I did not know how, but I would find a way to strike back at that man for what he had done to my people and, most importantly, to my brother.

That night, instead of roaming the woods, I went quietly to the house by the shed where I had been sleeping. When I was sure there were no neighbors to see me, I went quickly to the back door and knocked. I had no idea who would answer. Still, I was surprised when an elderly lady in a housecoat and apron opened the door.

She looked not the least bit surprised or upset, her face neutral as she looked me up and down, and then she stood aside, peering over my shoulder as she admitted me to a stark, scrubbed kitchen. Satisfied we had not been seen, she closed the door behind me and looked me over again.

"Too cold for the woods tonight?" she asked in Polish.

"No," I said. "I came to say thank you."

She considered this.

"Sit," she said. "I have cocoa. Powdered. No milk. But it is hot and sweet."

I did as I was told.

"You were in the mine?" she said, not looking at me.

"Yes, Ma'am."

"Just you, or you had family there?"

I opened my mouth to speak and found I could not. Since the moment my brother died, I had not spoken a word to another person. I stared at her, my eyes brimming with tears, shaking my head and stammering apologies.

She did not embrace me, but she laid her hands on my shoulders, and put her face close to mine and shushed me softly, as Ishmael might have done, so that for a long time I just sat there, weeping.

"What is your name, child?" she asked at last.

I hadn't thought of myself as a child for a long time, and not only because I was now almost fifteen. That dried my tears.

"Jerzy," I said.

"German?" she asked.

"Polish," I said.

She managed a half smile then.

"Welcome, Jerzy," she said. "I am Mrs. Habernicht, a name that has made the last five years a fraction easier around here, but you can call me Olga. My husband was German. Thank the Lord he died before all this," she said, breaking from me and bustling about the kitchen as she prepared the cocoa.

"They are leaving," I said.

"Soon," she said, "yes." Something in my face gave me away. She thrust the cup into my hands with a scowl. "And you want revenge before they go."

"Yes," I said, my former bitter anger returning so that the single word, "yes," had a hardness and certainty I had not believed myself capable of.

She nodded, thoughtfully.

"Understandable," she concluded. "The army will be here soon."

"The Russians?" I asked. I didn't like the idea. The Russians scared me. Before the war, my father had said it was only a matter of time before they came, with or without the Germans' support.

She shook her head dismissively.

"The Polish army!" she exclaimed. "They have been fighting in the East. They would have liberated Warsaw, if the Reds had delivered on their promises. They will be here soon. Then we shall see."

"There are things in the mine," I began, uncertain. "Dangerous things. The Germans will try to get them out."

She sipped her cocoa, and I imitated her. It was the most delicious thing I had tasted in years.

"Planning a little sabotage, eh?" she said.

"Yes," I agreed, though I hadn't been until that moment.

She nodded again, and I wondered if she might be a little bit crazy.

"We shall have to see about that," she said.

ALAN
Camp Leatherneck Marine, Helmund Province, Afghanistan

THE UNSIGNED RESIGNATION LETTER SAT IN HIS INSIDE pocket as the C-130J took off from Leatherneck. Hatcher hadn't asked for it, but as they took their seats, Alan's jacket had bulged, and the CIA man had smiled that distant, private smile of his and said nothing.

Alan had flown in C-130s modified to feel more like a civilian aircraft, with plush, forward facing seats, but this was a conventional troop flight operated by VMGR-252 that, in a series of hops, would eventually wend its way back to Cherry Point, North Carolina. The trip would refuel in Souda Bay, Greece. As long as they eventually made it stateside, or to wherever they had been FRAGG'd,

127

SEKRET MACHINES

the troops onboard didn't seem to care. Alan was edgy. He didn't like not knowing what was going on.

He sat in one of the red mesh troop seats that lined the bare fuselage walls, facing into the body of the aircraft where the luggage had been strapped to a plastic-wrapped pallet. The airplane was basic and functional, and if there was any question that they were in a military plane, in what was still technically a combat zone, the takeoff removed any doubt. Instead of the slow and graceful climb to altitude civilians enjoyed, the C-130J pulled up in a great stomach churning surge, like a roller coaster car clanking up to its highest point, but at 120 knots and accelerating. There had been no hostile fire on flights from Airbase NAIA in months, but the pilot was taking no chances. As the nose rose still higher, Alan tipped sideways in his seat. He gave Hatcher a sidelong glance, but if the gut-spinning climb was bothering the other man, he wasn't letting it show.

Alan closed his eyes. There were no windows, nothing to look at but the men sitting opposite him, and he had long since mastered the ability to sleep through the most turbulent of flights, but his mind was racing. He hadn't signed the letter of resignation, but even that token gesture of defiance was little more than a delaying tactic, while he waited to see what he was really being offered. Hatcher had told him nothing, beyond dangling a few vague and slightly mystical phrases, smiling cryptically and—more to the point—silently, when Alan pressed him for details. He would be fully briefed when he committed to the program. Not before.

It wasn't like he had a lot of options.

But a dawn flight out of Afghanistan felt strange, like he was sneaking out. It didn't sit right with him, and a part of Alan felt that Hatcher was playing games with him, with his hints about strange aircraft.

"Sign this," he had said, "and I'll show you."

Alan shifted in his seat, trying to hold onto his outrage and his skepticism, but part of him was curious, and nervous, the way a child feels, cautiously cranking the handle of a jack-in-the-box.

Around him, sleepy Marines nodded along to the tinny music that leaked out of their headphones and ear buds. Some played video games on their phones or tablets. Others thumbed through magazines. Two had thrown up, and several others were looking green, but there was still an overall sense of relief. They were going home. Alan didn't know where he was going.

If they were heading to Cherry Point, or even to the CIA headquarters in Langley, Virginia, they would fly through DC. When they touched down not in Greece but in Kuwait, he and Hatcher were the only passengers to disembark. There, they were met by a bald man in a suit, who shook Hatcher's hand and introduced himself to Alan as Agent Harvey Kenyon. His handshake was firm and dry, his manner brisk as he directed them to a solitary Gulfstream jet parked in a hardened shell just off the tarmac. "You can get aboard. We're just waiting for one more."

Alan took his seat. After the C-130, this was luxury itself, the Gulfstream's sleek and polished interior more posh and expensive than anything Alan had flown lately. And for all its luxury, nothing like as fun.

"Where are we heading?" he asked as Hatcher settled into the seat across the aisle and took out an iPad.

"Did you sign that letter yet, Major?" he replied, not taking his eyes off the screen in front of him.

"Not yet," said Alan.

"You're going to want to do so," said Hatcher. "Or we won't be taking you any further." His tone was abstracted, as if he were thinking of other things, but it had a finality to it that left Alan irritated. He turned away so that the CIA man—men, now that Kenyon was standing in the doorway—wouldn't see the color rise in his face, and said nothing. Then, a final passenger boarded.

"Major," said the asset known as Morat. "We seem to keep crossing paths, don't we?"

He tossed a non-regulation duffel bag onto the seat behind Alan and dropped into the chair next to it.

"You're heading to Langley too, huh?" asked Alan.

There was a momentary pause as Morat looked at Hatcher, who was studiously ignoring them both.

"Not unless they're planning on giving me a parachute," Morat said.

"We're not going to Langley?" Alan asked.

"Until you sign that document in your pocket," Hatcher said, still not looking up, "our destination is classified."

Alan frowned. The aircraft was a Gulfstream G650 designed for both speed and extreme range. They could reach a lot of places without stopping to refuel.

Morat grinned and rolled his eyes.

"CIA, man," he muttered to Alan. "We do like our little games."

"What's your position exactly?"

"Mr. Morat's identity and occupation are likewise classified," said Hatcher, deadpan.

And that, it seemed, was that. After years of being inside the loop, of being not just informed but consulted—his opinion solicited—Alan was now to be treated like a raw recruit, a know-nothing who couldn't be trusted with the most basic piece of intel . . .

"Guess I'll see you in the morning," said Morat. "Whenever the hell that is." Morat turned his shoulder in toward the window and pulled the blind down.

"Okay, Major," said Hatcher. He was standing over him, a ballpoint pen in one hand. "We're ready to close the door and get out of here. This is your last chance. Sign your letter to the Marine Corps, or this is as far as we go."

For all the earlier back and forth Hatcher seemed quite serious. Alan plucked the letter from his pocket and considered it. He was a Marine. If he stopped being one, what would be left of him? Who would he be?

"Where are we going?" Alan asked, stalling.

"Okay," Hatcher said with a shrug and a half smile. "We're going to Groom Lake, Nevada. AKA Homey Airport, AKA Dreamland, AKA Paradise Ranch, AKA Watertown, AKA . . ."

"Area 51," Alan completed for him, suddenly wide awake.

Hatcher gave him that fractional, knowing smile again. "That's an Air Force base," said Alan.

"Parts of it," said Hatcher. "I'm Operations Director for a separate portion. Special aircraft development and testing. Wanna see what we've got?" he asked, his voice low, almost teasing. "Sign here."

Alan blinked.

And signed.

ALAN WAS SHAKEN AWAKE BY HATCHER. THE FLIGHT HAD been uneventful and, for all his unease, exhaustion had gotten the better of him, two-thirds of the way into the flight. It was unlike him to sleep through a landing, but that was what seemed to have happened. He awoke groggy, his mouth dry, with an ache in the small of his back. Hatcher was the only person still aboard. The Gulfstream's cabin door was closed and all the window shades were down.

In a half daze, born of exhaustion and the enormity of his resignation from the Marine Corps, Alan followed Hatcher down the steps to the airfield. The runway was lined with blast-hardened hangars and concrete buildings, the base nondescript except for the eerie quiet and the parked buses with the blacked-out windows. A Humvee barreled towards them from the direction of the air traffic control tower, throwing up a rooster tail of sand and dust. A soldier in the gun port, half suspended in his five-point harness, manned a massive 50 cal machine gun. Alan gave Hatcher a look.

"Easy, Major," he said. "Just routine."

"I'm still a Major?"

"Would you rather be called Agent?"

Alan thought quickly and shook his head.

"Then Major it is," said Hatcher.

The Humvee pulled up some twenty yards short and the driver got out, careful to keep out of the .50 cal's field of fire. Hatcher held up his badge in one hand and the iPad in the other.

The soldier checked the ID and took the tablet back to the Humvee, where he made a phone call while he checked the mobile data terminal mounted on the vehicle's passenger side. Alan waited, conscious of the vast and silent blue of the Nevada desert sky above him, and of the eyes of the man watching him down the barrel of the machine gun. Overhead, a hawk called, high and shrill. The soldier returned Hatcher's things to him.

"That seems to be in order, sir," he said. "Sorry for making you wait. We have inbound in three minutes. Anyone below level seven must avert."

"I'm granting the Major here clearance level seven on a temporary basis," Hatcher said.

The soldier hesitated.

"Temporary, sir?" he said. "For how long?"

"Five minutes ought to do it," Hatcher said.

"Understood, sir," said the soldier.

Not by me, thought Alan. What was the point of being granted five minutes of high security clearance?

"This way, please, gentlemen," said the soldier, motioning them into the Humvee.

Hatcher sat up front, Alan in the back. He nodded an uncertain greeting to the machine gunner, but the other man did not respond. They dove towards the control tower, and then the air was torn apart by the shriek of a pulsing high-pitched siren. Red lights flashed in sync with the noise. In the distance, two uniformed men lay face down on the ground, hands around their heads.

"What the hell . . .?" Alan began, but he words died on his lips. All over the base, men were doing the same, either dashing into buildings or lying down in the dust and sand, arms over their heads. They weren't taking cover. They were effectively blindfolding themselves. It was so strange, so mesmerizing, that for a moment Alan did not see the ship.

It came out of nowhere, soundless, slipping through the air so easily that it was as if it had always been there, and he'd just noticed it. But that couldn't be.

Nothing about the ship could be.

Except, of course, that he had seen it—or something like it—only a few nights before.

16

JENNIFER
London

THE BUSINESS SUIT FELT RIDICULOUS. THE PENCIL SKIRT hugged her thighs so closely that she had to take tiny steps, though in her absurd high heels, it was no great loss, given that she could barely walk.

"No wonder women don't get anywhere in business," she muttered to her refection. "It takes them twice as long to go anywhere."

"I think you look most professional," said Deacon, sweeping an invisible fleck of lint from her shoulders with a brush apparently designed for the purpose. He considered the elegant French twist which had taken her a maddening half hour, and adjusted a fly away strand of hair.

"I think I look like an imposter," said Jennifer, "and so will everyone else."

It had been three days since the reading of the will. Jennifer had stalled as best she could, asking Deacon to deflect all phone calls and requests for informal meetings on the grounds of bereavement, but she was only postponing the inevitable. When she was told of the scheduled meeting of the Maynard Consortium's executive board, she knew she would have to go.

"Wouldn't Miss rather begin with one of the less . . . er . . . formidable bodies?" Deacon suggested. "A museum board or charitable trust, for instance? Dip your toes in, as it were. The men in the Maynard group are . . . powerful."

"I'm powerful," she said, not really believing it. "My father's will made me so."

"But you are also new to the world of finance," Deacon said gently. "These men take no quarter. I recommend you get your feet wet in rather less dangerous waters."

"Maybe I'll just cannonball into the pool and see how they handle it," she said.

"At the risk of belaboring the metaphor," Deacon replied, "I think it's less of a pool and more of a piranha tank."

"Then I'll be the shark," she said, determined to stay upbeat.

Deacon frowned. "Do sharks eat piranhas?" he mused. "I believe piranhas are fresh water fish . . ."

"Let's leave the marine biology lessons for another day, shall we Deacon?"

"As you wish, Miss," said the older man, with his patented gesture of acknowledgment—a fraction more than a nod, a fraction less than a bow, head tilted slightly, eyes almost closed for a moment. "Then I will find you the Consortium's latest reports. If, after perusing them, you want to delay the meeting . . ."

"I won't."

"As you say, Miss."

She'd sounded so confident, so sure of herself and her capacity to blend in. All that changed once she began to pore over the Consortium's various printouts and quarterly reports. Bafflingly, her father's computer files seemed to contain nothing on the Maynard group, despite it being his primary financial concern, so she had little that was personal to guide her through the publicity hype and acronym-cluttered business-speak.

Deacon brought her tea in a china cup and politely said nothing as she plowed through a hefty dictionary for phrases like "iterative empowerment," "backward compatibility," and "angel investors." Jennifer sipped absently—recognized the delicate aroma of Earl Grey—and looked up.

"What in God's name does it mean if a company has," she checked the brochure, "'*a little known equity tail to its bond managing body*?'"

"Perhaps we should start at the beginning," said Deacon.

A day later, she was still learning. Jennifer had been up half the night, getting Deacon's crash course in global finance, though as was always the case with complex information, the result had been to teach her how little she understood about the world. She had gone to bed with a raging headache and the nagging certainty that she would make a fool of herself at the board meeting, business suit or no business suit.

She had managed to squeeze in a morning run along the hedgerowed lanes of her childhood, but it hadn't been nearly enough to burn off all her pent-up agitation. Now she forced herself to sit still in the car, feeling the time tick by as they idled in the gridlock of central London.

"This is why we should have used the helicopter," Deacon remarked.

"Because the day wasn't sufficiently traumatic?" Jennifer shot back. She was starting to feel nauseated.

"You are so like your father," he remarked. It wasn't a compliment, and she gave him a sharp look, though she didn't have the energy to argue the point, ludicrous though it was. They passed the pale, restrained decorum of the Bank of England on Threadneedle Street and were soon in sight of Pater Noster Square and the London Stock Exchange. Jennifer spent her time checking off the head-quarters of companies that, in recent years, she had come to think of as the enemy: Lloyds, Old Mutual, Prudential, Ernst and Young, Standard Charter . . . This was her father's world, the world of suits and limousines, though whether she was entering as a spy, full of hostile intent, or a defector, she really wasn't sure.

Something else was on her mind as well. In her largely futile attempt to prepare for the day's meeting, Jennifer had scoured her father's files for details of his work with the Maynard group and had come up empty, and while she first thought this merely annoying, she soon realized that it was rather more than that.

It was strange. It made no sense. The Maynard Consortium had been a huge part of her father's life. Why would there be no trace of it after his death? A solution seemed to present itself when Deacon pointed out that all the Maynard data was on a separate laptop he kept in his study when he wasn't traveling.

But when she looked for the laptop, it wasn't there.

Jennifer stopped fiddling with her French twist, flexed her fingers until the knuckles cracked and stared out of the rain-misted car windows at the orderly façades of the city offices. Maybe the laptop had just been misplaced. Maybe it would turn up when she and the lawyers catalogued her father's things.

Or maybe it wouldn't. Maybe it was gone, spirited away by whomever had stood there in his study the day her father—inexplicably, impossibly—threw himself off the balcony. The police investigation had been perfunctory at best and that, it now occurred to her, was worrying. Her father had been a powerful man who dealt with vast amounts of money. The possibility that someone who ran in the same circles might have been able to influence the inquiry into his death was all too plausible. Who that might have been and why he had killed her father—if that was what had happened—she had no idea, but a thought was forming in one of the dark corners of her mind, something strange and shapeless and terrible to look at, something, she felt sure, that involved the Maynard Consortium.

Deacon checked his watch as they boarded the sleek steel elevator and gave her a look.

"Might I offer a piece of advice, Miss Jennifer?" he asked.

In other circumstances, the question might have irritated her, but she was rattled by how clearly out of her depth she was, and nodded.

"Be polite," said Deacon. "Accept their condolences gratefully. Then just listen. Most of what they discuss will be baffling, and all of it will be tedious, so just keep calm and we'll review after we've determined how long you are to stay involved in these meetings. Don't talk. You will only antagonize them and reveal how little you know. That will make it easier for them to outmaneuver you. Best to keep them guessing, as it were."

Shut up, in other words.

She nodded again, nausea swelling within her as the elevator slowed into position on the twenty-third floor, and the doors opened. Deacon gave her a quick look and, as if seeing something in her eyes he didn't like, added, "Really, Miss Jennifer. This is not the time for you to take on the *dominant social order*, or ask pointed questions about your father's death. Just sit still and listen."

She held his eyes for a moment with a touch of resentment, but she knew he was right. It was going to take all her strength, just to sit through the next couple of hours without being banned from the building.

"And stop touching your hair," he added, smiling. "It looks fine."

A secretary looked up from his desk, his bright, professional smile faltering when he saw Jennifer, then checked Deacon. Something wordless passed between the two men and the secretary rose, the professional smile back in place.

"Miss Quinn," he said, standing up but seeming unsure if he should reach out to shake her hand. "Welcome. Please follow me."

She murmured a *thank you*, but the words stuck in her throat and she didn't think he heard her. She turned to Deacon, who gave her an encouraging smile. They followed the secretary, who stopped at a heavy door of lacquered wood and knocked deferentially, head cocked to catch the voices within. She didn't hear whatever made him turn the handle and push the door open, but that was partly the blood rushing in her ears as she tried to shut down the panic that was rising inside her.

The room was bright, all windows onto the city, white walls and chrome furniture trimmed and padded in gray leather. There were a dozen chairs all occupied by men she had seen at the reading of the will, save one.

Hers.

She walked to the chair with deliberate, confident strides, one hand in her pocket so no one would see it tremble, ignoring the way they rose minutely from their chairs: a minuscule show of politeness that only served to reemphasize that she was the only woman there. Just before she sat, Deacon lowered his head and, in a voice no louder than a breath, whispered, "Be polite. Listen."

He addressed the table in general.

"I will await Miss Jennifer in the lobby."

"Thank you, Deacon," said a white-haired man at the end of the table. "And I'm sure I speak for the board when I say how grateful we are for your work easing the transition at this difficult time."

There was a rumble of agreement around the room, rich Old Etonian accents murmuring "hear, hear!" For all her anxiety, Jennifer had to bite her lip to keep from grinning at the absurdity of it all.

Deacon eased out and the door latched closed behind him. Jennifer shifted in her seat.

The white-haired man called the meeting to order. This was Archibald St. James. She recognized that jowly countenance and the basset hound eyes from the pictures Deacon had provided the evening before to aid her preparation. He was the chairman of the board, though Jennifer did not think she had met him before. In fact, the only people she knew, beyond Deacon's improvised gallery of mug shots, were Herman Saltzburg, the walking skeleton who had haunted her childhood dreams, and Ronald Harrington-Smythe, spilling out of his tailored suit like oil from one of the tankers by which he had made his money. Of the rest—based on their names, accents and appearances, she counted an American, two Germans, one Japanese, one who might have been Spanish or South American, and one Russian, all men. There was also the younger man with disheveled jet-black hair, whose name she did not know but who had nodded to her when she fled the reading of the will. Compared to the others, he looked vibrant, athletic even, and his eyes, when they looked at her, were bright with curiosity and amusement.

He reached across the table and offered his hand.

"Daniel Letrange," he said. "Call me Dan. Everyone does."

Jennifer took his hand and shook it, grateful for his deliberate welcome.

"Pleased to meet you," she said.

"Welcome to the lions' den," he whispered, grinning.

His accent—unlike the others—was hard to pinpoint. There were northern English vowels in there, but they were laid over something else, a different, non-English rhythm. Italian, perhaps? French? Letrange sounded French.

She looked away, busying herself with the attaché case she was having trouble opening. She scowled, trying to be inconspicuous as she fumbled with the catches.

Deacon had locked it and forgotten to give her the bloody key.

"Miss Quinn?" said St. James, giving her a look of labored patience. "Is there a problem?"

She blinked, momentarily frozen. For a moment, the room was still, and she felt their mood. They were satisfied that she was what they'd expected. Some were even a little bored by how right they'd been in their private whisperings before she'd arrived. Her fingers clenched, and in that instant, the briefcase clasps snapped open. She had been pulling the wrong way.

There was another watchful pause heavy with unspoken judgment, and then St. James continued.

"As I was saying, if you turn to the first item on the agenda . . ." And the meeting began.

It was, as Deacon had prophesied, dull stuff. Jennifer tried to keep up, but they frequently lapsed into the kind of jargon she had read in the printouts, language designed to exclude her. She quickly lost track of what was happening. When they voted on each item, she was the sole abstainer. The first time, it felt like a tiny act of honest defiance, but by the fifth time, it felt merely embarrassing.

The sixth item on the agenda was an African investment package. Saltzburg, the cadaver, mumbled his way through its details and everyone nodded dutifully as they moved toward a vote.

"I'm sorry," said Jennifer. "Can I just make sure I'm clear on something?"

The room turned to stare at her as if she were a cat who'd suddenly broken into song.

"Is there something you do not understand?" asked St. James, the question containing a poisonous joke at her expense. The others smiled.

"No. I think I understand completely," she answered, stiffening. "I just want to be clear you do."

There was a subtle shift in the quality of the air as they all bridled and adjusted. Only the young man with the black hair still seemed amused.

"I'm not sure I follow," said Saltzburg in his usual death rattle.

"You seem to be moving a sizeable investment into the extraction of crude oil from Chad despite that country's Failed State ranking, according to the Fund for Peace. With Bangladesh, it has been consistently rated one of the most corrupt political systems in the world."

It was Saltzburg's turn to blink, but he rallied quickly. "I assure you, the oil fields are extremely well-protected. I don't think it an especially risky investment . . ."

"Again," Jennifer cut in, "you misunderstand me. I'm talking about the ethics of supporting—however indirectly—a deeply problematic regime with a record of tribalism, cronyism, and a history of abuse of presidential authority in matters of government."

"I think you are overstating the case," said Saltzburg with a ghastly fake smile. "I can assure you that our shareholders have no serious reservations about . . ."

"Extrajudicial killings by government forces?" Jennifer chipped in. "What about rape of civilian women by members of the army and police? How do your shareholders feel about that?"

"Interference in the social infrastructure is not the matter at hand," Saltzburg began, but Jennifer cut him off.

"To invest in a country that severely limits free speech and freedom of assembly, which imprisons gays and lesbians, and which permits its security forces to arrest political activists without cause, to operate with total immunity on matters of . . ."

"Call the question."

It was St. James.

"I beg your pardon?" Jennifer said, turning to face the chairman.

"I'm moving that we proceed to a vote on the item," he said.

"I understand that," Jennifer returned. "But I haven't said my peace."

"Seconded," said Saltzburg, ignoring her.

"All in favor?" St. James asked, levelly.

Jennifer's mouth dropped open.

"Aye," said the room.

"No!" Jennifer gasped.

"Eleven in favor, one opposed," said St. James. "Motion carries."

"Ten," Letrange corrected. "I abstain."

"Are you sure?" St. James asked pointedly. "That would force us to table the motion."

"Yes, I'm sure," said Letrange.

St. James' eyes lingered on him for a half second, then returned to his papers on which he made a note, and, without looking up, said, "Very well. Motion tabled. Item seven, on the matter of the Greek currency."

Jennifer avoided Letrange's eyes. To show gratitude might make her look weak, so she focused her attention on Saltzburg whose skeletal face looked satisfied in ways she wanted to punch. He caught her eye and smiled, papery skin stretching wide around the thin mouth, eyes twinkling with pleasure at her defeat. For a moment she was ten years old again, hating him, wanting to run from any room that had him in it.

For the next few minutes, as the burble of conversation went on around her, she sat rigid, hearing nothing, feeling only an old rage at everything the room represented and toward the man whose death had put her there. Again she thought it, first as an outraged exclamation and then, after a pause and a breath, as a real question: What had he been thinking?

Was one of the men in this room involved in her father's death? It seemed impossible. In terms of what they did, they were, she was sure, global bullies, but if people died because of their decisions, it was indirectly, at a remote, untraceable distance. That was what made them so maddeningly respectable.

"Item eight," said St. James, in that same monotonous drawl, "continuation of the special aerospace initiative package at current funding levels. Discussion?"

"Yes," said a man two seats down from her. His name was Justin Hadley-Jones, though she knew little else about him. "I'd like to propose a friendly amendment to raise funding by twenty-eight percent to counter currency exchange fluctuations. I have figures, if anyone would like to see them."

"I think we trust your judgment, Justin," said St. James. "All in favor of the proposal as amended?"

Another rumble of ayes.

St. James hesitated a second and his eyes fell on Jennifer. "Miss Quinn?"

"What?" she said, irritably pulling hairpins from her French twist. "Oh. Abstain."

"Motion carries. May I suggest a coffee break? We have rather a lot still to get through."

As they filed out, Jennifer's heart sank. This was undermining the dominant world order? Investigating her father's death?

"How is it going?" asked Deacon, when he found her cradling a cup of rapidly cooling tea.

"Awful. Ghastly. It's only the tedium that's keeping me from killing them all," she added with a bleak smile.

"Well, we can be grateful for that," said Deacon. "By the way, we found your father's laptop. It was in the Jaguar."

"Did he often leave it there?"

"Never, to my knowledge," said Deacon, his face carefully blank.

"And he was planning to come to London by helicopter the day he died."

"That is correct," said Deacon.

Jennifer nodded thoughtfully, realizing, just in time, that Letrange—Dan—had materialized at her elbow.

"How are you holding up?" he asked.

"Let's just say it's not what I'm used to," she replied.

"Indeed. And can I say that I sympathize with your vote against the African deal. It must be harder for you, having been on the ground as it were, seeing the conditions there . . ."

"I wasn't in Chad or Nigeria," she said quickly, her irritation returning. "And I didn't see you voting against it."

Her obvious hostility gave him pause, but he gave a sideways nod of understanding and said, "I said I sympathized with your perspective. But there are others that sometimes take priority in a place like this."

"I don't agree."

"And I respect that. Perhaps at some point we can meet less formally to discuss it."

"You're asking me out?" she said, staring at him.

"Not at all," he said, still smiling genially. "I just thought you might like the opportunity to discuss ways in which you might strengthen your position. Or express yourself in ways men like this are more likely to listen to you."

"Aren't you one of them?" she said, voice hard with defiance.

"I think if you got to know me, you'd see that it's rather more complex than that."

"You know, Mr. Letrange, I think I have all the complexity I can handle right now."

She said it with a stiff and final politeness. His nod of acceptance was also somehow a shrug of defeat, though he produced a business card from a silver case.

"Should you change your mind," he said.

She pocketed the card without looking at it, and he left her. She found herself under Deacon's watchful gaze. She closed her eyes for a second and felt a little of the tension leech from her shoulders.

"That was rude of me, wasn't it?" she said.

"That is not for me to say, Miss," said Deacon. "But I would say that in this world, allies are to be nurtured."

"Assuming you can trust them."

"Trust has to be earned," Deacon agreed, "but it sometimes begins with, as you might say, a leap of faith."

Jennifer sighed. The board members were drifting back into the meeting room.

"Once more unto the breach," said Deacon, taking her untouched tea from her. "And please stop fussing with your hair."

"It's annoying."

"It's professional."

"Same thing."

She followed the others, closing the door behind her and taking her seat before she noticed that on her copy of the agenda, someone had underlined the last item they had approved in heavy black pen.

Special aerospace initiative package.

She stared at it, then glanced around the room in the hope that someone would give her a nod or a look that would acknowledge the curious message, if indeed that was what it was.

But everyone was looking at St. James as he began to work his way through the rest of the scheduled items. It was as if they had forgotten she was there.

Except that one of them hadn't, she was sure of it. Though what it meant, she had no idea.

17

TIMIKA
New Jersey

JUST OUTSIDE SPRINGFIELD, NEW JERSEY, TIMIKA pulled off the exit ramp and into a McDonald's parking lot, signed into their Wi-Fi on the burner phone, and typed "Jerzy Aaron Stern + New York" into a series of search engines—zabasearch, pipl, wink and zoominfo—her usual snooping starters. She got no one in the right age group, which meant that either the name was false or he was new to the area. She widened the search from New York to the Northeastern states, then the whole East Coast and eventually to the whole country. Nothing.

False name, then. No one could have that small a data footprint. The police would have other tools, of course, but she had only given them the name. She called Officer Brown, but hung up when the call went to voice mail, then tried reaching the other burner phone, hoping the cabbie had been as good as his word. If he hadn't, she had his license plate, though she doubted that would help.

Marvin answered. "What's going on?" he whispered.

"Can you talk? Without being overheard, I mean?" she asked.

"Sure. Where are you? *How* are you?"

"Okay. I'm fine, but I'm moving and I don't want anyone to know where, so keep this number to yourself and don't call anyone but me on that burner, okay?"

"Okay."

"I want you to see what you can find on a Jerzy Aaron Stern. Jerzy with a 'Z'. He'd be in his eighties, I think."

"And the nature of this search?" asked Marvin.

"Discreet but rigorous," said Timika. That meant he'd be hacking, but covering his tracks as he went. He was good at that.

"On it," he said.

"Thanks, Marvin," she said. "I appreciate it."

"Look after yourself, boss," he said.

"Planning to."

She paid cash at the drive-through and began working on a quarter-pounder with cheese like she was twelve, taking a large bite and wondering, vaguely, when she'd last permitted herself such an indulgence.

Yeah, well, she thought. *Get shot at, win a burger.*

She forced herself to chew slowly, deliberately putting the wrapped sandwich down when she was halfway through. She reached for Stern's ancient journal on the passenger seat and flipped the front cover. Under his name was an address in Pottsville, Pennsylvania. She considered it, picked up her phone, then opted to go old school, dragging a dog-eared atlas from the glove box and onto her lap. Pottsville was not far off 78, west of Allentown.

She pushed a french fry into her mouth and wondered what the hell she was doing or what she hoped to find.

"Sixty miles, give or take," she said aloud. It didn't sound too far, assuming the Corolla was up to it.

She turned the engine over and pulled back onto the interstate heading west. The day was warming as she left the city behind. Some of the trees showed the buds of new leaves.

Spring at last, she thought, deciding to take that as a good sign.

She came off the highway at the Pottsville exit and, wary of turning her phone back on, stopped at a Mobil station for directions. They led her through the center of town and into the surrounding hills. As she drove, she saw no black people and few cars significantly fancier than Dion's. The gated community at the top of the hill was therefore a surprise.

It was called The Hollows, set back from the road, surrounded by trees next to a golf course, but the wrought iron fence edging the property looked more than ornamental. Timika drove slowly past the security gate, then parked just beyond a row of closely planted Leyland Cypress, carefully manicured and dense as a wall. She got out and walked back. She considered pressing the buzzer by the electric gate. There was something strange about the place, its remoteness and its unexpected opulence, that gave her pause.

As she looked, a man emerged from a sentry box inside the gate. He was uniformed in black, and was younger and more athletic than she expected.

"Can I help you?" he asked. The words held no welcome.

"I'm here to see Mr. Stern," she answered. "Mr. Jerzy Stern."

The guard's face remained expressionless.

"I think you have the wrong development," he said. "There's no Stern here."

"You know all your residents' names?" asked Timika, trying to sound playful rather than confrontational.

"I do," he answered, unsmiling. The bulge under his sweater pulled down over his waistband suggested he was armed. "Is there anything else?"

"If this is the wrong place, perhaps you can point me in the right direction," she said, still trying to sound sweet. "1094 Poplar Road."

"That's here," said the guard, still giving nothing away. "You must have gotten it wrong. Where did you get the address?"

And now she knew she was in the right place. He was probing.

She pretended her phone was vibrating, put it to her ear with a vague wave of apology at the guard, and mouthed

"Thank you." As she jabbered randomly into the phone, she walked from the gate back to the car, conscious of the way the guard watched her go.

SHE DROVE A FEW HUNDRED YARDS AND STOPPED TO THINK. Stern had been elderly, frail even. The Hollows, for all its stateliness, had an institutional feel.

Retirement home?

Maybe. But then why deny he lived there? She Googled local food service providers, ignoring the party caterers, and made a series of calls. In each case, she tried to sound distracted, manic, and a little panicky, calling herself Ashley and asking if they had already processed their order for The Hollows. Two came up empty, but at the third, a company called Newman's, a man's voice, slightly exasperated, said, "Not yet. Why, what is it this time?"

"Need to make some changes to Mr. Stern's order," she tried, eyes closed, feeling her way through the deception.

"Hold on," said the voice. There was a sigh, some muffled movement and voices away from the phone, and then he was back. "Stern, you said?"

"That's right. Read me what you have there."

"Standard continental breakfast, pastrami club lunch with fruit cocktail, and chicken piccata with banana cream pudding dinner."

"Yes," said Timika, thinking hard.

"So? What needs changing?" asked the caterer, his irritation mounting. "You can't keep doing this, you know. Not without more notice."

"They're old people," Timika ventured. "We have to keep a close eye on their dietary needs."

"So what does he want?"

"Fish," said Timika.

"Type?" prompted the caterer, still more exasperated.

"Well, what's available?"

Another sigh.

"You know the drill. Long as you guys keep paying, we'll find it, catfish to swordfish and anything in between."

Timika frowned. The Hollows was turning out to be a very strange place.

"Salmon," she said. "Fillet. Poached."

"Okay. Anything else?"

"Hold on," she said, stalling. "Our system is down. Can you run down what else is coming today and for whom?"

"Just the two at The Hollows or all eight of them?"

Timika hesitated.

All eight of them?

"Better give me the lot," she said, pen and notebook poised.

More grumbling and sighing, followed by a list of names and some pretty fancy dinner entrées: filet mignon with goat cheese and pine nuts; Vienna schnitzel, wild mushroom risotto, red snapper and snow peas. With the exception of the only woman on the list who also lived at The Hollows, the other diners lived elsewhere, all separately by the sound of it, but he only mentioned one actual location as he absently worked through the list: a place called

The Silver Birches. Timika wrote the names down, thanked the caterer for his time and patience—not that he'd shown much—and hung up. She reviewed the names.

Horace Evers.

Stephen Albitz.

Katarina Lundergrass—the other Hollows resident.

Albert Billen.

Frederick Kaas.

Karl Jurgens.

Max Stiegler.

Eight elderly residents scattered across at least two rest homes being catered by a special service. It was odd. She called Marvin.

He answered quickly. She had to speak over his anxious questions.

"I want you to see what you can find about these people. Anything that might group them together," she said. "Also this place: The Hollows, in Pottsville, Pennsylvania. And another called The Silver Birches. Also near here." She asked if he'd turned up anything on Stern.

"Next to nothing," said Marvin. "It's weird, you know? I see a statement of citizenship from 1945, but after that, nothing. Like he's been wiped from the records, you know? I'll keep poking around."

Timika considered the list of names again, then redialed the caterer.

"Ashley again from The Hollows," she said. "What time will you be making your delivery today?"

"Usual time. Four," said the caterer.

"You wouldn't mind picking me up on the way, would you?" she asked. "I'm having car trouble."

Another sigh.

"Where?" asked the caterer.

SHE DROVE TO A COFFEE SHOP, ACROSS THE STREET FROM A bridal showroom full of lace and fake plastic lilies, yellowing in the sunlit window. She wondered if Jerzy Stern had ever been married. She wasn't sure why, but she doubted it. She was on her second coffee when the burner phone rang. Good old Marvin.

"So this is really weird," he said. "Those people you told me about? All the same as Stern. Citizenship records in the late 1940s and early '50s, but nothing else."

"What about The Hollows and The Silver Birches?"

"Retirement homes. No apparent connection."

Timika's heart sank.

"Something interesting with your caterer though."

"What?"

"Mr. Newman was trained in Paris and Florence but then joined the military. Lived for a few years in Las Vegas, but it's not clear where he worked. He's been out here ten years. His catering company is owned by something called Firelight Holdings, but I can't find any other properties, bank records or tax statements under that name."

"So it's a shell company."

"A well-hidden one."

Timika drummed her fingers on the edge of the table. "You're thinking government," she said.

"Not sure who else could bury tax info so completely," said Marvin. "And it looks like The Hollows was built on land that was bought in the late 1940s by what was then called The National Military Establishment."

"The DOD."

"Right. I'm going to pull some strings and see if I can get a peek inside their more covert files."

"Remember what I said, Marvin," Timika cautioned. "Discreet, yeah?"

"Call me Bond. James Bond."

"You mean you'll show up in a tux and a sports car that shoots people out the roof? Let's keep it under the radar, okay?"

"Understood," said Marvin.

TIMIKA PARKED AROUND THE CORNER FROM THE HOLLOWS, then walked a mile back toward town to the junction where she had arranged to meet Newman's van. The driver was middle-aged but silver-haired, white, and grumpy as expected. Timika opted for slightly ditzy bubbliness and chatty gratitude, beating away the caterer's suspicions—if he had any—with a flurry of talk that wasn't so much small as microscopic.

"I've been at that mechanic three times in a year, if you can believe that," she burbled. "The one with the sign outside? They did my friend Carlson's Camry when he got rear-ended by some hick from Kentucky. It was really too bad 'cause the car had to be completely repainted and the body shop couldn't match the blue exactly. It was like a teal kind of color with a bit of turquoise. Capri blue, they called it. That's an island near Italy. Or Greece, maybe. I'm not sure. I've never been to Europe. Have you?"

"No," he said, which Timika thought was interesting.

"How come you don't cook for the other residents? Just these two?"

"Different contract."

"But you deliver to other people at other places, too?"

"Yes."

"How come you don't just deliver to one place but, you know, feed everyone there?"

He was getting annoyed now. "Not everyone can afford what I make," he said. "Now, if you don't mind, I need to concentrate."

And that was that.

Timika tried a few questions that weren't as leading, but the driver gave her nothing more than grunts and monosyllabic replies, his eyes on the road, but he was bored rather than suspicious, and she'd take that. As they pulled up to The Hollows, Timika dropped her face to her purse and began fiddling with her compact conspicuously. It was the same guard on duty who had turned her away before.

Timika's heart raced. She had used deception to investigate stories before, but this felt different and entirely more dangerous. Newman lowered his window and took a clipboard from the guard with a nod of greeting. As he signed, Timika kept her face down, saying nothing.

Then the window closed and they were moving. She waited until the gate receded in the side view mirror before looking up. The house they were approaching was a sprawling mansion, windows set in olive-colored stone stained with age, though the result looked stately rather than dilapidated. The van rumbled on the gravel approach, swung around the front and slowed into a parking lot screened from the house by trimmed shrubs and a picket of tight conifers. Newman slid out, muttering, "Give me a hand with the food, will you?" without pausing to hear her response.

He dragged the back doors of the van open, pulled out a ramp, and released the clamps on a pair of hostess trolleys with racks of covered dishes.

"Take one of these to the kitchen," he said.

Timika didn't object as she moved towards the back door, shoving the trolley's reluctant casters across the gravel with difficulty. The door was locked. She was further dismayed to see a keypad with a red light next to the handle. She could sense Newman behind her, watching.

She tapped a series of random numbers into the keypad and tried the door, feigning puzzlement when it didn't open.

"Huh," she said, trying the numbers again. "That's weird."

Newman sighed, stomped across the gravel and reached past her irritably to the keypad.

"There," he said, as the light turned green.

"Sorry," said Timika, trying to look embarrassed. "I don't usually use this door."

"Well excuse me for bringing you to the tradesman's entrance," snapped Newman.

"Sorry," said Timika, meaning it this time. "I didn't mean . . ."

"It's fine. Just get that food inside, please."

She did so, pushing the trolley down a carpeted hallway flanked by doors, trying to guess which one was the kitchen.

"There!" said Newman, sensing her uncertainty and nodding towards one of the doors on the right. "Jesus!"

She managed not to turn on him, resolving to stay in character another minute or two. She gave him an inquiring look as he pushed past her to the end of the kitchen, where she saw a large commercial refrigerator. She dithered, checking her watch as if there was somewhere she needed to be, and he gave up.

"Go," he said, loading the fridge. "Do whatever it is you do."

She thanked him for the ride, but he just grunted.

In the hallway, she faced the same uncertainty, unclear where she was going or what she was trying to accomplish. She didn't think the guard at the gate had noticed her, but she couldn't be sure. If he'd decided to let her in, only to corner her until law enforcement arrived, she wouldn't have long. She moved down the hallway, listening for sounds beyond the clatter of Newman in the kitchen. She thought she caught a strain of music coming from a door at the far end of the corridor. Old-fashioned music. Big band. Pre-swing. She tried the door.

It opened onto a kind of conservatory, filled with lounge chairs, low tables and French windows looking out onto a well-manicured garden surrounded by high hedges. Half a dozen people sat around the room, some sleeping, two drinking coffee and chatting, one playing half a game of chess, and one—the only woman—sitting alone with a book in her hands. All were old, as old as Jerzy, possibly older. One of the men was asleep in a wheelchair.

It was eerily quiet, and yet no one noticed her entrance. The old woman was not turning the pages of her book, her gaze fixed on a point in space at a middle distance, as if she were seeing nothing at all.

Timika made for her, trying to recall the one female name on the list she'd given Marvin.

"Hi," she said, smiling. "Katarina, right?"

The old woman started, then sat back while her eyes focused.

"Who are you?" she demanded. There was a hauteur in her manner. Her eyes looked pink and swollen.

"I'm Ashley," Timika said. "I've come from New York."

"New York?" said the woman. "What are you doing here?"

Good question, Timika thought.

"I'm trying to find a friend of mine," she said, improvising. "Jerzy Stern. You didn't know him, did you?"

"I know him," she said, but warily.

Timika glanced around the room. Only the chess player seemed to be paying her any attention.

"Do you mind if I sit with you for a moment?" she asked.

"It's a free country," said the elderly woman, adjusting her shawl. "Or so we like to think."

Timika sat and leaned in. The woman smelled like lavender.

"What is this place?" she began, trying to make the question sound casual, an ice-breaker.

"Death's waiting room," said the woman. "There used to be twice as many of us as there are now."

"And who are you all?" Timika ventured. Someone could walk in at any minute. "And these others," she added, producing the list of names she had written down. "Where are they? What connects you?"

The old woman's eyes tightened shrewdly.

"I don't think I should be talking to you," she said. "Are you supposed to be here?"

Another reckless chance.

"No," said Timika. "I'm not."

"Then you should probably go. While you still can."

It wasn't a threat. More like a warning. Her manner was weary and sad.

"You were a friend of Jerzy's, weren't you?" said Timika.

Katarina's eyelids flickered and she turned momentarily away. When she looked back, her eyes were bright, but when she opened her mouth to speak, her jaw quivered, so that she shut it hurriedly and gave a single nod instead.

"I thought so," said Timika, kindly.

"Are you?" the old woman managed. "A friend of Jerzy's, I mean."

"Yes," said Timika with sudden certainty. "He entrusted me with something he wanted me to do. But it's about the past, and there's a lot I don't understand."

Katarina nodded again, slowly, thoughtfully.

"We can't talk about that," she said, with a wistful smile, adding in a conspiratorial whisper, "Against the rules."

"Right," said Timika. "I see. Tell me about Jerzy."

She smiled then, a sudden unexpected smile, like clouds parting over a meadow of wildflowers.

"He was a beautiful boy," she said. "Long ago. Before we came here. I could look into his eyes for hours. Even now . . ."

She faltered and Timika felt an unexpected panic, a fearful wave of grief rushing in on her heart as she took in the woman's face, the depth of feeling in her bloodshot eyes.

"You've known him a long time," said Timika.

Katarina nodded.

"He's gone, isn't he?" she said. "Dead. They said he was just going away for a while, but I knew. I felt it."

Timika looked down, humbled by the old woman's grief. "I'm so sorry," she breathed.

Katarina Lundergrass clenched her teeth together and patted Timika's hand with her own, as if it were the younger woman who needed comforting.

"Who are you all?" Timika asked again.

"The best fed inmates on the continent," said the older woman, wiping her eyes.

"You are prisoners here?" Timika said, wondering if the woman was entirely in her right mind. Dion's grandmother had developed a dementia that manifested as a persecution complex.

"Jerzy said so. He said that it looked like a resort, so we would forget we couldn't leave."

"Why not?"

Katarina leaned in suddenly so that her face was inches from Timika's.

"Some things are best kept in the shadows," she said. "People think they want to know everything these days. But they don't. They really don't. So we stay here."

"Who's we?"

Katarina glanced around the room, her eyes lingering on each of the old men in turn.

"Paper people," she said. "Hidden away in a drawer where no one can read us."

The phrase raised the hair on the back of Timika's neck, and somewhere deep in the dark parts of her memory, something chimed, though she could not say what. She brushed her unease aside.

"What line of work were you in, Katarina?"

"I can't tell you that."

"Jerzy did. He gave me a book."

The old woman looked at her, and Timika felt she'd overplayed her hand.

"I think you should go," said Katarina.

"Just tell me a little more about . . ."

"No," she responded forcefully. "I mean it. I really think you should go."

She nodded towards the French doors, where two men in suits and overcoats were approaching the house from across the lawn. Timika got unsteadily to her feet.

"I could give you my phone number . . ." she began, but the old woman shook her head vigorously.

"Go."

"Thank you," said Timika, taking her hand on impulse and squeezing it gently, feeling the paper-thin softness of the other woman's skin, the bones and raised veins.

"We have an outing tomorrow," said the old woman, apparently changing her mind. "Locust Lake State Park. There's a little Presbyterian church just off the road as you drive north from town. Be there at eleven."

For a moment, Timika stared at her, taken aback, but then Katarina was brushing her away. The two men had almost reached the house.

She slipped out the way she'd come in, back down the hallway toward the kitchen and out the door into the gravel lot, but instead of walking back along the drive to the main gate, she cut right, forcing her way through the tight coni- fers and out onto a concrete path skirting a golf course.

She broke into an unsteady run, keeping to the tree line and moving away from the building and into the woods out of bounds from the fairway. She heard a door slam, back at the house, and the sound of raised voices, male. She took a few more hurried steps into the densest part of the underbrush and dropped to the cold, damp earth in the partial cover of a wild, shapeless magnolia.

Another shout, and now the sounds of men running her way. She burrowed a little into the leaf litter, trying to blot out any of her clothing's bright colors that might give her away. She forced herself to keep very still.

A guard came down the cart path at a full run, his jacket open so she could see how his pistol holster swung at his hip. He was white, thirty something, athletic. He wore an earpiece, and his eyes surveyed the woods as he ran. He was also closer than she'd realized. Before his gaze could fall on her, she turned her face down and held her breath, conscious of how her heart was hammering. Her right leg was twisted. What had been merely awkward was getting painful, but she did not dare adjust her position.

"No," said the man.

For a split second, she thought he was talking to her, and nearly looked up, but then he added, "I'm going to track round to the third hole and cut east."

He was talking to a colleague through the wireless mike he wore on his ear.

She tried to remember if she had seen a hole number on the fairway, in the hope that she could figure out which way he was heading, but her memory was blank. Hole one? Wouldn't it make sense to have the first hole by the house? She thought so, but she knew nothing about golf, so that could be wrong.

"Yes."

After a long silence, he was running again, and Timika could breathe.

She waited, still forcing herself not to move, counting in silence until she reached fifty before, with agonizing slowness, she looked up. The path was clear.

But coming silently across the dewy grass of the golf course, looking directly at her, was another man, also suited, his right hand pressed to his ear, mouth moving. He had seen her.

JERZY
Poland, January 1945

MRS. HABERNICHT DID NOT REFER TO MY PROPOSED sabotage for two whole days, so that I began to think she had forgotten about it. The village was full of the evidence of the Nazi retreat, a chaos of men and machines and ransacked shops. You could hear the vehicle engines running all night, and the normally rigid blackout got a little more relaxed. I don't know how much of a factor that was, but on the third night, the bombers found us.

The village had been largely spared by the allied air raids, except for a few planes that, for whatever reason, released their bombs on the south side of the mountains, perhaps to lighten their load as the German fighters closed in. It took us a moment to realize what was happening when we heard the drone of the Lancasters overhead, just distinguishable above the noise of hasty loading of trucks and halftracks on the ground. Then the bombs started, producing great roaring flashes that lit the night.

"Will they destroy the mines?" I whispered to Mrs. Habernicht as we crouched in the dusty, damp space under the stairs, which passed for a cellar.

The old woman listened and shook her head.

"Too deep," she said. "Too many layers of rock. But I don't think they are trying to hit the underground factory. They probably don't even know for certain that it's there."

"Then what?"

"The railway lines and the bridge," she said.

And so it proved. There was enough confusion that I could risk a walk into the village proper, just as the sun came up. A few houses had been hit, and a concrete bunker housing an anti-tank gun, but most of the damage was clustered around the railway station. Several warehouses had burned and collapsed, but the biggest problem for the Germans would be the railroad tracks, which had suffered at least two direct hits close to the station. The tracks just stopped on either side of the craters, their rails blackened and twisted. In one place, a hopper wagon had been lifted clean off the rails by the blast and lay in splinters and mangled strips of metal twenty yards away.

Whatever was being hauled from the mine would not be going back to Berlin that way, and if the Nazis repaired the tracks, they would only be bombed again. I remembered the concrete strip where the woods had been cleared, the place where I had seen Ungerleider. I had often thought about the work detail I had seen there, and was sure they had been building a rudimentary airfield. The Luftwaffe might be bringing in fighters, but I had seen very few German planes in the last few months, and Mrs. Habernicht said that according to Mr. Starek, who ran the corner shop and who had friends in Warsaw, the allies could fly wherever they wanted now. That meant that the airstrip—which seemed far longer than anything fighters would need—was for cargo planes. Big ones.

I wondered if the Polish army or the resistance knew about it.

That evening over supper, I told Mrs. Habernicht what I had seen, and she watched me with that shrewd, thoughtful way of hers, so that I fell silent, self-conscious, while I waited for her to speak.

"Two new tanks came to the village two days ago," she said. "I don't know where they came from. Maybe they have been hidden away for a long time, waiting to be used. They are not usual tanks with a single big gun on top. These have a kind of box with four guns all firing the same direction. Bigger than machine guns. Anti-aircraft guns."

She said it conversationally, dipping her bread in her soup.

"People saw them," she added. "But by morning, they had gone. Mr. Starek says they are no good for shooting at the bombers because they fly too high."

I thought furiously. Ishmael and I had once been enthusiastic readers about military hardware, in the first weeks of the war. That was a long time ago now, a former life, but I had always paid attention to the equipment I had seen and heard of, and I knew that the British had taken to sending single fighters to patrol over German airfields. They would swoop in and attack aircraft during takeoff and landing, when they were most vulnerable. If the Germans were positioning *flakpanzers*—which is surely what Mrs. Habernicht had described—then they were looking to protect cargo planes from air attack.

"When will the Polish army be here?" I asked. I seemed to be asking that question every day.

"Soon," said Mrs. Habernicht, which is what she always said. "And the Russians."

"It will be too late," I said. "The mines are full of new weapons. I am sure of it. If the Nazis can move them somewhere else, the war will go on and on. Perhaps it will never end."

I felt the passion rise in my voice and had to look away. It was the memory of Ishmael. I could not bear to think that all we had gone through was for nothing.

"I will speak to Mr. Starek," said Mrs. Habernicht.

I stared at her. "What good will that do?" I demanded, angry now.

She said nothing, holding my eyes for a long moment. "Wash your bowl before you get ready for bed," she said.

And I understood. Starek the shopkeeper worked for the resistance. He knew people.

That night, I was too excited to sleep. I heard the planes as they came in. It was quite different from the allied raid that had been far away until the bombs dropped, when I felt no danger. This night, the sounds of the aircraft engines caused the hairs on the back of my neck to rise. The planes were big, and close, getting louder and lower in pitch as they descended.

I got up from my bed and dressed hurriedly. I was barely down the stairs before there was a knock at the door. Mrs. Habernicht opened it in her nightgown and shawl, motioning me into the kitchen, and I listened to muffled voices, heard the front door click shut, and then she was back with the shopkeeper from the corner and another man I did not recognize. He carried a Russian-made sub-machine gun. They all looked at me.

"You want me to lead you to the airfield," I said.

They looked at each other.

"Can you?" said Mr. Starek.

"This way," I said.

I HAD ONLY BEEN THERE ONCE. THE NIGHT WAS HEAVILY overcast, so that the darkness in the woods was almost total, but I found my way without undue difficulty. Once we had left the village, the man with the submachine gun made us wait under an oak tree while he went back the way we had come. We spent about ten minutes alone, just me, Mr. Starek and Mrs. Habernicht, the silence broken only when the shopkeeper remarked that it was starting to rain. Mrs. Habernicht said nothing, but squeezed my shoulder encouragingly. I was not scared. Not yet.

The gunman returned, bringing three others with him, two men and a woman. One had a rifle, the others had pistols, and the two men bore between them a crate with rope handles. They did not speak to me, though the woman—she must have been no more than twenty-two or twenty-three—gave me a long, appraising look, as if she had expected someone older.

"Okay," said the man with the submachine gun, nodding to me.

I began walking, my feet finding the trails I had paced for days without my having to think about it. We passed the log where I had slept, crossed a shallow stream in which the heavy rain drops were pattering through the leaves above, and eventually climbed a steep escarpment to a fence where the tree canopy opened to the sky. Even in the low light, you could sense the clearing, and as I crawled cautiously up to the lip, just inside the tree line, I felt the soft forest floor grow hard and cluttered with the scree of concrete and stone chippings.

There were lights out there. They were hooded, but you could see them when they moved. Men, walking about, but other things, too. Vehicles. Somewhere among them were those flakpanzers, with four twenty-millimeter cannons that could tear up ground targets better than they could aircraft.

I ducked back into the deep shade of the trees. Two of the resistance men had opened the crate, and one of them was using a hand cranked radio set to send coordinates from a map he was studying with a small hooded flashlight.

"Now what?" said Mr. Starek. We were all speaking in Polish.

"We wait," said the man with the submachine gun. "Mrs. Habernicht? You should take the boy home."

"No," I said. "I'm staying."

Again, the woman gave me a long look.

"Very well," he agreed, "but stay out of the way and keep down."

I peered into the crate. The contents were wrapped in oilcloth, but sitting on the top was a black, heavy-looking revolver.

"Don't even think about it," said the younger woman.

"I didn't say anything," I said.

"You were about to."

"I wasn't!" I protested.

"You want the gun."

"So? Why shouldn't I?"

"You are a child," she said dismissively, fishing a cigarette from the pack in her coat pocket.

"I'm not," I said, biting down on the fury in my voice so that for a second she stared, then shrugged.

"You need to learn how to use a gun before you get to carry one," she remarked, striking a match and cupping its flame against the rain with her fingers as she lit the cigarette. "And you need to earn the right to use it."

There was a momentary pause.

"That he has," said Mrs. Habernicht. The younger woman gave her a long, level look through the smoke of her cigarette, then shrugged again.

"No skin off my nose," she said, reaching into the crate. "You don't shoot until I tell you. Got it?"

I nodded.

"What?" she demanded.

"Yes, ma'am," I said. "I won't shoot until you tell me to."

She hefted the pistol at me and I took it, awed and dismayed by how heavy it was, though I tried not to show it.

"Six shots," she said. "Make them count."

I nodded, and she managed a bleak grin.

"What's your name, little soldier?"

I bridled at her condescension, but said "Jerzy."

"I am Maxine," she said. "This is Pierre, Franco, and Roberto." The last was the submachine gunner, who seemed to be in charge. The others all nodded at me. The names were all fake, of course, so no one minded that she had told them. These people were all Poles. "Maxine" had a Warsaw accent, but I thought "Roberto" sounded more local.

I just nodded and turned away, not looking at the gun, which felt like something strange and magical at my side. It terrified me.

"Roberto" had been peering over the rise, watching the comings and goings at the airstrip. I turned to look at him, just as the blackness behind him shifted suddenly. From where I was, I could see stanchions and tree trunks, pale and hard against the blackness of the night. Floodlights had been turned on.

Everyone but Mrs. Habernicht moved cautiously up the rise and gazed out toward the airstrip.

The lights were dazzling, lighting only a portion of the concrete runway. The rest was marked with green lanterns, arrowing into the darkness, straight and precise. The end to our right, where the lights were hard and bluish, showed clusters of trucks, and people, and equipment. Beyond them, one behind the other, their wings so vast that they almost reached the tree line on either side of the runway, were three of the largest aircraft I had ever seen.

They were vast, boxy planes with wings mounted high atop the fuselage, with six propeller engines, three on each side, which, as I watched, had just begun to turn with a distinctive, rising howl. Their fuselages ran low to the ground, and their front ends were open like the jaws of a hippo. Some kind of truck drove right inside, through the nose of one of the planes, and was swallowed.

"What are they?" I gasped.

"Messerschmitt 323 Gigants," said Maxine. "They are in short supply. Whatever came out of those mines must be important to the Nazis."

"And they are loaded to go," said the man she had called Franco, who spoke Polish but didn't sound Polish at all. "They are closing their loading ramps. They're not going to leave the runway lit up like a Christmas tree for long. Not with the allies this close. We need to move—now."

"We are supposed to wait for armed support," said Roberto, not happy about it. "They should be here by now."

"Well they aren't," said Franco. "And those planes are ready to go."

"And what are we supposed to do to stop them?" demanded Maxine. "There are six of us!"

"Seven," I said.

They ignored me. Suddenly, we heard the roar of a vehicle coming our way along the runway. It was one of the flakpanzers, essentially a tank with a pulpit-like box on the top, bristling with anti-aircraft cannon.

"*Wirbelwind*," muttered Roberto as it rumbled by and took up a position in the darkness at the end of the runway. In English, this would be "Whirlwind."

"The other will be near where the planes are," said Pierre. "Get caught between them and they'll cut us to pieces before we fire a shot."

Roberto seemed to think for a second, then, with an air of decision, flung back a tarp covering the contents of the crate. Beneath it were three metal tubes with bulbous tips, like sink plungers: *panzerfaust*. Hand-held anti-tank weapons.

"Where did you get those?" I asked.

"One of our cells hit a retreating convoy three nights ago," said Roberto, lifting one out and handing it to Franco. "Range is about sixty yards. The safety is here. Aim and squeeze here to fire. One shot only. Our priority is the Messerchmitts. We wait as long as we can for the Polish army. I don't want to lose people now."

But the army didn't come. We waited, but the only activity came from the Germans as they finished loading and readying the aircraft. For ten long minutes, we said nothing. Roberto checked his watch six times. Pierre monitored the radio, but no one called. I found myself torn between the desire to do something and the dread of the attempt. Apart from the flakpanzers, there was an armored car, a half-track, and a detachment of about twenty guards armed with rifles and submachine guns. We couldn't possibly hope to take them on. I began to dread the arrival of the Polish forces, which might force our hand, and I couldn't help thinking that with only enough firepower to destroy the planes and not the flakpanzers, we couldn't hope to survive the attack.

After about twenty minutes, the runway was cleared, and a man with colored flashlights motioned the lead aircraft into position. They were about to depart, and there was still no sign of the Polish army. I gave Roberto a sidelong look. He was biting his lip and fiddling with the safety catch on one of the panzerfausts. And then, as the first aircraft began lumbering forward like some great, fat goose laboring to get up enough momentum to launch itself into the air, he handed his submachine gun to Maxine, moved to the lip of the runway, and took aim.

The plane was still idling, though it would be a matter of seconds before it began its acceleration. When it passed us, Roberto would fire, and all manner of hell would let loose. I felt a sudden and violent urge to urinate, to vomit, to run, and the last of these I gave in to.

I moved down the slope and into the woods, ignoring Maxine when she called after me. I ran, but not back toward the village. I ran up through the woods flanking the airstrip, clutching the heavy pistol, and feeling the sweat from my brow mix with the rain running down my face. I didn't know this part of the forest as well as I knew the trail and had to be careful, but when I heard the pitch of the aircraft engine climb, I knew I didn't have much time.

I emerged a few hundred yards down the runway, at the point where the slick concrete became gravel, then uneven grass and bracken. I looked down the concrete strip towards the lights where the hulking plane was rocking forward like it was towing something immense. Between me and the plane was the silent bulk of the flakpanzer.

There would be four men inside, but only the one in the AA turret would be likely to hear me in the dark. I stared at the tank, not sure what I hoped to achieve, and I thought I heard a snatch of conversation from inside. For a moment, I tried to hear above the sound of the airplane's engines. It was all so strange, standing there in the night, a revolver in my hand, and the might of the Nazi army only feet away, oblivious. And then the plane picked up speed, and someone emerged from the darkness of the forest, shooting something squat from the crook of his arm.

I couldn't see where the charge went, but it must have caught the fuselage of the Messerschmitt a glancing blow near the top, because there was a flash and a plume of orange, but the plane kept coming. As it outran the cloud of smoke, I could see, in the floodlights, where the roof behind the cockpit was scored with a ragged—but superficial—tear. Roberto had missed.

Now the flakpanzer came to life, creaking and groaning as the gunner swung the turret round and opened fire with all four cannon so that tracers flashed towards where the resistance fighters and Mrs. Habernicht crouched in the undergrowth. The sound was like bombs going off beside me, and the blaze from the muzzles—fire and lightning mixed—was blinding. Trees snapped and exploded, cut in half as the shells tore into them, and Roberto—the only one I could see—dropped under the raging hail of gunfire.

I did not consciously decide to run at the tank or scale its hull, burning my hand on the exhaust pipe. I did not consciously choose to haul myself over the angled box of the turret sides. I do not believe I could have consciously shot the gunner down, but he saw me and he let go of the cannon grips, snatching for his machine pistol, and I saw in his eyes what he meant to do. I saw anger and hatred and maybe fear as well. Above all, I saw purpose, deliberation, the same kind of intent that had looked down the barrel of an MG 42 from a watchtower and cut my brother down. I pointed the revolver at his chest and fired.

Just once.

It was enough.

I dropped the pistol, hands shaking, wondering vaguely if the men in the tank below me realized what had happened. As I paused, momentarily entranced by what I had done, the first gigantic Messerschmitt pulled hard up over the end of the runway and roared directly overhead so that I ducked, hands over my face as it arced into the night. Despite Roberto and however many of the others who were dead, and despite anything I had done, it escaped. But there were two more, one of them already on its way.

The dead gunner was already half out of the seat, so with effort, I pulled him clear and took his place. Then I swiveled the turret a few degrees around until I saw the nose of the second aircraft just as its front wheels left the concrete, and I squeezed the trigger. The cannon shells raked the belly of the craft, and it juddered uncertainly, continuing to climb but wounded now. I kept shooting, shouting incoherently, tears rolling down my cheeks, awash in grief and horror and a terrible kind of joy I never want to feel again.

The massive plane limped up into the night sky above me, but it was barely above the trees when it began to tip to one side, stalling, falling, and then the sky flared once more, and what was left of it plummeted into the woods. I stared vaguely toward where it had gone down, absently wiping the tears from my eyes, and realized that I had heard movement from below. The tank's belly hatch had opened.

I snatched up the fallen machine pistol and peered over the canted walls of the turret. Three men scrambled out from beneath the tracks at the rear. One of them had an automatic pistol, and he rolled to his feet sighting along the barrel at me. I saw the surprise in his face, the doubt when he registered the machine pistol, and then, without a word, he dropped the gun and raised his hands.

I was too scared to trust him. My trigger finger twitched. But I took a breath, and in that moment, I saw that he was only a few years older than me. He looked pale, frightened. Of me. On instinct, I nodded toward the tree line and motioned with the gun. He and his fellows turned and ran into the darkness, not speaking or looking back, hands clasped behind their heads.

I watched them go, then got back into the gunner's seat. There was one more plane to come, but when I looked at the runway, it wasn't the Messerschmitt barreling towards me. It was the armored car, headlights blazing.

My fingers felt thick as I fumbled for the trigger mechanism. In that split second, I felt the staccato thud and rattle of machine gun rounds kicking off the sides of the tank as the armored car's weapons blazed. The shield around the AA mount buckled and popped as two holes punched through only inches from my shoulder.

Stricken with terror, I dropped from the gunner's seat and hugged the decking as round after round punctured the pulpit and ripped through the air above me. The metal shredded and tore, lighting the darkness around me with a frightful brilliance matched by the deafening roar of the gun and the clanging of its shells. Overwhelmed, my senses fogged. I was too scared to weep and lay flat, eyes shut, waiting for death.

And then there was another sound behind the others, a bang, deep and close and loud, after which there was a sudden silence and the light changed, flaring red and yellow, the air stinking of oil and smoke. I waited for more cannon rounds to come streaming into the AA pulpit from the armored car, but as the stillness stretched on, second after agonizing second, I rolled cautiously onto my back and, very slowly, lifted my head just high enough that I could see through a hole torn by the cannon fire. I saw flame and movement, and I heard voices calling, and not in German.

I sat up, peering over the savaged rim of the AA gun shield, my eyes prickling in the smoke. The armored car was burning, its turret crumpled impossibly. Behind it, hulking in the firelight, was a tank from which men were clambering. I knew its shape from the secret broadsheets which had been smuggled round the ghetto, though I had never seen one, the distinctive sloping armor which had given the Nazis such an unwelcome shock on the fields of Kursk. It was a T-34. And now I could hear the voices of the troops as they rounded up the German survivors, and there could be no mistake.

It was the Russians.

KATY
New Mexico, July 1947

KATY DIDN'T MIND THE DESERT. IT WAS WEIRD, LIKE another planet, but after the rubble they'd left behind, thousands of miles away, she could see the bright side. The only thing that was hard was the language, and the way some of the kids at school looked at her. Her English was okay. Her father's was better—perfect, it seemed to her—but then one of the boys in her class had told her the sign that had gone up in front of the house across from the playground that said, "Krauts go home" was supposed to be about her.

The idea meant nothing to her, at first, because she didn't understand it, even though the boy had whispered it under his breath without looking at her, his face flushed, which meant he thought it was true. She'd gone home and asked her father about it, and her father, who was good at explaining things, told her that some people around here didn't feel good about them being there, because this new country had been fighting Germany, their former country, for so long. Katy pointed out that that had all finished ages ago, but her father had smiled, in that way of his that showed he wasn't really happy, and said that it was only two years ago. Two years seemed like a long time to Katy, her father said, but to grownups, it was no time at all.

This was a worrying thought, all by itself, an idea as strange as the desert where it never rained and the birds and animals were unfamiliar. How could two years be no time at all? Was time as different here as its strange birds and lizards? Might she wake up tomorrow to find that a year had passed? What then? Would she grow old and weak, like the dark-skinned lady with the eagle face who sold blankets and jewelry by the side of the road just outside town?

She lay awake, her knitted dolly with the yellow wool hair in her hands, wondering, studying the wrist watch that had belonged to her mother, staring at it without blinking to see if the hands moved faster than they ought to. If her mother was here, she would explain it, but her mother had been in Dresden when the bombers came. It was just Katy and her father now, alone in the desert, where time moved faster and you didn't talk too much in case people heard and figured out where you were from.

Kraut.

It was a nickname, her father said, from sauerkraut, but that didn't make sense. When Maggie Philips said it, while they were lining up for assembly, Katy had explained—quite politely, she thought—that she did not like sauerkraut and never ate it. Her mother used to make it for her father, she remembered, but you couldn't buy it in New Mexico, so even her father didn't eat it anymore.

There were lots of things her father didn't have anymore. Perhaps that was why he seemed so sad. Of course, Katy knew that his sadness wasn't really about such things—sauerkraut and forests, castles and beer and the other things he talked about—but she was sure, in her heart, that if he could have them, he would feel better. Not about Dresden though. There was nothing that would make him feel better about that, and she had learned that it was best not to try.

She gazed at the ceiling one night, then told Hella—the yellow-haired doll—that she would speak to Mrs. Simms at the grocery store about ordering something her father would like. Not sauerkraut. Not beer. Some kind of sausage, perhaps. Her father liked sausage, the way they made it back home. There might be a way to get it.

Pleased with the idea, she rolled onto her side but had not fallen asleep when the phone rang. It rang for a long time before she heard her father half-falling out of bed and running heavily down the stairs, muttering to himself in German. He answered the phone in English, because that was what you had to do here, and then he went quiet for a while. When he spoke again, he sounded excited and a little confused, and it struck her as strange that he was speaking German again.

She got out of bed, taking Hella with her, and moved onto the landing so she could see him through the banisters, pacing up and down the hall as he talked. He was smoking, and the cigarette in his hand seemed to tremble very slightly, as if his whole body were cold. He turned suddenly and looked up, as if he had been thinking of her, and she saw the strange look in his eyes. She wasn't sure what the expression meant because she had never seen it before.

He finished the conversation and said to her—in German, "Get dressed, little Katy. We have to go out."

Katy stared at him, disbelieving. It was nighttime. She should be in bed.

"I have to go out and I can't leave you here alone," he replied. "You can bring Hella. Put on your dress and shoes."

Katy left the house after dark for the first time since those late night trips to the shelter two years ago, which had seemed so long ago, until she learned that time moved faster here. She asked where they were going, but her father just said, "Work," and hurried her into the car. Sometimes, when he wasn't too sad, they sang old songs in the car, but not tonight, perhaps because it was so late.

She had never been to her father's place of work, so she was surprised by how far it was, and she slept for part of the way, waking when someone shone a flashlight into the car and asked to see papers. It was a soldier with a gun and a helmet. Katy, who did not like soldiers no matter what kind of uniform they wore, kept very still and tried not to meet the man's eyes.

It felt like her father was being tested, like at school when they showed you the words on a card and you had to read them in front of everyone in your best American English, but if so, it was a test he passed. They were allowed to drive into an area with a lot of square buildings, lit with lights on high stands, dazzling lights that made the ground as bright and clear as lunchtime, though the sky above was black. Her father took her hand. She was surprised to note that his was sweaty, though the night was cool. He squeezed her fingers reassuringly and she smiled at him to make him feel better.

Pulling up beside their car where they'd parked was a pickup truck, its bed carrying a big, shiny balloon made of something like the foil wrapped around chocolate bars. There was string too, and some kind of big wooden box bound with pink tape that looked like it had been put together in someone's shed. Maybe it was a school project: a basket that you fastened to the balloon to see how high it would go. Something like that. The driver looked to her father, then threw a shiny cover, big as a rug, over the back of the truck before driving off.

Inside the building, there were more men in uniforms, and more questions, some of them directed at her. No one seemed to know what to do with her, but her father explained—five or six times in his perfect English—that he could not leave her at home. She had to stay with him.

"And anyway," he said, "who is she going to tell? She's a little girl, for God's sake!"

That meant he was serious. He did not say "God" unless he was very serious. Or sad.

But they wouldn't let her in so her father stopped her at the door.

"I need you to wait here now, Katy," her father had said, glancing over his shoulder, as if there was something there he desperately wanted to see. "Just for a few minutes."

"I want to see," she said.

"Maybe later," he replied. "But for now you must be patient and not come in. Is that clear?"

"Yes, father," she said, not happily. She turned away and began to walk in the direction he had nodded, but as she heard the door behind her open she turned and looked after him.

Her father was showing his papers again while other people took flash photographs and whispered to each other. The room beyond the door was so big that it wasn't really a room at all, more like a space with walls and a roof, big as a football field. Maybe bigger. In the middle, under multiple floodlights, more men stood with guns, guarding a strange metal object that flashed under the lights. It was big, like a giant's cake pan that had rolled off his table and landed upside down, and part of it was broken.

She stared past the soldiers and the men in white coats, but then the door closed again and she was alone.

It seemed like he was gone a long time, though she couldn't be sure because of the way the time ran differently in the desert. Her feet got tired from standing, and she sat down on the chilly concrete. Once he came to check on her, his face still pink and shiny with strange emotions, and someone gave her a chair, and that was all she remembered.

She woke up in the car, a mile from home. The sky was still dark, and her father was very quiet and thoughtful, but not sad. Not angry. When they reached their driveway, he turned off the engine and sat staring at his hands on the steering wheel, not looking at her, unaware that she was awake. When she spoke, he jumped and looked surprised. Then he took her in his arms and carried her inside. He clutched her tight to him as they walked so that Katy, a little frightened by his love, asked nothing about where they had been or why.

When they were in her room and she was sitting on her bed, he hesitated in the doorway, looking at her.

"No piano lesson for you tomorrow," he said. "Get into bed."

"But I have to go to my lesson," said Katy. "The teacher says so."

"I will speak to the teacher, little Katy," he said. "You have had a very tiring night and you need your sleep."

"I don't want to," she said. "I'm not sleepy."

She was, but she didn't want to say so. She didn't want him to leave. His peculiar excitement, the place with the soldiers, and the cake pan all made her feel strange, and she didn't want to be left alone in the dark, though she couldn't think of how to say so.

"I'll sit with you," he said. "And look. I brought you a present."

She snuggled under the thin blanket, face open and attentive to what she was going to get. From his pocket, he drew what she first thought was a candy wrapper. It was balled up tight, a little screw of paper, so that her excitement at being given a present disappeared, and she gave him a crestfallen look. As she did, he opened his hand and something remarkable happened. The patch of foil sprang open and went perfectly flat, showing not so much as a wrinkle in its surface.

Katy gasped, delighted, and put out her hand to receive it. Her father gave her the thin piece of foil and she gasped again as it pulsed with a soft blue radiance that spangled like water. It gave off enough light that she could see her father's eyes in the darkness. He reached out cautiously and touched his hand to hers, whereupon the bluish glow became pink as dawn. He let go, watching the light change back to blue, and his face was unreadable once more.

DAYS LATER, AFTER SHE HAD GONE BACK TO SCHOOL, THE schoolyard was abuzz about a crash. The newspaper showed the men in uniform with what they called the recovered debris. It was a weather balloon, the paper explained. It looked like the bits of wood and foil she'd glimpsed in the back of the pickup truck. Her father told her she wasn't supposed to say anything about it, and that she should forget, because the crash was not something worth remembering. But Katie remembered, and if she ever felt herself doubting what she had seen, she would take out the piece of strange metal foil that glowed when she touched it with her skin, and she would remember the look in her father's face, a mixture of delight and anxiety, confusion and horror.

ALAN
Dreamland, Nevada

THEY DIDN'T CALL IT AREA 51. NOT THE PEOPLE WHO worked there. They called it, appropriately enough, "Dreamland." It was a maze of blank corridors and windowless rooms, every door fitted with combination locks and badge-reading scanners. Armed guards stood at every corner and did not speak, such that Alan sometimes got the impression he was the only real person there. The truth was that they were just people who knew and did their jobs, unfazed by the strangeness of the place. Posters on every other wall read, "If you see something odd, don't wait: Report it!"

That ought to keep everyone busy, Alan thought.

Alan had been there a week, but for all its otherworldly interiors and the desolate exterior landscape, nothing so far had matched the excitement of that first five minutes. He still didn't know what exactly he had seen. His questions had been met with a disinterested silence. His glimpse of the ship had been little more than the reward he'd needed for resigning his commission as a Marine. That done, he'd immersed himself in a world of books and computer tutorials so abstract in their applications that half the time, he didn't know if he was learning to fly a plane or operate a high-tech washing machine. He read passages and filled out questionnaires, but there was frequently no clear relationship between the two, and often nothing about planes or flying at all. By the third day, he began to suspect it was all a test, or a bad joke at his expense, and that none of it really meant anything at all. The fourth and fifth days, he spent in a completely unremarkable classroom with a guard on the door armed with a purposeful looking M-4 carbine. He studied logs and tables, charts and diagrams, and from time to time, an instructor who did not give his name came in to talk him through the next pages, speaking in a steady monotone. Alan took multiple-choice tests late into the night, after which he was escorted to his quarters to sleep, until it all began again the next day.

He hadn't known what to expect, but the boredom surprised him. That was as much irony as Dreamland was going to give him.

Though he saw several other men undergoing similar instruction, he talked to no one but his instructors, who merely gave him lists of the day's tasks and took his written work in without comment. He didn't even know if they read it. The base was owned and operated by the Air Force, but it was compartmentalized and spread over a large area in separate units between which there was no traffic. While he occasionally glimpsed jets in the sky over to the northwest, he interacted with no Air Force personnel at all. The base guards were a separate security force and everyone else was CIA. Hatcher met him for dinner every night but kept the talk small: sports, mainly. And barbecue. Hatcher was a nut for barbecue.

"No politics, religion, or military intel," he said, the first time they sat down together.

Alan abided by the rules for as long as he could, until one night, he had to ask.

"That craft we saw when I first arrived," he asked Hatcher. "What was it?"

They were eating dinner, just the two of them in a canteen the size of warehouse: lobster and filet mignon, flown in from Vegas.

"You want to know if it was a flying saucer," Hatcher clarified.

Alan had been avoiding the term, even in his own mind. It was too loaded with impossible things, with craziness and zealotry. The problem was that the term fit all too well. The craft had been roughly saucer shaped, twenty feet across and windowless. It was bare metal, like brushed nickel or aluminum, and showed no lights except the large, central one on the underside which seemed to be its source of propulsion. The disk bulged upwards in the middle but was otherwise unmarked, so it was impossible to be sure if it was rotating or not. And it was flying, though not in any way Alan could recognize or make sense of.

He said nothing, pretending to be too busy chewing to answer directly, though Hatcher, who recognized the moment for what it was, just smiled.

"Yes," he said simply. "It was a flying saucer."

"So that means it's . . ." He searched for a word, one perhaps even more insane than *flying saucer*. "Alien?" he said at last.

Alan wasn't sure what he had expected from Hatcher, but the CIA man's laugh—which in other circumstances might have been scornfully dismissive—came as a welcome relief.

"Made in the USA," he said. "By people like you and me."

"But how?" said Alan. "I've been in aviation all my adult life, and I've never even heard of anything that looked or moved like that."

Hatcher grinned. "Because it's secret, Alan."

He didn't say it, but *dumbass* was implied.

"Okay," said Alan. "Why?"

"It's how we keep our edge," said Hatcher. "And this is a test facility. The R&D section here—a subdivision of a major commercial aerospace manufacturer whose sole client is the US government—is called Possum Plant. Ask me why."

"Why?"

"Because they are really good at playing dead when people get too close. These are secret machines, Alan, but they are ours."

"So why not show the world we have them, and stop any potential enemies in their tracks?"

"Like I said," answered Hatcher, spearing a hunk of steak with his fork. "We are a test facility. You know how long it took to get the U2 operational? Or the Blackbird? Wouldn't make sense to show our hand to the world before we had everything in working order, would it?"

"But I saw one of these things in Afghanistan," said Alan. "That's why I'm here. You took a chance on me because I'd already seen one."

"And because you're a damn fine pilot," said Hatcher.

"But my point," Alan pressed on, refusing to be deflected by the compliment, "is that one of those ships showed up and interfered with my mission. Right?"

Hatcher considered whether or not to answer this before nodding. "It would seem so," he said.

"So someone else has . . . whatever the hell those ships are, yeah? Someone other than the ordinary people of the USA who built the one I saw last week."

"We're entering classified territory again," said Hatcher, putting down his knife and fork.

"You're telling me a bunch of Afghan insurgents have access to aviation technology so advanced that our own country doesn't know it exists?"

"Of course not," said Hatcher.

"So?"

"So, think it through."

Alan frowned. "Someone else is supplying them, or interceding on their behalf."

Hatcher didn't deny it, returning his gaze to his plate and continuing his meal in silence.

"But who would have that kind of tech?"

Hatcher said nothing.

"They would also have an interest in either destabilizing the region," Alan continued, thinking aloud, "or of undermining US interests in the area."

Still Hatcher said nothing.

"And the technology the ground team at Safid Kuh went in to recover was connected to the development of these same craft, or you wouldn't have brought Morat out here with me. Which means we're in some kind of secret arms race."

At last Hatcher spoke. "You haven't figured out who we're dealing with, but you've answered your first question."

"Which was?"

"Why are we keeping the program secret? Because we aren't the only ones involved. Secrecy, like information, is currency. It's power, and it has to be protected at all costs. All arms races are secret, until they're not."

Alan digested this.

"The Russians," he said. "It has to be. Or the Chinese."

"You have room for dessert?" said Hatcher, as if they had been discussing the weather. "The chef does an excellent crème brûlée."

Alan opened his mouth to say more, but the CIA man raised one index finger, eyes on his plate. The conversation was over.

Dreamland was quiet at night, so quiet that Alan was unsure how many people were based there from one day to the next. He knew that a lot of the staff were bussed in daily, though he was not allowed to speak to them, and that regulations concerning leaving one's designated area— even one's quarters—were strictly enforced. Sometimes it felt like he was alone, the sole worker surrounded by security teams who had nothing else to do but watch him.

His lodging was a prefabricated trailer that sported an AC unit that sounded like a jet engine. At first, he assumed this was just because the device was working at maximum capacity to counter the extreme Nevada heat, but then he was summoned to one of the base's office complexes and noticed something strange. The décor was coolly, nondescriptly professional, and the windowless interior might have passed for the halls and offices of a major New York law firm, but the carpeted halls featured trim black wall-mounted speakers generating a soft, white noise hiss. It was a counter-surveillance mechanism. Even the most sophisticated listening devices would struggle to cut through the static. Maybe his air conditioner had been designed with the same secondary function in mind.

In his trailer, he read, listened to music or played video games—there was no Internet to connect him with the cyberworld off base—until summoned. Then he was escorted to wherever he would spend the bulk of the day, flashing his badge and scanning his palm print at every door, breaking for meals in the DFAC, which was invariably deserted except for whoever was serving him his gastronomic treat for the day. He turned in his dinner requests the night before, amusing himself by challenging the cooks with exotic dishes he had only read about. So far he had tried wild boar with roasted chestnuts and truffles, duck à l'orange and—just for devilment—vegan shepherd's pie. He hadn't tripped them up yet, though after the shepherd's pie, he'd asked for a rib eye steak, cooked rare, which might have been the greatest thing he ever tasted. He spent ninety minutes a day in the well-appointed gym while he waited for someone to tell him what the hell he was doing here.

The second week was spent in classes—again, by himself—being instructed on the nature of the craft he would be flying. Alan privately nicknamed his instructor Professor Beaker, after the Muppet. Half of what Alan was told comprised nodules of information coherent in their own right, but not clearly connected to each other, so that he felt he was learning about individual systems, the purpose of which remained a mystery. The other half was just techno-babble, and though he was good at parroting it back, it meant little to him.

The craft itself, according to its data manual, was triangular and was named the Astra-TR3B, "but we just call it the Locust," said Beaker with a smile. He was proud to be connected to it. The Locust had control layouts unlike those used in any aircraft he had ever seen, controls that were not just unfamiliar but counterintuitive to anyone with a basic sense of aviation or aerospace physics.

". . . which is why you can't think of space and time as separate entities," Professor Beaker was saying. "Is that clear, Major?"

Alan had to fight the urge to laugh. Clear? It was, to him, gibberish. It meant nothing. But did he understand the words themselves? Sure.

"Absolutely, professor," he said.

"You don't need to call me that," said Professor Beaker, looking slightly puzzled, before turning back to the diagram he had scribbled on the white board. "So you see the curvature in Space-Time can be exploited by applying, as it were, pressure here and here." He tapped the diagram and then noted Alan's raised hand. "Yes, Major?"

"So this is what?" said Alan. He tried not to sound skeptical. "Warp drive?"

Professor Beaker blinked like a baby bird in the sun, scowled, then finally smiled. It looked like it took real effort.

"Good one," he said. "It's good to keep a sense of humor. Warp drive. Very good, Major."

He smiled wider, as if he had made a joke. Alan appreciated that Professor Beaker was trying to help him, in his way. They just didn't speak the same language or, Alan thought ruefully, inhabit the same version of reality.

"We'll break for lunch," said Beaker. "Then we'll begin work on the Locust's weapon systems."

"Yes," said Alan, sitting up. "I was wondering about that. I can't make sense out of these design specs. There's no nose cannon?"

Again, Beaker's bird-like blink indicated he was unsure if Alan was trying to be funny. "Nose cannon?" said Beaker, as if he had never heard the words before.

"Right."

"Lasers," said Beaker, as if nothing could be more obvious. "In 1956 the pilot of a Grumman F11F-1 Tiger traveling at the speed of sound shot itself down when its speed allowed it to accidentally fly into the path of its own slowing bullets. We've been a little wary of conventional weapons for superfast aircraft ever since."

"So," said Alan, "we've got lasers."

Beaker smiled vaguely. "Nothing faster than light, is there? I'm sorry—was not that in the briefing?"

Alan, who had been staring in stunned silence, rallied.

"Not in those precise terms," he managed.

He was glad when lunch break arrived. He'd crossed over into a world that didn't make any real sense, however much everyone behaved as if it did. That sense stayed with him throughout the afternoon briefings. He listened, he studied, he aced his quizzes, but he felt like the only sober one at a party where everyone else was drunk or high.

Lasers?

It was nuts.

That night, he told Hatcher he was getting restless, that he didn't know what he was doing there, and that he was starting to think they had made a serious mistake.

"We'll see if you feel that way tomorrow," said Hatcher. "You've completed the first phase of your training."

So Beaker had given him a passing grade after all.

"What happens tomorrow?" Alan asked, unconvinced. He didn't see how he'd been "training" for anything.

"Brave new world," said Hatcher.

ALAN SLEPT LITTLE THAT NIGHT. WHEN HATCHER CAME for him the next morning, he'd been up and dressed for almost two hours.

"We're flying today?" he asked. It seemed like a long time since he'd been in a cockpit.

"Good morning to you too, Major," said Hatcher. "And no. Today we're in simulators."

Alan's heart sank. He was tired of being treated like a rookie.

"Is that really necessary?" he said. "I've racked up thousands of hours in the air. Are these ships so different that I have to start over?"

"Yes," said Hatcher, simply.

Outside was a yellow school bus with blacked-out windows and a driver in shades who verified their IDs before setting off without a word.

"Where are we going?" asked Alan.

"You ask too many questions," said Hatcher. "We're going to another part of the base. A separate, restricted part."

"I thought the whole area was restricted."

"There are levels. Where we're going is classified as S-4, Papoose Lake, south of the mountains. You'll be spending a lot of time there, and you won't be discussing it with any-one. Ever. Clear?"

"Crystal."

The bus rumbled over what felt like a dirt road. Alan could see nothing but the occasional bleed of white Nevada sunlight through scratches in the blacked-out windows.

When they stopped and got out, the terrain looked much as it had. Dry, pale ground, and another evaporated lake bed at the base of a wall of cliffs, utterly desolate, without any sign of human habitation, until they approached the cliff face, turned into a shaded alcove, and came to a door with a keypad. Alan did a double take. From a few feet away, the door was nearly invisible.

"Avert your eyes," said Hatcher, casual, but not messing around. Alan did so.

Inside, they walked down cool, white-noised cor-ridors, stopping at security doors that looked like they belonged in a submarine, sliding open only after Hatcher had entered codes and a palm print. Alan said nothing, oscillating between annoyance and a swelling sense of excitement.

Planes were planes. They had their varying quirks and capabilities, and it made sense that pilots specialized in particular models as a result, but at its core, flying was fly-ing. He knew—in his very bones—the essential elements of thrust and lift, of banking, acceleration, G-force, pitch, roll . . . you name it. It was a part of him. Who was Hatcher kidding with all this cloak-and-dagger teasing?

The CIA man walked him to a locker-room, opened one of the steel wall cabinets, and dragged out a flight suit not so very different from what Alan had worn over the mountains of Afghanistan. He dressed and Hatcher stood by, watching like a critical parent, poised to offer help or criticism. Alan welcomed neither.

When he was ready, they proceeded through another door, and Hatcher nodded towards a familiar dark-eyed man standing at a console, dressed in a matching flight suit.

"You already know Mr. Morat."

Alan didn't bother concealing his surprise.

"I didn't know you were a pilot," he said, assuming the man was here to monitor the simulator while Alan was inside.

"I'm many things," said Morat with a flat smile, "including your tutor for the day. I'll be monitoring your progress today and will be in constant radio contact."

"I'll be fine," said Alan, needled.

"No doubt," said Morat. "Through there."

He nodded towards another door.

"You ready?" asked Hatcher.

"For a simulator?" asked Alan, trying to keep the edge out of his voice. "Absolutely."

"Good," he said, smiling his slim, private smile that suggested he knew something Alan didn't. "Follow Mr. Morat's lead, and don't try to run before you can walk."

"Yes, sir," said Alan, eyes level, face impassive.

"And don't worry if it doesn't come to you right away," Hatcher added.

Alan didn't trust himself to say anything. He managed a curt nod and turned to Morat as the door to the simulator slid open with a pneumatic hiss.

He hesitated in the doorway. The room was large and unremarkable, save for the simulator that sat in the center like a giant spider, trailing cables and air hoses leading to various monitoring stations. Alan put on his helmet and scaled the gantry, waiting as the steel panel in front of him folded down on the hydraulics providing motion simulation. The simulators he was familiar with had high definition flat screens and speaker arrays, recreating the sights and sounds of being inside a plane, but the experience of flying, the tug in your gut, the sense of gravitational rightness or wrongness as you banked, turned and climbed, all came from the hydraulics.

But he'd never seen this model before. Assuming it was state of the art, he felt a tingle of anticipation. There was that Dutch simulator he'd read about called Desdemona that was supposed to be able to generate something like 3.5 Gs. That would be pretty cool. Maybe this would have the same capabilities.

His first response, as he stepped inside the simulator cockpit and closed the door behind him, was disappointment. The Martin-Baker ejection seat could have come straight out of an F-16. It was only as he climbed in that the strangeness of the controls struck him. The jets he knew had HOTAS systems, with all the significant control mounted on either the stick in his right hand or the throttle quadrant in his left. Here, the thrust control lever was on his right hand armrest, and on the left, there was a red sphere sitting in a cradle.

Okay . . .

He had seen the control layout before during Professor Beaker's tutorials, but he hadn't expected them to be real.

Not real. This is a simulator.

He belted himself into his seat. And put his hands instinctively on the unfamiliar controls. The consoles, which ran all the way round the cockpit in a series of lit panels, flickered to life, showing a range of digital displays that Alan knew from his classwork.

He heard the intercom system click on in his earphones, and a moment later, he heard Morat's voice.

"Poised to engage simulated environment. Do you have a preferred venue?"

"Does it matter?"

"If in doubt, I go to Paris," said Morat, deciding for him. "Charles de Gaul airport it is."

Alan rolled his eyes and tapped on the touch-sensitive console, watching the displays as he engaged the simulator's navigation systems. One of them displayed the Locust itself, another graphic he had seen during his two weeks of study but hadn't really believed. It was a perfect triangle with a couple of fins on the trailing edge, the only way you could determine for sure which corner was the nose. To Alan, the closest known aircraft that came to mind was the B2 Stealth bomber, but this was not so much a flying wing with the B2's characteristic jagged trailing edge as a perfectly equilateral triangle with soft, curved points. The sheer lines of the plane—if you could still call the Locust a plane—were just so unlike his awkward but trusty Harrier II that he could barely imagine himself getting inside it.

"I've never flown a stealth aircraft," he said, conscious that he was already covering his ass in case the simulation didn't go well. "Shouldn't you use pilots with that kind of training?"

"Trust me," said Morat over the radio, "it wouldn't help. This is . . . different."

THERE WAS A FLICKER OF LIGHT FROM ABOVE. ALAN LOOKED up, realizing, for the first time, that he had a continuous window all the way around the craft, looking out over its bizarre triangular shape. Overhead, he saw a patchy blue sky, while the horizon was cluttered with the radar towers, hangars, sheds and passenger terminals of a bustling modern airport.

He whistled. "That's quite a simulation."

"Thought it would be less than top of the line, Major?" said Hatcher's voice over the intercom. "I'm offended."

Alan said nothing. He felt under the microscope and didn't like it.

"The Eiffel Tower is just under forty clicks to your southwest," said Morat. "Why not take a look?"

"Okay," said Alan.

"Oh, and you're no longer Black Eagle," said Hatcher. "Your code name is now Phoenix. Your controller, who you know as Mr. Morat, is Night Bird One. Base out."

"Roger that, Base," said Alan. "Initiating take off."

"Welcome to the future, Phoenix," said Morat. "I'll talk you through this first time. As you know, the sphere on your left armrest is directional control. On the right, you've got acceleration and altitude adjustment. These can be overridden by entering preset coordinates into the console in the dialog box with the green rim. The temporal index controls arrival time. The computer will do the rest unless there's interference with the flight path. These dials set your customizable menu options for cruising speed, altitude, radar countermeasures, the works. Let's leave them as they are for now."

Alan was determined not to ask questions unless absolutely necessary. Gradually, the controls were making sense to him as everything he'd seen in two-dimensional abstract terms in Professor Beaker's classes became real.

Well, almost real. You are still in a simulator.

"You have to unlearn a few things about flying," said Morat. "But don't worry. It will make sense to your body. Let's get in the simulated air and you'll see what I mean."

"Wait, I don't understand . . ." Alan began, hating the way he sounded, so uncertain, so confused. It was only a damn simulator for God's sake.

"Okay, so let's take her up," said Morat. "Straight up. No runway. As a Harrier pilot, you should like this. You're used to a single engine directed by multiple movable nozzles so you can direct the thrust straight down, behind, or at an angle that changes the plane's attitude, right?"

"Right," said Alan, feeling a little more comfortable. This was stuff he knew.

"Yeah," said Morat, and Alan could just hear the grin in his voice. "This is totally different."

Alan bit his lip.

"I think I can take it from here, thanks, Night Bird One," he said. More switches, then a push of vertical thrust. The ship gave the distinct wobble of a craft leaving the ground, but slowly, moving on a rising column of force. Through the cockpit viewers, Alan saw the simulated Parisian tarmac fall away beneath him, and then the ship hung motionless in the perfectly faked afternoon light.

It was an impossible climb, straight and quick and easy, quite unlike the bronco ride of a Harrier. Nothing flew like this. Alan's faith in the simulator took a hit.

He forced himself to look around the inside of the single seat craft, and the display panels surrounding the unconventionally roomy interior, and he saw what Morat meant. The interface was uncommonly commonsensical, the screens overlaying the live digital diagrams of the ship's attitude clear, requiring neither training nor complex explanation. Despite the lights and scrolling displays, it was all remarkably self-evident and intuitive, though it was hard to imagine that it mirrored the interior of the actual craft.

"When you're happy with the altitude," said Morat over the headset, "move towards the coordinates on your nav display."

Alan turned the sphere under his hand and the craft rotated cleanly—too cleanly—in the air. He applied a little thrust and he was moving, the landmarks of Paris—including the Eiffel Tower—zipping past them in a blur.

He pursed his lips. State of the art it might be, but it didn't feel like flight. No aircraft could pivot on a dime like he had just done.

Then he registered the heads up display.

"That can't be right," he muttered. "Phoenix to Night Bird One. I've got some read out anomalies."

"Go ahead, Phoenix."

"The console says we just went from zero to four hundred knots in under a second."

"Not in a Harrier now, Major," said Morat.

"No," Alan agreed. "I'm in a simulator."

"The best in the business," said Morat.

"If you say so," said Alan, increasing speed. He felt the pull of G-force on his face and the pressure in his chest, but it was nothing like what he should be feeling at this speed.

"How's that?" asked Morat.

"Fine," said Alan, refusing to be impressed, and not only because he felt the honor of his beloved Harriers had been called into question. "But there's a lot of things you can do in a simulator that would pull you apart if you were really in the air."

In response, Morat's voice came over the headset.

"Why do I feel like it's us who are being tested?"

"Just want to see how wide of reality we really are," said Alan.

"You need to work on your outlook, Phoenix. It's very cynical."

"Sorry about that, Night Bird One," said Alan, pushing the craft faster still. They were now going well beyond

Mach 1 but the simulator felt as smooth as ever, even when he jinked the directional sphere back and forth, half rolling the little digital triangle which showed the Locust's imaginary attitude. "I just like simulators that actually, you know, *simulate* what the act of flying feels like. It's an eccentricity of mine."

"You're going to have to trust me that it is doing exactly that."

"Right. Okay, Night Bird One, what tricks do you want to show me?"

"Let's try a hard left. Really hard. Like ninety degrees."

"Ninety degrees?"

"Yeah. Point at Africa and go."

Alan, annoyed, did so, pushing the ball hard so that the great triangle slewed around without losing a single notch of speed.

"See?" said Morat.

"Uh huh," said Alan, "though I'm pretty sure I could do that in an X-Wing on Play Station."

"Can your X-Wing do a vertical climb at Mach 5, make a right angle turn and come to a dead stop?" asked Morat.

"Probably not," said Alan, his irritation getting the better of him, "but that's my point. Nothing can. So why am I wasting time pulling impossible stunts? Are you going to use me as an actual pilot, or are we just playing video games?"

"You hear that, Base?" said Morat. "I think we've been issued a challenge. Requesting an unscheduled shift to phase two."

There was a moment of radio silence and then Hatcher's voice came in over the intercom.

"Let me see what I can arrange, gentlemen. Ascertaining full phase two clearance. Stand by."

"Wait," said Alan. "What? I don't understand."

"Something has come up," said Morat. "We need to accelerate your training."

"Meaning what?"

"I think it's time you got out of the simulator and up in the air."

21

JENNIFER
Hampshire

"**W**ELL?" JENNIFER ASKED.

"Details are proving difficult to locate," said Deacon.

"That's the understatement of the fucking year," she answered. "Sorry," she added, noting the shock on the older man's face. "But it's like they go out of their way to bury any useful information about what they are actually doing."

They were back at the house, huddled in the glow of computer screens and a single desk light, where they had been for almost two hours as darkness fell on the gardens outside. Jennifer had changed into jeans and a sweatshirt, and had hastily disassembled the maddening French twist so that she kept having to brush her hair out of her face. She didn't care.

"And you are absolutely sure that this is your copy of the agenda?" asked Deacon.

They had had this conversation twice since the board meeting. Deacon had thought that perhaps she'd absent-mindedly underlined the item referring to the special aerospace package herself, or had picked up someone else's copy.

"If it's supposed to be a message to you," he said when she protested, "it is singularly unhelpful."

But then again, it was all unhelpful. The Maynard Consortium had a snappy website, and brochures, and interminable files detailing its various accounts and investments, but it all seemed to end in cascades of numbers. What they were actually investing in was anybody's guess.

The numbers were not exclusively misleading, however. Whatever that aerospace investment was, it was expensive. Billions of dollars, funneled over the last six months alone, but to fund what? Even her father's laptop had been unable to shed light on that.

"These files make no sense," she remarked to Deacon as she pored over them. "Most of the directories are empty, and the accounts they do show explain only about a tenth of the funding." She sighed then whistled. "Nigeria has a space agency? And Saudi Arabia? This is weird."

Deacon materialized at her shoulder.

"Maynard is funding the Nigerian Space Agency?" he asked.

"And the Sri Lankan Space Agency, if you can believe that. And the ones in Bangladesh, Tunisia and Pakistan. That's a pretty strange list of bedfellows, even without the space agency bit."

"But the funding levels are low," Deacon mused, peering at the screen.

"So where is the rest of it going? And why can't we see it?"

"Perhaps there's nothing to see," said Deacon. "Let's be honest, Miss Jennifer. We don't even know we're reading the data correctly. This may just be an accounting convention, or a matter of how money is transferred through channels. If the bulk of the money goes to UK interests, it could be recorded differently, routed through companies with strong governmental ties, such as British Aerospace, whose records are confidential or classified."

"Or maybe someone doctored the laptop to remove whatever they thought we'd find interesting," Jennifer countered.

Deacon sat beside her and, for a moment, said nothing. When she turned to look at him, he was watching her with a troubled frown.

"What?" she said.

"Miss Jennifer . . ."

"Just call me Jennifer, please," she said. "This 'Miss' thing makes me feel like I'm twelve years old."

"Jennifer," he said, laying the word out like it was a gift, wrapped and ribboned for Christmas. "Have you considered the possibility that there's nothing to find? That you are hunting for something you want to be there, because it will give your father's death a sense of purpose it doesn't really have?"

She had considered that. Of course she had. But she was surprised to hear him say it.

"Someone wanted me to look into this," she said, indicating the agenda item someone on the Maynard Consortium board had underlined.

"Perhaps," said Deacon. "But if so, it's more likely to be a rather mean-spirited joke at your expense than a pointer towards nefarious activities."

She would have bristled, but this use of the word nefarious brought her up short, and she couldn't help but grin.

"Did I say something amusing?" he asked.

She shook her head and patted his hand. It was cool, ridged with bone, liver spotted and latticed with prominent veins. Old hands.

"I don't know," she said. "Maybe you're right. I just feel like . . ." But she didn't know what she felt. Not really.

She pushed the rolling chair away from her father's heavy desk and stretched out.

"Perhaps you should call it a night," said Deacon. "Get some rest, and take a look with fresh eyes tomorrow."

"When I'll see that I've lost my mind?" Jennifer said. "And give up?"

"Not precisely what I meant," said Deacon, conceding the half-truth. He saw the disappointment in her face and relented. "Do you mind if I just check something?" he asked, nodding at the laptop.

Jennifer shrugged, got up and perched on the edge of the desk, staring absently at the little wooden lion she'd wanted to believe was significant. He had probably stopped facing it towards him a decade ago. She wouldn't know. She hadn't really known him for years.

She might have lapsed further into nostalgia and sadness, but something in Deacon's manner had changed. He was sitting very still, as his focus on the computer sharpened.

"What?" asked Jennifer.

"There's a keystroke logger he installed," said Deacon, not looking at her. "A month ago. He said he was growing forgetful and wanted to keep track of what he had been doing and when. You have to know exactly where to go to find it. He hid it because he said he'd hate to have someone else spot it and think he was losing mental acumen. I didn't think much of it at the time, though it did strike me as out of character."

"And?"

"According to this, the computer was active for two hours, the day *after* he died. And again, for four more, the day after that."

"So someone took it and rifled its contents. Possibly deleting as they went."

"But inexpertly," Deacon mused.

"You think any deleted data might be recoverable?" Jennifer asked.

"In the right hands and with time, possibly, though that is beyond my area of expertise," said Deacon. "Which is suggestive. A professional would surely destroy the machine and replace it. The person who did this doesn't seem to know that deleted material doesn't truly go away, or assumed no one would look too closely."

"Meaning me," said Jennifer, with bitter amusement.

"Indeed," said Deacon. "But then someone sends you a cryptic message that guarantees you will. So either you have two different people, pulling you in different directions . . ."

"Or one person, laying out breadcrumbs," she concluded for him.

"Precisely," said Deacon. "I'm not sure which possibility is more troubling."

"Don't breadcrumbs lead to the gingerbread house and the witch's oven?"

"I believe that is the traditional outcome, yes," Deacon agreed.

"Then let's pull for option one," said Jennifer. "I assume you've already got everything relating to Dad's business interests out of the safe?"

"And his various safety deposit boxes, yes," said Deacon. "If he hid pertinent information elsewhere, I'm afraid I don't know where."

For a moment Jennifer grew very still, and her eyes glazed.

Surely not . . .

"Miss Jennifer?" Deacon prompted.

"Nothing," she said, shaking off the reverie. "I suppose I'm more exhausted than I thought. Time for me to turn in."

He hesitated for a half-second, and there was the beginning of a question on his lips, but he thought better of it.

"Anything I can bring you before bed?" he asked, standing.

"No," she said. "Wait. Yes. Whisky. The Lagavulin."

Her father's favorite.

"Certainly," said Deacon. "I'll bring it to your room."

JENNIFER SHOWERED AND CHANGED INTO FLANNEL PAJAMAS and a terrycloth dressing gown. For all its opulence, the house was always cold, even in summer. The alternative was a heating system that made the place stuffy and humid. She sipped the scotch Deacon had left on her nightstand but made no move to go to bed, waiting, instead, for the noises of the house to still.

Twenty minutes later, she went barefoot along the hall, feeling the chill from the polished wood floors as she went past her father's study, past his bedroom and past what had been her play room, to what had been, effectively, his. She took a sip of the whisky she was still cradling, savoring its complex, heady flavors, feeling strange to be here, like a kid awoken by a nightmare, looking for her father.

Once more, the memory of disturbing her father in his study that night, the one night he had shouted, came back to her, but she didn't know what it meant. Not wanting to remember him like that, she shrugged it off. Instead, she tried the door. For the briefest anguished moment, she felt sure she would find him inside.

If Edward's Quinn's office had been his inner sanctum, this was his secret treasure trove, the one place he never discussed with his business colleagues, his hideout, where he could indulge all he was not in daily life. In here, he had been, she imagined, a boy again.

It contained one thing only, vast and glorious though it was: a model railway, painstakingly built, remodeled and maintained for decades. It was where he had gone when everyone was in bed and he needed to escape his work. It was, she supposed, where they'd had their last truly intimate connections. Here, she had sat in silence, painting minuscule cows and gluing bits of lichen to trees while he soldered points and fiddled with signal gantries.

Quality time, they would call it now. She hated the glibness of the words, the easy way they pigeonholed and made ordinary what had once been special.

It was all still here, as she knew it would be. She snapped the switch beside the outlet and turned on the transformer, as if she'd done it yesterday and the day before, though it had in fact been—what?—fifteen years?

Something like that.

She turned the dial, familiar as her own hand, and heard a train stir. On the far side, in a siding beside the village she had childishly christened "Christmas," because that portion of the layout was laid out in snow around a frozen pond, the Flying Scotsman—always her favorite— emerged with its tender and a pair of passenger coaches. She gave it a little more speed to get it up the incline, and, as it hit the great outer loop, watched with an old and poignant delight that brought tears to her eyes.

For five minutes, she just let it run, absorbing the familiar sound of the wheels on the track, and then she moved to the carefully molded hill, with the model mine and its beautifully crafted elevator tower and hopper loaders. It looked perfect, meticulously executed, like a real place seen from a great height.

She reached across the track to where a tunnel bore into the side of the hill, its rocky escarpments cunningly made of plaster and cork bark, took hold of the escarpment with her hand spread wide, and tested it. It shifted slightly and, with a little pressure from side to side, lifted free. The hill was hollow.

The idea had first been to give access to the track inside the tunnel in case carriages derailed or faults developed on the line, but it had quickly become their secret hiding place, the spot he would leave cream eggs and other forbidden goodies for her to find.

She reached inside, feeling around with the care of someone accustomed to dealing with delicate parts and tiny electronics, but felt nothing but plywood, papier mâché, and dust. She was withdrawing her hand when something small and hard dislodged and skittered away. Fingers spread, she tried again, slower this time, and came out clutching . . .

A thumb drive.

TIMIKA
Pottsville, PA

THE MAN IN THE SUIT WAS COMING FOR HER ACROSS The Hollows' golf course. She did not think. She rolled up onto her feet and broke into a run back into the woods. Somewhere, there would be a wrought iron fence, and beyond it, a road. If her estimation of her position was right, she wouldn't have to go far to reach Dion's car.

Unless they'd already found it.

Unless they caught her first.

Unless the fence was too high to climb, or the gate keeper was waiting for her on the other side . . .

She had no choice. She ran.

The ground was uneven, strewn with branches and rotting leaves, so that every step was ragged, and every jump risked a fall. She checked over her shoulder. The man was moving faster now and had already reached the cart path. He was also reaching under his jacket.

Wide-eyed, she ran, plunging up through the woods, desperation driving her forward. She could see nothing but trees ahead. He was gaining on her, and now he had his pistol drawn.

God.

She wove her way through the trees in case he started shooting. Yet though she heard him shouting as he ran, there was no gunfire.

She thought wildly about the man who had chased her through the streets of Manhattan, dressed as a cop. He had fired at her, even with crowds of people around, people who could have been hit, people who could have been witnesses. So why hadn't this guy started shooting yet?

And then, looming ahead of her was a wrought iron fence. The perimeter of The Hollows estate. It was perhaps ten feet high, with no handholds. She felt her pace flag as something like despair threatened to overcome her, but she ran on, looking for a tree she could climb, a limb that might get her over the fence.

There was one. It was a ragged, blackened spindly thing, leafless and blasted, as if it had been struck by lightning. Timika made for it, vaulting and scrabbling as soon as she reached it, dragging herself awkwardly up and out, going just high enough to inch out over the fence, each railing tipped with a fleur-de-lis spear point.

Her pursuer had nearly caught her, his shouts now directed at her.

"Stop where you are!" he called.

But even now, he did not shoot. Timika was suddenly sure he was quite different from the man calling himself Cook who'd pursued her in New York. She kept moving. Just as he reached the foot of the tree, she dropped over the fence into a ditch.

The road was there. She ran until she saw her car parked where she had left it. It was the most beautiful thing she had ever seen. She glanced in the rear view mirror as she sped away.

SHE CHECKED INTO A MOTEL WHERE THE DESK CLERK, thankfully, didn't ask a lot of questions, and took a long hot shower, watching the detritus of mud and leaves she rinsed from her hair go slowly down the drain. She was not very hungry, and decided she would rather not risk being out and about, only a few miles from The Hollows, so she curled up on the uneven mattress and read from Jerzy Stern's journal.

It made strange reading. She began to wonder if she had been crazy to put so much stock in the old man and his poignant but insane ramblings. But then, the people who had come after her were more than serious.

Could it all be true? And if so, what did it finally mean?

She took a pair of nail scissors from her purse and used them to slit the lining of the Navy Officer's coat just to the side of the vent in the back, then slipped the journal inside. It wouldn't stand up to a thorough search, but if someone was in a rush and just checked the pockets or gave her a pat down, she might get away with it. She put the coat on, feeling the weight of the book in the back as she considered herself in the mirror.

Not bad, all things considered.

She thought again about the difference between the feel of the two chases she'd gone through. The fake cops who had come after her in Manhattan had wanted her dead. There was no doubt about that. At The Hollows, the pursuit had felt somehow more restrained, even law-abiding. Despite her attempts to conceal herself in the caterer's van, she was pretty sure the gate guard had spotted her, but he'd let her through.

Why?

He'd called for backup. They'd hoped to corner her in the house. It meant they'd wanted to catch her. Even when she'd gotten away from them, they hadn't opened fire.

So. Two different groups were after her. One wanted her dead, the other—at least for a while—alive. One was reckless and had no concern for the law. The other . . . She wasn't sure. Those suits and earpieces seemed authentic in ways the fake cops hadn't, and that meant . . .

Government?

She frowned and thought back to Katarina's evasion when she'd been asked what line of work she'd been in.

What had she said, that strange phrase that so unsettled Timika?

Paper people. Hidden away in a drawer where no one can read us . . .

At the time, it had reminded her of something, but she wasn't sure what. Like there was another word, just beyond her memory's reach, an ordinary word, but somehow loaded with meaning.

Paper people.

She thought of Jerzy's journal, and something struck her. She flipped through her notebook and found the list of names the caterer had given her.

Horace Evers.

Stephen Albitz.

Katarina Lundergrass.

Albert Billen.

Frederick Kaas.

Karl Jurgens.

Max Stiegler.

She looked at them again and realized that most of them—perhaps even all of them—sounded German. Coincidence? She doubted it.

Paper people . . .

Suddenly her memory chimed once more, and this time, she had the word she had been groping for.

She called Marvin.

He answered on the first ring, babbling inquiries about her health and welfare.

"I'm fine," she answered. "How are things there?"

"Quiet," he said. "Audrey called in sick so it's just me."

"Question," she said. "What do you know about Operation Paperclip?"

She could almost hear his mind focus, like the mechanism of a microscope adjusting, creating sharpness and clarity where there had been a blurry nothingness. Marvin was a computer whiz kid, but that was only half his value to Debunktion. He was also a fount of wisdom on conspiracy theories, and an expert at sifting through the hype, the mysticism and the drama, for kernels of truth.

He pulled up some pertinent data as he talked, but in spite of his technological gifts, Marvin was very much a book guy when it came to hard data.

"Books aren't slippery like websites," he liked to say. "You know where they come from and what they're worth. No one vets what you post online."

But he didn't need either to recall Operation Paperclip.

"There's still some stuff we don't know about the scale of the program and exactly who was in it," he said, "but there's also a lot we do know."

"Know or guess?" Timika prompted.

"Know," said Marvin, with none of his usual stoner vagueness. "It's a matter of historical record. There may be conspiracies attached to it, but the core has been public and verified for decades."

"Give me the gist."

"At the end of World War II, the Nazis were frantically developing high-tech weapons to turn the tide. Jet planes. Ballistic missiles. Stuff like that. In many ways, they were well ahead of the allies. They didn't have an A bomb, but a lot of people in the States—including Einstein—thought they were close, and that scared the crap out of everyone. When it looked like Germany would fall, everyone started looking at Russia. It was already clear they were going to be the next enemy. Some top brass thought that war with them would follow, pretty much right after beating the Nazis. It was also clear that the Russians would reach Berlin first and would take whatever tech the Germans had built, and the people who built them."

Timika sat very still, holding the phone. This was it. She could just feel it.

"The short version?" Marvin continued. "We wanted to get what we could and keep it out of Russian hands. That included people: the scientists, technical assistants, lab staff who had been working for the Nazis, not just in weapons development but research and experimentation, some of it seriously illegal. And I'm talking war crimes illegal. Like, the Nazis had been building these jet- and rocket-powered aircraft, right? They were traveling faster and faster. So they wanted to know what that kind of velocity and pressure would do to a pilot. They built ways to test that stuff, using animals or—at first—the scientists themselves, but that was slow and cautious, as you'd imagine. Why experiment on yourself when you had millions of people who you'd decided weren't really people at all?"

"The concentration camps," said Timika with a kind of numb horror.

"Exactly," said Marvin. "Seriously heavy shit. We don't even know how many people died in the process. A lot. And then the war ended. We liberated the camps, rounded up the people who had been doing all this stuff, whisked them away before they could be tried at Nüremberg, wiped their records clean, gave them made-up bios and made them US citizens. When Truman set the program up, it was called Operation Overcast, but it was renamed Paperclip later. We took their data, their research, their ideas, their technology, and we slotted them right into our own weapons and aerospace programs. When everyone started freaking out about Sputnik and the Soviet space program, guess who led NASA's charge to put men on the moon? The Operation Paperclip boys. Werner Von Braun, who designed the Saturn V rockets for the Apollo missions, had spent the war building V2 missiles for the Nazis. He went from devastating London to being hailed as a US national hero practically overnight. He wasn't the only one. Debus. Rudolph. Strughold. All these guys had been high on the allies' wanted lists because they were integral to the Nazi war effort. Then they were working for us, and everyone conveniently forgot how they'd been using their talents before. Some worked for NASA, some went to White Sands in New Mexico to work on missile systems, some went to the rocket fuel lab in Louisiana, or Missouri. A whole bunch of engineers went into combat aircraft development . . ."

"But we don't have complete lists of all the people we brought over?" Timika asked. "What are we talking? Ten? Twenty?"

231

Marvin laughed.

"Last estimates I saw said something in the region of fifteen hundred."

Timika gasped. "And this is real, right, Marvin? It's not the tinfoil-hat crowd stuff?"

"Absolutely real. The authorities—though they are still pretty stingy with specifics—came clean on this long ago. Truman said they shouldn't include known Nazis—I mean, people affiliated with the SS, or actual Nazi party members—just Germans who worked for their country's war effort, but the Pentagon ignored him. To cover their tracks, a lot of records got lost or buried."

"Are any of these people still alive?" Timika asked, picturing the lounge at The Hollows and its dozing geriatrics.

"I doubt it," said Marvin. "They would've had to have been in their twenties or thirties at the earliest during the war, so they'd be like a hundred now. So it's possible, I guess, but it's unlikely."

"Any women?"

"Not that I've ever seen," said Marvin. "Like I said, the records are incomplete, but there are pictures. I've never heard of any women being involved. Why?"

"Just wondering," said Timika. "Anything new on Katarina Lundergrass or any of the others?"

"Not yet. I've got someone poking around in military archives though. I'll let you know if I hear anything."

"Just remember . . ."

"Yeah, yeah. Discretion. My middle name."

"One more thing," said Timika. "If Paperclip is public knowledge, why would anyone want to hide away people connected to the program?"

"Today? No reason. Plus, as you say, they're all dead now. Sounds like you're dealing with something else."

"Yeah," Timika agreed vaguely. "I guess so. Thanks, Marvin."

She hung up and lay for a long time, staring at the stained ceiling, her mind turning over everything she'd learned so far. She felt like an archaeologist, trying to reassemble a pot, piece by fractured piece. Nothing made sense. She turned out the light and missed Dion's presence beside her for the first time since she'd left New York. She wondered if she was still in the same world as she'd been in only yesterday, when she'd been confidently giving interviews and writing copy about the idiocy and credulity of others. Was this what it was like, the special madness of the conspiracy theorist, surrounded by fragments of something you can't quite see and which might only exist in your own mind? Well, tomorrow, she thought, remembering Katarina Lundergrass' plan to meet her in the church at Locust Lake, she would find out.

23

JERZY
Poland, 1945

THE RUSSIANS SLAPPED ME ON THE BACK AND CALLED ME *geroy malchika*, which I took to mean child hero or something similar. I did not feel heroic. When Mrs. Habernicht battled her way through the throng, all of them drinking and singing, I buried my face in her apron and would not look at anyone. She had a few words of Russian, and one of the soldiers spoke a little Polish, and she answered what questions she could. She called herself Bronikowski now, her name before she married, she whispered to me.

"Easier that way," she said.

I nodded. I asked her about the resistance fighters, but she winced at the memory, and shook her head.

"All of them?" I gasped, tears starting to my eyes once more, though I had spent no more than a few minutes with them. I thought of the one who had called herself Maxine, and though I tried to tell myself that they would not have minded dying fighting the Germans, I could not believe it.

The Russians impounded everything they could find, including the remaining cargo plane. The German crew and soldiers who had survived the firefight with the Soviet troops had been rounded up and were being kept in paddocks at the end of the airstrip, under heavy guard. Many Germans had been killed, their bodies heaped for mass burial. I saw no sign of Ungerleider, the man who had ordered my brother's death. Either he got away on the first plane, or died at my hands on the second. The thought left me numb, feeling nothing, as if some part of me had been shot away in the fight and I would never be of any use again. Mrs. Habernicht—now Bronikowski—told me that the war, our war, was finally over. One of the soldiers gave me a glass of vodka to celebrate, but I neither smiled nor sang as the others danced drunkenly around. I kept staring at my hands, as if they might have belonged to someone else, wanting only to forget the last hours, the last years, even my past before the war.

I was afraid of the Russians. It was clear that they were here to stay, and that Poland, as I had known it before the war, was gone. With nothing to hold me there, I resolved to escape to France or England and start over. But even as I prepared my final escape, I was still haunted by the memories of my family and by the possibility that some of them may have survived. I needed to be sure, and that meant going East.

I told Mrs. Bronikowski/Habernicht of my plan, and though I had expected her to try to talk me out of it, she just nodded sadly and told me she would get together some food and clothes for my journey. When it came time to part, she pressed a piece of paper with her address printed carefully on it, so that I could send word of what she called "my adventures," and kissed me once on the cheek. She wept for both of us and then, when she went to the shop to buy soap, I slipped away, leaving a note that contained the thanks I could not speak.

I moved through the pine-scented woods as I had first come, sleeping rough for two nights until I found a village where I could catch a ride on a freight train toward Kraków. I spent a week there, found the place we had lived, even spoke to old Mrs. Liszka, who had raised poultry for the shops and restaurants my parents had frequented before the war. She looked different now. Everyone did. But she remembered me and wished she had good news, or any news. When I told her about Ishmael, she put her hands up in front of her face, her fingers splayed as if she was catching a ball, and closed her eyes. She stood like that so long that I did not know what to do, and when she looked at me again she seemed older and sadder than ever. So I thanked her, though she had told me nothing, and left.

I fought the crowds outside the temporary offices—the awkward alliance of the old Polish bureaucracy that had been absorbed into the new Soviet order—and stood in lines for three days, reciting my parents' names and those of every relative I knew, no matter how distant. At first, I was cheered that they had records of where they had gone, but as each one was chased down, the awful truth became harder and harder to avoid. I had not dared seriously consider the possibility, and the fact of those stamped documents, presented to me by a hard-faced woman whose eyes betrayed only weariness, left me hollow, emptied out of feeling, of self, so that for the next few days, I experienced a kind of madness.

My family was gone. All of them.

As the stories of the camps came out and the full horror of the Nazi occupation came to light, what little hope I had left faded to nothing, so that all that was left was a kind of hard kernel, made of defiance, rather than faith. When everything is lost, it is better not to remember what you had.

And I had nothing.

A week later, I left Kraków forever.

The Russian chokehold on the borders was tightening every day, and it was getting harder to move around, so I went where I could without going through checkpoints and waiting for my papers to be approved. In my case, this meant the long trek north to Gdansk, cushioned as best I could in an empty boxcar. Once in the port, I would find a container ship bound for the West.

I boarded the first ship I could, stowing away below decks, but two of the crew found me and threw me back on the dock, leaving me with a bloody lip and an empty purse. I was more cautious thereafter, watching the moored ships and trying to get a sense of their schedules before risking another attempt. There was nothing directly bound for France or England, but I eventually got one to Gothenburg, which would do for a start. My food rations were getting low, and though I had grown used to eating little, I would need to replenish my supplies somehow in Sweden, though I knew nothing of the language or customs of the place, so finding work seemed unlikely.

They found me on the third day, and though they did not beat me, they would not feed me, and said I had to get off before they reached port. The captain, a Lithuanian who stank of alcohol at all hours, would not, he said, be responsible for smuggling undocumented immigrants, no matter how much I argued that the Swedes would not turn me away. In sight of the cranes and warehouses of the Gothenburg docks, he put me on a smoky tug that moored alongside for the purpose and sent me to another ship that was about to leave port. It was an altogether bigger, sleeker, more modern looking vessel than I had left, and it had guns.

"This is a warship!" I protested. "I am not a soldier."

"Or a sailor," said the Lithuanian, sucking on a ragged cigarette. "And therefore not my problem."

The men on board spoke English, and for a moment I thought I had been lucky, that I would be disembarking in London, but when I was called before the duty officer, I learned otherwise. He was perhaps thirty, athletic and clean-cut, with bright blue eyes that considered me with a touch of humor. His uniform was crisply pressed and spotless except for a smear of oil on one sleeve that he kept dabbing at irritably.

"Speak English?" he demanded.

"A little," I said. Before the war, one of our neighbors had married a pretty English girl who had made a game of learning Polish from the local kids. In the process, because I liked words, I had picked up some of her own language. The language of Shakespeare, she had called it. I do not know if she survived the war.

"You might want to work on that," he said. He smirked, as if at a private joke, considering me, then extended a strong hand. I took it, my own hand feeling small and feeble in his, and he gave it a single brisk shake. He spoke again, but I did not understand all he said, and instead framed a single question.

"Where are we going?"

"We're an escort destroyer," he said. "The *USS Kitchener*. We'll be joining a troop ship out of Cherbourg, bound for New York City."

I stared at him. "America?" I said.

"The one and only. No other stops. Take it or leave it."

AND SO I CROSSED THE ATLANTIC. I PLANNED TO TAKE THE next ship back to Europe as soon as we reached port, but I was well fed on the journey, well treated by the sailors, and the feared encounters with lost U-boats never happened, so that by the time we reached the extraordinary skyline of New York, I could not remember why I had not planned to stay.

I had also made good progress with my English, speaking with the crew whenever I could, and reading voraciously throughout the voyage. The Captain had given me some dog-eared miniature paperbacks—mysteries and a couple of classics by Twain and Dickens—and these I consumed, the hard work of reading turning to pleasure as my vocabulary expanded. When the weather was calm, I sat in the sun on the deck with my books, the pages bubbled and uneven from the salt spray, and when I ran into a word I didn't know, I'd approach one of the crew and ask. It got so they saw me coming and competed with each other to provide the best definitions, bickering good-humoredly, working their way up the chain of command when they needed a ruling. Somehow, without really meaning to, I had become the *USS Kitchener*'s mascot.

The crew talked about their hometowns, their sweethearts, the things they had seen in the war, but no one ever asked me what I had been through, and I started to suspect that they had been ordered not to talk to me about it. The Captain knew about my family, the ghetto, the Wenceslas mine, even that fateful day when the planes tried to leave and the Russians came, because I had told him in my first meeting with him, blurting it all out in the hope that he wouldn't send me back.

I came through Ellis Island on the last day of August 1945, throwing my Polish papers over the side of the ferry, and saying that I was nineteen so I could work. Captain Jennings sponsored my citizenship, and no one seemed to doubt that I was as old as I had claimed, though I was still slightly built.

"It's the eyes," said one crewman. "It's like they came from someone else, or they've seen . . . I don't know."

He was grinning when he started speaking, his tone light, like he was merely remarking on a curiosity, but something happened to the smile midway through the thought and it went away, leaving him with an awkward, haunted look, and though he was talking about my eyes, he couldn't hold them.

I felt strange. It reinforced the idea that I was not one of them, though what I was now, I did not know. I had been a Polish Jew, a child. I wasn't sure which of those things still applied in this vast and unfamiliar land, and when I thought about it for long, I felt a tide of panic rising in my chest. I had no friends, no family, no sense of who I was, and no way of putting food in my belly, let alone of building any kind of real life here.

As if to prove the point, I struggled in my dealings with the immigration people. Though my English was much improved, I did not understand everything they said to me, and the result was frustrating and humiliating. How was I supposed to function in this society when I lacked even the basic means of communication? I was still housed on the destroyer for now—illegally, I suspected, and solely at the discretion of the Captain. Since he had taken me under his wing, I threw myself on his mercy, requesting that he come with me to my next interview. To my immense relief, he did not hesitate. He accompanied me through the form-filling and interviewing. The immigration official did not seem cowed by him exactly, but he tended to loom over the proceedings, and I never seriously doubted that they would let me into the country. The surprise came after.

Telling me he had something to discuss with me, the Captain took me to a bar where the sailors gathered, and ordered me a beer, "you being a grown up and all," he said. I said nothing, sipping at the yellow liquid and trying to hide my wince of distaste.

"Tell me about the mine," he said at last.

I shrugged, not wanting to go over it all again. America was to be my new beginning. I didn't want to rehash my past anymore.

"I already told you," I said.

"Tell me about the henge and what you saw under it," he said. He had always been friendly in his dealings with me, and he still was, but for all his feigned casualness, his eyes now held an intensity I had never seen before. There was something specific he wanted to know.

I didn't care, and thinking that the sooner I got past it, the faster I could leave it behind, I told him everything in detail: the concrete flytrap henge, the power system, the bell below it and the strange material it was made of. I told him the odd behavior of the guards, the heightened layers of secrecy, and the ruthless way in which Ungerleider had attempted to eradicate the work detail as soon as our task was complete.

He frowned thoughtfully, staring at his beer glass, and said nothing for a long moment before nodding.

"There's someone I want you to meet," he said.

I immediately began to shake my head, but he raised a hand.

"There might be work in it," he said. "Pay."

"I don't need it," I said. It was a lie, and he knew it, but he let that slide.

"It's not about what you need, Jerzy," he said, and his manner was different now, as if he had decided to say something he had hoped he wouldn't have to. "A few weeks ago everyone in this city was celebrating the end of the war."

"Yes," I said. "So?"

"So what if it isn't over?"

I stared at him.

"What do you mean?" I asked. "The Japanese . . ."

"I'm not talking about the Japanese," he interrupted. "Or the Italians. Or even the Germans. I'm talking about the Nazis."

I made a face. "What's the difference?" I said.

"The Germans are a people. They are bound by blood and geography and history. The Nazis are something quite different. What binds them is an ideology, a worldview, and a purpose. The Germans were defeated. In time, they will rebuild as a functioning nation, and their sense of who they are will change. But the Nazis . . . We killed a lot of them, and some of the survivors will turn back into Germans, like people waking from a nightmare. But we did not cut the head off the snake. Some of them live on, in Germany and . . ." he shifted in his seat, and I sensed his nervousness, "elsewhere."

"Where?" I asked.

"You said there were three planes," he said. Reading my confusion, he pressed on, his voice low and urgent. "At the

Wenceslas mine. Three big cargo planes, loaded with what-ever came out of the underground factory."

"Yes," I said, wary of his sudden intensity, unnerved by it.

"You shot one down," he said. "One was captured by the Russians. What happened to the other?"

"I told you. It got away," I said. "I don't want to talk about this." The memory and his mood were getting to me.

"But where did it go?"

"I don't know. Berlin?"

"No, that's just it," he said, his eyes bright, his voice now barely above a whisper. A huddle of sailors at the bar burst into raucous laughter, and the sudden sound actually made me jump, but Captain Jennings' eyes did not leave mine. "There's no record of it going there or being shot down. Allied air superiority was close to total by then. We know what was in the air over Germany. We spent the last months of the war in the waters of the Flensburg Firth, in the Schleswig-Holstein region of Northwest Germany, where the last Nazi government holed up in the final weeks, after Berlin fell and Hitler killed himself. The British have the airfield now, and I think your Messerschmitt Gigant may have gone there."

I thought this through. "If that was one of the last places to fall, that makes sense," I agreed. "But why does it matter?"

Captain Jennings took a sip of his beer, glanced over his shoulder and leaned forward.

"Because it wasn't the only cargo plane that went into Flensburg that remains unaccounted for," he said.

"So it was hidden away?"

He shook his head. "You know what else Flensburg was famous for?" he asked. "Why we were in the area in the first place?"

I shook my head, my apprehension mounting.

"Submarine yards," he said. "When the Germans surrendered, all U-boats that were at sea—according to the official story—were ordered to surrender. Many did not. Some were at large for months. Some remain unaccounted for. Some made for South America."

"No," I scoffed. "It's too far. We would have been told."

He smiled at that and shook his head slowly. When he spoke, it was in a measured tone, the information coming easily, as if he had spent a long time considering it.

"We have people in South America," he said.

"What do they say?"

"They say the U-530, a type 9C/40 submarine commanded by Otto Wermuth, reached Mar del Plata, in Argentina, on July tenth. U-977, a type 7C, commanded by Heinz Schaffer, got there two weeks ago, having been off the radar for more than two months. No one knows exactly what route he took or where he went along the way. The last known base for the sub was Flensburg."

He sat back.

"Why would the Nazis go to Argentina?" I asked, intrigued in spite of myself.

Jennings' face broke into a rueful smile.

"Because they can," he said. "Perón is welcoming them with open arms. Especially if they can pay, and a lot of them can."

I stared at him, and he, knowing what I was thinking, nodded. The Nazi coffers were stuffed with all they had looted from Europe, particularly from its Jews.

"They go via Spain, because Franco lets them," said Jennings. "Or Genoa. There are Nazi sympathizers who cover for them, hide them, and there are others who just don't care who they are or what they have done, so long as they can pay. Either way, there are ratlines right to Buenos Aires. And Rio. Other places that we haven't found out about yet. Paraguay, maybe Chile. Who knows where else? They go because they know what will happen if they stay."

"The war is over," I said.

He seemed to consider that for a moment, then shrugged it off.

"The Allies have been saying for years that defeating the Nazis won't be the end for them," he said. "There will be trials before the year's out. You know better than most, what the Nazis did. There were crimes committed that go beyond simple war crimes. They know that. And they're bolting."

"Why are you telling me this?" I asked.

"Because," he said, "I think that some of what you saw in the Wenceslas mine made it out of Germany. I have no idea if it made it onto one of those submarines, but I'd like to find out. And I'd like to be involved in making sure that the Nazis don't rise up—armed with whatever they were building in those underground factories—in South America."

"That still doesn't explain why you are telling *me*," I said, though I suspected the answer.

"Because it matters to you," he said. "You pretend it doesn't, but it does."

I shook my head, but I feared that if I tried to speak, my voice would break.

"We're going," he said. "The crew of the *Kitchener*. Got our orders today. A long trip south, to escort a pair of captured Nazi submarines back to New York. Come with us."

I found my voice. "What? I've been at sea for months! I finally get some solid ground under my feet and you want me go back on the water? Why do I have to keep telling people I'm not a sailor?"

"You could be," said Jennings. "You've seen things, people, including some who are doing their damnedest to disappear. You're a witness, which could be useful in making sure that doesn't happen. You're also a citizen, or as near as makes no difference. Out of work. About to be dropped in a country you don't know, without friends or family to cushion the fall. And what better way to repay the government of the great nation that hauled your sorry Polish ass out of the water than to join up and serve on the very vessel that saved your hide? Sounds kinda poetic, don't you think?"

He grinned then and I found myself—ridiculously, impossibly, grinning back. It must have been the beer.

ALAN
Dreamland, Nevada

"PHASE 2," AS MORAT CALLED IT, REQUIRED ANOTHER bus ride and hours of sitting around waiting for clearance. By the time Alan—still annoyed by the implausibility of the flight simulator—went through his fourth security checkpoint, he'd decided that nothing could be worth the wait.

He was wrong.

Alan stood on an expanse of runway as the moon rose over the dark Nevada cliffs, staring. He had known the Astra TR3B "Locust" was supposed to be triangular, but seeing it still caught him off guard. Seen at from above it would look like an equilateral triangle with a pair of vertical fins at the back. Standing on the airstrip and looking at it from the side it was slim, with only a central bulge for the cockpit on the triangle's topside, its lines smooth, even elegant, and its edge was blade-like.

And it was black as the night itself. Indeed, the light from the floods above the hangar seemed to fall into it.

With a low hiss of air, a panel near the center of the ship folded down, revealing three steps into the body of the craft. Morat pulled his helmet on and checked his coms as he led the way, stooping beneath what Alan still wanted to call the wing, though the whole ship was a kind of wing. The struts of the landing gear were tall and slender, not designed for conventional takeoff or landing, but sturdy enough to roll the ship out into the open. Alan tried not to stare, to give away his fascination with each new aspect of the craft that he discovered, and took refuge in pulling his helmet over his head as he climbed the stairs into the belly of the Locust.

There were two seats, side by side. The inside of the cockpit was exactly as the simulator had promised, which came as something of a surprise given how skeptical he had been of the machine he had just left. Alan wore a flight helmet unlike any he'd ever worn before, though he'd heard similar devices had been developed for the F-35. It was snug and new smelling, and it gave him the option of seeing beyond the aircraft itself, via a complex set of digital projections effectively making the ship around him transparent. In any other circumstances, he would have found the possibilities thrilling, but tonight he wanted to stay focused on the Locust itself. Absurd though the simulator had been, he was sure the Locust was capable of maneuvers his Harrier was not. He took his seat, buckled himself in with a five-point harness, then tapped the silvery rectangle.

Once buckled in, Morat turned his seat to face Alan and began touching control buttons, talking as he did so.

"This is the stand-by mode, which brings online your communication and navigation systems. See this here? This is the home preset. If you get into difficulties, hit this button here; wherever you are in the world, at whatever altitude, the craft will return to this point by the fastest, safest available route. It's designed to tap into any available satellite system to track air traffic and adjust its flight path accordingly. Best autopilot function ever devised."

"And if the system is compromised?"

"You'd be amazed how much it takes to stop that function from working. Multiple built-in redundancies. But if it really can't get you home, it will let you know. If that happens, and I've never known it to, you'll have other things to worry about." He paused, then spoke. "Preflights check out?" Morat asked into his headset.

"You're green," flight control responded.

"Night Bird One primed for departure."

"Roger that, Night Bird One," said the flight controller. "When you're ready."

"Much appreciated," said Morat.

"Kick the tires and light the fires," Alan said. "Old pilot saying."

After all, for all its mystery, the Locust was still just a plane.

Morat was talking again. "This light indicates when you are in free space—where there's room to lift off. You have proximity detectors here, which will alert you to any interference—birds, power lines—you name it, though bird strikes aren't usually an issue. There's no air intake, like on a conventional jet, so you don't suck geese through your fans. Not that they come near anyway."

"Why not?"

"They just sense us. Not sure why. Of course, if you're moving very fast, bird strikes are still possible, but they don't endanger the ship's performance."

He reached for one of the wall consoles and popped it out of its housing like a tablet computer. "This is your main power readout," he said. "It won't activate if surrounding conditions are unfavorable, but we're clear of the hanger now so . . . Watch this sequence."

He tapped a series of buttons, replaced the tablet in the console and reached for a silvery rectangle glowing beside it.

"Night Bird One to flight control," he said into his headset mike. "Permission to activate flight systems."

"Granted, Night Bird One," said the voice in Alan's earphones. "Happy flying."

Morat gave Alan a nod and, with the thrill of understanding, Alan reached for the console and touched the blinking amber square of light till it turned green. With a faint hum that resonated through his body, the ship became something subtly different from what it had been.

That made no sense, he knew, but that was how it felt.

The Locust was still sitting on its spindly landing gear, but—Alan thought—not really. They were touching the ground, but that, it seemed, was a choice, and not the result of basic gravitational physics. For all intents and purposes, Alan thought, they were already flying. Retract the gear, and the ship would just hang there, he was sure of it, dangling in empty space, not so much hovering—since that took thrust—as floating. He could feel it, a curious and inexplicable weightlessness about the ship, unlike anything he had ever felt in a plane before.

"Let's give her a little altitude, shall we?" said Morat.

Alan swallowed, then did what Beaker had told him, pushing slightly on the vertical thrust lever. He watched all around—instruments, scanners, windows—as he set the craft into its vertical ascent, but still he couldn't believe his eyes.

The Locust rose steadily into the desert sky, but there was no sense of the force doing the lifting, no pressure, no registering, in his body that they were moving at all beyond a slight oscillation of the craft as it climbed, as if it were floating on a rippling cushion of air. Strangest of all for a pilot used to the bellow and shriek of jet engines, there was no sound, other than a low, cycling hum that was less a noise than a vague awareness, something felt in the pit of the stomach and the bones of the skull.

This can't be.

It had to be an illusion, another bad simulation. The Locust continued to rise, but Alan's body felt nothing. The ship just drifted up to—according to the readout—56 meters, then stopped. There had been a fractional shudder as they left the ground and then only that minute undulation, like they were a cork on a still sea, rising and falling so slightly that you could barely sense it at all.

"Landing gear away," said Morat, pulling a little lever. The dull whir and snuck of the wheels being stowed sounded loud in the stillness. He paused and looked at Alan. The visors on their helmets were still up and Morat met his eyes. "You okay?"

"Sure," said Alan. More fake casualness. "No sweat."

"Don't want to know what's holding us up?"

Alan's hesitation was so small he doubted Morat saw it.

"Will we crash if I don't know?" he asked.

"No."

"Then let's go. I want to see what this thing can do."

If it had been a test, Morat's grin said he had passed.

"We'll stay over the base tonight," said Morat, all business again. "But you can practice some maneuvering."

"How long can we stay airborne like this?"

"Without moving? Indefinitely. Turn off the directional acceleration systems and we go dark. No external lights would be visible from the ground. We're just here. Going dark also turns off detection counter measures, however, so though we're invisible to the naked eye, we'll show up on radar. But yeah: power everything down and we can hang here in the air forever."

Alan wanted to ask how that was possible, but buried the thought.

"Take her up to two thousand feet," said Morat, "and you can see how she handles."

They did, and Alan moved the craft out around Papoose Mountain, first manually, then using preset coordinates entered automatically as the ship moved. They moved at a steady 300 knots but there was, as before, no sense of drag, thrust or turbulence as they moved. Alan was reminded of a hot air balloon, drifting, its weight somehow canceled out so they moved like dandelion seeds.

Alan realized he was holding his breath, and deliberately let it out again.

"Hold it here," said Morat.

Alan cut the thrust, mouth dry, speechless. The craft hung in the sky in a controlled drift, level but rippling fractionally. Years ago, when Alan had still been with Lacey, he had taken her up in a hot air balloon in the foothills of the Blue Ridge mountains, his last great romantic gesture, complete with champagne and strawberries. It hadn't worked, and a month later she was gone for good, but he remembered what it had been like in the balloon, moving soundlessly (when the burner wasn't roaring) through the sky, unobserved by the deer and rabbits who went about their business below, oblivious. That's what this felt like, an entirely different experience from being in any kind of plane.

"Looking good from here Night Bird One," said the voice of flight control. "Sending coordinates to your nav system now."

"Roger that flight control," said Morat. "Coordinates received. Engaging directional control and locking on."

Alan watched the console as the navigational computer processed the input.

"Take her over there on your mark, Phoenix," said Morat. "Nice and easy."

Alan adjusted the controls, and the Locust suddenly slipped sideways, speeding east at something close to five hundred knots, so that the world below was a nauseating blur.

Or should have been. In fact, there was no nausea at all, and though he was moving too fast for his eyes to make sense of anything, Alan's body remained cool, unfazed, as if he was sitting in a bar, watching the world go by, but at supersonic speeds.

"There now, Phoenix," said Morat. "That wasn't so bad, was it? You're in safe mode now and practically invisible to any technology we know of. Try moving the ship around to get the feel of the controls. Your nav screen will show you the safe zone. Your operational shelf tonight is between five thousand and twenty five thousand feet. Let's try some manual control."

"Roger that," said Alan, still trying to wrap his mind around the way the Locust had moved.

He engaged the manual system and cupped his hand over the red track ball on his armrest. He rolled it gently and the Locust pivoted in place. He did it again, this time applying a little thrust with his other hand, and the ship changed direction again, leaping hard to the west and then climbing in a dizzying spiral before screaming back to the southeast. Of course, there was no screaming, except perhaps inside Alan's head as the laws of physics seemed to implode with each movement the craft made. No sound, no torque, no G-force, no inertia.

It was, if anything, smoother than the simulator had been. Which was impossible.

As the ship moved at Alan's bidding, he gaped and stared, mouth parched, eyes dry because he didn't blink for fear of missing something. And even though he was the one piloting the craft, he felt strangely irrelevant, all his knowledge and experience of flying rendered null and void by the way the Locust handled. The word that had slid unsummoned into his head already ricocheted around like cannon fire: "impossible." All of it. It couldn't be true, but it was, and it changed everything.

Alan gazed at the land beneath him and the sky above, his mind chasing the vectors, acceleration and related calculations the ship seemed to make with an ease so complete that it did not even register on the inside.

It was, in every possible sense of the word, awesome.

When Morat's voice came in over the headset Alan realized that he had almost forgotten the other man sitting beside him entirely.

"You okay, Major?"

"Yeah," said Alan. "Or at least, I will be."

"Understood," said Morat. "I think that's enough for your first night. I think you get the idea."

Except of course, that Alan didn't. Not really.

Back on the ground, Alan was silent as they left in the blacked-out bus. There was something about the way

Hatcher patted him understandingly on the shoulder which said that his mood was not unexpected. They were used to it, this stunned sense that reality was not what it seemed.

"Let's take the rest of the night off," said Hatcher. "Mr. Morat, take the Major for a beer."

ALAN WAS RELIEVED THAT THE PLANNED BEER WOULD NOT be on the base, but there were things to say first, things that could not be said anywhere but Dreamland. He requested a debriefing room, a place, he said, where they could talk openly and without fear of being overheard. Hatcher did not hesitate, but neither did he ask what was on Alan's mind, or if he could sit in. This was pilot talk.

He led them down a series of hallways, swiped his badge through three separate doors, and showed their clearance IDs to the guard with the submachine gun on duty outside the designated meeting room.

"And remember, gentlemen," he said, showing them into the comfortably appointed—but predictably deserted—lounge. "Careless talk . . ."

Costs lives, Alan thought, recalling the old wartime motto. "Say what you like in here," Hatcher concluded. "But only here. Then get your beer, like a regular person. Just remember that you aren't one. Not anymore."

And with that, he left them.

Morat took bottled water from a fridge, tossed one to Alan and waited. The room hummed with the textured hiss of the white noise speakers on the walls.

"How can you live with it?" Alan asked.

Morat gave him a level stare. "With what?"

"The . . ." Alan fought for the word. "The sheer *physics* of it?"

Morat glanced fractionally around before answering, making sure no one had come in. "I don't need to understand digital recording, or sound compression and reproduction to enjoy a bit of Taylor Swift on my iPod," he said with a shrug. "I'm a pilot, not an engineer."

Alan scowled. "You listen to Taylor Swift?"

Morat shrugged and grinned, but Alan didn't let him derail his train of thought.

"No one ever told you Taylor Swift on an iPod was a theoretical impossibility," he said. "You haven't lived your life according to—premised on—that assumption."

"True," said Morat, taking a sip of his water. "You lived your life on the premise that there could be no more advanced form of flight than what you've been trained to do in a Harrier. What if you grew up flying a Spitfire or a Sopwith Camel, and then someone showed you the Harrier? Would that change your view of the world?"

"No," said Alan. "Yes. Kind of. But this is a different order of magnitude." He leaned in, lowering his voice. "This isn't just going faster or higher than we thought we could. This is a fundamentally different notion of travel. According to everything I've ever heard, it's not possible. Those aerial maneuvers I just did, the changes of direction, the acceleration, that's . . ."

"What?"

"That's not flying."

"It's just a different kind of flying."

Alan shook his head. "I don't know what that means," he said.

"No, and if I'm really honest," said Morat, "neither do I, but you know what? It works. You've seen it."

"I just don't understand how it's possible that . . ."

"Yeah, yeah," said Morat, and his smile was brittle now. "So you keep saying. Let me see your phone."

"What?"

"Your phone, let me see it."

Alan fished in his pocket and pushed the iPhone across the table.

"State of the art," said Morat, impressed.

"For now," Alan replied.

"Right," said the other man with a meaningful stare. "But even if it wasn't, what do you have here? A communication device that allows you to talk to people all over the world. This phone is a computer that can process more data in less time than anything involved in the Apollo space program that put men on the moon. You've got digital pictures and video, music . . ."

"I know. So?"

"So imagine taking this back in time a thousand years, or less, say a couple of hundred. Imagine you could walk into the house of George Washington, with all your networks and servers functioning, and show him what that little device could do. What do you think the people of the time would say?"

Alan frowned. "I guess they'd be pretty impressed," he said, grudgingly, guessing where Morat was going.

"No," Morat replied. "Not impressed. They'd freak the fuck out. They'd be terrified. They'd say it was witchcraft. They'd say it wasn't possible, that such a thing could not exist in the world as they knew it."

Alan said nothing.

"What you saw today is a leap forward—a quantum leap, if you like—but a leap forward in technology and theoretical understanding way beyond our pay grade. But it ain't witchcraft."

"I get that," said Alan, "but I'm a pilot. I know about flying."

"Sure you do," said Morat. "Thrust against drag; lift and angle of attack to generate turn Gs, right? You are dead-on: a Sopwith Camel pilot could get his head around a Harrier. Action and reaction, objects in motion stay in motion unless acted on by a force—that's what Newton figured out right? And invented calculus to analyze? A fighter pilot has Newtonian physics baked into our muscle memory. But think on this: Didn't Einstein already grasp that Newtonian physics are just a useful approximation for the world and speeds we live in? Or that space and time are a continuum, and both bend and curve? Astrophysicists can see the evidence—around neutron stars and black holes; Einstein lenses bending space. But the useful engineering of non-Newtonian physics into applied technology—why that's as far out as telling old Ben Franklin that your iPhone is just the engineering of the electricity he is experimenting with in his kites and Leyden jars. Bend space and time under commanded control, non-Newtonian, and there's no action/reaction; no force needed to equal acceleration you'd feel in the cockpit. The engineering of such technology? Well, that's more than you need to know. But it ain't magic, and the sooner you get used to the idea that it's real, the longer you'll last up there, *capisce?*"

Alan blinked, looked at him and nodded. It hadn't been a threat. Not really. A caution, perhaps, and a useful one.

AFTER THE BUS RIDE BACK TO GROOM LAKE, THE TWO OF them sitting silently in the cool interior, looking at nothing, the driver took them to their respective quarters to change out of their flight gear, asking them politely to return in civilian attire. For Morat, this meant jeans and a worn open necked shirt that made him look like someone Alan had never seen before. Alan ruffled his hair a bit and pushed the sleeves up on his wrinkle-free no-iron Oxford shirt, but he knew that anyone with half a brain would spot him for military.

The bus driver looked them over as if inspecting them, then drove them to a carpool near the main gate where Morat signed for the keys to a tan Lincoln Town Car. The driver started to offer directions but Morat cut him off.

"I know the way."

They could hardly get lost. Once through a series of security check points, they drove northwest on Highway 375 for a couple of miles, twice navigating around black steers that watched them curiously, until they came to what had to be the smallest town Alan had ever seen.

"Say hello to Rachel," said Morat. "Population 50, give or take. There's no point trying not to stand out, because you're gonna, whatever you do. But let's not advertise what we do, okay?"

Alan nodded.

As to where they would get the promised beer, their choice was not so much limited as nonexistent. There was a single-story white building, surrounded by mobile homes, which Alan took to be guest rooms, set on a piece of barren land by the service road, the main building flying a US flag. It proclaimed itself the "Little A'Le Inn: Restaurant, Bar, Motel." A classic big-eyed alien-head logo, painted roughly beneath, said "Earthlings welcome." A couple of big rig tractor trailers were parked out front and across the road there was a pickup truck with a small crane in the bed, from which a model flying saucer was suspended.

"Seriously?" said Alan.

"Welcome to the Extraterrestrial Highway," said Morat, with a sideways grin and an eye roll. "Don't tell anyone what you were doing this morning, or the entire place will have a heart attack."

Alan would have preferred something big and loud, where he could hole up in a corner with frosty mug, regularly refilled, and not think about what he'd seen today, but the inn looked homey and welcoming enough. The place was a theme park of alien paraphernalia and kitsch, and its menu matched. The kitchens were about to close for the night so Alan ordered an alien burger with macaroni salad, which was good, but not as good as the fries Morat got.

The beer was standard domestic—which was fine by Alan, though Morat sneered—but it was ice cold. Alan ordered two more, as soon as the first ones arrived.

They talked about nothing: baseball and Bruce Springsteen, cars, and whether the first *Alien* film was better than the second. Conversation was pleasant enough, even if Morat knew surprisingly little about what Alan thought was common knowledge (how did anyone not know that the Jets were football and the Rangers were hockey?), but it was also intentionally empty and guarded. They were careful to say nothing about where they worked or what they did, which meant that—at least from Alan's perspective—the conversation had no weight, no substance. His gaze flicked away and landed on the windowpane, where a pale banded gecko clung to the glass with the ridges of its padded toes.

"How those burgers working out for you, hon?" the waitress chirped.

"Great," said Morat. "Perfect."

Alan managed a nod and a smile, but as soon as she sauntered away, he went back to watching the gecko.

What had Hatcher said?

"Get your beer like a regular person. Just remember that you aren't one. Not anymore."

That was about the size of it.

They finished their beers in silence, and though Alan ordered another, the two men did not speak again until they were ready to drive back to the base, nicknamed, Alan recalled—both ironically and aptly—Dreamland.

25

JENNIFER
Hampshire, England

BACK IN HER ROOM, JENNIFER INSERTED THE FLASH DRIVE she'd found concealed in her father's model railway landscape into her laptop and tried to make sense of what she saw. There were no letters to her, no narratives of any kind, just spreadsheets of names and dates and account numbers, none of it familiar to her, according to what she had seen on her father's laptop. She knew the numbers represented money. Lots of it. Billions of pounds, moved around by the Maynard Consortium across nation states and through corporations whose names she did not know. Most of it seemed to funnel, eventually, into an entity called, simply, SWEEP. Nothing in the documents gave any sign as to what SWEEP was, what it made or sold, where it was, or who ran it. It was just a name, possibly an acronym. She looked the company up, but there was nothing online, no trace of it at all.

She had assumed the flash drive would answer all her questions, but it had only raised others, and given her larger mysteries to work with. Some of the names in the files were not companies. They were people, individuals in a variety of professions and places, which simple online searches quickly revealed: English lawyers, German financiers, Russian industrialists, even one US Senator who she remembered visiting Steadings when she was an adolescent. A "friend of her fathers." They probably all had ties—of some sort—to SWEEP, whatever that was, and none of it had shown up in any of the Maynard group's records or files or—for that matter—their boardroom discussions.

It smelled wrong.

But smell, she thought, as she sipped the last of her father's Lagavulin, wasn't nearly enough to go on. She was going to have to do some exploring, but where to start? In this utterly unfamiliar world, she couldn't imagine. She doubted Deacon would have any more insights than she had, unless he knew more about her father's dealings than he'd let on. She was about to close the drive when she saw a notepad app. She clicked on it, and it opened, revealing a single three-word message.

"Talk to Letrange."

The handsome face of the young man at the Maynard group came to mind. Letrange. He'd asked her to call him Dan. She reread those three loaded words. Was it her father making a note to himself, a plan? A decision? Was it a message to her from beyond the grave, a place to start getting answers? Or was it none of these, a fraction of a memo that had accidentally been included among all this secret data.

No, she thought. The flash drive had been stowed in a hurry, a desperate act designed for no one but her. And her father was a careful man. The message was intended for her. It had to be. Did that make the dark-eyed man merely a source of information, or was he someone her father had trusted? Someone *she* should trust?

No, she thought again. He had been nicer to her than the other board members, felt different from them, but that was just his relative youth and manner. It was no reason to take him into her confidence.

But someone in that room had wanted her to poke around. She felt sure of it. And, with the half message from her father still glowing on the screen in front of her, it seemed more likely Letrange than any of the other ten. What had Deacon said about making leaps of faith as the beginning of trust? She reached for the suit jacket she'd thrown over the back of a chair, fished in the pocket for Letrange's business card, picked up her mobile and dialed the number before she could change her mind.

He answered immediately, but there was wariness in his voice as he gave his name.

"This is Jennifer Quinn," she said. "I was wondering if we might meet."

SHE DIDN'T TELL DEACON, NOT BECAUSE SHE DIDN'T TRUST him, but because she knew he would caution her against doing anything rash. She felt like being rash. Needed it. She had spent the last few days in what felt like a fog, feeling her way cautiously, led by other people who assumed she had no place even being there. She had to take decisive action.

But she was not an idiot. The meeting was to test the waters, nothing more. She would not tell Letrange—Dan—about the data her father had squirreled away for her and her alone, no matter how charming he was.

She spent the morning poring over the files on the flash drive, tracking Maynard's investments, going all the way back to the year it was founded in the late forties, a quarter of a century before her father got involved, its finance emerging from Swiss accounts. Records from those days were only partial, but even then, the primary recipients of the Consortium's funding seemed to have been shadow corporations that had left no trace on the Internet. The companies and their assets were always global, scattered across the world but seemingly unconnected, and they tended to melt away after a few years. Until SWEEP appeared in 1964. It looked like it grew out of a conglomeration of previous corporations, though the historical record was so tangled at this point that she couldn't be sure. It seemed to quietly swallow up the other companies, until it was moving hundreds of billions of dollars, pounds, euros and other currencies through the Caymans and Seychelles, through Liechtenstein, Vanuatu, Belize, and Singapore. There was no record of it in any public documentation, though its various activities must clearly have put an invisible hand on various world markets and stock exchanges. That was more than strange. It was either all nonsense, or it was criminal.

Dad, she thought, the fact of it settling in her gut like a stone. *What did you do?*

She let Letrange choose the place, a pub close to the Earls Court tube station called—bafflingly—the Prince of Teck. He offered no explanation for his choice except to say that he would be "in the area," and though its ordinariness surprised her, she was glad she was meeting him in a place where she didn't feel like she had to behave like some under-accessorized Sloane Ranger. She ordered a glass of Glenmorangie Signet at the bar, took a stool at a plain wooden table by the window and watched the traffic on Earls Court Road. Letrange, when he arrived, was casual chic in a close fitting dark suit without a tie, but if he was a regular in the pub, no one greeted him as such. He carried an attaché case, which he slid under the table.

"You came," he said.

"We made the plan only a few hours ago," Jennifer answered, slightly defensive. "Of course I came."

He smiled at that, then took a step closer to the bar and, with a single word—"pint"—and a nod at one of the pumps, ordered. It was an easy confident gesture, the action of a man accustomed to being in charge. Jennifer decided to be unimpressed.

"I hadn't expected your call," he said, sipping his beer. "To be honest, I thought I'd pissed you off."

Jennifer shrugged. "Partly, I was just in a bad mood," she conceded.

"Understandable," he answered.

"But also," she said, recovering her steel, "well, you know, the company you keep."

He smiled. "It's a not a crime to be rich, Miss Quinn. I thought you would understand that."

"Because I am, you mean? I don't think that follows. Inheriting my father's money just means I know more than most people do about how it was acquired. What it does and doesn't do, and who it supports, and who it keeps in their place. It's not a pretty picture."

"I think you're the richest socialist I know," he answered.

"Because I have a conscience *and* resources, that's supposed to be a contradiction?"

Her words were clipped, but she could feel the heat in her face. This wasn't the way she'd intended the meeting to go.

"I just think," he said, "that when you champion the underclasses from a position of privilege, you wind up pleasing neither those you are trying to help—who resent you as a *noblesse oblige* do-gooder who goes home to a palace at the end of the day—nor your own people, who think you're a class traitor. Must make for a pretty miserable and lonely existence."

"If by *my own people,* you mean the kinds I went to school with, the ones who spend their time shopping or watching horse shows, I was never one of them. And for all his other faults, my father knew it."

"And accepted it?"

"Eventually."

"And yet here you are," he said. He wasn't smiling now and the air was sharp with tension.

"Here I am," she said. "Because he's dead, and he wanted me to take over for him. And maybe bring my socialist sensibility to his work, and undo some of the things he'd been complicit in."

"You can't know that," said Letrange.

"You just don't want to think he had second thoughts about the kinds of business you did with him."

"Oh, please," snapped Letrange. "Don't canonize him, now that he's not around to disappoint you."

If she had been holding her glass as he said it, she would have thrown it in his face. As it was, she had to reach for it, and that split second gave her the moment she needed to restrain herself. She gripped the glass and held it deliberately in place, but the speed of her action had already spoken volumes.

"I'm sorry," said Letrange. "That was out of line. Perhaps I should leave you to finish your drink in peace."

She considered the offer seriously, but the heat was already draining, as if his apology had released the pressure, and she was suddenly herself again. She shook her head wearily.

"I'm sorry too," she said. "I have not been myself lately, and this is all very stressful. I hope I haven't disrupted your day too much. This was clearly a mistake."

She rose to leave, but his hand was suddenly on hers, gentle, tentative.

"Don't go," he said. "This was entirely my fault. I'm afraid I'm not used to having the ethics of my profession called into question. You touched a nerve. But that's my problem, not yours. And since you obviously didn't call me so that you could bask in my charming personality, why don't you tell me why you wanted to see me?"

For a moment she hesitated, feeling the creeping exhaustion of the last few days, and then she sat, staring at her half-empty glass to avoid his eyes. He sat too, giving her a moment to collect herself.

"What do you know about SWEEP?" she asked, only looking at him as she uttered the final word.

She hadn't intended to mention the name. She knew it would reveal that she had access to information someone had tried to keep from her, but she didn't know how else to proceed.

And she was curious. She wanted to see how he reacted.

SWEEP. Possibly an acronym, possibly a front, but certainly the recipient of a lot of Maynard Corporation money. She watched his face.

For a moment he did not react at all, as if he were waiting for more information, then he frowned and shook his head.

"Sweep?" he repeated. "I don't understand. Is that a thing, or some kind of practice?"

"A thing," she answered. If he was lying, he was good at it. "A company. It's where a lot of Maynard's money has been going."

His frown deepened, and there was something else in his eyes now: doubt, incredulity.

"Since when?" he said.

"The name first appears in the mid-sixties, but I think it existed before then, under other names."

"I've never heard of it," he said. "You must have something wrong. If Maynard had serious investments in this SWEEP—whatever it is . . ."

"Not just serious investments," she cut in. "Massive."

"If that were the case, I'd know."

"You're what, thirty-five, thirty-eight? A good fifteen years younger than anyone else on the board."

"Until you showed up. So?"

"And you've been a member for . . ."

"Two years. You're saying that I'm not senior enough to know what's going on?"

He sounded stung.

"Sometimes there are inner circles within organizations," said Jennifer. "They don't always share the most important material with the more junior . . ."

"Thanks." He glared at her. "You know, a better solution to all this—frankly, rather rude—skepticism about my position on the board, and your implication of cloak and dagger funding, which would almost certainly be in violation of all manner of international laws, is that you have bad data. Where did you get this SWEEP nonsense?"

"I found it among my father's things."

"In what form? A note? A letter? Maybe you misinterpreted . . ."

"Files detailing thousands of money transfers," she said. "Names, places, account details. The lot. Hidden away where he knew only I would find it."

"Why would he do that?"

"Because he knew he was in danger and didn't trust anyone else," she said. The idea hadn't registered with quite that much hard-edged clarity before, but she saw it now, and it touched something in her heart, so that her voice quavered on the last word. "Whatever this SWEEP is, Dad was murdered for it."

Letrange stared at her, but when he spoke, it was with a kind of resignation.

"His suicide was . . . unexpected," he said. "I don't think I really believed it. You're sure?"

"Pretty sure," she said. "I wasn't before, because I didn't know why someone might want him dead, but now . . . And he said I should talk to you."

This time, the surprise really did register in Letrange's face, though it was quickly doused, such that she couldn't tell how he felt about the revelation. At last, he smiled mirthlessly, acknowledging that she had indeed thrown him a bone.

"Which is why you're here," he said.

"Yes," she answered. "My father thought you knew something that would help. And perhaps he thought you were not in as deep as the others. He thought I could trust you."

She said it stiffly, conceding nothing, and at last he nodded.

"SWEEP," he said. His voice was still musing, baffled, but he took a swallow of his beer and came up with something like resolution in his eyes. "What do you want me to do? I could speak to the board . . ."

"No," she said. "That wouldn't achieve anything. It might even be dangerous."

"Dangerous?" he echoed, his black eyes wide and alarmed. "You don't really think . . .?"

"The first thing to do," she said, ignoring the question, "is make sure we know what we're dealing with. I can't make sense out of all the data, but maybe if you took a look at the files . . .?"

"Certainly," he said. "Who else have you told?"

Jennifer hesitated for only a second. "No one," she said.

"Not even Deacon?"

She shook her head, but the question tripped some vague alarm. Was it obvious that she might confide in her dead father's manservant? Would anyone make that guess, or did it suggest Letrange knew more than he'd let on?

"I need to make a phone call," he said.

"Who to?"

She was wary now, suddenly and inexplicably doubtful that she had done the right thing. She hadn't meant to confide this much, and some part of her worried that it had been a mistake to do so. He seemed to see something in her face and, as if in response, squeezed his eyes shut in furious thought for a moment.

"My name is not Letrange," he said.

Of all the things he might have said, this was something she'd been unprepared for. She blinked but said nothing.

He reached under the table to his attaché case, opened it and drew out a wallet, which he flipped open. The blue card inside showed his picture, but the name below it read Robert Chevalier. It was followed by an agent number. The card bore a crest featuring a globe with a sword behind it. The white capital letters across the top read "Interpol."

26

TIMIKA
Pottsville, PA

THE MOTEL OFFERED NO COMPLIMENTARY BREAKFAST, so Timika loaded up the car and stopped off at a Dunkin' Donuts, three blocks from the Yuengling Brewery, in downtown Pottsville, before heading north on Route 61 towards the wooded hills of Locust Lake State Park. She found the little Presbyterian church, set back from the road, surrounded by pine trees. It was white clapboard with a tower for a single bell, and the sign out front advertised a bake sale and a children's Sunday service. It looked like the kind of rural church that would be featured on Hallmark Christmas cards, surrounded by snow and an artfully positioned minister. A white church, Timika thought, in both senses of the word. She felt conspicuous, trying the door and pushing her way inside.

It was dimly lit, bathed in the glow from tall, narrow stained-glass windows. It smelled of furniture oils and brass polish, and its pews were straight and regular, equipped with ancient hymnals, all exactly as the exterior promised, simple and plain. There was no one there. The silence felt heavy, like accumulated dust, or the memory of something long finished. The only sign that this was still an active house of worship, and not some recreated "living museum" like Old Sturbridge, was the string of paper dolls looped between the half-columns molded into the walls, and trailing along the benches. They'd been cut out of white cardstock, the way people used to make holiday trimmings, the paper folded many times so that each scissor snip made cuts that echoed through the stack. As a kid, she'd always been delighted and amazed when she did it right and opened up the folded mass to reveal the streamer of repeated shapes. She assumed they had been made for the children's service advertised outside, strings of paper children holding hands. It was a cheap old-fashioned display, in keeping with the rest of the chapel, but it touched something in her and made her thoughtful.

She sat at the back in a corner pew and waited, but the hour came and went without any sign of Katarina or anyone else from The Hollows. She waited fifty minutes before deciding the old woman wasn't coming. As she waited, the paper dolls acquired an altogether different aspect, their skeletal whiteness in the empty church standing in for all the people who weren't there, a ghostly echo chilling by virtue of its childishness. Timika closed the church door behind her and stepped out into the cool air with something like relief.

She considered driving out to the lake, but there was no reason to believe Katarina had been telling the truth about the outing. The appointment at the church had probably been a ruse to get rid of her. Whatever kind of strange, luxurious prison The Hollows was, the old woman wanted no help from Timika in escaping it. For a moment, she considered driving back there, but the guards would surely be watching for her, and she wouldn't be as lucky today as she'd been yesterday.

She got into her car and called Marvin, but he didn't pick up, and she could think of nothing to say in a message. Having no idea of where to go, she read from Jerzy's journal for a half hour. She kept one eye open for the van that might still bring Katarina Lundergrass to her meeting, but the two or three cars she saw in the next ten minutes did not slow.

The phone rang. Marvin.

"Hey," she said.

"Nothing much to report," he said. "But I have the address of that other old folks' home for you, The Silver Birches. Want it?"

She had forgotten that the caterer had revealed one of the other locations he delivered to. It might be nothing, but since she had no other leads, it was worth a look.

She drove back towards Pottsville, following Marvin's directions. She missed one turn as she swung into the west side of town, but doubled back easily and found herself face-to face with The Silver Birches. It was a more modern building, in the Swiss chalet style, and the gardens looked younger, the trees showing something of the nursery's evenness, arranged with military regularity, like little green nutcrackers. A sign by the drive advertised the assisted living facility's pool, and another said that there was now a vacancy, which suggested—Timika thought bleakly—that someone had recently died. It felt quite different from The Hollows, but there was another of those Checkpoint Charlie-style gates, with a friendly looking uniformed officer complete with radio and sidearm. Timika drove past without making eye contact.

At The Hollows, she'd talked her way in and improvised her way out over the wall, but that wouldn't work this time. If there was a connection between the two residencies, they would be watching for her. In the absence of any better ideas, she opted to simply reverse the process.

Over the wall in, talk your way out.

So she drove, keeping the brick perimeter on her right in her peripheral vision, slowing when the brick wall became the stone blocks of a different neighboring facility. A hundred yards further down was another gate, broad and unguarded, its driveway leading to what was advertised as a private tennis club and spa.

Good enough.

She drove in, parked in the lot, then walked not towards the glass and chrome gym—where she would probably need a pass—but into the trees that lined the wall separating the spa from The Silver Birches.

This is becoming a habit, she thought, as she checked over her shoulder, then shinnied up a tree, breathing heavily, and hopped the wall. *Still, better to do it when you're not being chased by armed guards . . .*

As soon as she dropped into the grounds of The Silver Birches, she could smell the tang of charcoal smoke and something sweet that made her mouth water: grilling meat. In spite of the chill, someone was determined to treat spring as spring.

There were no wooded landscapes, as there had been at The Hollows, just the trimly regimented trees mulched and spaced to give them room to grow. The garden wouldn't look its best for another five years. It meant she had no cover. She made for the house, taking in the numerous cars and vans parked outside. Perhaps the barbecue—informal, outdoors, mingly—would be the perfect way to slip in. She followed her nose down the side of the house, past the obligatory conservatory and round to an extensive rear patio with potted plants and a fire pit.

And people. Seven of them. Six men and one . . .

Katarina Lundergrass.

Timika turned on her heel before she was observed and tried the closest door into the house, thinking furiously.

She was in the conservatory, and she was not alone. It looked a lot like the common room at The Hollows: lots of indoor greenery and old people chatting, drinking coffee, and playing cards. She moved with her back to the windows, slipping around a healthy ficus, and sat down next to an old white man. They were all old and white. She could forget about being inconspicuous.

"Hello," she said.

To her surprise, the man beamed at her, his smile peeling off a good fifteen years.

"Hello, my dear," he said. "And what's your name?"

"I'm Ashley," said Timika reflexively, "I'm from social services. Routine inspection."

"Social services? Here?" he said. "Well, I suppose you have to make sure they aren't poisoning us for our estates. Not that there's much left to inherit, once all this has been paid for."

Timika nodded and smiled.

"So you're happy with your care, Mr . . .?"

"Sanderson," he answered. "Call me Chuck."

He took her hand and, to her amazement, raised it quickly to his lips.

"*Enchanté*," he said. "What lovely skin you have."

If that was his way of signaling that he wasn't a racist, Timika thought, it was clumsy. But nicer than most. She found herself smiling.

"Not joining the barbecue, Chuck?" she asked, turning so that she could shoot a furtive look at Katarina through the window.

"Private party," said Chuck with a shrug. "Not invited. Never."

"Never?" said Timika with mock amazement.

"Fred's buddies," said Chuck.

Timika thought.

"Frederick Kaas?" she asked.

"That's the fella. Traveling salesman, or so he says."

"You don't believe him?"

"Once told me he sold vacuum cleaners door-to-door," he said. "Now, my old man worked for Sears. As a kid, I knew more about vacuum cleaners than was good for a boy, so I start firing model names and numbers at old Fred there, and I'd swear on my old man's grave he never heard of any of 'em."

"So what do you think he did?"

Chuck Sanderson shrugged expansively. "He used to have a pal who visited him every few days. Funny fella by the name of Siegfried something. Mahr? Maier? Something like that. Engineer. Bit of a drinker, just between us. You could smell it on him. He'd come couple of times a week, and they'd huddle up in the corner and mutter to each other. One time, he came when Fred was sick in his room, and sat around down here by himself instead. Got talking to a couple of the other residents. Told them all kinds of nonsense, about how he used to work on special aircraft or something. Barking mad. Nobody believed a word of it. But then, a couple days later, these others fellas came, young guys in suits. Talked to everyone who had been there, wanted to know what this Siegfried character had been saying. Very bizarre. We never saw him again. Poof. Just like that. Gone."

Timika looked suitably shocked.

"What did Fred say about it?"

"Said they'd had a falling out," said Chuck, skeptically. "Weird. He doesn't get visitors anymore. Just this crowd who come over for a barbecue once a month. Rain or shine. Like the damn postal service. What do they say? Neither rain nor snow nor heat nor gloom of night will stay these couriers of . . . something or other? Well, that's what these guys are like.

Nothing stops their precious barbecue. And the rest of us have to sit inside, just to avoid the smell. But then someone opens the window and. . . . Well, you can imagine. Steak. I could murder a steak."

"This man who disappeared," Timika said, trying to redirect the conversation. "Maier?"

"Maher, maybe. Something like that."

"You said he worked on special aircraft?"

"That's what *he* said. I didn't say jack."

"What do you think he meant by that?"

"Something about how they performed, how they flew, I guess. But he never said he flew them. He was an engineer. I said that, right? Built the materials the planes were made of. Bragged about it, you might say, though I try not to judge."

"How they flew?"

"I don't know. He told this one story about how these R&D guys brought him a blue tile, made of some weird material. Said you couldn't tell if it was metal or plastic or ceramic. They told him to figure out what it was and build some more. He asked where they had got it from, and they told him that didn't matter. He was all 'How am I gonna figure out what the stuff is if you won't tell me anything about where it came from?' And they said, 'That's why you make the big bucks.' He liked telling everyone he made a mint, like we'd be impressed."

"Did he say where he thought the tile came from?"

"Russia. Maybe China," said Chuck. "Somewhere secret, from people who didn't want us to have it. Like it was recovered in some James Bond mission and he couldn't really talk about it. Except that he did. Thought it made him cool. Jackass. Now he's off the barbecue list. Not so cool now, huh?"

Timika nodded thoughtfully and looked out to where Katarina and the others were huddled round the grill in their coats.

"You know where he went?"

"Never heard from him again."

"And no one saw him arguing with your friend, Fred?"

"There was no argument that I saw. And a falling out doesn't explain those other guys who showed up asking questions."

"Who did you think they were?"

"No clue. Corporate security or government types, I'd say. Engineering is a high dollar line of work. Someone wanted their secrets protected."

Unbidden, the thought of the paper dolls trailing across the empty church came to mind. Children. German names. The protected secrets of scientists imported from the ashes of Berlin.

And the last piece of the puzzle slotted into place.

German children.

The offspring of all those Operation Paperclip researchers and engineers who perhaps saw or heard things deemed classified long ago. Was that possible?

Timika stood up abruptly, the idea clear and sharp in her head, and turned to the window and the exclusive barbecue beyond.

Katarina, half in and half out of a group who were talking and laughing, was looking directly at her.

JERZY
Guantanamo, Cuba, July 1946

I STILL DON'T KNOW WHAT PART CAPTAIN JENNINGS PLAYED in fast-tracking my sudden commitment to the navy, but within weeks of our arrival in New York I was in basic training at the Great Lakes facility north of Chicago. Early the next year I was in Guantanamo, Cuba, for further training while the *USS Kitchener* was being refitted, and spent my leisure time on deck drinking Coke. It was, of course, no accident that I would continue my career under Captain Jennings' command, though he kept his distance to avoid the appearance of favoritism. For all the hardships of training, life among the palm trees and haciendas where the sailors cracked open green, freshly harvested coconuts filled with sweet milk on the beaches of the base's Windward Point was like being on another planet. There's lots to say about life on a destroyer, but it's not relevant to my larger story so, at least for now, I'm going to skip over it.

We left port at the beginning of September 1946, heading south between Haiti and Jamaica, then down the east coast of Venezuela and Guyana. In the vast openness of the South Atlantic, we lost sight of land entirely, and went many days at a time without glimpsing another vessel as we skirted the great coastline of Brazil, finally pulling west again in time to spy the coastal buildings of Montevideo looming off our starboard bow. I was told by a shipmate about the scuttling of the German pocket battleship, *Graf Spee*, in the first year of the war, and we peered over the side, hoping to see the shadowy outline of its wreckage as we sailed over it, but there was nothing.

We entered Argentine waters and came to a full stop less than a mile from La Plata's shipyards, where the two German submarines were moored. We were met by a patrol boat flying the Argentine triband of pale blue and white, the escort for a pair of US officials, one of whom, I was told, was an ambassador or consul.

The ship was tense. There were, including officers, a little over three hundred of us aboard, and we had been at sea for weeks. On deck, it was hot, and below deck it was hotter, unventilated and saturated with the stench of unwashed bodies. We slept on deck, where it was cooler, if we could, or in bunks four high, seeing the same faces, doing the same chores. We were waiting for something—anything—to happen, and, more importantly, waiting to get off the damn ship. We'd come all this way, and now we were sitting in the harbor, waiting for some goddamned diplomats to say we could get on with our job or—better still—go ashore for a while.

But we waited that first day, and one hour turned into two, and there was no sign of progress. When a hatch opened, it was only Billy Ray, the mess steward, a burly black man who ran the galley with an impatient efficiency that terrified me.

"Stern!" he bellowed, glaring at me. "Get your ass up here."

I stared at him. He had never spoken to me directly before. Even the fact that he knew who I was thrilled me, though I felt something between pride and panic.

"Me?" I said, getting hesitantly to my feet.

"You," he said. "Why, God only knows."

"What . . . ?"

"Captain requested you by name," he said, moving back to the galley and not bothering to see if I was following. "There's a tray of coffee. Take it to the state room."

"Coffee?" I muttered, stupidly.

"Yeah, you know what coffee is, don't you?" Billy Ray shot back, turning to give me the kind of level glower that would freeze a charging bear. "They grow it right here. In fact, offering our dried crap to these Argy diplomats is like bringing the Governor of Maine aboard and serving him canned lobster. But what the hell do I know? I'm just the damn cook. That tray there. You see it?"

"Yes sir," I said, staring at the tray with its cups and polished brass coffee pot.

"So take it," he said. "And don't call me sir, boy. What's wrong with you?"

"Yes, sir. Sorry, sir," I stammered.

Billy Ray held the hatch open and watched me unblinkingly as I took the laden tray gingerly and stepped over the threshold.

"And don't spill it," he said, adding as I moved unsteadily away, "Boy don't have the brain God gave a lemon."

I was used to following orders without question, but the fact that I should have been singled out for this particular job was odd. When I reached the Captain's state room—having just about managed to tip the contents of the tray all over myself as I made it up the metal gangway and got the door open—he showed no sign of recognizing me.

"Just set it there, Seaman," he said, nodding to the table upon which I saw various papers spread out, and a sheaf of black and white photographs.

The small room felt crowded. The captain and his first officer were joined by the two diplomats in suits, an Argentine military officer in sunglasses and a pale blue jacket trimmed with heavy gold braid and epaulettes, and two other uniformed men who were squeezed in against the wall. I did not know if I was supposed to offer coffee to everyone. There weren't enough cups.

The Captain spread the photographs out as he made room for the mugs, and I had to make my way round the table, pouring coffee over the shoulders of the seated men like a waiter. It irritated me, and I risked a look at the Captain, though he did not look back. The Argentine officer spoke languidly in Spanish, splaying the fingers of one tanned hand for casual emphasis. As he finished, the slimmer of the two diplomats translated in clipped tones.

"The internal arrangements of the US Navy are not his concern, he says. This is a matter of sovereignty. The vessels in question were surrendered to Argentina, not to the United States, and their extradition has not been cleared by Presidente Perón's government."

The Captain sat impassive as the Argentine officer put down his cup and continued his speech. This in turn was given in English by the increasingly frustrated translator.

"He says that your crew are welcome to the hospitality of his great city, subject—of course—to all local rules and ordinances, and he suggests that they avail themselves of the opportunity, since your ship will not be permitted to take the aforementioned submarines back to your home country any time soon. He compliments you on the standard of your coffee," the translator concluded, "though he is, of course, lying."

If that last was a joke, no one reacted as such. Instead they nodded sagely, and it struck me that the dynamic reminded me of some of the crew's poker games. I moved to top off the Argentine officer's cup and froze.

In front of him was one of the photographs. It showed three men in conversation. In the background, other people in what looked like German naval uniforms, but only the three in the foreground were in sharp focus, showing no awareness of the camera, as if it had been taken with a powerful lens from a distance. Two of them, I did not recognize. The third, though out of uniform, had a distinctive sideways smile that I knew instantly. It was the ranking officer who had been visiting the Wenceslas mine, the day Ishmael died. He had been talking to the scientists in the bell chamber. Ungerleider had saluted him. I would have recognized him anywhere.

"That's all, Seaman," said the Captain, sweeping the pictures back into a manila folder as if annoyed that I had seen them. "Leave us."

He said it roughly, as if I had done something wrong, and the Argentine officer gave me a look of amused condescension as I bustled out, my head swimming.

"So?" Billy Ray demanded when I returned the tray to the galley.

"What?" I asked, only half coming out of my reverie.

"We going home with those subs or what?"

I shook my head vaguely.

"No," I said, in answer to his stare. "I don't think so. But we may be able to go ashore."

"Better than nothing," he said. "You okay boy? Look like you've seen a ghost."

"Yeah," I said, unsure which remark I was agreeing with.

THE ARGENTINE OFFICIAL LEFT WITHIN THE NEXT TEN minutes, but the US diplomats stayed an hour more. I was watching from below the bridge when the hatch opened and the Captain showed them out. He watched them go, then looked down and around the deck. I was sure he was looking for me. I stepped sideways into the sun, and he nodded toward me once. It was, I believed, an invitation.

He closed the door behind me as soon as I reached the stateroom.

"Sit down, Jerzy," he said. "I'm sorry if I was brusque with you before. I didn't want anyone to recognize what I'd seen in your face."

"That I knew one of the men in the pictures," I said.

"Exactly," he said.

The table had been cleared and the pictures were gone.

"The photos were taken by a US journalist, shortly after the U-boats arrived in La Plata. I've had them since Guantanamo. Was it just the one man you knew?" he asked.

I thought, trying to recall the photographs, but nodded. "I think so," I said.

"From Wenceslas?" he asked.

"I only saw him once," I said. "For a few minutes."

"But you are sure it was him?"

"Positive," I said. I would never forget that face.

"You know his name?"

I shook my head. "I do not think he was stationed at the mine," I said.

Jennings smiled ruefully at that. "No," he said. "He was not. An *Obergruppenführer* of the SS would not be stationed in a mine."

I stared at him in disbelief until he inclined his head.

"His name is Hans Kammler," he said. "An engineer by training, Nazi by ideology. Worked his way up to command a host of construction projects and facilities. Concentration camps, extermination procedures, special weapons testing and construction. Under that last category, he ended the war in charge of the Nazi jet aircraft and V2 rocket program. A very powerful man, and one who is supposed to have died of self-induced cyanide poisoning near Prague in May of last year. Yet here he is, walking around, big as life."

For a moment, his eyes narrowed, and he stared thoughtfully at nothing.

"Captain," I said, framing something I had wanted to say for a long time. "What are we doing here?"

Captain Jennings gave me a shrewd look. "We are here to escort those two U-boats up to Virginia," he said. "You know that."

"Yes, sir," I said.

"And? Is there something on your mind, Seaman?"

"Well, sir, if you don't mind me saying so, sir," I said, "and meaning no disrespect, sir, that sounds like bullshit. Sir."

He didn't shout me down or throw me out. He didn't even glare. But his right eyebrow raised in mildly quizzical surprise.

"Is that right?" he said.

"Sir, yes sir, if you don't mind me saying so, sir."

"At ease, Jerzy," he said, fishing a cigarette packet from his breast pocket. "Smoke?"

"No, sir. Thank you, sir," I said, still a little stiff.

He lit up and took a long, slow drag, exhaled and considered the smoke, as if he were trying to read what he would say next in its gunmetal grayness.

"You are right, to a point," he said. "Though I could have you up for insubordination for saying so. Our official mission remains to escort the U-boats stateside, but the paperwork hasn't cleared yet."

"We came anyway," I said.

"We're a little early," he conceded.

"Giving us time to do what?" I asked.

"Well, now," he mused aloud. "That seems to be the question."

"Is this strictly a Navy mission?" I asked, emboldened by his confessional manner.

"Escorting the U-boats is a navy mission, yes," he said. "But there are other objectives in play which are best addressed by other elements of the government and armed forces."

"Such as?"

"Have you ever heard of the National Intelligence Authority?" he asked.

I shook my head.

"No," he said. "It didn't exist last year. What about MI6? The British intelligence gathering service?"

Again I shook my head.

"Spies, Jerzy," said Jennings. "It's the beginning of a new world order. President Truman was impressed by what the British commandos accomplished in what they were calling 'covert warfare' against the Nazis. And he was, to say the least, dismayed by what happened at Pearl Harbor. By what we didn't see coming. Now we have the Soviets to deal with . . . So resources are being diverted, agencies created, so that we'll be able to fight the coming intelligence and information wars."

I blinked at him.

"Intelligence?" I repeated, unsure of how he was using the word.

"Secrecy," he said. "Not battles and uniforms and flags. People who watch. Who listen. Who mislead the enemy . . ."

"And you work for one of these agencies?" I asked.

"You know what we learned from Pearl Harbor?" he said, ignoring my question. "The same thing the Italians learned from Taranto in 1940. The same lesson taught by every Kamikaze attack that sent one of our ships to the bottom of the ocean. We learned that the days of the Navy are gone. Ernie King might tell you different, but the days of wars—nations—being won and lost by ships have passed. We now live in the age of the air power. One airplane, cheaply made, and flown by a single pilot can destroy a state-of-the-art battleship and everyone on board. One airplane, carrying an atomic bomb, can end a war. And I'm a career Navy man. I wish I didn't have to admit the Navy is finished, but I do."

I said nothing. His voice was level, but it was taking an effort to keep it so.

"A version of the world is passing away," he said, "and a new one will take its place."

"So this . . . National Intelligence Authority," I said. "You work for them?"

"As long as it doesn't run contrary to my Naval duties," he admitted, "yes. Unofficially."

I frowned, unsure what to do with this new information.

"I'm still the captain of this vessel," he said, "until my superiors decide there's a conflict of interest in my being associated with both entities."

"Which superiors?" I asked, tartly. I could not help feeling betrayed. I had joined the Navy because of him, and all the time, he had been taking orders from someone else.

"As I said, there is, as yet, no conflict of interest," he said it firmly, but relented a little when he saw my face. "I'm sorry if you feel misled, Jerzy. This is all confidential, and I must ask you to keep it that way. My concern here is that prominent Nazis, officers, engineers—and possibly some of their most dangerous equipment—escaped the fall of Berlin. Some of what was salvaged may be here. And some of these men may feel their defeat is only temporary."

"What could they have brought that you are so worried about?" I shot back. "The war is over."

"The battles are over," he said. "But if you're fighting a war of minds and hearts, it's never truly over. And if you no longer need those tanks and thousands of uniformed soldiers . . ."

"How are you going to win a war without soldiers?" I asked.

"Same way we forced a surrender from the Japanese," he said, grimly. "With weapons so appalling that no one will fight against them."

For a second I just gaped at him.

"You think the Nazis were building an A-bomb at Wenceslas?" I said.

"It would fit Kammler's profile," he said. "The technology was clearly already under development. We don't know how far along they were, or what they may have been able to build. But imagine if they had one. We dropped ours from bombers. But they already had rockets that flew hundreds of miles—the V2s the Nazis fired at London, a program that fell under Kammler's control. Imagine those rockets, equipped with nuclear warheads. You got that image in your head?"

"Yes, sir."

"Good. Keep it there while you consider your answer to my next question. How would you like to be a secret agent?"

I did not hesitate. "What do you need to me to do?" I said.

28

WILFRIED DEBROUWER
Belgium, November 29, 1989 to March 30, 1990

T BEGAN IN NOVEMBER NEAR LIEGE, A LARGELY FRENCH-speaking city in Wallonia. The medieval town-turned-modern steel producer sits close to the Dutch and German borders where the rivers Meuse and Ourthe meet. It is, depending on how you calculate such things, the third- or fourth-largest city in Belgium. It fell to the Germans during both World Wars, and was pummeled by V1 and V2 missile strikes between its liberation by the Allies and the final Nazi collapse. Forty-five years later, its people turned their eyes to the night sky once more, this time in wonder and disbelief.

Twelve miles to the east of Liege, across low, rolling country on the road between Eupen and Kettenis, a pair of policeman were on routine patrol when they observed what seemed to be a large triangular object with white lights at its corners and a red light in the center moving slowly over a field, perhaps two hundred meters from the road, at an altitude of a little more than that. As they watched, the shape seemed to change direction, moving directly overhead and on to the village of Eupen, where it hovered in almost complete silence over the Lac de la Gileppe dam for the better part of an hour, before heading southwest towards Baelen-Spa, and then quickly out of sight.

The police officers called the sighting in and, since their report was corroborated by other policeman and the general public, the air force base at Bierset was alerted. Having already detected the object on radar, an AWACS aircraft was dispatched to investigate, coming into the area from Gelsenkirchen. Sightings continued to come in for the next two hours, from locations throughout the Liege region and from border towns in Holland and Germany. Thirty groups of witnesses and three separate police patrols claimed to observe the lights in the sky. Later, the original two officers reported seeing a considerably larger triangle rise up from behind some trees and ascend quickly before moving in the direction of the road at about fifty miles an hour.

This was how it began.

It continued through the ensuing weeks and months, culminating on the thirtieth of March, the following year, when, approaching midnight, local police stations in Wavre near Brussels were flooded with calls reporting strange lights in the sky that seemed to indicate a triangular object. The police reported the sightings to the Glons radar station, part of the NATO defense group, which confirmed that they were reading an object apparently cruising at about three thousand meters. The Glons readings were further confirmed by the air base at Semmerzake. These were the last days of the Soviet Union, only weeks after the non-Russian states of Moldova and Lithuania had voted to throw the Communists out of their governments, acts to which the Soviet army responded with a military and economic blockade, allegedly to protect the rights of ethnic Russians like those killed earlier in the year in Azerbaijan. It was only a few months since the Berlin wall had been torn down, and Western Europe was watching closely for signs of old-school Soviets attempting a counter-coup that might have included smash-and-grab military actions.

Fearing a hostile incursion, and detecting no identifying transponder signal from what looked like a slow moving aircraft, Belgian Air Force Colonel Wilfried DeBrouwer scrambled two Belgian F-16 fighters stationed at Brevocom. The pilots of these planes, guided by the Glons radar, were unable to make visual contact with the triangles, but their instruments showed the presence of an unidentifiable mass moving at speed through the sky. They attempted to lock their chase radar onto the target, but when their instruments indicated a successful target acquisition permitting the deployment of missiles, the target dropped precipitously, disabling the weapons lock.

The object then moved erratically, seeming to take evasive action each time the fighters attempted to lock on, moving at speeds in excess of fifteen hundred kilometers an hour, in ways that would produce unendurable G-forces on the pilot of a conventional aircraft. The object moved to the skies above Brussels, changing direction at speeds the F-16s couldn't begin to match, appearing and disappearing from radar in ways suggesting either a failure of the F-16s' onboard systems, or else it had dropped too low to be detected, vanishing in the lights of the city below. To Colonel DeBrouwer, the movement seemed deliberate, because at such low altitudes, the density of the air limited the F-16s to speeds under 1300 KPH. Three times, the cat-and-mouse game played out over the next seventy-five minutes, the object diving to safety just as the fighters were about to complete their weapons lock. Numerous witnesses on the ground, including police officers, reported watching the whole encounter, though the object generated no supersonic boom, and no windows were blown out, as would be expected at that altitude and velocity, suggesting some form of propulsion that defied conventional analysis.

After the events of that night, the data accumulated by the Belgian Air Force was, for the first time, shared with scientists and research groups who attempted to explain what had happened with a range of possible scenarios. Could the object have been some form of balloon? No, said the expert witnesses. The meteorological conditions had been thoroughly analyzed and could in no way account for the movement of the object. They asked if it could it have been a meteor or piece of falling space junk, but were told that the trajectory of such things did not fall into accord with the unidentified object, whose recorded radar signature indicated numerous changes of directions as it zigzagged across the sky. Neither could the object have been the undocumented incursion of a known stealth aircraft such as an F-117, due to the absence of the sonic boom, and the moments when the object flew at no more than 40 KPH, more than 200 KPH slower than the stealth fighter's minimum operating velocity. Moreover, the military attaché to the American embassy expressly denied that any such US stealth aircraft had been stationed in Belgium or had operated in its airspace. Several prominent scientists issued outlandish statements saying that the only logical conclusion was that the object was of extra-terrestrial origin.

Countless pictures and videos were shot in the course of the various events over Belgium, some of them generating impressive images of triangular craft with lights at the corners, some suggesting infrared beams. Many were too small or blurred to present useful detail, and those that did were accused of fakery, though some remain compelling to this day, at least to believers. Whatever actually happened, the Belgian triangle wave remains one of the most witnessed and best-documented UFO sightings in human history. Its true nature remains a mystery.

29

ALAN
Dreamland, Nevada

IT WAS TWO DAYS BEFORE ALAN SET FOOT IN THE LOCUST again. No explanation was offered for the delay. He found that for all his existential angst about the nature of the craft, he wanted nothing more than to be in it again, to explore its strange capabilities, and to test his own. He worried that the powers that be were having serious doubts about his continuation in the program.

That was his new greatest fear. That he'd flunk out. That he'd never be allowed up there again.

Forty-eight hours after his beer with Morat at the Little A'Le Inn, there was a knock at the door of his room. An orderly he didn't recognize saluted, a flight suit folded in his arms.

"Time to suit up, Major," he said without preamble. "I'll wait."

Alan closed the door and dressed, splashing water on his face and staring hard at himself in the bathroom mirror. He looked pale in spite of his spell in the desert. Too much time indoors. He looked tired too, and there had been a slight quiver in his fingers when he zipped up the suit. That would not do. Alan had been shown the future the last time he'd stepped into that strange black triangle. He'd seen it in all its dazzling glory and wonder, and he'd flinched, at least at first. Morat and Hatcher had seen it, that mental twitch that said I don't think I'm ready for this. He would not do that again.

The decision hardened his blue-green eyes.

He splashed a little more of the cool tap water on his face, toweled himself dry and left his room, nodding curtly to the orderly as if he were being given a ride to the airport.

He rode alone in the blacked-out bus during the twenty-minute ride to Papoose Lake. The ride took longer than he thought, and he couldn't help worrying. Was he not going to fly tonight? Was he to be quizzed or reprimanded first? Surely if he was being thrown out, disciplined, or even just subjected to more of those maddening tests, they wouldn't have made him suit up first.

The bus stopped and Alan got out. They were close to the cliffs. He inhaled the early evening air and gazed off over the dry lakebed, his flight helmet dangling from his right hand. It would be another clear Nevada night. Cloudless. A good night for flying . . . The back of his neck prickled with the thrill of hope.

He turned towards the outcrop concealing the door into the cliff face, but the orderly said, "This way, Major," and walked along the cliff face itself towards, as far as Alan could see, nothing. Alan went with him, the two men silent as the daylight faded in the west and the rocks cast their long shadows across the desert floor. They walked a hundred and fifty yards, and then the orderly stopped and pointed back to the mountain ridge they had just driven around on the bus.

"Do you see that peak right there, sir?" said the orderly. "The highest one?"

"Yes," said Alan, thinking that this was an odd time for a lesson on local geology.

"I respectfully invite you to fix your eyes on it."

"What?" Alan said, half turning to face the man.

"Please?"

Alan did so. In his peripheral vision, he saw the orderly reach to the cliff wall. There was a click, a hum, and a long, drawn-out hiss.

"You may look," said the orderly.

Alan turned back to him, irritated at being treated this way. His annoyance instantly vanished. Where the cliff wall had been, there was an open hangar, lit with the flat greenish light of florescent strips hung from a high ceiling and the harder, blue-white spotlights angled from above the hangar door into the great space in the cliff side. The floor was clean smooth concrete, the walls immaculately white, and the concealed room was perhaps two hundred feet across and fifty feet deep. Doors at either end suggested that there were perhaps similar chambers on either side of it.

Four Locusts sat on the polished concrete, balanced on tall, spindly landing gear ending in little wheels. Morat, dressed in his flight suit and cradling his helmet in the crook of one arm, stood beside one of them, talking to three men in dark blue overalls and a man in a suit with a narrow, old-fashioned black tie and horn-rimmed glasses. One of the men in overalls glanced over his shoulder, considered Alan for a second, then looked away. No one spoke to him until Morat turned.

"Major," he said, nodding. "Ready?"

"When you are," said Alan, trying to sound casual. One of the engineers turned and gave him a slightly quizzical look as if he had said something funny, or weird, or . . . something, then turned away. The man in the suit was considering a clipboard as if Alan wasn't there, then he nodded, and one of the Locusts was hitched to an electric cart for towing outside.

"I have to warn you, Major," Morat said. "What we are about to do may test your nerves."

"I'm sure I can handle it," he said, sounding more confident than he felt. It was difficult to imagine what would be more unsettling, more alarming, more thrilling than last time.

He found out soon enough. They went through the same preflight checklist and guided the Locust out and into a steady, silent hover over Groom Lake as the sun went down.

"Now," said Morat, "let's get some miles under your belt."

"Where to?" said Alan, excitement crackling within him like electricity.

"East," Morat answered. "We want to stay in the dark. Watch this gauge here for indications of the sun's position in your current location and any destination coordinates you program in. This map screen will home in on any location in the world. Once input, this dialog box here will let you know your flight route, any necessary changes to cabin pressure, and any potential interferences or risks."

"Including passing through foreign air space?"

"We're off the grid up here, Alan. If we can get there, the high ground is ours. There's not a conventional fighter flying for any nation in the world that can catch us. Most of them don't have the equipment required to even see us if we don't want them to."

"Okay," said Alan, registering the word *conventional* and trying not to give away the kid-in-a-candy-store exhilaration he was feeling. "What do you think? Boston? New York?"

"We can come back that way. But the UK won't see sunrise for another half-hour or so. Let's check it out."

Alan's hesitation was only momentary. He tapped London on the world map, leaving the altitude, speed and other navigational concerns at their default settings.

He gave Morat a look, and the other man nodded. They were both still wearing the visors of their helmets up. Alan assumed that the cockpit had automatically pressurized, though in ways more efficient and unobtrusive than on any aircraft he had ever been on.

He began moving the Locust manually, guiding it with the toggle controls on his arm rest, increasing the speed to 600 knots, then 850, turning into the craft's new direction as it sped across the dark sky. He saw their movement on the consoles and the windows, but it felt like they were sitting in someone's oddly decorated living room, albeit one that throbbed slightly, like they were over a laundry room.

After a couple of minutes, he tried the preset coordinates, hitting the auto-guidance engagement under Morat's watchful eye. The ship seemed to shimmer slightly, and for a moment the speed gauge registered an astonishing speed: 1200 knots, then 2,000, then 4,000. The sensors indicating the view below winked out, and the stars Alan could see through the cockpit canopy seemed to move. He checked the map, and saw their breathtaking trajectory, arrowing out over the Virginia shore and the featureless waters of the Atlantic.

Alan stared at the readouts around him. According to the speed gauge they were doing something in the vicinity of Mach 7, which—even without the complete lack of G- force trying to peel the skin and muscle from his face—was impossible. Nothing could go that fast.

Morat watched him, reading his eyes. Alan decided to shift focus.

"What's this display?" he said.

"Weapons systems. I thought you'd studied them."

"In a classroom," said Alan. "Lasers. Kind of different up here in the Millennium Falcon."

"The what?" asked Morat.

"Seriously?" said Alan. "*Star Wars*?"

"Oh," said Morat. "Don't think I ever saw it."

"Them."

"There's more than one?"

"You need to get out more," said Alan.

"Speaking of which," said Morat, "mind if we give London a miss? The pubs will be closed, and it's too early for the great British breakfast."

"Sure," said Alan. "What had you in mind?"

"Wiltshire," said Morat, tapping a point on his map some ways west of the capital.

Alan had never heard of it.

"What's there?" he asked.

"Quiet," said Morat, and for a second Alan wasn't sure if the word was a demand or an answer to his question.

They had been traveling, according to the internal chronometers and readouts—assuming they could be trusted—for forty-seven minutes, when the craft suddenly slowed to a drifting, hovering halt.

"Bring her below the cloud deck," said Morat.

Alan did so, dropping the Locust to a thousand feet, finding the canopy overhead spotted and streaked with rain.

"England," said Morat. "Typically cold and miserable."

It could be just a hose or showerhead, thought Alan madly. *Maybe we never left the hangar . . .*

"Check this out," said Morat, nodding to one of the lower windows. Alan looked. Through the misty, rain-streaked darkness, he saw what he took to be hills rolling out below them, gray in the darkness save where a single pale shape seemed to leap across the turf. It looked like it had been sketched from above by a confident painter, a few disconnected flicks of his brush capturing—what? A deer? No. A horse.

"What the hell?" said Alan, staring.

"The Uffington White Horse," said Morat. "Cut into the chalk hillside a few thousand years ago. Like a sign post."

"To what?" asked Alan, all his skepticism momentarily forgotten.

Morat shrugged.

"Stonehenge is that way," he said, gesturing vaguely. "But I don't like to go there. Too many gawkers at all hours."

"Stonehenge?" said Alan. "Are you serious?"

"Of course."

"Let's go."

Morat started to shake his head, but he saw the seriousness in Alan's face and knew that this was about more than sightseeing.

"Suit yourself," said Morat, frowning. "It's less than forty miles. You can drive."

Alan ignored the deliberate incongruity of that last word, and maneuvered the Locust north, tracking their location on the scrolling map as he did so, using a ribbon of road—marked on the map as the A346—to guide them at an easy 120 knots per hour. As they got close, Morat shifted in his seat.

"Turn the lights off," he said. "This is farm country. Even without sky-watching tourists, people are up at all hours."

Alan did so, slowing the craft, and dropping it to two hundred feet.

"Where can we set down?" he asked.

"We're not landing!" said Morat. For the first time since Alan had met him, he looked out of his element, anxious.

"Sure we are," said Alan, his gaze fixed on the map screen which he had toggled to show what the ship's sensors actually saw: a video feed marked with spots of glowing color overlaid with heat-sensors not unlike weapons targeting systems Alan had used many times. "This part of the field looks pretty level."

"If anyone sees us here . . ."

"There's no one around," said Alan, gazing out over the circle of standing stones. "Look for yourself."

"There's a perimeter rail around the walkway," said Morat. He sounded petulant as well as uncertain.

"Then I'll land inside it," said Alan. He wouldn't really. But he felt in control for the first time in weeks and was taking a vindictive delight in watching Morat squirm. "Don't worry. I won't scratch the paintwork."

"Or destroy a world heritage site."

"That either," said Alan. "If I can land a Harrier on a carrier, I think I can do this."

"I don't think that's the issue," said Morat. "Come on, Alan. Don't make me override your controls."

The radio came to life.

"Come in, Phoenix, this is flight control. Over."

"There goes our shore leave," said Alan with a sigh. The relief on Morat's face was unmistakable. "Phoenix here, flight control. What can I do for you?"

"Location and altitude looking strange to us, Phoenix. Time to return to base."

"Roger that, flight control," said Alan, punching the controls and shooting Morat a grin. "Be right there."

30

JENNIFER
London

ENNIFER'S EYES MOVED FROM THE INTERPOL ID TO Letrange's—or Chevalier's—handsome face and back.

"So when you accused me of being all cloak and dagger . . ." she began.

"Touché," he said. The word changed him, made him sound French in ways he hadn't before. Jennifer found that she did not know what to say. She'd barely known the man who had called himself Letrange, but she knew the man in front of her—the *agent*—even less.

"You want to tell me what's going on?" she said at last.

"This couldn't have come at a worse time," he said. "Maynard has been under police scrutiny for years: insider

310

trading, smuggling, money laundering, financing hostile groups . . ."

"Terrorists?"

"Indirectly," said Chevalier.

"Why?"

"That's what we've been trying to find out. I was assigned to the task force three years ago and got a seat on the board a year after that."

"How?"

"Contacts, most of them spurious. Payoffs. And the ability to be useful. An international police force can open a lot of doors, get things done."

She didn't know what that meant, and when she looked at him, he shrugged and looked away, not proud of himself, even if he was one of the good guys.

"They were wary of me," he said, "as you so shrewdly observed. I haven't been admitted to every hall of the inner sanctum yet."

"And you're thinking that with my father's data, you might not need to?"

"No," he said quickly. "I'm thinking that if anyone hears you have access to that data, your life won't be worth the price of a pint. I'm trying to verify the scale of the threat. You are sure no one knows you have seen these files?"

"Only you."

He nodded and then, apparently on impulse, said, "Why me?"

"What do you mean?" Jennifer replied, coloring slightly.

"I mean that if you had chosen any of the other men from that boardroom to confide in, you would almost certainly be dead soon after. So why did you choose me?"

Jennifer looked out on Earls Court Road, watching a woman with a pushchair and plastic bags of groceries cautiously crossing the street.

"Something my father said," she replied absently. "And you were kind to me at the meeting."

Under the circumstances, given the risk she had taken, it sounded absurd, but he smiled, apparently pleased, and gave a Gallic shrug of acceptance. It wasn't a great explanation, said the shrug, but it would do.

"So what do you know about SWEEP?" asked Jennifer, keen to push past the moment.

"Not much, to be honest. It's a very specific network of funding streams tied to various aerospace concerns dotted all over the globe, mainly R&D, but also, we think, operation."

"Operation of what?"

"I was hoping you could tell me."

"Me?" Jennifer exclaimed. "Why would I know anything about it? I just found out it existed."

"You were around your father a lot growing up, Miss Quinn. Did you never see or hear anything that might connect him to this kind of thing?"

"What kind of thing? Aerospace? You mean rockets and stuff? No."

"Anything of that sort. Aircraft development, perhaps."

She shook her head, but even as she did so something tugged at the edge of her memory, something old and indistinct from a long time ago. She was quite small. It was night and she was standing outside her father's office, cold in her nightdress, looking through the crack of the door. She didn't want to bother him when he was busy.

"What?" asked Chevalier. "You looked miles away."

"Sorry," she said. "Nothing." The half memory had unsettled her for reasons she couldn't recall and she wanted to change the subject. "What do we do now?"

"I talk to my superiors and we get you somewhere safe," said Chevalier. "If these men find out you are about to expose them, you'd have no more than an hour. Their resources are as limitless as their ruthlessness. Give me a moment."

She blinked again. The situation felt surreal, like something out of a movie.

"Okay," she said.

Minutes later, Jennifer was in the passenger seat of Chevalier's black BMW, speeding out of central London westbound on the M4, Taylor Swift playing on the stereo. The Interpol agent had said very little since shepherding her to the car, his manner now all business. As they left the pub, he'd taken her arm, guiding her step by step, his eyes flashing around the street, alert and watchful as a president's security detail. It should have made her feel safe, but it didn't. She felt like a target.

First time I've been alone with a man close to my age in weeks and he's my bodyguard.

"Was my father involved?" she asked him as they drove past Chiswick and left the river behind. "In the money laundering and the rest of it, I mean?"

Chevalier gave her a swift sidelong glance then returned his eyes to the road. "He may not have known the extent of it until recently," he said. "And I think he decided he wanted no further part of it. One of our operatives approached him, but he was . . . suspicious, I guess."

"Did he know about you?"

"I don't think so, but he knew something was going on. I think he was willing to turn. In another few weeks, we would have known for sure."

"But someone got to him first."

"So far as we know, he killed himself. We assumed he wanted out, but didn't dare try to take the rest of them down."

"He didn't kill himself."

"You have evidence for that?"

"Nothing that would stand up in court," said Jennifer sadly, "but I'm sure of it."

Chevalier said nothing. He seemed to be checking his mirrors a lot, and he was certainly the fastest car on the road. He was very calm in the driver's seat, weaving around other vehicles with little more a twist of his wrists. It made him seem efficient, professional. It made her feel the opposite: clumsy, amateurish. Vulnerable.

"Where are we going?" she asked.

"Somewhere safe. Do you have the files with you?"

"Yes."

"And you didn't copy them?"

"Not yet. Should I have?"

"We can make a safety copy," he said.

A pause.

"So this safe place," she began. "Where is it?"

"Near Heathrow," he said. "There's someone I want you to talk to. One of my colleagues, who can look after you. You can't stay with me without blowing my cover. You may have to go to ground for a little while. You can send Deacon a text saying you've been called back to Africa. That will explain your absence. And why no one can reach you."

"How long?"

"Weeks? Months? I'm not sure. But it will be somewhere nice."

That last was added because he sensed her resistance.

Months?

They turned south at a roundabout and headed towards the airport, then left the main road. The area was built up in a desultory, suburban way. There were hedgerows lining the highway, playing fields, a school, and then, as he slowed, across the road to her left, the silos, gantries, and hoppers of a cement works. They turned in and circled around, past industrial trucks, across a paved parking lot, and then down a dusty road that led alongside the works to a sudden opening, where she saw a clutter of silent shacks of weathered scrap wood and corrugated iron. Gravel roared under the tires. The car slowed and stopped, and suddenly, the world was very quiet.

"We are to wait in there," said Chevalier, nodding to one of the storage sheds, as he unsnapped his seat belt. The rusted shed door hung half open. He reached into the back seat for his attaché case, then got out of the car, closing the door behind him with a soft *thunk*.

Jennifer climbed out slowly, thinking hard. The cement works, several hundred yards away, was a snarling, clanking cacophony of sound. The great open space she'd seen flashing in front of them as they drove in was a flooded quarry, steep-sided, the water black, thick, and still.

Suddenly, she didn't like the situation she found herself in.

It was no more than that, a feeling, an impulse, but it hit her hard, and suddenly everything felt wrong. She checked the ignition, but he'd taken the keys. Of course he had. Why wouldn't he? She studied the shed he'd gone into, its turquoise paint stained orange with rust, and she wondered why he hadn't waited for her. He'd been so attentive in the city, but here, it was like he'd wanted to reach the shed before her.

To make sure it was safe?

Or something else. She thought back to the pub, the way he'd feigned bewilderment when she first mentioned SWEEP. *"Is that a thing, or some kind of practice?"* A good dodge. A practiced liar . . .

And then he had produced his Interpol card, and she decided to trust him, which is what she'd wanted to do. Had he guessed as much?

She looked over to the shed.

He hadn't asked her to bring her purse, the handbag that now held the flash drive, tucked into a zippered pouch to the shed. That was odd, wasn't it? If they were meeting someone and the data was vital, wouldn't he want to be sure she had it with her?

But he had asked if she had the files with her, so maybe he just assumed she wasn't an idiot.

Maybe.

She took a step toward the hut, conscious of how alone they were. A plane soared overhead, its engines a thundering bellow that drowned out the steady growl of the cement works.

"Jennifer!"

He called to her from inside the shed. He didn't come to the door and look out. He stayed inside, deep in the shadowy recesses and called to her. It was the first time he had used her first name.

And then she knew.

She knew before she saw him, before the gun with its long suppressor screwed into its barrel came up, and before the muzzle flashed. She knew and she ran.

The silencer didn't do the job she expected it to do. There was no discreet *phut* like in the movies. It was a bang. Anywhere else, it would have drawn attention. He fired again.

She was moving, first instinctively back toward the car, then changing her mind and dashing around the side of the hut so that he would have to come after her if he was to keep shooting.

He did. She knew he would. She broke hard to the right, through a gateway and across another road of baked mud. Behind her, he fired again, and this time she heard the bullet, a thrumming streak through the air, inches from her head. It was followed by a muffled curse.

She was still running, big staggering strides. The road curved up toward the motorway, but the land around it was open and would provide no cover. She risked a look back but could not see him. Then she heard the BMW's engine turn over and the car screech into reverse.

She was already breathless, heart banging against her ribs, though that had more to do with panic than fitness. But even if she could get a hold of herself mentally, her runner's legs couldn't beat out the BMW. She thought wildly about throwing herself in the turgid waters of the quarry and swimming to the other side, but that was stupid. It would just give him time to pick his shot. She ducked where a large field was screened from the cement works by a dense hedge of Hawthorne brambles and low, ancient trees. The thicket was only a few feet deep, though it stretched all around the field. If he saw her before she made it into cover, she was dead.

She leapt the boggy ditch on the other side of the thicket and clawed her way through stinging nettles into the shade of a stunted beech tree, then pressed south through the densest part of the skinny strip of woods, back the way they had driven. Above her, a jet roared. Ignoring the hammering of her heart and the shriek of blood that rang in her ears, she forced herself to think of the purse, thrown ragged and flapping over her shoulder.

Yes, she thought, as the car tore up the gravel road towards the motorway. Her passport would still be inside.

He would soon realize he'd lost her and turn back. If she could keep moving, and stay hidden when he came hunting for her, she might make it to the airport.

It was clear that Chevalier, or Letrange, or whatever the hell his real name was, was no Interpol agent. It was also clear that she wasn't safe where she was. She wasn't safe anywhere in England. Surprisingly, the thought calmed her. She hadn't been comfortable in Chevalier's "protection," but then she hadn't been comfortable in the Maynard boardroom, or even in her father's house. At least now she knew she could trust no one but herself. The idea was comforting.

The BMW came roaring back. She had made it no more than a couple of hundred yards before he'd realized he was on the wrong trail. The narrow copse was as dense as before, the light dim and patchy, and she was as sure as she could be that he couldn't see her from the road unless she moved. She threw herself face down in the bracken, feeling a prickly vine lash her face, knowing she would get up nettled and bruised.

She didn't move.

The car barreled past in a flurry of dust and chippings, then braked hard. For a moment, it idled in the road, and she could almost hear his fury. She stayed exactly where she was, breathing shallowly out of the corner of her mouth, hands tucked in, the red purse concealed beneath her. Then the car was rolling slowly backwards, a soft panther creep that took it twenty or thirty yards past her. Then it stopped.

She waited, her heart rate mounting again as she heard the clunk of the car door. He'd gotten out.

She listened.

She could hear the grumble of the cement works in the distance, and the flat cawing of rooks in the field, but if he was walking toward her, stalking her, looking in her direction, she couldn't say.

Was this how her father had died? Some strange, absurd game of cat and mouse that led to him plummeting from his office balcony? Had he been forced off by a man with a gun? This man?

She closed her eyes and balled her fists.

She heard footsteps on the road, then the car door, and then the BMW executed a rough and hurried three-point turn, ramming its front end into the hawthorn that overhung the ditch. Then he was racing north again, and she was moving south.

After five full minutes, timed on her watch, with no sign of the car, she allowed herself to venture into the field proper so that her progress would be faster. In another four, she'd crossed a road and was running hard across open country toward a far line of hedges. Ten more minutes and she was pushing through a perimeter fence into a nursery, surrounded by ornamental cypresses and Japanese maples in oversized pots. Then there were houses, cut-price generic hotels, and a taxi rank. Ten minutes later, she was walking purposefully through the ticketing area of

Heathrow airport, looking for a restroom where she could clean up, and scanning the departure boards for a suitable destination.

Doesn't really matter, she thought. *So long as it's away from here.*

31

HERMAN SALTZBURG
London

IN A WARM, EXPENSIVELY-PANELED OFFICE IN MAYFAIR, Herman Saltzburg extended his long legs under his desk and smiled a wide, slightly ghoulish smile. For a big man, he carried almost no body fat and gave the impression of being all sinew and bone, which was why the daughter of the late Edward Quinn had dubbed him "The Skeleton Man." He hadn't minded, though he'd thought the child impertinent. He'd always liked the idea of scaring her. The skin of his face, sallow and close to the bone, stretched improbably so that the grin looked like the death's head motif SS officers had once worn on their peaked caps. He didn't mind that either.

But little Jennifer Quinn had become more than impertinent of late and things had come to a head.

"Tell me again," he purred into the phone, his eyes resting on the man sitting silently and patiently across the desk from him.

"There's nothing more to say," said Letrange, made defiant by failure. "She got away."

"That, *Daniel*," said Saltzburg in his most unctuous voice, "is the part I don't seem to be comprehending. That she escaped from you is regrettable, to say the least, given what she apparently suspects, but the fact that you seem to have no notion of where she might have gone is unacceptable."

He said it quietly, without rancor. He didn't need to do more.

"Yes, sir," said Letrange. "If she made it to the airport, I'll be able to find where she went."

"A consummation devoutly to be wished," said Saltzburg. "I suggest you do so. Immediately. Call me back."

He hung up without another word and smiled at his companion, before continuing their interrupted conversation in measured German.

"*Wird es ein probleme sein?*" asked Herr Manning, one of Maynard's other board members.

"No, it won't be a problem," said Saltzburg. "You've seen Miss Quinn's tenacity, first hand, but you've also seen her blundering cluelessness. This is not her world. *We* are not. She will scurry about, turning over the wrong stones, until we stub her out like a spent cigar. Though I doubt she will unearth anything particularly sensitive, it remains unclear how much she knows. Or remembers."

"That was very long ago, surely," said Manning. "You can't think she recalls that?"

"I had a hobby-horse when I was four," said Saltzburg. "It was white with blue glass eyes and an improbably orange mane. I rode it everywhere, though I had no recollection of it until some workmen stumbled upon it while clearing out a lumber room a few years ago. As soon as I saw it, I was transported back to a very particular day when I saw my father beating my mother for something involving the gardener. My mother was, I knew even then, not some-one to be trusted. But the incident came back to me with extraordinary clarity. Which cane he used. The sprinkle of blood on the hearth where she fell. It was really quite remarkable."

He said this with the same eerie and unflinching smile, so that even Manning, who was used to him, looked momentarily unnerved.

"The mind is a curious thing," Saltzburg concluded. "You never know what discarded details might float to the surface."

His phone rang. Letrange again.

"Well?" Saltzburg demanded.

"Washington, DC," said Letrange. "She tried to throw us off track by buying a ticket to Jamaica on her credit card, but then paying cash to change the destination. Fortunately our people got into the passenger manifest."

"Ah," said Saltzburg, satisfied. "Then all may be dealt with expeditiously. We have some good people in the United States, and they are already alerted because of the so-called *web journalist*, Timika Mars."

"You need me to go after her?" asked Letrange. "I have, as you know, other duties."

"Indeed," Saltzburg replied. "And I only hope that you perform those with greater professionalism. But no. Leave her alone for now. Other operatives will tidy up your mess. But . . . wait one moment."

He pressed the phone to his breast pocket and said to the man opposite him,

"Herr Manning, how would you feel about a journey across the Atlantic?"

Manning shrugged and nodded.

"Excellent," said Saltzburg. He spoke into the phone. "You are in luck, Daniel. Herr Manning and myself will be following in Miss Quinn's blundering wake."

Letrange's half-suppressed gasp of surprise amused Saltzburg, whose skeletal grin spread wider than ever.

"You? You are going yourselves?" said Letrange.

"Things are moving rather more swiftly than I had anticipated," he said. "We would need to go, sooner or later. It may as well be sooner. I would hate not to be on hand to see it all in person."

"Right," said Letrange. "Okay."

"Oh, and Daniel?" said Saltzburg, still beaming at Manning.

"Yes?"

"No more mistakes, yes?" he said. "And do not allow yourself, even for the briefest of moments, to forget where your loyalties lie. That would be most unwise."

The momentary hesitation at the end of the phone before Letrange's babbled "Of course" spoke volumes about the operative's sudden terror. Saltzburg's smile grew even wider.

32

TIMIKA
Pottsville, PA

KATARINA LUNDERGRASS HAD CORNERED TIMIKA IN THE hallway as the younger woman tried to slip out of the retirement home unnoticed.

"You don't give up, do you?" she said, the firmness of her voice and steadiness of her gaze completely belying her age.

"Did you want me to?"

"What does that mean?"

"You sent me to a church full of paper children," said Timika. "I remembered what you said when I first asked you about the people at The Hollows. *Paper people*, you said."

Katarina smiled a little sadly.

"Stupid of me," she said. "An old weakness of mine. I can't resist giving hints just oblique enough to keep me on the windy side of the law."

"Your father was an Operation Paperclip scientist," said Timika.

"Yes," said the old woman simply. "A low-ranking rocket propulsion technician at Kummersdorf. He wasn't a Nazi. Ever. He worked briefly at the Langley Aeronautical Laboratory and a few other places."

"And this is why you are here, all of you? Why? That work is a matter of public record."

"It is," she said. "As the policemen would say, nothing to see here."

"Are you prisoners here?"

She smiled again at that, wide but slightly rueful. "Jerzy came to think so, but no, not really. We are . . . looked after. The government considers it a debt they owe to our fathers."

"It can't be that simple," said Timika, her voice low, her eyes on the end of the hallway where someone less friendly might appear at any moment. "There's too much secrecy."

"Look," said Katarina with a shrug, "some of what our fathers worked on was classified. Some of it is still considered sensitive. My father worked on rockets. Some of that helped put men into space, but it was also tied to missile systems. He consulted at Los Alamos in the late forties. People don't want to be reminded that the US had German specialists working on their nuclear weapons right after the war. It's . . ." she searched for the word. "*Ungehörig.* Unseemly."

"But everyone already knows that," Timika persisted. "There's got to be more to it. Ms. Lundergrass, I think you liked Jerzy a lot. Maybe you were in love with him. He wanted to tell me about his past, and someone killed him for it. There must be something you can tell me, something that would help me figure out where to look next. For his sake."

For a long moment the old woman just looked at her. Then someone called her name from the kitchen.

"Be right there!" she sang back, her eyes never leaving Timika's.

"Please," said Timika. "Someone came after me, shot at me. Probably the same person who killed Jerzy."

"Finding out why won't save you," said Katarina.

"It might," said Timika. "And if it doesn't, at least I'll die knowing what I got involved in."

Katarina's eyes narrowed. "You think that will be a consolation?" she said. "Knowing something no one wants you to know? It won't. Trust me. It really won't."

Timika frowned.

"I'd like to make that decision for myself," she said.

Katarina considered her. The noises in the kitchen were getting louder, closer.

"There is a second-story window at the back of The Hollows, under a copper cupola. And a ladder by the greenhouse, down the side of the house. The window will

329

be open at eleven o' clock tonight. I will give you thirty minutes."

TIMIKA LEFT THE RETIREMENT HOME THE WAY SHE'D COME and drove away from town, stopping to eat at the second exit advertising food and gas. She bought both, then considered her remaining funds. She couldn't live off the rent money she had withdrawn in New York indefinitely, and daren't try using her credit cards. Most of her family and friends were in New York. She knew no one around here who might help her out. If she abandoned the idea of returning to New York, her closest family was her cousin Tonya, who worked for a museum in Atlanta. Maybe she would head in that direction and see what she could borrow. Depending, of course, on what—if anything—Katarina offered her tonight.

As the terror of the chase receded, she found herself almost forgetting that she was still in real danger, and that there was something out there she needed to find. Maybe, she reasoned as she munched on yet another generic burger, it was all over already. Maybe she should get on with her life. But what had her life been, to this point, if it wasn't chasing after truth amongst the misdirection and clutter, the wishful thinking and the outright lies of the contemporary world? And maybe, just maybe, she was chasing the story of her career. Not for *Debunktion*, but for *Time Magazine* or *Newsweek*. This might be what her professional life—and her bank account—needed, a jumpstart.

She called Dion but he didn't pick up. She kept her message short and unspecific. She'd be back soon but didn't know when. She missed him. After she hung up and turned off her phone, she wondered a little about that last remark. She missed a lot of things about her life in New York, including him, but did she miss him the way lovers were supposed to, like she might miss a part of herself, a constant, burning absence that made her feel somehow incomplete? It had never occurred to her to share what she was doing with him, not because she was being secretive, but because she knew how his eyes would glaze over, how he would tune her out and make noises into the phone while his eyes strayed to the muted basketball game on the TV, or the *Call of Duty* game he was playing on the Xbox.

She shook her head. This wasn't the time to dwell on such things. She considered calling her cousin Tonya, just to take her mind off it all and to prime the pump, as it were, in case she needed to recruit her help, but Atlanta was far away. Surely, it wouldn't come to that.

She parked under the scrawny, neglected trees of a strip mall, and sat listening to Motown on an oldies station as the sun started to set. Then she turned the key and set off for The Hollows, humming along to Marvin Gaye's "What's Going On?"

Seems appropriate, she thought, as the weary Corolla nosed its way into the gathering night.

She drove past The Hollows' entry gate, trying to find her way around to the fence she had scaled on her way out. It wasn't easy in the dark. She couldn't help thinking that the lack of street lighting around the old house was deliberate. There would be cameras, she imagined. Whether there was night vision or thermal imaging equipment depended on just how protective the government wanted to be about keeping any foxes out of their geriatric hen house. Assuming it was the government. Assuming Katarina hadn't spun a pack of lies to lure Timika to who knew what . . .

Get on with it, she told herself.

There would be time to agonize over what it all meant later.

Very existential.

She shook herself. All this solitude and driving was making her crazy. She checked her watch and parked on the shoulder, tucking one fender into a screen of densely packed cedar. She wondered if she needed a gun, but had no idea how she would have gone about acquiring one here. In New York, she knew exactly where she would have gone. Then again, if she needed to go directly to the cops, she didn't want a sketchy handgun receipt and a glove box full of ammo complicating the conversation.

And besides, she thought as she began the slow walk along the dark and narrow road to The Hollows, she didn't like guns. Dion had one, but she insisted he keep it locked up at all times. It made her nervous. She could always tell when he was carrying it. It gave him a swaggering confidence she didn't like.

The black outlines of the trees ahead parted for a second, and she saw the steep gables of The Hollows, set back from the road. Timika checked the position of the crescent moon to get her bearings and pushed along until she found the spot in the fence where she had clambered over from the other side. If a car came by, she would be conspicuous.

And climbing the fence was easier said than done. She'd gotten out by shinnying up a tree, but there was no such vegetation on this side. She could just about reach the top of the fence when she stood on her tiptoes, but she didn't have the arm strength to haul herself up and the fence provided no obliging crevices in which she might wedge a shoe for leverage.

She tried a standing leap but succeeded only in bashing her knees before dropping into a ditch. She was suddenly struck by a memory she hadn't recalled in years: climbing those damned ropes in high school gym while the teacher, Ms. Keyton, smirked at her and told her she might want to go easy on the cheeseburgers.

Good thing she didn't see what I had for dinner, Timika thought, scowling at the fence in the darkness. She cursed under her breath and looked around for an object she might use as a step. Something lay in the ditch, to her left. She picked her way toward it and found a section of sawn-off telephone pole, about three feet long. She tried to pick it up, feeling the wet coldness underneath it when she slid her hands around it. It was surprisingly heavy. She flipped it around and rolled it to where the fence was most accessible, pushing it with her feet and wheezing slightly, muttering with each shove:

"I. Was. Not. Built. To. Be. A. Spy."

She propped it up against the fence, took a moment to get her breath back and then climbed up with one foot, boosting herself up. As she adjusted her weight, the fragment of telephone pole pushed out from under her and rolled into the ditch, but she had her elbows on the top railing and, with a struggle, was able to hoist her way up. With another concerted effort, she climbed up and over.

It wasn't a graceful landing, but she did herself no serious injury. She was in.

You see that, Ms. Keyton, you sanctimonious crone? You owe me a burger.

The woods were dense. Finally the house rose into view. Even then, it was difficult to make out exactly where she was because there were no lights on. Everyone, it seemed, had turned in for the night.

Old people, she thought.

She skulked her way to the edge by the golf course and approached the house from the side, breaking into a low trot as she crossed the open space leading to the greenhouse. The ladder rested on a pair of hooks fastened into the wall. She was relieved to find it was made of lightweight aluminum. One of the old wooden kind would have been impossible to lift. She got it balanced and carried it toward the house, eying the copper cupola Katarina had told her about. The window below it was closed.

Another wild goose chase?

Or worse?

She consulted her watch. Ten fifty-eight. She'd made good time. As she watched, the window was pushed discreetly open an inch and a half. There was no sign of the hand that did it. This was no time for hesitation.

In for a penny, her grandmother used to say, *in for a pound.*

She lifted the end of the ladder, raised it above her head like a weightlifter switching grips, and walked under it, moving down the rungs till the ladder was vertical. With a series of little steps, her gaze up so that the ladder wouldn't overbalance, she walked it to within a few feet of the wall and lowered the top of the ladder against the house. It made a slight clatter on contact, but that couldn't be helped. She waited. No one seemed to have heard.

She began to climb, slowly, carefully, quietly, feeling the ladder shift and groan slightly under her weight, so that for a second, she stopped, her heart in her throat.

She heard nothing.

Timika pressed on, rung by rung and hand over hand, staring fixedly up at her goal, then pulled the window open, slowly, quietly, slid her head under it and pushed it wider with her back and shoulders.

As with the dismount from the fence, there was no elegant way to finish her entrance, and she wound up half walking on her hands across the carpet until her feet fell in after her.

"At least I'm not wearing a dress," she muttered as she got upright and flopped heavily into a wingback armchair.

Katarina Lundergrass turned on her bedside lamp and pulled the heavy drapes closed. She was wearing a flannel nightgown under a heavy bathrobe, belted with a silk sash, and looked ghostly in the thin light. She was unsmiling, but she was also alone and, as far as Timika could see, unarmed.

"So," Timika hissed. "What in God's name do you have to tell me that makes all of that worth it?"

"Not to tell," said the old woman. "To show."

She opened a drawer in the cabinet by her bed, reached into the back, and drew out what looked like a cloth package. She unwrapped it carefully, lovingly, revealing a patch of silvery metal, about four inches long and diamond shaped, though the edges were ragged and crumpled. It glowed softly in the lamplight, so that Timika could make out odd symbols etched—or rather polished—into the dull surface.

"What is that?" asked Timika.

"Here," said Katarina, scrunching it up like a candy wrapper. "Feel it."

Timika reached out, palm up. Katarina lay the little screw of foil on it, but as soon as she let go, it sprang open again, showing not a single crease or fold. Timika stared at it, caught up in a sudden unexpected sense of strangeness. The metal felt odd, light and pliable but strong. It was also slightly warm. As she held it, she thought the strange symbols glowed faintly, as if catching some distant firelight.

"See?" said Katarina, reaching out, and sweeping one gnarled finger along the length of the metal. The touch seemed to bring the metal to life in Timika's hands. It blushed a cool blue color that cast shadows around the room. Timika gasped and almost dropped it, as if it were too hot to hold.

It wasn't. But it felt curiously charged, as if it somehow contained something of Katarina's energy, or her own.

"What the hell is this?" Timika whispered. "Where did you get it?"

"My father gave it to me," Katarina said. "A souvenir."

"Of something he built?"

The old woman shook her head. Her hair, which had been pinned back before, now hung long and white, almost to her waist. In the strange blue glow of the metal, it shone like a halo.

"He didn't build it," she said. "He found it."

"When? Where?"

"I told you he worked in Los Alamos, in New Mexico, in the forties, yes?"

Timika nodded, barely able to take her eyes off the pulsing scrap of metal.

"He was called in to examine some materials," she said, smiling wistfully at the memory. "It was all very hush-hush, and he really shouldn't have shown it to me, let alone brought a piece of it from the facility, but he knew I would love it. I've kept it ever since. My secret. My little piece of the past. Apart from Jerzy, you are the only person I've ever shown it to."

"And it came from Los Alamos?" Timika pressed, feeling the warmth ripple around the metal fragment as if blood surged within it.

Like it's alive.

"No," said Katarina. "He was called over from Los Alamos. It was July 8, 1947. I remember him getting the call, and the two of us driving out in the middle of the night. 'Get dressed, little Katy,' he said. 'We have to go out.'"

She looked suddenly sad, wistful, the memory stirring something complicated that had more to do with her father than with the scrap of metal they were talking about.

"Where did you go?" asked Timika.

"What?" said Katarina, coming back to the moment with an effort.

"The two of you drove out at night and came back with this," said Timika, patiently, holding the metal fragment up. "Where did you go?"

Katarina looked up from the metal, her face mildly surprised, unearthly in the shifting blue glow coming from Timika's hands.

"Oh, I assumed you knew that," she said. "It came from Roswell."

JERZY
La Plata, Argentina, October 1946

I**T WAS FOUR DAYS SINCE THE** *USS KITCHENER* **HAD ARRIVED**
in Argentine waters. The Captain had met with the various officials and diplomats, and it was two days since
he told me of his dual loyalties to the Navy and to this
new "intelligence" service. I had not spoken to him since
then, and had said nothing of my conversation with him
to anyone else.

Not that anyone cared. The crew had been given shore
leave, released to the bars and dance halls of Buenos Aires,
and none of my shipmates were in any great hurry to get
back to open water. I stayed onboard, reading a collection of speeches from Shakespeare and enjoying the rare

silence of the crew quarters. No one—so far as I knew—had guessed that I was younger than I claimed to be, but at times like this, with the rest of the crew hankering after liquor and women, I felt like a child.

My English was much improved now, but old books—Dickens, say—still gave me difficulties from time to time, and the Shakespeare was especially hard, since many of the words were not in the dictionary I kept at hand. When I heard movement on the gangway, my first impulse was to ask a question without even looking up from the pages in my hand.

"What does *interred* mean?" I called out. "*The evil that men do lives after them. The good is oft interred with their bones.*"

"Buried," said the Captain's voice.

I swung down from my bunk and stood at attention.

"At ease, Seaman," said Captain Jennings. He considered the empty berths. "Just you?"

"Everyone went to town," I said.

"Not you though?" he said.

I raised the book in explanation and he smiled.

"*Julius Caesar*, eh?" he said, peering at the text.

"Yes, sir."

"Treachery and ambition," he summarized. "Don't you get enough of that onboard?"

"No one has been stabbed to death," I said. "Though if they weren't able to get ashore . . ."

"Indeed," said Jennings. "Which is what I wanted to speak to you about."

"Sir?"

"I wonder if you would go inland for me. Let's call it 'recon.'"

"Of what?"

"Not what," he qualified. "Who."

"The SS officer," I said. "Kammler?"

"I want to know where they went," he replied. "Our diplomatic friends had some leads, but Perón and his government aren't saying anything. You're going to have to poke around a bit."

"I don't speak Spanish."

"You won't be alone. One of the diplomats from the meeting the other day—Hartsfeld, the translator—will be with you, and I'm going to assign another crewman, Petty Officer Belasco. Hartsfeld will supply a local driver, so language won't be a problem."

"A driver? Are we going far?" I asked.

"Frankly, yes. If our information is correct, Kammler and some others, probably Nazis, some of whom were part of the crew of the Graf Spee who spent most of the war here—we think they went inland and north, close to Paraguay. It's a good four hundred miles on difficult roads, which is why you need to make a start as soon as possible. It looks like we'll be tied up in red tape for a week or more here, but once we get our orders, we'll have to ship out right away. I want you and the others off at first light and, if possible, back here in four days."

"Yes, sir."

"And Jerzy," he added. "Keep your wits about you."

Something in his manner got my attention.

"Who don't you trust?" I asked.

"The Nazis have not just had help inside Perón's regime. Someone has been covering for them diplomatically too. Someone we consider one of ours."

"You think it could be Hartsfeld."

"I don't know," he said. "But as I say, keep your wits about you."

I DIDN'T LIKE BELASCO. HE WAS MEXICAN BY HERITAGE, but while some of the other Hispanics aboard were shy, unsure of themselves among the largely white crew, he was a meaty, swaggering brute, a bully with a crude sense of humor who'd taken my copy of *Bleak House* and thrown it over the side during our first week at sea.

"Books?" he had scoffed. "What are you, a girl?"

His buddies had laughed and made pouty lips and kissy noises at me, but he hadn't done it to amuse them, and that somehow made it worse. I avoided him for the bulk of the voyage and had watched him push down the gangplank toward the dance halls of Buenos Aires with something like relief. The prospect of traveling four hundred miles in the back of a jeep with him settled in my gut like nausea and kept me awake much of the night.

I hid my nervousness as best I could when meeting with the Captain before we embarked, but he spotted it and gave me an encouraging pat on the shoulder.

"Remember that for some of the men you are looking for," he said, "the war is not over. Never will be. I just want a good sense of where they are. That's all. Do not engage or make any attempt to capture or communicate."

"Yes, sir," we answered in unison.

"Mark Hartsfeld is to be treated as mission commander," he added. "You will treat his word as if it is mine."

"Yes, sir."

He caught my eye but didn't hold it. Whatever concerns he might have about Hartsfeld were clearly not to be shared.

"And be on your guard in the jungle," he said. "There are more than Nazis to worry about."

It was supposed to be a joke, but it didn't quite come across that way. I wanted to ask about how to deal with Belasco but didn't know how to frame the question. He was older—in his late twenties—more experienced and more confident than I, and as a Petty Officer, he outranked me. In my heart, I thought him less intelligent, but even then, I knew that stupidity wasn't necessarily a hindrance to command, and in fact, it made some things a lot easier. I was, I'd decided with a teenager's hubris, more like Hamlet, deeper and more reflective, paralyzed by my own complexity.

Thank God I didn't try to say such a thing to Captain Jennings or, for that matter, anyone else.

The fact remained. I say I didn't like Belasco, but the truth was that I was afraid of him. I didn't think he would stab me in my sleep or otherwise do me serious injury, but he oozed a constant low grade capricious malice that could, I felt, turn nasty at any moment. I worried more about him—my comrade in arms—than about the Nazis I was hunting.

Briefed—though less fully than I'd expected, given what I already knew—we left the Captain's office with our packs slung over our shoulders. We had each been issued M1911 automatics but were ordered not to wear them on our belts until we were away from the city. I could feel the extra weight in my pack.

As we descended the gangplank to the launch that would ferry us ashore, Belasco gave me a sidelong look and grinned maliciously.

"Ready for a little adventure, Polack?" he said. "Won't be no reading on this trip."

"Shut up, Belasco," I said, casually, not looking at him. He chuckled at my feigned defiance.

"Oh yeah," he said, not even bothering to address my insubordination. "We're gonna have a high time."

HARTSFELD—THE DIPLOMAT AND TRANSLATOR—MET US AT the quay. He was a thin man with wire-rimmed glasses and a lawyerly air, in a pale linen suit and a blue shirt. He looked ordinary, but I was wary of him because of what Captain Jennings had said, even if he hadn't pinned his doubts on Hartsfeld exactly. His driver, whom he introduced simply as Ignacio—was my age, heavily tanned with lank, black hair that fell to his shoulders in ways I had never seen on a boy before. He spoke no English and seemed taken aback by Belasco, who made a joke in Spanish as they loaded the truck. Hartsfeld had procured a long-bodied four-wheel-drive vehicle, like a Willys Jeep, but with an extra storage row behind the rear seats. It was built for rough terrain and tended to bounce, something Ignacio—who was no taller than I and almost as slight, dwarfed by the steering wheel and gearshift—seemed to relish.

It was a pleasant day in Buenos Aires, the cold Southern Hemisphere winter long over, and the city enjoying the last mild days of spring as the weather warmed. I loved it, and not only because we would be pressing north into the steamy heat of the jungle. It reminded me of my boyhood in Poland, even the buildings recalling something of an old European grandeur . . .

"Look at the tits on her," remarked Belasco, pointing at a girl in a red dress who was crossing the street. He whistled, shouting something in Spanish that made Ignacio laugh, but Hartsfeld, who also spoke Spanish, turned from the passenger seat and gave him a disapproving look. For her part, the girl glared at the car, and when Belasco made more lewd noises, she fired back a stream of invective. That just made him laugh harder than ever.

We left behind the broad, tree-lined avenidas with their elaborate, classicist buildings, obelisks and equestrian statues, finding our way north, out of the city proper and up Highway 12 along the Uruguayan border. The road deteriorated quickly, and within a few hours, we were jolting along lanes of packed earth where hard ruts and hollows suggested serious flooding in the rainy season, but the land was flat and we made good speed.

"Pampas," said Ignacio, playing tour guide, nodding at the grassy planes on either side of the long straight road.

Near Paysandu, we stopped to eat at a roadside steak-house populated by Argentine cowboys called *gauchos*, saving the rations we'd brought for less populated regions ahead. Belasco bought beer, staring Hartsfeld down when the diplomat gave him a look.

"What?" he said. "Not on board. Not on base. Hell, I don't even know whether we're on mission."

"You are," said Hartsfeld. "And I'm in command. I thought that was clear."

Belasco shrugged. "Okay," he said, pointedly draining his bottle in three long swallows. "See? No beer."

Hartsfeld's lip twitched, as if he had been about to say something else, but he let it go.

Somewhere north of Salto, the road began to deteriorate even further. Soon we dropped to half the speed we'd been doing, and within another hour, half that again. Belasco, squeezed in beside me and flexed his shoulders so he took up three quarters of the room, cursing in Spanish and English. Hartsfeld checked his watch. We had only another hour or so of daylight remaining and were seeing fewer and fewer signs of civilization as we climbed. In the storage rack at the back of the vehicle, we had a canvas tent and bedrolls, but we'd hoped to stay in hotels where possible. We gave it another forty-five minutes, but Hartsfeld had clearly been getting antsy as the sun got lower in the sky, and I wasn't surprised when he called it.

"Pull over there," he said. "We'll camp for the night and get back on the road at sun up."

Belasco was, predictably, unhappy.

"I don't see why we can't drive for another hour or two," he said. "So it gets dark? Big deal."

"We can't pitch a tent in the kind of darkness they have out here," said Hartsfeld.

"*You* can't," muttered Belasco. "I can do all kinds of things in the dark. Right, Polack?"

I said nothing, unsure if that was supposed to be a joke or a threat. Maybe he didn't know either.

So we pitched the tent in a clearing beside the road, Belasco giving the orders throughout, and made a fire on which we put a kettle of water, which tasted of the iron jerry can. There was some bread, cheese and apples—the only perishable food we had brought with us—and whatever we chose to supplement it with from our own rations. While the rest of us worked, Hartsfeld set up the radio and sent a message in Morse code, presumably to the Captain. He saw me watching him and hesitated before giving me a nod.

"Something I can help you with, Seaman?"

"No, sir," I said.

It was a warm night, warmer than it had been in Buenos Aires. The open plains had given way to low hills and patchy woodland. It wasn't jungle—certainly not the impenetrable and swampy wall of vegetation that I associated with the term—but we were getting there slowly. You could hear the difference in the night air, the birdcalls and other unfamiliar, unnerving shrieks. And it was at least as dark as it had been in those Polish forests, when even the neighboring villages had been blacked out. I didn't want to go into the tent with Belasco, but sitting out in the night by myself, eating canned beans with a spoon, was starting to get to me. As we drove, Belasco had told stories of the vampire bats that crawled up to you as you slept and slashed your ear or your wrist with their teeth, lapping at the blood with their tongues. Ignacio, the boy driver, confirmed Belasco's tales in enthusiastic Spanish.

"Sometimes they come back to the same cow or donkey, night after night, until it bleeds to death," Belasco said. "If they hit a major artery, it will be over a lot sooner."

He made gushing noises and gestured from his throat with a splayed hand, and laughed as I turned away. At the time, I'd been more revolted than scared, but now, sitting in the dark, I felt a sudden longing to be back in Europe, far from the reach of such strange creatures. At least I had already emptied my bladder. Now I was just killing time, hoping that if I waited long enough, Belasco would be asleep when I crawled into the tent.

I listened to the shifting and grunting under the canvas, keeping still, my flashlight off. There would be snakes up here. Dangerous ones. Would they come out at night, or only during the day? I had no idea.

I looked up at the night sky, the constellations so bright and distinct this far from the city lights, and the milky wash of other stars beyond them, clustered in their millions like specks of dust. I was gazing blankly up, when one of the stars began to move.

34

ALAN
Dreamland, Nevada

"**Y**OU WENT TO FUCKING *STONEHENGE*?" HATCHER bellowed.

Morat and Alan were standing at attention for the first time in weeks.

"Yes, sir," said Alan.

"I take full responsibility, sir," said Morat.

"It's not like we were going to land or anything," Alan said. Morat glanced at him and Hatcher saw it.

"You have got to be kidding me," he said. "Did your last commanding officer have such a lax attitude toward orders that you felt empowered to do this?"

"No sir," said Morat. "It won't happen again, sir."

"It was my idea," Alan inserted. "I insisted."

"And did you visit any more of the UFO club's favorite places?" Hatcher barked. "A flyover of the great pyramids, maybe?"

"Sir, no sir," said Morat, humorless, eyes front.

"I was gonna do that next time," said Alan.

There was a frosty silence and Hatcher came very close to Alan.

"You think this is funny, Major?" he demanded.

"Just trying to lighten the mood, sir," Alan confessed in a low voice.

It hadn't worked.

"You think this is a game, Alan?" Hatcher shot back. "You think we're playing with toys here?"

Alan thought for a second, then dropped something of the stiffness in his back and shoulders.

"To be honest, sir, I really have no idea *what* we're doing," he said.

Surprised, Hatcher blinked and Morat shot Alan a sideways look.

"What's that supposed to mean?" Hatcher asked, but something of his rage had dissipated and the question was not rhetorical.

"I mean," said Alan, carefully, "you have these amazing crafts, and I'm delighted that you let me go up in them, but I don't understand what they're for, operationally. I don't know how we built them, or how they work, or why we aren't telling anyone else about them, and that's fine, sir. Most of it is fine, I guess, but when you ask me if we're playing, I genuinely don't know."

"We are absolutely not playing, Major," said Hatcher, giving him a level stare.

Alan's hesitation was only fractional, but it was loaded nonetheless.

"Good to get that straight, sir," Alan replied.

The CIA man looked poised to press the matter further, but decided to accept this at face value.

"No more grandstanding nocturnal landings," said Hatcher.

"Understood, sir."

"And you follow orders to the letter."

"Yes, sir. Absolutely, sir."

"Good."

"And sir?"

"Yes, Major?" said Hatcher, unwinding a little.

"What exactly are our orders?"

HATCHER NEVER ANSWERED ALAN'S QUESTION. THE following day, he was sent up with Morat in the great black triangle with a preset flight plan, but at no point did Hatcher so much as hint at what their larger mission might be. The day after that, Alan did not fly at all, spending his waking hours in a briefing room, going over the various readouts and procedures associated with the Locust. He was dining alone in the mess— veal saltimbocca with angel hair pasta—when a man came in.

Alan had gotten used to not looking too closely at the people he saw on base, but sharing mess was so rare that he looked up, the forkful of food freezing en route to his mouth as he took in the bullish frame of a large black man: Staff Sgt. Barry Regis, the FAC he had last seen at Camp Leatherneck in Afghanistan.

He just stood there, head bowed, his eyes on Alan who, reflexively got to his feet so he could defend himself if necessary. The two men had not parted on good terms.

"I was told I'd find you here," said Regis.

"You were told right," said Alan, watching him.

"I was told a bunch of other stuff, too," said Regis. "About what you do here, and why they took you out of the Marines. They showed me what you fly. Told me what you saw back in Afghanistan. What happened."

"Yeah?" said Alan.

"Yeah." He muttered, "I'm sorry about Safid Kuh. You should have said what happened."

Alan heard the disbelief in his voice, and couldn't help grinning. Regis matched his smile, and suddenly the two of them were laughing, and Regis was crossing the room and taking his hand.

"You wouldn't have believed me," said Alan. "I don't think I believed it. Not really. Not until I came here."

"I get that," said Regis, sitting at Alan's table. "Still. You should have said. And I should have trusted you. I was just angry, man. I felt like those guys depended on me and I let them down. Guess I was looking for someone else to blame."

"It's okay. What's a little awkward silence and pent up aggression between Redhawks, right?"

Regis grinned with relief. "You still were the best pocket passer I ever protected," he said, glad to change the subject.

"Too bad I couldn't scramble worth a damn," said Alan.

"That's why you're in the cockpit and I'm on the ground."

"Wasn't just physical though, was it?" said Alan ruefully. "When you guys were around me, when I could sit back in the pocket and pick out my targets, I was fine. As soon as I felt it collapsing. . . . Panic. Cluelessness. I got sacked more than a week of groceries."

Regis laughed.

"Wasn't so bad," he said, adding before Alan could protest, "and if you were, that was us. That's what the offensive line is for. You didn't let us down."

Alan nodded gratefully, knowing they were talking about more than football.

"And what about you?" said Alan. "Your job here, I mean. You still a Marine?"

"Technically, I'm private security for Dreamland, employed, as of two days ago, by the CI fucking A. Specialized Skills Officer. Not exactly what I was trained for, and I doubt I'll do much flying anymore, but they think my experience coordinating air and ground forces will be useful. Gotta say, Alan: this is some seriously wild shit."

"You got that right," said Alan.

Suddenly they were laughing again as the tension dissipated, for Alan's part with a sense of relief he hadn't realized he needed. Seeing Regis was like having a piece of the real world come back and agree with him about the strangeness of the universe. It was like finding a star to navigate by, and it calmed a dreadful loneliness he had not been aware he'd been feeling.

It wasn't until later that he wondered if that had also been a factor in the decision to bring Regis inside Dreamland's cone of secrecy, a strategy to help their new pilot adjust to the strangeness of his new environment. He immediately rejected the idea as arrogant, but it left him uneasy nonetheless.

THE FOLLOWING DAY, ALAN WAS CALLED OUT TO PAPOOSE Lake again, and this time he was surprised to learn he would be flying alone, in a single-seat version of the two-man craft he'd flown on his last mission. He'd handled the controls by himself on his last flight, and had a good sense of how to activate all the craft's automated systems if he felt out of his depth. Having the cockpit to himself shouldn't have felt like a big deal, but it did. He suited up, climbed into the single-seat Locust and went through the preflight protocols, feeling, again, a sense of glee. It was his now, like the Harrier he'd flown over Afghanistan was his.

Alan was not a romantic. He did not refer to the planes he flew as if they were lovers, or pets, or any of the other terms he sometimes heard pilots use. An airplane was a machine, albeit a complex, even quirky one, and the Locust was no different. Yet it was also somehow alive, as all air-craft were, and it needed feeding and coaxing, reigning in and urging on, tethering and unleashing. It was bigger than he was, and stronger, but he had to have mastery over it. He couldn't do that with a copilot or trainer sitting beside him.

So he smiled as the hatch door latched closed. He entered the starting coordinates for today's mission.

"Today you'll be flying in formation with Night Bird One," said Hatcher's voice over his head set. "He will rendezvous with you at the assigned location."

The assigned location was directly above Groom Lake, but they were to meet at 40,000 feet, considerably higher than Alan had been flying so far, and the craft was pressurizing around him as he climbed. Morat's voice came through his cans moments before he reached the rendezvous.

"I have a visual on you now, Phoenix. Can you see me?"

Alan checked his radar, spotted the point of light on the screen, and oriented to the appropriate window. The other black Locust sat motionless in the bright air above him.

"Got you," he said. "Where are we headed?"

"Up," said Morat simply.

"Come again?"

"We're going high," said Morat, "where you can't land and freak out the locals. We're going so far up that the word will stop meaning what you think it does."

"I don't think I follow."

"You will," said Morat. "In every sense."

Alan grinned at the weak pun. "Right behind you," he said.

There was a momentary pause and then Morat's voice came back.

"Okay, Phoenix, first thing you're going to do is angle one point of your triangle directly up, perpendicular to the ground."

"We can't just drift up the way we came?" asked Alan, feeling an edge of unease. This was new territory.

"Not this time."

"What are we doing exactly?"

"Leaving the atmosphere," said Morat.

Alan put one hand to the earphone and pressed it to his head.

"Can you repeat that?" he said.

"You heard me," said Morat.

"I don't understand," said Alan, feeling numb, dazed.

"Sure you do," Morat answered. "Congratulations, Phoenix. You're going into space."

"Wait," said Alan. "I'm not sure . . ."

"Just do as I say and you'll be fine," said Morat.

Alan did as he was told, his fingers suddenly clumsy. Morat talked him through the next stages, the engagement of an entirely different thrust and navigation system accessed through a console that had been dark on his previous flights. Now it blazed with illuminated digital diagrams, graphs and gauges. As Alan's mind raced, Morat kept talking in a level, matter-of-fact voice.

"Okay," said Morat. "I'm synced with your systems remotely so I can see your status. I'll let you know if anything doesn't look right. And don't worry. The Locust is designed to protect itself and there'll be no thermal build up as we go. The ship won't let you do anything crazy or incompetent without making you jump through a whole lot of clarifications and overrides."

"Thanks for that vote of confidence," said Alan. He was, he knew, tipped up on his back, the earth behind him, but he felt quite level, normal even, though his arms felt lighter than usual when he moved them. "Where exactly are we heading?"

"The upper thermosphere, assuming we don't burn up en route."

"What?"

"Kidding," said Morat. He was enjoying himself. "Like I said, friction is for ordinary pilots. Enter the following coordinates and set your speed range to yellow. As we cross over the mesosphere, another set of sub-controls will activate and heat shields will close over your windows. You don't need to do anything, but as we emerge, the ship will shift to an entirely different propulsion system. It will feel a little different, but it's quite normal and you don't need to do anything. These things practically fly themselves."

"So why am I here?" asked Alan. He was genuinely nervous now. Even frightened.

Morat just laughed. "Good one," he said. "Okay. Engage when ready. I'll see you on the other side."

Alan closed his eyes for a second, took a breath, and hit what he continued to think of as the ignition. Rightly or not, he had no idea.

The ship leapt forward, which was to say—he had to remind himself—that it leapt up, an impossible vertical surge of gravity defying acceleration accompanied, for once, by a distinct rumble of energy. Ignition, he decided, was right after all.

The Locust's speed was staggering. It didn't so much fly out of the troposphere and into the stratosphere as punch through, getting faster still as it hit the rarefied air of the mesosphere. He was sixty miles above the earth and climbing at the same staggering rate, the altimeter flashing a constant stream of numbers: 200 knots. 350. 500. And then, at last, with the thermosphere falling away below, the engines powered down and Alan, sweating for reasons that had nothing to do with the external temperature any ordinary ship would have just generated, looked out.

All was suddenly still and silent. Above him was blackness. And stars. Below was a pale blue ball, swirled with white, the earth itself, incandescent in the dark. It was breathtaking.

"This is Night Bird One," said Morat's voice over the headset. "All okay, Phoenix?"

Alan cleared his throat.

"I think so," he said. "Everything looks good."

It was easily the most inadequate thing he had ever said, and that—as Lacey would have pointed out—was saying something. He gazed out into the furthest reaches of space, taking it all in—or trying to—as Morat's voice talked him through what he called the LEO—low earth orbit—operating systems.

"You've got to be more conscious of fuel levels up here," he was saying. "Little bursts are all you need. And try to get the heading right the first time. Constant adjustment reduces dwell time."

Alan was barely listening. He was in orbit—higher, in fact, than the International Space Station, and outside his cockpit, the air was so thin its properties were not very different from the vacuum of space. He was gazing down from what had been called "the heavens" for thousands of years, a view few men or women had ever seen with their own eyes, and if someone on the planet's surface somehow got a glimpse of him, he would appear as a star. He had been a pilot. Now he was an astronaut.

". . . which is why all counter-detection measures are automatically engaged as you leave the lower atmosphere, though that means you have to be alert to your own proximity warnings." Morat explained. "Satellites won't move for you because they won't see you coming. You got that, Major? Phoenix, do you read?"

"Yeah," said Alan, absently. "Yes, Night Bird One, I'm here. Just . . . taking it all in."

Insofar as anyone could.

"Okay," said Morat. "Let's try some maneuvering exercises."

He either hadn't heard the awe in Alan's voice or chose to ignore it.

For the next hour Alan flexed the Locust's LOE capabilities, moving from point to point, stopping, turning, changing altitudes and executing a range of rolls and banks, dives and climbs. Surprisingly, and in spite of the fact that every thrust had to be countered by another just to bring the vessel to a halt or change its direction, the Locust functioned more like a conventional aircraft up here. Banks of nozzles along each edge lit like jet or rocket engines, glowing bluish as they fired, so that following Morat it was almost possible to imagine they were flying in formation over foreign seas. It was a relief to find something up here that took the edge off the strangeness. Alan found his nervous apprehension draining away as they soared through the blackness over the rolling planet.

They kept well clear of the International Space Station, "In case someone happens to be looking out the window," Morat said, but they navigated their way through an array of satellites, most of them strange, ungainly things glittering with gold and sprouting wing-like solar panels of cobalt blue. Many of them bristled with antennae and dishes, but others looked like the shiny innards of oversized domestic appliances—housings of coils and struts, drums and irregular boxes, disks and tubes—their functions impossible to guess at. None of them would detect the Locusts "unless you actually hit them," Morat deadpanned, "which we try not to do." What were they worth, Alan wondered, these drifting hunks of technology? Billions, maybe more. All hanging in their orbits for him to waltz around, like a child in a museum after dark. A burst of weapons fire and he could cripple the business interests or surveillance systems of a dozen countries. In any future conflict involving the USA, the Locust would surely play a part up here.

The streak of light came from above, arcing across the blackness, a point of light with a tail.

"What's that?" he said.

"What do you see, Phoenix?" Morat returned.

"Bogey at eleven o clock. Now ten. Wait . . ." He checked his instruments but no movement registered. "I've lost it."

"Negative on that, Phoenix," said Morat. "Probably a meteor or a piece of space trash burning up on re-entry."

Alan craned his neck to stare through the window, bringing the Locust about almost absentmindedly as he did so. His instruments were, after all, showing him nothing. He pivoted the Locust.

"You're changing heading, Phoenix," Morat said.

"Just seeing if I can get a better look," said Alan.

"It was nothing. Leave it."

"Hold on," Alan mused, firing the Locust's thrusters and shooting forward in the direction of the light he'd seen. For a moment it was like he was back at Safid Kuh, the brilliant light burning in the sky in front of him, his weapons jammed, men—his men—dying on the ground below . . .

"Hold your position, Phoenix," said Morat.

"One second," said Alan. Nothing was shutting his systems down today, not in the Locust, and he wasn't about to let the bogey slip away. He sped toward it, adjusting to go round a satellite that hung like a great shining metal insect in the sky, all legs and antennae.

"Phoenix, we have a mission to perform. You need to return . . ."

Alan, barely hearing him, said nothing. His attention was riveted to the other vessel up here in the black where nothing should be. Because he could see it again now. As he had come around the ungainly satellite he had seen it, a sleek silver arrowhead with three blue white flares on its trailing edge.

Engines.

"That's no meteor," he whispered.

"Phoenix, I insist that you hold your position," came Morat's voice over his headset.

"There's something up here," Alan replied, staring at it. The ship—it was a ship, it had to be—banked and accelerated away. His right hand strayed to the console and, with a touch, activated his weapon systems. "I'm going after it."

35

JENNIFER
Heathrow Airport, London

JENNIFER HAD BOOKED HER FLIGHT FROM A VISIBLY uneasy ticketing agent whose eyes kept straying to the smears of dirt she hadn't been able to get off her clothes when she cleaned up. Jennifer thought how lucky it was that her passport was still in her purse. She kept an eye on the airport police, staying close to them where possible, but she did not speak to them. Her mission was to get out of the country, and nothing was to get in the way of that.

She had just enough time, before her flight, to buy a carry-on suitcase and enough over-priced clothes in the airport shops to last her a week. She didn't relax until the plane backed away from the jetway and began to taxi.

She flew British Airways to Washington, DC, landing at Dulles Airport. The destination had almost been selected at random, but not quite. On the plane, she opened up her laptop, paid for Wi-Fi, and read everything she could find on Senator Tom Powers, the Nevada Republican whose name had been in her father's files, a man who had visited their house in her teen years. He looked much the same now as he did then: pale, well-groomed, with ice blue eyes and a handsome bearing that was as much attitude and confidence as it was bone structure. He was in his late sixties now, what the media called a Washington insider. She e-mailed his office, saying who she was and requesting a meeting.

More misplaced trust?

No. Powers' connection to her father was real and proven over time. And she would be more careful about what she told him than she had been with Letrange.

The thought of him needled her. She'd been duped, her instincts manipulated by a skilled liar. How could someone be that good at deception? It was more than work skills. He was a sociopath. She wondered if he was working for anyone other than the Maynard Consortium, but could find only the thinnest of professional profiles online, and nothing telling. Of the Interpol agent Chevalier, there was no online trace at all. She kicked herself again, feeling the old angry spike of humiliation that she had been so completely played.

At least he didn't get you into bed first, she thought.

Had that been a possibility, part of his long game? She shuddered at the thought, not so much with revulsion, but at the horror of it being all too plausible. She'd considered it. Under other circumstances, it may already have happened.

She pushed the thought away, studying her computer and making mental notes, until her eyes ached with the strain and she closed them for a moment, waking an hour and a half later over the Atlantic ocean. She woke up her laptop and sent Deacon an e-mail, in which she told him everything except where she was going, asking him to report all that had happened directly to the police. She was taking no chances now.

```
I'm e-mailing the police the whole story and
will call them myself, once I get settled.
I'm sorry. I hope this all blows over soon.
I'd like to come home and see you.
```

The rest of the flight was uneventful. Awake now, she stared uncomprehendingly at two different movies, was rude to the middle-aged businessman beside her who tried to flirt with her, and finally slept for the last two hours. She was hungry enough to eat whatever they put in front of her and, as they came in to land, drank a Diet Coke. She wanted to be wide awake when they touched down.

They landed in Washington at two in the morning, East Coast time. She saw no sign that anyone was anticipating her arrival, and made her way directly to ground transportation, where she boarded the first hotel shuttle she saw. The driver said there were rooms available at the

Westin in Weston Heights. She had no idea where that was, but it didn't matter. She signed in as a Miss Andrea Bell, though she had to use her credit card to cover her costs, so she doubted that would stand too much scrutiny if anyone was looking for her. The room was on the fifth floor, elegantly modern and spacious in ways hotels in England almost never were. She set the alarm for seven and slept. By the time she awoke, there was an e-mail from the office of Senator Tom Powers waiting in her inbox. She read it, changed her clothes, and called a cab.

Jennifer had never been to the US capital before. She was underwhelmed. The hotel district was new and featureless, and the highway could have been any busy city artery during morning rush hour. It was with something of a shock when she caught her first glimpse of the Washington Monument, stabbing upwards out of the trees over the Potomac. By the time her taxi had left her outside the Hart Building on Constitution Avenue, there was no doubt that she was in the heart of the world's most powerful government, and was meant to feel its presence.

The Hart Building, in spite of its marble façade, was blockish and modern-looking, without the neo-classical elegance of its surroundings. It felt utilitarian, which was fine as far as Jennifer was concerned. She didn't want to be overawed any more than was strictly necessary.

Powers' office was on the third floor, above the Central Hearings chamber. Jennifer looked for an elevator, crossing the great atrium with its static mobile of dark, cloud-like shapes suspended over spiky metal mountains. The

Senator's secretary announced her, and she was ushered in almost immediately.

He was older than the pictures on his web page suggested, and without the careful lighting and photoshopping, he looked haggard. The smile he gave her was weary and a little sad.

"Miss Quinn," he said, rising and extending his hand. "You have no idea how sorry I was to hear about your father's passing. I sent flowers to the funeral but my schedule . . ."

"They were much appreciated, Senator, thank you," said Jennifer, who had not known about the flowers.

"So what can I do for you? I can arrange a tour of the building, including a trip on our rather exclusive little monorail, if you like, but maybe you're a bit old for that now. It's been what, ten years since I saw you last?"

"About that."

"Edward doted on you. You must feel his loss very deeply."

Jennifer nodded and smiled but she was keeping a tight rein on her feelings so that she could watch him. "I was wondering if you could tell me something about your business dealings?" she said, sitting as he did.

"With Edward?"

"Or with the Maynard Consortium generally."

She said it lightly, as if the distinction didn't matter, but she saw the caution in his face immediately.

"I'm not sure I have had any direct dealings with Maynard," he said.

She smiled at his use of *direct*. Of course he hadn't. Maynard was all about indirection, money passing through multiple hands before it reached its destination.

"Was there a specific transaction you were interested in?"

He was testing the waters, she thought. Trying to find how much she knew.

"Well, on November the fourth of last year, a political action committee supporting you received a contribution of forty-thousand dollars from a Nate Hapsel."

Powers performed a memory search and smiled.

"Ah yes. Nate is a rancher in my home state," he said. "Very successful and committed to staying so. You understand, of course, that my re-election committee had nothing to do with any PACs supporting me. That would be illegal. I believe Nate had concerns about federal encroachment into private lands…"

"No doubt," Jennifer interrupted. "But the money wasn't really his, was it? It came via an account in Singapore, through his hands, but the transaction originated with Maynard."

"Oh, I think it's very hard to say what dollars belong to whom, once they come out of someone's bank," said Powers, smiling his politician's smile. "It was still Mr. Hapsel's money, however he came by it. Do you mind my asking what this is all about? We have inquiries set up to look into campaign finance, and I have been cleared at every level. I hope you aren't suggesting anything untoward."

"Not at all," said Jennifer, matching his smile. "I'm really just trying to fill in some details about my father's interests. For personal reasons."

"Quite," said the Senator, nodding thoughtfully.

"When did you last speak to him?" Jennifer asked.

"Oh, a month or so before he passed. He seemed in good spirits. A real tragedy and a shock to hear . . ."

"What did you talk about?"

"Oh, this and that. The implications of a trade deal, I think. I really don't remember very well."

"So it wasn't specifically a SWEEP project?"

Again, her approach was light, conversational, but the Senator was not as good a liar as Chevalier/Letrange. He blanched, and his eyes flashed to the door in case someone might overhear. When he spoke his voice was low and hoarse.

"I'm not familiar with that er . . . entity."

"Yes, Senator, you are," said Jennifer, "and I have the files to prove it."

He stared at her and his fingers began to drum on the edge of his desk.

"What do you want?" he said at last.

"Information," she said.

"About SWEEP? Out of the question."

"Senator, I am not looking to make life difficult for you, but I think my father had become involved in something he wanted to step away from. Something involving investments of which he did not approve. I need to find out what. I owe him that much. I suspect you do too."

"Me?"

"Those contributions to your election campaign began a long time ago. As we were saying, there are laws against foreign campaign contributions, and there are ways around those laws. Your first successful run depended on them, if I'm not mistaken. My father was part of the decision to support you. I have proof of that."

Powers sagged visibly, and the hand he raised to his face was momentarily unsteady. He shut his eyes and massaged his brow for a second, and the weary, haggard aura she had first noticed seemed to intensify.

"All right," he said. "But not here. Meet me . . ." he checked his watch, "at ten-thirty this evening on the steps of the Jefferson Memorial. It will be quiet then. We can walk somewhere from there."

SHE ATE IN WHAT CALLED ITSELF A PUB, SURROUNDED BY young people in suits who, she supposed, had government jobs. They had the brash confidence of people sure of their futures. Jennifer had taken the quietest corner she could find and spoke to no one. She was pretty sure she had not been followed, and while the Mall surely deployed all kinds of covert surveillance, she saw no sign of anyone paying particular attention to her.

Powers was right. Once the sun set, the crowds on the National Mall thinned to a trickle and the Jefferson Memorial, set back as it was away from the other monuments, was almost deserted. The Jefferson Memorial sat atop a series of broad steps, looking across the Tidal

Basin to the Washington monument and, distantly visible through the trees, the White House, all lit up with a blue-white light that made it seem spectral and unearthly. The Memorial itself was eerily quiet, apart from a lone police-man in shorts and on a bicycle but wearing a sidearm, who gave her a respectful nod as she gazed up through the imposing pillars to the statue of the man himself. But the bronze figure was less compelling than the words inscribed on the walls. One panel, less familiar to her than the others, particularly stood out. It read:

> I AM NOT AN ADVOCATE FOR FREQUENT CHANGES IN LAWS AND CONSTITUTIONS, BUT LAWS AND INSTITUTIONS MUST GO HAND IN HAND WITH THE PROGRESS OF THE HUMAN MIND. AS THAT BECOMES MORE DEVELOPED, MORE ENLIGHTENED, AS NEW DISCOVERIES ARE MADE, NEW TRUTHS DISCOVERED AND MANNERS AND OPINIONS CHANGE, WITH THE CHANGE OF CIRCUMSTANCES, INSTITUTIONS MUST ADVANCE ALSO TO KEEP PACE WITH THE TIMES. WE MIGHT AS WELL REQUIRE A MAN TO WEAR STILL THE COAT WHICH FITTED HIM WHEN A BOY AS CIVILIZED SOCIETY TO REMAIN EVER UNDER THE REGIMEN OF THEIR BARBAROUS ANCESTORS.

She read it twice, lingering over the penultimate sentence and marveling at the foresightedness and humility that could devise laws designed to change as civilization evolved. Coupled with the other panels' words on freedom and equality, it made a powerful statement, so that the statue of the man himself seemed to her almost an afterthought. This was a monument to an idea, something the likes of which she could not recall in England, for all its ancient palaces and monuments.

Powers arrived seven minutes late. He seemed tired and distracted, and instead of leading her away to some quiet late night café or discreet bench, he eased himself slowly onto the hard steps on the side of the monument itself, and breathed out a long, slow sigh.

"Well, Miss Quinn, you have disrupted my day."

He said it without malice, looking from her to the vista across the waters of the Potomac, which glittered black under the lights of the mall.

"I'm sorry," said Jennifer.

"No you're not," he said. "Nor should you be. Beautiful, isn't it?" he said, taking in the monuments around him, the broad, sparsely trafficked walkway and the vista of muted splendor. "It deserves better. We all do."

"Is that the conclusion my father came to?"

"I don't know. Perhaps. So. What do you know, Miss Quinn, about unidentified aerial phenomena?"

Jennifer gave him a baffled look. "What?"

"I'm talking about UFOs."

The bafflement lasted only a moment, and with it came a fragmentary memory too dark to see, something about being a child in her father's study . . . It wouldn't come into the light and she was suddenly angry.

"Seriously?" she said. "This is what you thought would fob off on me? I've been killing hours, waiting for you, and you give me little green men in flying saucers? What happened to *we all deserve better*? Come on, Senator, you can do better than that."

"I didn't say anything about little green men or flying saucers."

"Aliens then. Whatever."

"Not them either."

"Can you just tell me what you *are* saying so that we can get this sham over?"

"There's not much I can tell you."

"Figures," snapped Jennifer, who was already resigned to her trip being wasted.

"You don't understand," he said, and now he turned to look at her, and his eyes were alive with a young man's fire. "This isn't about money—or not merely. It's about things I am forbidden to discuss."

"Forbidden by whom?"

"By my allegiance to the American people and the oaths I swore to serve them."

"Which means what exactly?"

"Do you understand the concept of black budgets?"

Jennifer felt like they had been driving along a straight road when the car had swung off onto a track she hadn't known was there, traveling in a completely different direction.

"You mean . . .?"

"I mean taxpayer money, earmarked for projects so secret they cannot be publicly discussed. While all budgets are subjected to congressional oversight there are special provisos for sensitive military projects. Title 10 section 119 of the US Code states—and yes, I can quote it from memory—*The Secretary of Defense may waive any requirement under subsection (a), (b), or (c) that certain information be included in a report under that subsection if the Secretary determines that inclusion of that information in the report would adversely affect the national security. Any such waiver shall be made on a case-by-case basis*. And that, Miss Quinn, is the Pentagon's get-out-of-jail-free card, though it is not, believe me, free in any sense for the rest of us."

"Why is this relevant? The Maynard money wasn't government money. It was private funding, originating outside the United States."

"Exactly so."

"I don't understand."

"When projects are black, and they cannot be discussed in any public forum, they can slip through the cracks of all government monitoring. Sometimes public interest has to rely on private funding."

"Maynard was paying you to give them classified information?"

"Absolutely not!" said the Senator, and his tone was— for the first time—loaded with self-righteousness. "I am no traitor, Miss Quinn. I am a loyal patriot determined to serve my country, its people, and its laws . . ."

"So what did they get for their money?"

The Senator hesitated, and the hauteur faded.

"A line of communication—not from me or my office," he added quickly, recovering a little of his defiance.

"From whom and about what?"

"The rancher I mentioned before, Nate Hapsel, owns a great deal of land. Some of it is very close to facilities in my senatorial district, which utilize those classified budgets we were just discussing. The money I received enabled me to have parts of Hapsel's land included in an environmental survey that identified a number of endangered species native to the area, some fish—the Ash Meadows Speckled Dace and the charmingly named Devils Hole pupfish—along with the Southwestern willow flycatcher and, for good measure, that old favorite, the gray wolf."

"None of which are actually there."

"I can't say that for sure. But their appearance on the endangered species record means that the Hapsel land is effectively protected wilderness, a no-go zone for everyone, including the government. Anyone—including the army—needs a permit to go onto those lands, and the screening process is set up to flag my office."

"So what is really going on there?"

Powers smiled ruefully. "Just a little private monitoring of public expenditure, all quite legal. A little interdepartmental monitoring is good for the body politic."

Jennifer gave him a long appraising look. "You think this is about rival government agencies?" she said.

"I shouldn't be talking about it," he said. "And I only agreed to meet with you because I had a lot of respect for your old man. But I'll tell you what any person with a half a brain would tell you after looking at a map of Hapsel's land in Nevada. The government owns a lot of territory down there. For years they denied it, but they eventually came clean. Area 51, Miss Quinn. A flight development and test center run, I suspect, by the CIA, possibly partnered with the Air Force, the NSA and DARPA and God knows what other alphabet soup government organizations. SWEEP is just another, a government watchdog, if you like, designed to keep black budgets in check."

"No," said Jennifer. "It's not and I can prove it. It's a network of private interests, and if I was in your shoes I'd be wanting to know why the people in charge of those interests feel the need to be so close to a top secret government installation. You've been manipulated, Senator, and not by private US citizens."

For the first time since they had begun speaking he looked genuinely unsettled.

"SWEEP has never requested anything that would bend even the most liberal definition of propriety," he said. "I'm sure this is all a simple misunderstanding."

"If it's not, Senator, you have a serious problem," said Jennifer. "We all do."

36

TIMIKA
Pottsville, PA

S HE WROTE IT ALL DOWN, THE FRAGMENT OF PECULIAR metal, the story of a nine-year-old girl whose father was called to Roswell to investigate a crash site, a government program to protect and silence the girl and others like her, the children of Operation Paperclip scientists. All of it. She sat in her car in the parking lot of a 24-hour Dunkin' Donuts, working by the thin blue light of her laptop's screen, driven by a fierce need to share all she had discovered. It would be a story unlike anything ever posted on *Debunktion*, not an exposé of hoaxes and the stupidity of conspiracy theorists, relayed in teeth-rattling sarcasm, but something quite different,

something with weight and seriousness and a genuine—
if uncertain—curiosity. The site was all about exposing
false truths, but that only meant it stood for the genuine
truth, she told herself as she formatted the document and
hit "post." This was no different, even though it might
involve a degree of retraction of earlier stories, and that
would certainly come as something of a surprise to their
readership.

It was after two in the morning by the time she finished. As the adrenaline faded, she found she was very
tired. Sleeping in the car was not an appealing prospect.
Driving around looking for somewhere safe to stay, risking getting pulled over for a DWB or worse, was even less
attractive. Suddenly, and for the first time since she'd left
the city, she wanted to be back in her own apartment, in
her own bed. Maybe it was time to go there. Maybe her
post would blow the lid off whatever the guys who had
come after her wanted to keep quiet. Maybe now the game
was up for them. Maybe this was where she got on the
highway to normality.

There was one thing to do first. She finished reading
Jerzy's journal, turning the pages with feverish curiosity
and mounting amazement. A week ago, she would have
laughed it all off, but now . . .?

She stared at the final page in baffled excitement and
then, with the distinct air of violation, tore the page out.
Bending the book cover as far as it would go, she located
the slit in the fabric and the hard shape beneath it.

A key.

Small and brass. She wrapped it up in the page she had torn out, and tucked it into her bra, replacing the book in the lining of her swanky new coat.

She remembered that she had turned off her phone before going back to The Hollows, and switched it back on. There were three texts from Audrey.

"Site hacked totes," said the first one. "Office ransacked."

She caught her breath and read the second one.

"Dion called. Your apartment raided last night. He's fine but you must NOT go home. He's leaving town. Won't say where."

Her hands were unsteady now. She scrolled to the bottom to see the third text.

"Don't call. Don't post to the site. They are watching. Marvin missing."

Timika stared at the glowing phone. Somewhere in the distance, a police siren wailed.

Marvin missing.

This was on her. If anything had happened to him because of her . . .

She waited only long enough to pull up the *Debunktion* site. Her story—which should have been front and center on the home page—was nowhere to be seen. In its place was a crappy photoshopped image of a flying saucer that looked like a lampshade. The headline read, "Roswell's Aliens Found!" She stared, momentarily captivated, trying to decide if the story was supposed to be funny, but the more she read, the more straight-faced it seemed. The words popped off the screen: UFO, alien autopsy, government cover-up. It was all presented as serious and was all ludicrously fake, without even the self-awareness to be a good hoax. Beneath it was a story from yesterday, demonstrating how crop circles could only be created by a complex pattern of lasers from a thousand feet above the ground, and another terrible picture of what looked like a plastic dinosaur model emerging from a pool of water and captioned "Hard evidence for Nessie at last!"

What the hell?

The comment section was full of mocking outrage from their regular subscribers. What had happened to *Debunktion*'s snarky objectivity? How could they go from taking crappy conspiracy theories to pieces to endorsing it all, without so much as an announcement? One commenting troll, even as he vowed never to visit the site again, charged them with pandering to the basest instincts of the Internet for advertising dollars. Saddest of all were the commentators praising them for abandoning their former skepticism and embracing the truth of unexplained phenomena.

Timika stared, speechless, tears welling in her eyes. Her life's work had been dismantled and made a mockery of. Just like that.

She took a long, shuddering breath, wiped her eyes and gripped the steering wheel.

"Okay," she said aloud. "Okay."

Don't post to the site . . .

She had. Could that give them a lock on her position? She'd been using the Dunkin' Donuts Wi-Fi signal, logged in as herself . . .

380

Stupid.

She thought the siren was getting closer. She snapped the ignition key twice, listening to the groan of the engine.

"Come on," she muttered.

She tried a third time, and the car rumbled into reluctant life. It lurched out of the parking lot, settling into its familiar rhythms as it warmed up. She was cruising comfortably by the time she turned onto route 209 and headed southwest toward Tremont. Her plans were unclear. Hell, she thought, they weren't plans at all. They were instincts, panicky, irrational and uncertain. She looked at the road map from her glove compartment. She would take Interstate 81 southbound, to where it joined 78, then head west to Harrisburg. That would give her time to think, to make some decisions. She could stay on the interstate all the way to Roanoke or Knoxville, or maybe drop further south and make for Atlanta and her cousin Tonya, praying that the Corolla lasted that long. Then what? New Mexico, to sniff around for clues to one of the world's most familiar mysteries?

Not that she had ever thought it a mystery. Roswell was the UFO conspiracy theorists' Shangri-La, but all the official evidence said it was merely the site of a high-tech balloon crash, and she had never seen anything to make her think otherwise. It was all nonsense, and had in fact been central to what had driven *Debunktion* from the start.

Now this. An old woman and a twisted fragment of strange metal.

It proved nothing. Timika would keep looking. She was, as ever, a skeptic. But people were looking for her, trashing her office, destroying everything she'd built, discrediting her, painting her as a fraud and a crank and endangering the people who worked with her. Maybe worse.

Every car behind her might be a cop, or worse. There was a car a couple of hundred yards back that had been there since she left Pottsville. She could see nothing but headlights, so she had no idea if the car was marked in some way, or even what color it was, but it lingered in her rear-view mirror like a threat. She tried accelerating, and then slowing down again, just to see what the other driver would do, but the car maintained its distance, and with each half mile, Timika's unease mounted.

Before reaching Tremont, she turned left towards the interstate on a secondary road shaded by forest and sign-posted to Echo Valley. There were no streetlights, and she had to stay focused on the road ahead, but she was pretty sure the car behind had not followed her.

Unless the driver turned off its headlamps.

That would be bad.

She swallowed and concentrated on driving. The road was narrow, lined by trees with pale bark that flashed in the glare of her high beams. At this time of night, the road was utterly empty. She wouldn't be able to evade drones or helicopters, but there was no point worrying about such things. Somehow, she doubted the men who'd come after her in New York had that kind of organizational reach. If they came for her, it would be a couple of guys in a car with a shotgun in the trunk, their headlights turned off so they could get nice and close before running her off the road and into the woods. Not as a drone, operated out of some Nevada control center.

The thought didn't make her feel better.

The country road had been a mistake. It wasn't going to save her time, and it was doing nothing for her nerves. The darkness was absolute, the forest on either side of the road impenetrable, and it occurred to her that if the Corolla died on her, this might not be the best place to be a single black female. And there might be bears in the woods. The sooner she got back to civilization, the better.

The thought had just registered when the Corolla's engine stopped. It didn't groan or fight or idle. It just turned off, as if she'd turned off the ignition. The car went silent, the power vanished, and she was just rolling on inertia. She pushed the gas pedal and waggled the steering wheel, but it made no difference. She had no brakes and no power steering. A hundred yards later, the Corolla rounded a curve and came to a halt on the shoulder.

"No, no, no," she muttered. "Not here. Not now."

But no matter how many times she turned the key, the car did not revive. The radio crackled on for a moment, spewing static and scrambled pop songs, and then died completely. So did her headlights.

Timika sat in the sudden silent dark, flipping switches, turning dials, muttering pleas and prayers, but nothing happened. It was as if the car was no more than a piece of furniture.

She was stuck.

Reaching behind her, she manually locked all the doors, then fumbled under the passenger seat for a flashlight, but before she turned it on, her eyes locked onto her rear view mirror. If that car were to reappear, rolling up behind her with its lights off, she was dead. Hell, parked where she was, she wouldn't need anyone to have a particularly sinister intent. They could come round the corner and plow right into her before they knew she was there.

But no one came. That was almost worse.

She was going to have to get out of the car and walk, and hope someone came. The right someone. It felt like a gamble because it was. Under other circumstances—perhaps if she lived through it all and could retell the story back home one day—it would be funny, this tale of a New York City girl lost in the Pennsylvania woods at night . . . She unlatched her door and put her shoulder to it.

And in that instant, the darkness was torn asunder by a brilliant blue white glare that seemed to come from all around, a light so bright that Timika hid her head in her hands. The cars lights and radio both flickered back into life for a second, then went out, but the light outside, the light that painted the trees impossibly green and white so that they seemed to leap close and hard, packing in around the car, stayed constant.

She squeezed her eyes shut, her head down. One second. Two.

She opened her eyes again, and the world was rational again. Normal. The light was gone and she was alone in Dion's crap-box car, marooned in the Pennsylvania woods.

What the hell?

She hadn't imagined the light. Could it have been someone's high beams weirdly bouncing off her mirrors, the sky-slashing searchlights of some car dealership display just the other side of the trees?

She pushed the car door wide and slid out, registering a strange silence as if the world had been muted. As she did so she snagged the bridge officer's coat on the seatbelt, and as she tugged herself free watched as a brass button popped off and felt to the road.

Except that it didn't land.

It hovered in the air eighteen inches above the ground, spinning.

Timika froze mid stoop, staring at it. She moved one hand through the air above the suspended button as if it might be snagged on some invisible thread.

Nothing.

And then she felt it, a strange pool of darkness like the shadow of something directly above her. Something vast.

Slowly, reluctantly, she tore her eyes off the spinning button and looked directly up into the blackness of the sky.

And then the Pennsylvania night tore open again, blasting her sight with the lightning glare of a thousand bursting stars.

37

JERZY
Argentina, October 1946

O NE MOMENT, THE MOONLESS SKY WAS CLEAR AND STILL, and the next, it was a mere backdrop to the one star that was in motion. I'd seen shooting stars in the mountains in Poland, and I knew immediately that this was not one of them. It seemed to drift sideways and then, as my attention fixed on it, it pulsed with a swelling, brighter light that doubled its overall size before shooting across the sky, flashing once more, and vanishing from sight.

I got to my feet, staring open mouthed, trying to make sense of what I had seen, heart racing, muttering to myself in excited Polish. I was so fixated on the sky that I did not notice that I was no longer alone.

"Jerzy?"

It was Hartsfeld.

"Did you see that?" I asked in a breathless whisper.

"See what?"

"A star. Or a plane. Something. It came from over there and then streaked that way."

"A meteor, perhaps," said Hartsfeld.

"No," I said. "It changed speeds, maybe direction too. And it got brighter."

"I think you're half asleep," he said, with a little smile. "You should get some rest. Long day tomorrow."

"No," I said. "I really saw it. Maybe if we wait, we'll see another."

"Sleep time, Seaman," said Hartsfeld, still smiling. "That's an order."

I scowled, then nodded.

"Are the others asleep?" I asked, trying to sound casual.

The diplomat gave me a curious look, removing his glasses, and he seemed to read my concern about Belasco.

"Does that matter?" he asked, and there was something hard in his face.

"No, sir," I said. "Good night."

He just watched me, saying nothing, and I had the distinct impression that he didn't like me, though I didn't think I had given him any cause.

I crawled into the tent, careful to make no noise or brush up against the other sleeping bags. In the dark, I wasn't sure which one was Belasco and which was Ignacio, so I unrolled my bag with the delicacy of defusing a bomb and slid inside.

Only when I was secure on my side, huddled into a defensive curl with the sleeping bag pulled up around my head, did I permit myself to replay what I had seen in the sky. I feel asleep thinking about it, managing to forget Belasco and the other dangers of our mission until morning.

I SAID NOTHING ABOUT WHAT I HAD SEEN THE NIGHT before as we ate our furtive little breakfasts and reloaded the jeep. Belasco must have gotten hold of a bottle of spirits somewhere. The tent smelled of his acrid breath, and he was surly all morning, shouldering me aside as he climbed aboard. It was warmer than it had been, and the further north we drove, the hotter it became. The road turned to a pitted track, overgrown with potholes deep enough to drown a goat, and the trees crowded in, until we were covered by a towering canopy. It still wasn't the jungle of *King Solomon's Mines*, but it was close, heavy with humidity and the cries of strange wild things. Once a troupe of peculiar, long-nosed, ring-tailed creatures the size of large housecats came out onto the path in front of us and, when we stopped, crowded around the jeep, peering in with bright eyes, holding their sides with paws more like hands than any non-human creature I had ever seen. Ignacio called them coati. Belasco gave them a blank stare and shooed them roughly away.

"Let's just get wherever the hell we are going," he muttered, closing his eyes and trying to sleep.

We were getting close. Hartsfeld studied his map and twice ordered that we stop so he could listen for water.

Eventually he consulted his compass and directed us off the main road, such as it was, and onto a still smaller path that crawled deeper into the forest to the northwest in a region he referred to as Corrientes.

"There should be a village up here," he said. "We will ask there."

I was forcefully struck by the strangeness of our mission, its seeming randomness. We had not been told how much Hartsfeld knew, or suspected, about the location of Kammler and the other Nazi officers. The idea that we were now going to start questioning whoever we found living in these remote woods seemed bizarre in the extreme.

"Is that not risky?" I said. "Asking local people who may have been paid off already by the men we are looking for."

"I think I can manage, thank you, Seaman," said Hartsfeld, not looking up from his map. "If I've learned anything in the foreign services, dealing with these people, it's how to get what I want without actually asking for it."

His use of the phrase "these people" bothered me, and not only because I doubted the people he dealt with in the offices of Buenos Aires were the same as the ones up here in the rainforest. But it was also the kind of phrase the Nazis had used about people like me. I shaded my eyes from the glare and watched an unreasonably iridescent bird with long, trailing tail feathers.

Soon, I was using my hands to protect my face and arms from the great leaves pressing in on the car, and swatting at the constant buzz of insects around my head.

"This," said Belasco, confidingly, "is bullshit."

Something in his irritated grumpiness amused me, and for once I actually laughed so that he, surprised, grinned back, as if we were friends, united in misery.

WE FOUND THE VILLAGE—OR *A* VILLAGE—AS WE PUSHED deeper into the forest, but our first attempts to get information from the locals met with an unexpected snag. The woman we found grinding maize, her children gathered around her on the dirt floor of her open house, did not speak Spanish. The other three jabbered away at her, but got nothing useful in return.

"Guarani," Ignacio pronounced with casual scorn. "Tupí."

Belasco demanded something of Ignacio—presumably whether he knew any words of these other languages—but the Argentine shook his head emphatically, and then a flicker of amusement at his employers' stupidity.

Hartsfeld scowled, then gave him another slew of instructions, whereupon the boy set the vehicle in motion again. Twice more, we stopped to talk to the natives, but made no headway, so that eventually we drove on, hoping for better luck at the next settlement we found.

We were rewarded on the shores of a long sparkling lake, where, for a few coins, a Spanish-speaking fisherman agreed to serve as interpreter with the locals in the village. So we drove back, hot and irritable now, but at least with a sense of progress made.

It was hard going, and I saw a lot of head shaking and blank looks. What I didn't see, however, was deception.

These people just didn't know anything about the men we were looking for. They did, however, verify where we were, and when we got back into the car, Hartsfeld looked pleased.

"Eight miles north of here," he said. "We'll get more information there."

"And when we find them?" asked Belasco. "What do we do then? Take down the map coordinates and drive back to Buenos Aires? What is the point, if you already know where they are?"

"We don't," said Hartsfeld, not turning round. "Not precisely. We need a good fix on where they are, and how many of them there are, and what they have with them."

"So we can do what?" Belasco pressed. "Drop the US Airborne on them? Bomb the shit out of the whole area?"

"That's not your concern," said Hartsfeld, haughtily.

"If we're gonna restart the Second World War in the goddamned jungles of Argentina, I'd like to know about it," Belasco shot back.

"Just follow your orders," said Hartsfeld, "and we'll have no problems."

Belasco said nothing, but I couldn't help worrying just how far Hartsfeld's authority would stretch out here in the jungle.

WE CAME UPON THE NEXT VILLAGE THAT AFTERNOON. Despite offers of more money, our fisherman translator had refused to come with us, so we were faced once more with the prospect of trying to make ourselves understood. We found a Spanish speaker on our second attempt. Half the village gathered to hear what was going on, and there was a lot of arguing and pointing off into the forest as Hartsfeld probed them. Again, I saw no signs that anyone was keeping anything secret, and it struck me that the Nazis would want as few dealings as possible with people such as these.

At last Hartsfeld seemed satisfied.

"White people were seen going in this direction two weeks ago," he said, pointing along a trail far too narrow for the jeep.

"Two weeks?" Belasco scoffed. "They could be anywhere by now."

Hartsfeld shook his head.

"That was only the most recent group," he said. "Apparently they have been coming here for several years, bringing things with them. The boys in the village have been out to where they went and say there is something there. Something we are going to want to see. I think, gentlemen, that we've found what we came for."

WE UNLOADED THE CAR WHERE IT STOOD, OPENING UP THE equipment crates, but leaving the tent and all but a little of the food and water. We would carry no more than we needed and, if possible, would be back within a few hours. The crate included a .45 caliber Thompson submachine gun and an M1 Garand. Belasco took the sub, so I got the rifle, a weapon I hadn't fired since Boot Camp.

"Not to be used unless absolutely necessary," said Hartsfeld, eying Belasco significantly. "This is a recon mission only. You shoot to keep yourself alive. That's all."

Belasco gave me an unreadable look. He didn't like Nazis. I didn't either, but for all his machismo and swagger, I don't think he knew what it was like to kill one. I did.

"Keep the flashlights off unless absolutely necessary," said Hartsfeld, as we began our trek along the path. For now, we didn't need them, but after an hour's hike, the sun was almost down and the jungle was giving itself over to a deep green darkness. Ignacio eyed the rifle slung across my back warily. I didn't know why he was still with us, instead of waiting at the car, but Hartsfeld had insisted.

"Wouldn't want to walk into the jungle and vanish without trace," he remarked to me.

I scowled, but nodded. It made about as much sense as the rest of this mission.

NIGHT CAME ON FAST IN THE RAINFOREST. HOWLER monkeys screamed in the treetops, and strange birds, with heavy-looking beaks as long as their bodies, flew off to their roosts. For all I knew, we were watched by jaguars, though I saw no sign of them. What we saw instead was far stranger and more unexpected.

At first I thought it was a house, looming out of the darkness of the trees, but then I realized it was far larger than any house, and of a completely different style of construction than anything we had seen in the last few days. It was more like the curtain wall of a stone castle, with high shuttered windows that leaked light and a great barred door set in a heavy arch, and it was no more native to these steamy woods than I was. In fact, the building was so unlike the jungle around it that the whole felt more than imposing—it felt dreamlike, as if the structure had been picked up from somewhere else and dropped here.

"What the hell?" breathed Belasco, dropping into a crouch.

I moved to the other side of the path, unslinging the rifle and bringing its muzzle to bear on the uncanny door. Ignacio hung back, looking suddenly very unsure of himself.

Hartsfeld, however, just smiled.

"Cover me," he said to Belasco, reaching inside his sweat-stained jacket as he approached the door.

Hartsfeld moved casually, walking upright, no trace of caution in his gait, no attempt to make himself small in case gunfire erupted from one of those upper windows. It felt . . . wrong. As Belasco edged out towards him, I found myself almost overwhelmed by the urge to call him back.

Hartsfeld reached the door, and I realized what he had drawn from his pocket.

It was a key. I didn't see it, not at first, but I heard the snap of a lock, and the creak of the door, and suddenly the darkness of the jungle was lit by a soft, yellowish glow from within. Hartsfeld spoke, and it took me a moment to process the significance of what he had said. The words—"I'm here, but I have brought guests"—were less important, perhaps, than the fact that he said them in German: *"Ich bin hier, aber ich habe die Gäste gebracht."*

And now I did call to Belasco, but Hartsfeld was already turning, pocketing the key, and drawing a black automatic pistol. He aimed it squarely at Belasco who, finally realizing what was happening, pointed the submachine gun at the diplomat in the doorway, and squeezed the trigger.

There was a click, but nothing else happened, and silhouetted in the unearthly arch and with his Nazi comrades at his back, Hartsfeld gave a little grunt that was almost a laugh.

"I'm afraid I took the liberty of removing the firing pins from your weapons last night," he said.

And then he started shooting.

BARNEY AND BETTY HILL
White Mountains, NH, September 1961

I T HAD BEEN A LONG TRIP, AND THERE WERE STILL SEV-
eral hours to go to before they reached Portsmouth, but
the New Hampshire roads were quiet, and the night
was clear. Barney Hill checked his side view mirrors and
shifted in the driver's seat, feeling the weight of the pistol
in his pocket. It would normally stay in the trunk, but they
had picnicked near Twin Mountain, and Betty was afraid
of bears.

Niagara had been something to see. The height, the
sheer volume of the water crashing down the cliff face. Just
amazing, and alone worth the drive, even though the air
pollution made it hard to see. The picnic at Twin Mountain

had been his idea. He hadn't said as much to Betty, but he was tired of the sidelong looks in the diners, the probing mixtures of curiosity and shock, gazes turned quickly away when he looked around. Betty didn't seem to notice, though he wondered if that was a choice, a blind spot she had developed to get through the day. Every day, Barney was reminded that it was still unusual to see a black man with a white wife, but it wore on him like the teeth of a saw rasped along barbed wire. And that was just the polite folk, the ones who averted their eyes or forced a smile as if nothing were wrong, but there were others, the ones who stared, or waited for you to look at them before spitting pointedly on the ground. Sometimes it was worse. Betty ignored it, but the revolver in his pocket was there to keep more than bears away, and it was no accident that their vacations took them north, not south.

Patsy Kline was crooning "I Fall to Pieces" on the radio, turned down so low that Barney could barely hear it, and then Bobby Vee singing "Take Good Care of My Baby." Chicago White Sox second baseman Nellie Fox had driven in two runs to beat the Red Sox 5-1 earlier that day, the news said. Barney turned to his wife to see if she was sleeping and, as she smiled drowsily at him, took her hand for a moment.

"Watch the road, lover boy," she said in her flat New England voice, grinning before turning to the dark, wooded hills outside.

"Just a couple more hours now," he said. "You can sleep if you want."

"Okay," she said. She sounded vague, as if she were already drifting off. In her lap, Delsey, their overindulged pet dachshund, shifted and looked up, tongue lolling and eyes hopeful. Barney wanted to get a few more miles under their belts before stopping to let the dog go out, but she was clearly getting restless.

He settled back, turning the big Chevy's steering wheel with a firm but easy grip as he angled it round the winding country road. It was a good car. A classic already. The kind that never went out of style and, with a little loving care, would run forever.

They passed through Lancaster, following Route 3 south towards White Mountain National Forest, with Mount Washington looming on their left. It was a region infamous for erratic weather and lost hikers—over a hundred fatalities, it was said—and Barney was glad that they were making the trip now, before the cold weather set in. He checked the Bel Air's gas gauge. The last thing he wanted was to get stranded up here. He didn't think they'd be in any real danger, but his buddies at the post office—who'd been calling him the Fearless Explorer ever since he'd told them about the trip north of the border—would never let him live it down

He grinned at the thought.

"What's that?"

Betty was, apparently, still awake.

"What's what?" he said.

"Over there," she said. She popped the glove compartment open and pulled out the field glasses they had used to look at the waterfall earlier. "Slow down," she said. "I can't see it."

"See what?" he said, easing off on the gas.

"Up there," said Betty. "Look. There's a light. See? Just to the side of the moon. It's moving."

"I don't see it."

"Right there. Look, it's getting brighter."

"Shooting star, maybe."

"It's going up."

"Plane then."

"Pull over," said Betty. "I want to use the binoculars."

"Oh, come on, Betty," Barney replied. "We still have a ways to go."

"Going to have let Delsey out soon," said Betty. "May as well be now."

Barney sighed and shot the dog a sour look.

"Fine," he said, turning the wheel and applying the brakes. He wasn't sure why they'd brought the damn dog in the first place. It wasn't like she needed to see the sights. They could have kenneled her for a night or two. Wouldn't have been the end of the world. But Betty wouldn't hear of it.

Part of the family, she'd said. Barney rolled his eyes, but he smiled at the same time. People didn't get them, but he loved his wife very much, and for all the looks they got, he had never doubted, for one moment, that marrying her had been the right thing to do.

While Betty fussed with the binoculars, he watched the dog do its business on the grass shoulder, inhaling the cool of the forest air and listening to the chirp of insects and thanking God it wasn't black fly season. He'd turned the headlights off, and the mountains and trees were dark to the point of blackness.

"It's crossing in front of the moon," said Betty, tracking with her binoculars. "It has lights on it."

"Probably a jetliner headed to Montreal," said Barney.

"It's not the right shape. Look."

She handed him the binoculars. At first he couldn't find it. There was nothing to focus on, but when he saw the light tracking northwest with his naked eye, he was able to home in with the field glasses.

"Plane," he said, peering at the lighted craft as it angled steadily up the way they had come. "Gotta be."

And then, without warning, it changed direction, a sharp turn and hard descent, a move unlike any plane he had ever seen before. He lowered the binoculars so he could find the craft again, and tried to refocus on it, but it was moving too quickly.

"It's coming right for us," he said, baffled. For a moment, the two of them watched, their disinterested dog snuffling at their feet, and then Barney felt a slow but rising unease that he could not explain. "Pick up Delsey," he said. "Get back in the car."

Betty gave him a quizzical look, but she didn't hesitate, and he knew she could feel it too: a muffled and unspecific urgency, just this side of alarm.

But once they were back in the car, headlights on, moving toward Franconia Notch, the feeling turned into a kind of childish excitement. Betty had heard talk of flying saucers from her sister, and the idea that they might have seen one was exhilarating. Barney wasn't so sure, but he had to admit that the way the craft had moved was about the damnedest thing he'd ever seen.

It took a moment to realize it was still there, and that it seemed to have descended, and if he were a fanciful kind of guy, which he wasn't, Barney would have sworn it was following them. It had been heading north before. Not any-more. Now it was slipping south, lower and lower in the sky, so that from time to time, it would be screened out entirely by the craggy landscape of mountains and the tall pines that lined the road. As they passed Cannon Mountain, the object seemed to scud through the air only a couple of hun-dred yards above them. It was now clearly not a plane. It had no wings, and resembled a flattened yo-yo with lights along the edge, which seemed to be rotating.

It was also big.

When it passed the great granite outcrop known locally as The Old Man of the Mountain, because of how it looked, in profile, like a head sticking out of the cliff—eyes, mouth, forehead and chin all quite visible—Barney finally got a sense of scale. The thing must have been close to sixty feet across. It was also, as far as he could tell over the noise of the car engine, completely silent, moving in looping bounds, little surges of acceleration that took it up and down, weaving effortlessly from side to side, so that in spite of the dread he'd felt before, Barney couldn't help sensing something playful in the craft's pursuit.

He wondered about that word. Was it really pursuing them? Tracking them, certainly. Watching. Maybe they should find some place where they could call the police or the Air Force.

But Barney didn't like showing up in places he wasn't expected. Not at night, a black man with a white woman in the American backcountry. He'd wait until they saw familiar faces. And maybe even then . . .? Barney knew how to fight from his corner. As a leading member of the Portsmouth NAACP, he was proud of who he was, but he had also learned to pick his battles. He knew that white people looked for a reason not to take him seriously. Telling the world he'd spent the evening playing hide and seek with a flying saucer was as good as dressing up as Uncle Remus and sitting on the porch with a hay stalk between his teeth.

The disk slid into the night behind them and vanished. Then, a mile south of Indian Head, it returned, in front of them now and lower than ever, so that it seemed to sit motionless above the road directly ahead. Barney slowed the Bel Air to a crawl, and eventually came to a halt. The saucer hovered in front of them, no more than eighty feet in the air. Barney, his earlier apprehension returning tenfold, was sure that he did not want to drive the car under the craft.

"Stay here," he said. He reached over and took the binoculars from his wife's lap.

"What are you doing?" asked Betty.

"Just wait here," he said, checking the pistol in his pocket, shouldering the door open and stepping out onto the road.

"Barney, you get back in here," said Betty, her voice shrill with fear.

"One second," he said.

He walked up the road, slowly, bathed in the hard white light from the craft in front of him. As he got closer, he found that it seemed to be angled down toward him, and at its rim, he could see windows tilted at the road. At him. As he stepped inside the glare, he could make out shapes at the windows. Figures in what he took to be black uniforms. His sense was that they were human-like but not human. He raised the binoculars to see better, but as he did so, the object seemed to change. Structures descended smoothly from the sides and underbelly, things that might have been legs and some kind of access chute. Barney turned quickly back to the car, suddenly sure that they had to get out of there. Now.

He dragged the Bel Air's door open and fell into the driver's seat, hands trembling as he turned the ignition key.

"They're going to take us!" he babbled. "They're trying to capture us!"

"God!" Betty exclaimed.

"Watch for them," Barney commanded as he gunned the engine.

"It's moving!"

The legs, or whatever they had been, retracted again. The ship moved directly overhead. For a moment, the car was full of its strange, hard light. Betty was crying. Delsey was whimpering. Barney floored the accelerator, sending them rocketing away down the road as fast as he dared go.

"Are they still behind us?" he asked.

Betty wound down her window and leaned out, craning her neck and looking all around.

"I don't see it," she shouted into the wind. "I don't see anything."

But then the noise started, a strange rhythmic plinking that seemed to come from the Bel Air's trunk. The car seemed to hum with energy. Barney touched the metal of the door gingerly, expecting to feel the bite of static electricity, but got only a dull vibration, quite separate from what the Bel Air's engine was doing. Almost immediately, the long drive and all the mental focus required to operate the car through hundreds of miles of empty road seemed to weigh on him. His eyelids drooped, his head lolled, and he felt the leaden pressure of sleep swallow him.

HE CAME TO WITH A START.

He blinked and shifted deliberately.

That had been close. Falling asleep at the wheel had always been one of his greatest fears. Out here in the woods, that could only end badly. He felt Betty stir beside him and saw she was waking up from a nap too.

There had been something they had been talking about, but he couldn't remember what it was, and that meant he really had fallen asleep, which was terrifying. Maybe he should get a cup of coffee somewhere. He checked his watch, but it had stopped, and that was weird, because he knew he had wound it that morning.

"What time is it?" he asked.

"It's . . . oh, damn."

"What?"

"Looks like my watch stopped," Betty answered. "Where are we?"

"Indian Head, right?" said Barney, less sure than he would have liked.

Betty paused.

"That sign said Tilton," she said.

"Can't be," said Barney. "That's over thirty miles away. We haven't gone through Plymouth yet."

But the town that they drove through was indeed Tilton.

"That's not possible," said Barney. "I can't have been that tired and not wrecked the car. You remember going through Plymouth?"

Betty shook her head. She looked rattled.

"I don't remember anything since . . ." she reached into her memory, then shook her head. "I don't know. Something. There was a light in the sky."

"We stopped," said Barney, dragging the memory back to the surface as if he were reeling in some strange fish, dark and nightmarish, from the deep sea.

"We set off again," said Betty. "But there was another light. A roadblock."

Barney nodded, his skin starting to creep, the hair on his neck rising.

"This isn't right," he said. "Let's stop. I need to get gas and a cup of coffee."

"And a shower," said Betty. It was a bizarre thing to say, and she laughed, but it turned into a gasp, almost a sob and there was something haunted in her eyes.

"Yes," said Barney, sensing it too. "A shower. Yes."

He felt . . . unclean. He couldn't explain it. It was as if something had happened that he could not recall, something had been done to him.

"My dress," said Betty. Her voice was at once absent and fearful. "It's torn. When did that happen?"

Barney looked at her, fingering the ragged hem of her dress, and he felt it again, that there was something just out of reach of his memory. He glanced down. His carefully polished shoes were scuffed and dirty.

What the hell?

They stopped at the first all night gas station they could find, and both went inside to use the restroom, to wash—no to *scrub*—as much of their bodies as they could. They didn't know why. It was while they were paying for the gas that Betty tried to set her watch to the clock above the register. The watch wouldn't restart. Neither would Barney's. But that was nothing compared to the shock of discovering that it was almost dawn.

They had lost nearly three hours. What had happened in that time was a dark, narrow hole in their memories. No matter how hard they stared into it, they could not see the bottom.

ALAN
Dreamland, Nevada

"**W**HAT THE HELL WERE YOU THINKING?" HATCHER demanded. "First tourist flights to Stonehenge, now this! When you are on a mission with Morat, he is your commanding officer and you do as he tells you. You do not go chasing imaginary lights across the sky on a whim."

"Wasn't imaginary," said Alan. "Or a whim."

"Did I ask you to speak, Major? Then shut up."

Alan did not reply.

"Your instruments show no record of any other craft," Hatcher continued, his voice lower, but his eyes as hard and level as ever. "Things are different up there. They look different. What you think you are seeing isn't always what you are seeing. You don't yet have the experience to distinguish between the things you see. You need to learn to ignore the irrelevant stuff."

"Forgive me for saying so, but it looked like . . ."

"Are you arguing with me, Major?" Hatcher roared, the color rising in his cheeks.

"No, sir, but I've had twelve years combat air experience and have logged thousands of hours in the air. My instincts should count for something. If they don't, why am I here?"

"Your talent is not in doubt, Major," said Hatcher. "But to answer your question, you're here to learn. Remember that. You were in charge of a craft that costs as much as the GNP of several small countries, flying it for the first time, God help you, in low earth orbit. Do you know what would have happened if you'd lost control of it, or hit something? You are not God, Alan. It may hurt to admit it, but in spite of all your experience, this is a new field for you. You are, effectively, a cadet. I've listened to the recordings. You disobeyed three direct orders and put your craft in peril, on what amounted to no more than a sensory hunch, a glitch. In any other program, you'd not only be grounded, you'd be out. You know that?"

Alan hesitated, then nodded.

Hatcher looked at him for a long moment, then nodded back.

"I don't think I need to tell you to keep your nose clean from here on," said Hatcher, returning to his desk. "You will not be given another chance."

▼   ▼   ▼

THE NEXT DAY, ALAN TOLD REGIS WHAT HAD HAPPENED, or as much of it as security protocols permitted. The big man shook his head in wonder.

"I can't believe they didn't ground you," he said.

"Me too," said Alan.

In fact, he wasn't even given a day off. That evening, he was summoned to the Papoose Lake hangar and directed back to the Locust. There was no sign of either Hatcher or Morat. The man who gave him his instructions was the suited man with the clipboard he'd seen before but did not know. The man was freckled, red headed, and his name badge said "Riordan."

"Stay in US air space and do not leave the troposphere."

"That's it?" said Alan. "Nothing more specific?"

"Consider it free flight practice," said Riordan. If he knew Alan was in the doghouse, he gave no sign of it.

The ground crew wore helmets that partly covered their faces. Alan was struck, as he boarded the ship, by how, apart from Regis, with whom he was still rebuilding his friendship, he knew almost no one at the base except for the people who seemed most pissed off at him. It was a depressing thought, not because he was a particularly social animal. He never had been. It was one of the things Lacey had found hardest to deal with about him. He didn't ordinarily crave company, and was happiest, he'd once stupidly admitted to her, when he was alone. But now he felt a strange urge to talk to someone—anyone—about what he was going through, about the world he had discovered, and the ship he was flying. He wanted to discuss its strangeness and the truly awesome feeling of being at the helm. He wanted to describe what it was like to dart across the sky at Mach 7 over the Atlantic, or angle his way between satellites as the earth turned slowly beneath him, but he couldn't. The only people he could talk to about his experiences were watching him for signs that he couldn't handle his assignment, waiting for him to screw up one more time . . . He should get a beer with Regis after the mission. Off base. As old friends.

He took the Locust up, turned its lights out and put the craft through a series of maneuvers over the Rockies and out over Utah's Great Salt Lake before selecting the coordinates for Riverside, Iowa, the fictional home of Star Trek's Captain James T. Kirk. If he was going to be accused of acting on a whim, he may as well do the thing right. He moved over it at twenty thousand feet, watching for air traffic, then found a solitary farm and settled into a dead air hover only six hundred feet above its barn. The sky was moonless, but there were lights on in the house. Alan watched as a young man came home in an old pickup, went inside, then came out again with a beer and sat on the stoop to drink it. The young man was oblivious, sipping his beer and gazing up at the stars, unaware that a portion of them above the house had been blotted out by an impossible triangular ship.

Hatcher had warned Alan that he wasn't God. Obviously. So obvious, in fact, that at the time, Alan was surprised that the CIA man had troubled to say it at all.

But here he was, watching from the silent heavens as the man on his porch wiped his mouth, took his empty beer bottle inside and closed up the house for the night.

"Of course I'm not God," Alan reminded himself aloud. "But sometimes it sure does feel like it."

ALAN MADE FOUR FLIGHTS IN THE NEXT WEEK, TWO INTO low earth orbit. At no time did he glimpse anything like the arrowhead craft he'd seen that first time with Morat. The strange ship tugged at the edge of Alan's memory, a delta-shaped question mark that made him wonder what was still being kept from him.

That week, Alan saw Hatcher only once and Morat not at all. When he asked about him, he was told only that agent Morat was "not on base at this time," though whether he'd gone via Gulfstream to Andrews Air Force Base, or by Locust to the Congo basin, or to the International Space Station, no one was saying. He saw Riordan, the red-haired man, twice, but still did not know his precise rank or function. His orders were sent by encrypted e-mail to his tablet, which he then inserted into a dock in the cockpit of the Locust.

He spent what free time he had with Barry Regis, reminiscing, playing cards, low stress, non-classified stuff, and he relished it all the more because he knew that friendship was virtually unknown on the base. There were other pilots, he knew, but he had never been introduced to them. People came in to work and were bussed out. Those who stayed on kept to themselves, as they were told to, life going on in intentional isolation. Twice as he sat with Regis, Alan had seen Hatcher, and twice he'd read in Hatcher's face a kind of deliberate permission. Alan's mental health was being looked after.

He was okay with that.

His missions were generally just getting familiar with the craft. They also had a reconnaissance component, though it was not always clear what he was looking for. He was given coordinates, and sometimes a fight plan, told to engage his sensors and recording devices at key moments. All of the flights were in darkness, the sensors gathering far more information than Alan could actually get with his own senses. The missions were as dull as could be in such a futuristic ship with quirks and capabilities that were still new to him.

Even so, a pattern emerged.

Every location patrolled—cautiously and at altitude, lights out and counter measures engaged—took place over a single icy swatch of the globe: Mongolia, Kazakhstan and Russia. Each mission avoided population centers—not hard, where the territory was vast and the population small and nomadic—and focused on remote facilities accessed by long, lonely roads, characterized by windowless concrete structures, security walls and minor airfields. Some of them showed circular structures that might have been the tops of missile silos, but the places might just as easily have been training camps or nuclear power stations. There was no way of knowing, from what he could see, and the viewers—even with night vision mode enabled—gave him little to go on. The Locust, often sitting motionless in the sky for minutes or even hours, shot ultra-high resolution footage that an onboard computer processed, using a complex algorithm that analyzed minute vibrations in ordinary objects: plants, glass windows, cans of soda. These could, Professor Beaker had told him, be decoded into speech, recreating any conversations that took place in proximity to those objects. Much of it would be unusable, some of it would be coherent but useless, "but a tiny fraction," said Beaker, "would be gold."

After each mission, as Alan slouched off to debriefing, and another day of classes and simulations, the same nameless tech in a blue flight suit boarded the ship, downloaded the data to a hand-held computer, and deleted and wrote over all records from the Locust's hard drive. Alan had gone, he thought bleakly, from being a god, to being a drone.

He said as much to Hatcher when they met to debrief at the end of the week.

"The work is not sufficiently interesting for you, Major?" asked Hatcher, dry as the desert air.

"It's not that, sir," said Alan. "It just feels like I'm doing a job you could do just as well with a Reaper controlled from one of those Vegas trailers the media loves to talk about, rather than risk exposing of the Locust."

"What makes you think it's the *bases* we're surveilling?"

"As opposed to what?" Alan replied.

For a moment, Hatcher said nothing, watching Alan, smiling slightly as realization dawned in the pilot's face.

"Me," Alan said. "It's not about the ground locations at all. You're monitoring me."

Hatcher's fractional shrug conceded the point. "Partly," he said. "We have to be sure you can follow orders and operate safely in foreign airspace. And the data you have been collecting has been very useful. No one is wasting your time, Major."

This was in response to Alan's frown and the way he looked into the corner of the room.

"So I passed?" he said, at last.

"It wasn't a test," said Hatcher, though he chuckled at Alan's raised eyebrow. "Okay. It was kind of a test. And yes, you passed. And before you can ask what you won for doing so, I'd like to give you your new assignment."

He handed over his tablet and Alan scrolled through the details. Half way through he looked up, shocked.

"This is a daylight op,'" he said.

"Yes."

"Over Moscow."

"Yes. We have an agent waiting to upload some data."

"I'll get shot down."

"You know the craft's evasive capacity and speed," said Hatcher. "And there are countermeasures we have not yet revealed to you which will help."

"Such as?"

Hatcher thought for a moment, then decided.

"Come with me," he said.

THEY RODE THE EMPTY, BLACKED-OUT SCHOOL BUS TO the Papoose facility but walked further, to a different door in the cliff, and another hangar. Hatcher led the way, typing his codes and going through weight and retinal checks at each door. The crew inside still looked up with surprise when he entered, Alan a half step behind. They were working on a pair of Locusts, though whether they were the ones he and Morat had flown, Alan couldn't tell. The craft bore no insignia or identifying marks. One was partially disassembled, the skin of its great angular wing peeled back in panels to reveal the workings within.

Beyond it was another door. It was open, showing another hangar and, sitting alone in the middle, a silvery disk, a classic "flying saucer," sleek and round, with a central bulge that seemed to have windows, the rest clad in steel or aluminum, bright as chrome. It seemed to sit in mid-air, though at this distance, it was impossible to be sure it wasn't suspended or otherwise held up by something Alan couldn't see. He angled his head to get a better look, and one of the ground crew was suddenly in his face and shouting, his hands up.

It took a second for Alan to realize he wasn't the one being yelled at. A soldier, standing behind the first Locust, came around its long, knife-like wing with his M4 at the ready. Alan hastily turned back to face the door they'd come in through, raising his hands. When he turned back, the door into the hangar beyond had been rolled shut and the saucer—whatever it was—had vanished.

Hatcher gave him a thoughtful look, then snapped a smile into place.

"Sorry about that," he said, as the place went back to work as if nothing had happened. "Prototype. Best to put it out of your mind."

"I can try," said Alan.

"So," said Hatcher, walking purposefully to the tech who'd raised the alarm. "I'm here to show Major Young the cloak. He'll be using it this afternoon. My clearance," he added, showing his tablet. "And his."

The tech scanned the computer documents and then double-checked them on a device of his own, while a single word bounced around in Alan's head.

Cloak.

He watched the technician climb the stairs into the cockpit, blinking as one of the craft's power systems engaged and a light ran around the triangular wing. Alan shot Hatcher a dubious look, a half-smile that said this was all a kind of joke that he was already in on. Cloaking? They couldn't be serious. It must be some kind of radar counter measure, something that confused ground arrays, bouncing the signal to make it shift, or cause it to be mistaken for a flock of birds, or . . .

The closest Locust vanished.

One moment it had been there. The next, without a sound, the air seemed to ripple, and it was gone.

Or very nearly. Alan could see through the space where the ship had been to the partially disassembled craft behind it, and the wall of the hangar with its now carefully closed door. But there was something very slightly off about the image. It wasn't just that his brain rebelled against the idea of seeing through something so obviously solid. The ripple effect that had marked the ship's disappearance hadn't gone completely, and when he looked to the other Locust, it seemed like things were not exactly in the right place. Close. Very close, in fact, but not quite.

He followed a seam in the concrete floor and watched the way it seemed to break and continue an inch or two out of place before reconnecting with its proper line on the other side. The ship was clearly still there, but somehow, something was bending his sight around it.

My eyes are made the fools of the other senses, he thought, a line from Shakespeare that some part of his brain had retained since high school. It had never made sense to him until now. He shifted from foot to foot, watching the way his vision changed so that it was just possible to imagine the shape that was so bizarrely lost to sight. Without turning away, he asked the question he always seemed to be asking these days.

"How is this possible?"

He got the usual answer.

"Doesn't really matter, does it?" said Hatcher. "If it helps, it's all about bending light. Light normally travels in straight lines, and you see along those lines. If they can be distorted around an object, the eye—following the curved lines—can be fooled into thinking it's seeing normally, when in fact the system has created a visual dead space in the center. And just so you know, it will disengage if you go above Mach 1. It's not flawless, but it is, as they say, close enough for government work."

Alan gaped at him, then—as the cloak was disengaged—back at the ship that seemed somehow even more magical, now that he could see it again.

"This gentleman will show you how to engage the system and when to use it," said Hatcher. "And don't get overconfident. The cloak generates an ion signature of its own that could actually make it easier for certain sophisticated tracking systems to lock onto it, so don't assume you're truly invisible. We'll activate the onboard computer's vocal interface so that you can simply speak commands: the voice recognition software is state of the art, but then you'd expect that."

"Yes."

"You won't be able to talk to us, however. Not with the cloak engaged."

"Understood."

"If you see evidence that you've been detected," Hatcher said, "you hit the home button. I don't care how much of the mission has been completed. You return to base immediately by the fastest safe route. You got that, Major? *Immediately*. This is your primary directive. Hesitate, dodge, decide to go exploring, discharge your weapons or otherwise disobey that fundamental principle, and you will never fly in this or any similar craft again. Are we clear?"

"Crystal," said Alan.

"Okay," said Hatcher. "Bring us back some nice pictures of the Kremlin."

THE FIRST PART OF THE MISSION WENT FINE. ALAN ENGAGED the cloak twenty minutes before sunrise, crossing into

Russian airspace at ten minutes after nine a.m. local. An hour later, he was over Moscow, his multi-source, situational awareness display swarming with aircraft—most of them civilian—but he saw no evidence that any of them knew he was there. His orders required him to drop to a thousand feet over Red Square, where he would have to hold position for exactly six minutes while his systems uploaded the data being transmitted to him from an operative below.

It was utterly surreal. The Locust hung there in the bright morning sun, and below him, Alan could see the colorful onion bulb minarets of Saint Basil's Cathedral and the long, angular brick wall and towers surrounding the Kremlin complex. Alan was old enough to recall those tedious, terrifying Soviet armored parades from the Reagan era, all those olive green tanks and missile carriers driving slowly past the balcony while politburo officials stood ramrod straight. And now he was here, in a different age but still, in a sense, an invader.

Alan did not pay attention to politics. He had long since decided it was best for someone in his position not to. It muddied the waters. But he was curious as to what was going on, and what he was participating in, however unwittingly.

He checked the onboard chronometer. Three minutes and ten seconds.

He drummed his fingers on his armrest. The silence of his engines unnerved him, as did the flickers of light from his MSSA scanner as yet another plane headed out of the city. He toggled between the political, topographical and multispectral settings that formed the background to the transponder, IFF and other integrated feeds. The Locust avoided the easily detectable pinging of radar by operating passive interferemetrics utilizing the ambient radio frequencies from all other transmissions to discover, ID and track those surface contacts and unknowns that were collectively known as *skunks*.

There was a long white building with an ornamental gilded roof along one side of the square. People were coming and going, though there was less bustle than he had expected.

Four minutes. The upload bar was filling slowly. Alan had asked Hatcher why their operative couldn't just upload to Dropbox or something, like everybody else, but Hatcher had only smiled and shook his head.

"Because the Internet is so secure, you mean?" he said.

Three minutes.

Something flashed on his MSSA screen. Two somethings. They were coming towards him, though that was surely coincidence. Alan looked to adjust position without breaking the upload connection, sliding the ship to the side and lowering another hundred feet.

The two craft on the MSSA made the same adjustment. And now a siren shrieked through the cockpit. There was no doubt about it. The two planes—if that was what they were—were on an intercept course.

Someone could see him.

Some kind of bistatic radar designed to spot low observable platforms? Perhaps, though it was surprising.

Cursing, Alan disengaged the upload with 87 seconds still on the clock. The cockpit rang with the cycling siren, and a serene female voice came through his headphones from the onboard computer.

"Two aircraft on attack vector. Configuration matches: Sukhoi SU-30. Engaging avoidance systems."

Alan grimaced. The SU-30—what he was used to calling a Flanker-C—was a fast and maneuverable fighter. But it was no match for the speed of the Locust. He sent the craft into a near vertical climb and gunned the engine to just below Mach 1 to keep the cloak intact as long as he dared. Moscow fell away beneath him as he pushed the ship as close to the speed of sound as he could. He scanned the MSSA. The fighters were closing fast. In seconds, they would be in combat range.

He waited, shooting out over the suburban sprawl north of Moscow, then pulling east, where there were few towns. There was a lake showing on his map. The Flankers were almost on him.

"Incoming aircraft weapons systems online and searching for target," said the computer evenly.

One more second . . .

He breathed.

"Missile away and incoming," said the computer.

Another half second . . .

Alan slid his speed gauge to Mach 4 and punched the controls.

He felt it this time, the slide and pop as he shed the cloak and tore across the sky, climbing all the time. The missiles fell behind him and the fighters that released them immediately slowed, banking, as if they thought they'd overshot him.

Alan released a whoop of triumph, suddenly conscious of the sweat on his upper lip.

The lake was already behind him. He'd need to decide whether to keep going east or double back over Europe and the Atlantic. He began some hasty mental calculations, tracking the position of the sun. If we were going home with his tail between his legs and hostile fighters on the sniff, he'd be better doing it in darkness.

"Incoming craft," said the computer. "Attack vector."

"I already lost them," he muttered.

"New contact," said the computer.

"What?" Alan gasped. "Where? I don't see it! How can they follow me at this speed?"

"That is unknown at this time."

"What kind of aircraft are they?" he said, correcting his course and increasing speed to almost Mach 5.

"Nonconventional," said the computer.

Alan hesitated, shaking his head as if to clear it.

"What does that mean?"

"Configuration of pursuing aircraft is classified," said the computer placidly.

He saw it now, a blip on his MSSA, in his slipstream, no more than four nautical miles behind him. It was matching his speed.

Alan stared.

"Okay," he said. "Let's see how you like heights."

And he pointed the Locust straight up.

"You might be fast," he snarled, "but I'm pretty sure you can't handle space . . ."

"Intercept aircraft closing," said the computer.

It wasn't possible. Alan swung his chair around and stared through what was now the Locust's rear window. There, bursting through the cloud layer into the bright blue stratosphere, hard on his tail, was a ship, chrome bright and shaped like an arrowhead. As Alan gazed, aghast, he saw the unmistakable flash of something in the nose. He was under fire.

He pulled the Locust hard to the left, rolling it and changing direction. There was no point trying to lose his pursuer in space. He had already seen the ship—or one very like it—up there, and knew it could match him turn for turn. As the Locust rolled, he saw a flash of light stab past him.

Lasers.

He dived, reaching for the red homing button, and turned on the auto-flight-planner, thinking furiously about Hatcher's order that he not engage his weapons.

"Decrease speed before engaging homing device," said the computer.

"Not really an option," said Alan, corkscrewing the Locust away from another flash of enemy fire. He came out of the roll and checked his six. The arrowhead was still in pursuit. If its weapons were locked on, he was about to find out.

He pulled the Locust's front point up, spiraled the body of the ship around and pushed it as hard as it would go back towards the pursuing ship. He passed it, no more than thirty yards below his right wing tip, and its bright metal body filled his window as the arrowhead tried to pivot into a chase. Alan slammed the heel of his hand on the all stop, and in the micro second following, hit the homing button.

The Locust seemed to hang motionless for a second, and then was tearing away, sliding out of the world and becoming not plane or bird but the air itself. Alan felt a drag in his guts as the craft leapt away, faster than anything should ever move. Even so, even in that tiny fraction of a second, he saw the pop of console lights, the sudden bangs and screams of something impossible tearing through his hull and knew, in the flare of fire light at his side, the shriek of pain in his face and hand, that he had been hit.

40

JENNIFER
Washington, DC

I T TOOK JENNIFER A LONG TIME TO GET TO SLEEP. SHE woke late in her DC hotel, her head brimming with the follow-up questions she wanted to take to Senator Powers. She brewed coffee in her room while she took a blisteringly hot shower, and now sat sipping the coffee unenthusiastically as she clicked through her e-mail. Nothing. She flipped on the muted TV while she dressed. A local news station was detailing some personal tragedy and showing footage of police cars, their flashers rolling blue and red, intercut with an image of a young, professional-looking woman and an older man in a suit. A familiar man.

Powers.

She stared. Then turned on the sound.

". . . the sixty-eight-year-old senator from Nevada was found in the rented townhouse by his cleaning lady at nine o'clock this morning. Though police have refused to comment on the case at this stage, the apparent suicide seems motivated by a pending story in the *Washington Post* detailing Senator Powers' affair with a junior aide. His family could not be reached for comment, but several members of his staff have expressed their shock and grief at this morning's developments."

Jennifer was frozen in the act of buttoning up her blouse, hands stuck as if her fingers had forgotten what to do. Her mouth and eyes were dry. She blinked deliberately and something of the spell broke, allowing her to sit on the foot of the bed as the images from the television washed over her.

There was, as she supposed there always was, a barely suppressed predatory glee about the reporters, like jackals stumbling on an unattended leopard kill. This only intensified when it was revealed that the *Washington Post*, which had supposedly been about to reveal the Senator's affair, had only gotten wind of the story, from an anonymous source, an hour before the alleged suicide had taken place. A spokesman from the paper, perhaps trying to mitigate his own responsibility, said he thought it unlikely that the Senator's alleged suicide stemmed from any upcoming negative publicity, and that the newspaper had not even begun to verify the accusations made by the anonymous caller.

"We get a dozen of these every week," said the reporter. "There's no reason to assume the story was going anywhere, at least in the short term."

So the story developed a tang of intrigue as well. She could imagine the newsroom's delight as national interest focused on the story.

Jennifer felt a kind of numb disbelief and, trailing it, a gnawing sense of responsibility for the death of the man she had met the night before. Could his conversation with her, there on the steps of the Jefferson Memorial, shrine to all that America was supposed to stand for, have left him with such a profound sense of failure that he'd taken his own life, only hours later?

But then, the official reports of her own father's death, a man who'd been the Senator's friend, said that he had also taken his own life, and she didn't believe that for a minute. If the two deaths were related, caused by the same people, it wasn't so great a leap to think her visit somehow precipitated the Senator's demise.

She shuddered at the thought, her anxiety undercut by a pang of sadness originating in her father's death, but somehow made fresh by this new tragedy. The two men had been similar in age, in temperament, even in their politics. For a moment, it was like she had lost her father again.

There was a knock at the door.

"Housekeeping," said a woman's voice.

Jennifer stiffened.

If her presence had in any way hastened Senator Powers' death, they—Maynard or whoever—would know where she was staying, even though she had signed in with a fake name. It was absurd to hope otherwise.

"Can you come back later, please?" she said, still taut and watchful.

"No problem," said the voice. It had a lilt that might have been Hispanic. Jennifer listened for the sound of feet in the hallway but heard nothing. She pressed her eye to the view-hole and saw, through the distorting fish-eye lens, the back of a middle-aged woman pushing a cart loaded with towels and cleaning products, her head bound demurely with a scarf.

Safe.

For now.

She snatched up the few things she'd brought with her and stuffed them into her bag. Twenty minutes later, Jennifer had checked out and was aboard the shuttle back to the airport. This time, she knew where she should be flying, but what she would find there when she arrived, she couldn't begin to guess.

IT WAS HOT IN LAS VEGAS. SHE'D ASSUMED IT WOULD BE, but it was still only spring and this was Africa hot, a searing, stifling heat, like standing beside a fire close enough to feel your skin cooking whenever you stopped moving. She rented a car from the Alamo stand in the airport, remembering, only a second before the bored attendant asked for it, that she did not have a US license. Fortunately, her International Driver's License, which she'd obtained before going to Swaziland, was still folded up with her passport.

The attendant—barely college age and ill at ease in a jacket and tie—peered at it dubiously but didn't care enough to make trouble. He pushed the keys to a Chevy Impala across the counter to her and sighed pointedly when, as an afterthought, she requested a GPS system. She had an address, but it wasn't like she knew where she was going, though she had studied a Google map on the plane and had a fair idea of where the government protected wilderness land was supposed to be.

Nate Hapsel's ranch bordered Nevada State Route 375 west of Crystal Springs, but it wasn't until she started driving and the GPS calculated the route that she got a sense of just how big America was. The flight from Washington made the point in one way, and she'd amused herself speculating where a flight of comparable length would have taken her from London—Russia? Turkey? Algeria? But it was only sitting in the driver's seat of the rented Impala, watching the miles go by, that the full scale of the place registered. The map she'd studied on her laptop had made it look like Las Vegas was right next to Crystal Springs, but even traveling nearly double the speed limit of all but the fastest UK roads, it took two hours to get there, crossing an unforgiving barren beige landscape of basin and range desert as forbidding as anything she'd seen in Africa.

She worried about being followed. It seemed unlikely. Frequent rear-view mirror checks showed nothing unusual, but if her intuition was correct, the people looking for her had access to serious resources. If some drone lazily circling a couple of thousand feet above her was tracking her car's every mile across the desert, she had no way of knowing.

And if that drone is carrying a missile like the ones they use to take out terrorists in Iraq?

Well, there was no point thinking about that.

She thought of the words inscribed on the wall of the Jefferson Memorial, those high ideals about freedom and equality expanding as society evolved . . .

Surely things couldn't be so far gone that a civilized and democratically elected government would target a visitor like her for elimination because she had asked a few questions?

It should have been a rhetorical question, but she thought of Senator Tom Powers, whose sudden suicide, according the NPR report she had just heard, was being met with incredulity and suspicion from those who had worked with him. But then it didn't need to be a government pulling the strings of deceit, surveillance and murder, did it? She had seen how much money the Maynard Consortium moved around. They could buy and sell most countries. However much people griped about governments and politicians, the power of corporate money had always scared her more. Nations turned on each other, fought bloody and devastating wars, but corporations somehow remained. Her father had taught her that. The Nazis had driven through the war in BMWs, Mercedes and Daimlers. Porsche had designed their tiger tanks. Fiat had done something similar for Mussolini's Italians. Mitsubishi, who built the pleasant, sporty looking passenger sedan that just passed her, had spent the war years building the Japanese its most infamous fighter, the Zero. Corporations were society's cockroaches: they always survived.

She would have forgotten these examples years ago if they had not become part of her anti-capitalist litany, rehearsed in many a university bar and charity work camp over the years. She suspected she was living that corporate reality now, and while she was used to the idea making her angry, its full terrifying potential was just beginning to register.

It was like a breakaway civilization, she thought, a powerful, moneyed organization that owed no allegiance to geography or the other outmoded trappings of the nation state, an entity that lived in the Internet, in anonymous boardrooms, in the interconnected invisible spaghetti of revenue streams and offshore accounts, unnoticed and impossibly powerful, a force moving beneath global affairs for its own ends. She knew the social media graphics about how the world's wealth was distributed, the less than one-percent who controlled over half the world's resources, and she knew how corporate interests had long shaped the most violent shifts in human history. We still think in terms of nations, ethnicities and elected governments when we think of foreign policy and war, she mused, but what if that's all a blind? What if the driving interest is solely economic? That would be no great surprise. Middle Eastern oil, Russian gas pipelines: these things were clearly at the heart of recent conflicts.

She thought of the Maynard group's jowly chairman, and of Herman Saltzburg, the cadaver who had haunted the dreams of her childhood, and the man who had called himself Letrange. All those men sitting around tables, amassing their fortunes and changing the world to suit their whims with the stroke of a pen, the click of a mouse, the plummy "aye" of a vote only the dozen people in that room even knew was happening.

She shifted in the seat. The hot plastic interior of the car was starting to smell. She turned the AC up higher and wondered how anyone would choose to live in the desert, but then, choice wasn't something most people had, was it? They chose which brand of sneakers to buy, or where to take their vacation, but other people controlled whether the places they worked stayed open, where they got their food from, or how much it would cost them to get on a plane. Real choice, choice in the ways the Maynard Consortium understood the term—the power to control your own destiny—that was denied most people.

She scowled. These were familiar ideas. There was something pompous about replaying them in her head, pompous and self-protective. She didn't want to think about what had happened to Tom Powers in DC, or what had happened to her back in the shed, a stone's throw from Heathrow airport, or what had happened to her own father. And she certainly didn't want to think about that peculiar phrase Powers had left dangling on the steps of the Jefferson Memorial.

Unidentified aerial phenomena.

What the hell was that supposed to mean? Money and politics, however appalling, she could understand, but if there was anything to that tantalizing, ridiculous three-word phrase, or if it had anything to do with what had happened to Powers, or her father, or her, it was beyond her ken.

UFOs? The badge of crazy people. The insignia of the lunatic fringe. No, she would not go there.

Choice, she thought bleakly. She'd chosen to be here, to chase down what she could find, like a mongoose going after a rat. Her money—her father's money—had allowed her to do that. She might be on the side of the ordinary people—she knew the term was condescending—but she wasn't one of them. She turned the radio on and found a country music station. The sounds were almost as alien to her as the landscape she was driving through. She left it on, figuring it was good to be reminded of just how far outside her comfort zone she was.

The Hapsel place was set back from the main road along a long dusty track marked with a battered rural mailbox: she drove past twice before finding it, slowing the rental car to a rolling stop. This was no African jeep, and she didn't want a fight with the Alamo people over the state of the chassis when she took it back. There was fencing on either side of the road, strands of barbed wire strung and rusting from wooden posts. It didn't look like it would keep anything in or out, but then there was no livestock she could see, just barren range. If anything grew here, this was clearly not its season. There were no signs designating that the land was in any way protected, nothing saying it was home to any endangered species. Two slow miles from the highway, she came to a metal gate, its white paint flaking and stained with pinkish clay. She got out, swung the gate open, drove through and dutifully closed it beside her, as if she were out for a ramble across green English farms.

The house—or rather homestead, a word which popped into her mind the moment she saw the place—was a two-story clapboard, painted white but a very long time ago, no better maintained than the rest of the place, with a wooden porch where an elderly couple sat in matching rocking chairs, as if they had been waiting to have their picture taken for *Life* magazine sixty years ago. The man was grizzled, wearing sweat-stained overalls. The woman was grandmotherly, wearing a dress that would have not been considered attractive even in the days when these territories were first settled by whites. There was a pitcher of lemonade, the glass sweating in the heat. For a moment, Jennifer wanted a drink from it more than anything else in the world.

"Afternoon," said the old man, not getting up but smiling. "Help you with something?"

"Well," said Jennifer, who realized she should have spent less time in the car thinking about global inequality and more about planning her rhetorical strategy, "I was hoping to find Mr. Nate Hapsel."

"Then you found him," said the old man, his smile widening. "Nate Hapsel, guilty as charged. What can I do you for?"

"Nate Hapsel," his wife scolded, "are you going to keep a young lady standing out there in the heat on a day like this?"

"Well, no," said the old man. "I was just getting through the pleasantries there."

"I think they'd be a good deal more pleasant sitting up here in the shade with a cold glass of lemonade, wouldn't you say, dear?" said the old woman, turning to Jennifer.

"Well," said Jennifer. "It has been a long drive. Thank you. That would be lovely."

"You sound funny," Hapsel teased as Jennifer climbed onto the porch. "Where you from? Australia?"

"England," said Jennifer.

"She's from England," Hapsel to his wife.

"I heard," the old woman replied. "Welcome to Nevada," she said to Jennifer, her smile touched with amazement. "I saw England once. Some of my people came from there. I'll get you a glass."

Jennifer settled into a rocker—a third, set out as if they had been expecting her—feeling a little dazed by her unexpected welcome.

"All the way from England to see me?" said Hapsel. "What's on your mind?"

He didn't add, *little lady*, but it wouldn't have been unexpected. Jennifer looked at the sun-bleached porch, the hot, dusty land and the massive expanse of blue sky overhead. It was like she'd wandered onto the set of some old-time Western.

"Well, I assume you know a Mr. Tom Powers, the Senator?" she said.

Hapsel frowned. "Can't say that I do," he said.

"Yes, you do!" called his wife from inside. "The senator. The one who visited the high school, seven years ago. Wanted to know if we would vote for him. You remember? Nate Hapsel, you don't have the memory of a housefly."

"She may be right," said Hapsel, still smiling genially. "So what about this senator?"

"Well, you heard he died?"

"Is that right? Ella?" Hapsel called back. "The senator died."

"You knew that!" his wife returned. "It was on O'Reilly. Senator Tom Powers. He died in Washington, DC."

Hapsel nodded thoughtfully.

"Guess I did hear that," he said.

Jennifer blinked. This was not how she'd expected things to go. A long silence passed. She eyed the pitcher on the table and looked for Mrs. Hapsel, who was still in the back.

"Okay," she said at last. "Well, the Senator was responsible—partly, at least, for securing a preservation order for parts of your ranch, on the grounds of its ecological sensitivity. That it was the home to some endangered species. He told me you made a sizable contribution to his election campaign."

The old man's smile did not falter.

"I don't know how it is in England," he said, "but here, what a man does with his money is his own business."

"Absolutely," said Jennifer, back pedaling. "It just seems odd that you didn't remember who he was, after giving him thirty thousand dollars."

"You heard the wife," said Hapsel, still grinning. "I don't remember nothing."

"And the protected environment?" Jennifer tried. "I didn't see any signs."

"Oh, that's up a ways," said Hapsel. "Two miles or more."

"Could I see it?"

"Not much to see. Buncha fences and signs. It's not like you can go in. That's kinda the point. Protected, right?"

"Right," said Jennifer. The pitcher of lemonade was continuing to bead with condensation and she still had no glass. "What sort of ranch is this, Mr. Hapsel?"

"Why?"

"I just didn't see any livestock."

"Nope."

"I saw tracks in the dust on the side of the road," she said. "It looked like heavy vehicles had come along the path. Lots of them. Recently. But if you don't have live-stock, then I guess they weren't cattle trucks."

Hapsel's smile, if anything, got wider, and he nodded as if reflecting on something fascinating she had said.

"What might cause those tracks, Mr. Hapsel?" Jennifer pressed.

The old man gazed out over the dry fields and sipped his lemonade. At last, he turned back toward the house and called, "You got that glass yet, Ella? The lady will be parched."

His wife emerged almost at once with a tall glass that, after setting down the phone in her other hand, she filled from the pitcher and then handed the glass to Jennifer.

"You'll just have time to drink it before they get here," said the old woman, pleasantly.

"What?" asked Jennifer, the glass half way to her lips, her eyes flashing from Mrs. Hapsel to the phone and back. "Who?"

The old woman turned and gazed back along the dirt road, shading her eyes with one hand.

"See?" she said. "Here they come now."

Jennifer got awkwardly to her feet and followed Mrs. Hapsel's gaze to where a black SUV was barreling along the road towards them, churning up orange dust in a long, billowing cloud behind it. She turned an anxious look on the old man in his rocker.

"Drink up," he said. "They're generally not as hospitable as we are."

TIMIKA
Location Unknown

TIMIKA MARS AWOKE SLOWLY, HER SENSES RETURNING bit by bit, hearing first, then smell, then touch, and finally sight. The process took several, unnatural minutes. It took all that and more for her mind to guess that she had been drugged.

And restrained.

Just before her eyes opened, she tried rolling onto her side, aware that she was lying on her back on a cool, hard surface, her upper body slightly elevated. She could not move. It was another few minutes before she realized that this was the result of something other than her body's strange lethargy. Her wrists were anchored at her sides to whatever she was lying on, and when she tried to flex them, she felt a flash of muted pain, as if some of her skin had been rubbed raw.

Her memory returned, but only in bits and pieces. She'd been driving along a deserted Pennsylvania road in the dark. There were trees and road markings. She recalled a nagging anxiety about what would come out of the woods.

No, she amended. That wasn't it. She'd been worried about being followed. That was it. She had been . . . somewhere. There was something just out of reach of her mind, something as dark as the forest she'd been driving through, but when she reached for it, it slipped away. And now she was . . .

Here.

Her eyes were open but her vision remained blurry, unfocused. There were monitors with lights that strobed or blinked periodically on either side of her. She had a sudden recollection of being fourteen, when she had been playing outside for eight hours in a hot New York summer and had collapsed from dehydration, hitting her head on the curb. It was the only time she'd ever been hospitalized, and the first time a doctor had hinted that she could stand to lose a few pounds. She hadn't thought of it for years. The vividness of the memory distressed her, like she'd somehow gone back to that day, waking groggily to find herself *an inconvenience who had brought this on herself.*

She squeezed her eyes shut, then opened them again, and this time the room came into sharper focus.

It was not the room in the hospital where she had woken up.

The machines were similar, but the room itself was blank and white, more like an emergency surgical operating room. Or a lab.

Something in her stirred with unease.

You were driving through trees. The car. Something about the car.

Some kind of accident?

No. The car had stopped. Then there'd been a light. All around her . . . from above.

God.

She tried moving again, testing to see what she could feel, whether there was numbness, or an absence where a limb should be, but felt only the tension in her wrist again, the discomfort edging into pain. She looked down at it, her head swimming. A thin nylon strap, like a zip tie, was looped around her hand on the proximal side of her thumb and then through the metal slats of the gurney, or whatever it was she was lying on. The skin looked pink and swollen as she twisted it. The act focused her mind.

She was still wearing the same clothes, though her jacket was missing. Tubes and wires snaked around her. Some were clustered between the cups of her bra, stuck in place with sticky pads that rose and fell as she breathed. One seemed to actually go into her left arm. An IV, she thought, dimly, trailing from a bag of colorless fluid on a stand. The room itself was hexagonal, like the cell of a bee hive, the floor matted with some dark rubbery substance, the walls white to waist height, then a broad stripe of dark, smoky glass she couldn't see through. What looked like a door, without a handle or knob, was set in the wall to her right. Her head was filled with a strange white noise, part static, part layered harmonics, almost music that did not seem to change, no matter how she moved her head. As she looked around, still too sleepy and confused to be truly scared, two monitors set into the wall, above the band of dark glass, began to flash with a bright, unsettling light, an uncanny, poisonous green.

Gradually, she registered that this was somehow connected to her waking. And now the smoky glass was not quite as opaque as it had been. There were shapes on the other side of the glass, two, possibly three, barely visible except when they moved. She wanted to think they were people, but something in the shape of their heads . . .

The fear that simmered unrecognized within her grew hotter, more urgent. She uttered a low moan, but she heard nothing but the strange ambient sound that coursed through her skull.

"Who are you?" she tried to say. "What do you want?"

Her lips felt rubbery, her mouth dry, but that didn't account for how distant and muted her own voice sounded. Something had happened to her. It was still happening. She clamped her teeth together, then tried again, this time working her jaw until she caught a little fold of her cheek between her teeth. She pressed down hard, and the pain worked on her mind like the ache in her wrist had. She tasted blood, but she could feel her body coming back to life, brightening, fading, then brightening again. She bit down, and a slow pulse of energy rippled from her toes to her knees, pelvis, torso, shoulders. She felt it in her arms where, apart from the restrained wrists, she had the most freedom of motion. She stirred, and it was like rousing a sleeping animal. Fear and anxiety were momentarily replaced by something else: anger, hostility, rage. . . .

These were good things, she thought, as her brain fought to control what it had awoken. They might keep her alive.

"*WHAT isss youra Na-em?*"

The sound was suddenly all around her, arcing out of the static as if the voice were coming from the machines to which she was connected. It was terrifying, a strange, slow hiss that blurred the oddly accented words together, distorting the sound, rolling it like waves so that each sound faded in and out without ever truly beginning or ending.

She gasped, but said nothing coherent, and a moment later, the strange, unearthly voice came back.

"*WHAT isss youra Na-em?*"

"My name is Timika Mars," she answered, though she could barely hear herself. "Where am I?"

There was no reply, only the strange oscillation of sound that was almost music in her head.

"*Where were you going?*"

It was clearer this time, though the distortion was as before, with the same curious foreign lilt, as if the speaker were not using his mouth.

His, she thought, struck by the pronoun her mind had offered.

Yes. The voice, for all its strangeness, sounded male.

The light behind the smoked glass seemed to brighten, and the figures beyond moved, shadowy and unreal. Their heads were too large, elongated. Thoughtless with dread, Timika fought with her bonds, pulling back and forth where she felt the zip tie snag against the underside of the table.

"*Where were you going?*" the voice demanded again, the same flat tone, the inflection all wrong. It didn't feel like she was hearing it. It was just there, in her head, like it came from deep inside her own mind.

"I don't remember," she said, fear making her honest. "I was driving through a forest. I had been to see . . . some-one. An old lady. But I don't know . . ."

She stopped as more pieces of memory slotted into place. The Hollows, and a dead man called Jerzy, who had once been a prisoner . . .

Like her.

She fought the zip ties once more.

"*Do nottt struggle*," said the voice. "*You will become injurrred.*"

The last word had three syllables. Someone who did not speak English fluently.

Someone. Yes.

Because the alternative was too terrible to acknowledge. She continued to pull at her wrist ties, raising her whole body from the reclined table and shaking it, thrashing her head and shoulders as much as her restraints would let her. She felt the blood run from her right wrist and, glorying in her rage, because it felt so much better than the skulking terror which would otherwise overwhelm her, roared her defiance. Still, her voice sounded muted and far away, but as she twisted her head violently one way then the other, something popped out of her right ear and landed on her chest.

An ear bud with a thin yellow wire.

She stopped thrashing and stared at it, anger lessening as logic took over. The voice was not in her head. It was being piped through to her from outside. With that, some of her fear abated. This was not metaphysics. It was communication. She forced herself to think, to analyze.

That was what she was known for, right?

The thought came to her, a piece of her past that she'd forgotten, and with it came a word she knew: *Debunktion.*

Yes. That was who she was. That was what she did. She dismantled fictions and fairy tales, cheats, ruses, hoaxes . . . But then the lights in the strange hexagonal cell dimmed, and silently, awfully, the door panel she'd almost forgotten slid aside. The three strange figures were watching her. And now one of them was coming in.

She saw the gangly gray frame, the long, impossible fingers, the bulbous head with the vast insect eyes, and all her former terror returned, blotting out any sense of who she was, leaving only a mad dread of what would happen next. It moved gracelessly, a shuffling, shambling step, and though it angled its head to one side, then the other as it considered her, it moved awkwardly, turning its whole body in the direction it was, as if it couldn't see well.

Timika's eyes flashed around the room in search of salvation. As she did so, she wrestled with her restraints, tugging, stretching, making the underside of the tabletop into a saw. Now that one ear was free of the headset through which they had been speaking to her, she could hear her own panic, the wordless grunting exertion, the labored breathing, the cringing, whimpering dread as the creature came near her.

Creature was wrong. She knew what she was looking at, even if she couldn't bring herself to say the word. Anybody would. Certainly anybody who had spent years mocking every account of these *X-Files* extras.

It came closer, its cautious, shuffling steps suddenly the only sound in the room, reaching towards her, its long fingers so terrible, so . . .

Alien.

And there it was. Her brain finally uttered the word, and it acted upon her system like adrenaline.

Alien, she thought again.

"Alien," she allowed, like it was the beginning of a spell, a magical, talismanic word. And suddenly she was still, her heart rate a fraction slower, breathing a little less ragged and heavy, looking directly at the creature who had, she thought, hesitated, as if something had passed between them. Then it moved again, stooping to the side of the bed. It was inches away now, close enough to touch. Its long, slender fingers groped under the side of the bed and pulled out a metal side table, arrayed with gleaming surgical implements.

Timika's horror returned, but it was different now: specific, rational, no nameless dread of the unknown implications of a universe she'd never accepted. This was different. This was surgery.

She roared and fought and tugged wilder than ever, though even as she did, she noted the strange way the alien had to rotate its whole body to look at what it was doing, like a far-sighted woman peering over her spectacles as she tried to knit. Suddenly the tie on her right wrist snapped free and her hand, bloody at the pulse point, swung up in a wild arc, pulling at the zip tie. The release sent her arm flailing, catching the creature lightly on the side of the head.

It staggered, disoriented, gazing around the room as if there might be someone else there, and in that instant Timika reached back to the side table with her now free hand and came up with a scalpel. She swept it across the tie on her left wrist, then sat up, tugged the IV from her arm and reached for her ankles. The alien had turned back to her now, and its careful deliberation was gone. It slammed one rubbery hand across her chest, trying to pin her down, but it was clumsy, and the head didn't turn with any speed or flexibility, still oddly blind.

Revolted by the creature's touch, Timika shrugged it off, jabbing at it with the heel of her left hand as the right cut her ankles free. The flesh of the alien's head was spongy. Her hand seemed to sink into it before hitting anything solid. Again, it didn't seem to see the blow coming, and it staggered back, she thought, more in surprise than because she had hit it particularly hard. Still sitting on the bed, she pulled her legs up, pivoted around and caught the creature with a firm two-footed kick in the middle of its chest that sent it sprawling.

Again, its movements were ungainly, unnatural, as if it were unused to moving around, at odds with its own physical form. One splayed hand tried to catch itself against the wall and failed, the hand bending in weird, irregular ways, as if there were no bones in the long fingers. Timika stopped at the door, still holding the scalpel's little half-moon blade out in front of her, staring at the alien and its strange hands.

Rubbery . . . glove-like hands . . .

She forced herself to look at it. It wasn't unconscious, but it couldn't get up, and it writhed for a second before she put one foot on the small of its back and pinned it to the ground. She checked the door. The others hadn't come yet, but they would be watching. She stooped to the one at her feet, reached down with her free hand and traced the almost imperceptible ribbon that ran down its spine from neck to waist. She pressed and teased at it with her fingertips until the rubbery fabric parted to reveal . . .

A zipper.

JERZY
Parque Teyú Cuare, Argentina, October 1946

BELASCO CRIED OUT AND DROPPED TO THE LEAF-STREWN floor. I stepped instinctively behind a tree, dropping the useless rifle and shrugging out of my backpack. Behind me, Ignacio, eyes wide with shock and horror, threw himself down into the underbrush behind a fallen tree.

It wasn't just Hartsfeld—assuming that was his real name—shooting at them from the Nazi jungle compound. The diplomat was still framed in the soft light of the doorway, but one of the high shuttered windows had kicked open, and from inside, a machine pistol had opened up. The flash was too bright to look at, but I could hear the bullets thrumming through the air, tearing through leaves and pocking into wood and loamy earth. There would be more coming, but in the near total darkness, I didn't dare move. The tree I hid behind was not quite as wide as my body. It had smooth, gray bark and waxy leaves. Even if I didn't move, a lucky shot could find me.

I stooped to my fallen pack, untoggling the cords that held it closed with fumbling hands, and rummaged through the cans of food and books and folded T-shirts. Surely, Hartsfeld couldn't have gotten to the sidearms we'd taken from the *Kitchener*?

Come on . . .

I found the heavy automatic at the bottom, but not the spare clip.

Seven shots then.

Dropping the pack, I crawled back to the tree, turning against it with my shoulder to reduce my profile. There was another crackle of gunfire from the window, but Hartsfeld seemed to be holding his fire, looking to make his shots count.

Belasco groaned in the darkness. I had no idea how badly hurt he was. He was also the most exposed and closest to the door. I cocked the slide on the .45 and clicked the safety off as I sighted on the arch. Catching the distinctive shadow of Hartsfeld's arm as it extended, the squat pistol trained on Belasco's head, I fired.

The .45 sounded like a cannon in the night, a round deafening blast compared to the smaller caliber weapons the Nazis were using. In Hartsfeld's cry of pain, I heard a hint of panic. There was a pause in the shooting, and then garbled voices calling to each other in German from inside the house. We weren't supposed to be armed.

I took the opportunity. Turning to where Ignacio had peered up from behind the mossy log, I gestured with one hand.

Stay down.

Then I sprinted twenty yards for the doorway, meeting it with the weight of my charge just as it was about to latch closed. I slammed into it and sent Hartsfeld sprawling on the other side. He'd dropped his weapon, and his arm was bleeding. As he started to get up, I kicked the counterfeit Nazi hard in the face, and he went down again.

I was in a small gatehouse that gave onto a small courtyard, paved with stones and concrete and lit by a yellowish floodlight in the center. Across the courtyard was a pair of two-story buildings accessed by doors and shuttered windows, and one three-story tower. I peered around, and another submachine gun opened up from the other side, sending a wild spray of bullets that zinged and sparked against the stone so that I ducked back under the arch.

At least two more shooters then. Possibly more.

A light snapped on in the tower, a searchlight, hard and bright, sweeping the courtyard, searching for me. It was a long shot, but I sighted along the barrel of the .45 and fired once. Twice. The light shattered and died, but I was down to four rounds.

Another rattle of gunfire. I mashed myself hard against the stone. When I looked out, I saw the shooter running towards me, machine pistol slung low and gripped in both hands. He was a big man, shirtless and muscled, hair cut short, chiseled features set in grim determination. He saw me and pulled the trigger even as he came on, peppering the gatehouse like he was playing a hose over a fire.

I sank deliberately to one knee, aimed, waited—hearing the zing and pop of his bullets in the air around me— and fired. I knew I had hit him before his weapon slipped forgotten from his hands. Blood ran down his chest as he crumpled to the ground.

For a long moment, I aimed at the spot where the man had been, breathing in the smell of oil and gun smoke, feeling my heart race. I was so focused on him that I did not sense Hartsfeld moving until he had gathered up his pistol and gotten to his feet behind me.

I turned in time to see his face beyond the muzzle of the pistol, the bitter anger written across his features.

"You think people like you can stop us, Jew?" he said.

And then came the bang of the gun, and I rocked back, amazed that I was not dead. Only as Hartsfeld slumped heavily to the ground did I see Belasco on his belly, his face smeared with blood, his pack open and both hands wrapped around the grip of his .45. Our eyes met briefly, and then he slumped down again, and whether he was still breathing or not, I could not say, because I heard the sounds of footsteps behind me and had no time for my shipmate.

I WONDERED IF THE MEN IN THE COMPOUND REALIZED that Belasco's shot had come from a different place, that there were more than one of us. It probably wouldn't matter either way. They had nowhere to go. They would fight to the last man to make sure we couldn't confirm their presence here to our superiors, and come after us if we tried to withdraw.

I took a long, steadying breath, stooped to Hartsfeld's body, and shoved his compact automatic into my belt. I would need every round I could find.

The courtyard was still lit, and I could hear voices calling to each other in German. I still had no sense of how many there were, but it seemed clear that I could not take them on alone.

I was thinking this through when the stone inches from my head exploded. I winced away, ears ringing and face stinging from the stone shards, spotting the rifleman inching down the left side of the courtyard. I fired wildly, missing, and pulled back into the shaded cover of the arch. This couldn't go on much longer.

More voices. They were coordinating now. Another door opened, this time on the right. Probably the machine gunner from the front window. Then another from the foot of the tower, where I saw a man with a pistol.

I fired a warning shot, but he ducked away. The effort nearly got me killed. I shrank deeper into the arch as another flurry of machine pistol rounds sang past me, and my eyes fell on Belasco. He was probably already dead. Would be soon. And Ignacio. And me. I just couldn't stop them. I risked another shot at the rifleman, then one more at the machine gunner, and then the gun was empty.

I dropped it, hands trembling as I snatched out Hartsfeld's little Walther. After the .45, it felt light, ineffectual, and I reminded myself that I had no idea how many rounds were still inside.

I took a step back towards the main entrance.

I could run, I thought. *They will come after me, but I might get away.*

They'd get Belasco though.

He's probably already dead. And you hated him.

Not relevant, I thought. Wouldn't be even if he hadn't just saved my life, but he had, and that meant I couldn't leave him. And there was Ignacio. It occurred to me that Hartsfeld had only brought the boy along to make sure there were no witnesses, and I felt a surge of anger.

I dropped back further. I could hear the Germans talking to each other on either side of the archway, picking their moment to round the corner shooting. I edged clumsily back through the door Hartsfeld had unlocked, eyes on the courtyard, pistol raised, so that I didn't see Belasco until I stumbled into him. I dropped to him, my left hand feeling for his throat as my right kept the gun up. I felt Belasco's blood slick on his neck, but I also felt the faint throb of a pulse. In the same instant, one of the Germans leaned around the corner. I fired twice before he could get a shot off, and he ducked back, but my third shot clicked on nothing. Another gun empty.

I had only seconds left.

I looked down, momentarily blind in the dark, trying to find Belasco's .45, but before I could locate it, the world went white.

It happened in silence, I think, though I could not be sure, because it affected me like sound, something powerful and shrill that only dogs could hear, perhaps, which shut down my brain entirely. One moment, I was there, waiting to die, and then the sky was aflame with a white light, hard and flat and intense, like the very heart of a flare, so that the jungle leapt into brilliant, impossible, day-lit green.

And then it was gone.

It was nothing and—after the briefest of pauses—it was somehow morning.

The birds were singing and I was alive.

So was Belasco—just—and Ignacio. I waited a good twenty or thirty minutes to be sure, then returned to the compound to investigate. The Nazis were gone, even their corpses. The compound was empty. There was furniture, bookcases with volumes of Schiller and Göethe and Hitler's *Mein Kampf* in German, even stacks of German newspapers and magazines, some of them only a few weeks old. There were crates of abandoned equipment, food and supplies, including boxes of Third Reich money marked with swastikas, but of the men, there was no sign, nor any trace of how they'd left the area. A half-eaten meal still spread on a table, unmade beds, and an open book marked with family photographs suggested that they had left very quickly and with little preparation.

Belasco had lost a lot of blood from a shoulder wound. He'd also been hit in his right forearm, but Ignacio bandaged him tight with strips of fabric torn from sheets in one of the compound's bedrooms. The shot that should have killed him had hit the useless Thompson he had been carrying. He could barely move, but he was conscious and, barring infection, would probably make it. The next forty-eight hours would be key, and I wished we were anywhere but where we were.

We scoured the compound for anything we might use to keep him comfortable while I tried to decide if we should go back to the car and begin the long drive back to Buenos Aires or wait until he was more stable. Ignacio found a sophisticated med kit containing iodine and used it to clean Belasco's wounds. The bullet injuring his forearm had passed right through, but the second bullet was still in his shoulder. I didn't dare try to retrieve it, so we closed the hole as best we could and bound it with sterile bandages.

I couldn't communicate with Ignacio with anything more than rudimentary sign language and Belasco was too weak to talk, so I had said nothing about what had actually happened the night before, not that I knew what to say. There had been a dazzling light over the compound. It came without warning and had, somehow, *filled* the sky. It had also overwhelmed my senses and pushed me into unconsciousness. That was all I knew. Did I connect it to the strange lights I had seen in the sky the night before? Not at first, but then I remembered the way Hartsfeld had tried to dismiss what I had seen as merely a kind of waking dream. My heart told me that the two strange incidents were connected, possibly even the same phenomenon. I still had doubts, of course. Ignacio had a strained, haunted look that had nothing to do with Belasco's wounds or the horror of the firefight. If we needed further evidence that something very strange had happened to us the night before, we only needed to look at each other. We were, after all, still alive.

The place felt abandoned, as if our arrival had merely accelerated something that had been about to happen anyway. Perhaps that was why Hartsfeld had been so keen to get here: so he could go with them when they left.

As to where they might have gone, we found one tantalizing clue. In the room below the tower, we found a series of crates packed with fur-lined jackets with hoods and goggles, snow boots and face masks for serious, cold weather conditions. We also found a chart pinned to one of the walls, on which a carefully drawn land mass had been marked with red pencil.

"Antartida," said Ignacio.

Antarctica.

It was the first word he had said that I understood, but it left me, ironically, with only a deeper sense of confusion and dread.

43

ALAN
US airspace

"I AM UNDER FIRE AND TAKING DAMAGE," SAID ALAN into the radio. He had lost the Locust's cloaking capability, but since that had not made him invisible to his enemy, that didn't much matter, and now at least he could talk to Dreamland. "Repeat. I am under fire. A single ultra-high-tech bogey matching my capabilities and velocity."

"Roger that, Phoenix," came the voice from ground control. "Arranging welcoming party. Make for home. Do not engage. Repeat, do not engage."

Alan had continued to drive the battered Locust into low earth orbit, but the unidentified arrowhead craft had kept pace with him every step of the way. He'd pushed the

Locust to the limits of its remarkable performance, but the arrowhead stayed with him.

A fine machine. And a finer pilot, Alan thought ruefully.

He wasn't used to being unable to outfly his opponent and, under other circumstances, would have resented the idea that he had to be rescued by the rest of the squadron.

Not today.

His face still stung from the electrical fire triggered by the enemy's lasers, but the Locust's hull was intact and the fire was out. The arrowhead hadn't used its lasers since leaving the lower atmosphere, but as Alan banked hard, racing through a sea of space junk, his controls lit up with warnings, and he saw the other craft coming right at him. Something pulsed yellow in its wing roots and the Locust shuddered in response, his console shrieking and flashing as automated emergency systems initiated counter measures. His vision through the port side had shimmered when the craft fired. Alan watched with horror as one of the Locust's corners seemed to shrink and buckle, like plastic exposed to massive heat.

In space, where there was no friction and aerodynamics didn't matter, the distortion to what Alan persisted in thinking of as the ship's wing wouldn't affect its flight characteristics, but once he reentered the atmosphere, he wasn't sure. He couldn't guess how much internal damage had been done by whatever weapon the arrowhead had used, but the damage to the shape of the flight surface alone would send any conventional aircraft corkscrewing into the ground. What it would do to a ship like this . . . ?

Guess I'm about to find out.

He made for Dreamland, noting that several systems were already off line, and that he had lost a good deal of power, so it was a good thing that his pursuer seemed to have opted to break off the chase. Where the Locust usually felt like the literal manifestation of what the old spitfire pilots used to say—the aircraft becoming inseparable from your own body, reacting to your every movement and desire without effort, so that you forgot you were in a machine—the craft was now very clearly a device around him, one he was fighting. It was subtle at first, sounds it didn't usually make, listing with an unusual mechanical heaviness that tried to tug the ship out of his control, but as they re-entered the atmosphere—heat flashing from every surface—the extent of the damage to the Locust was clear.

It slewed out of its flight path, tipping, spinning, and while Alan usually felt no movement at all in the pilot's seat, he felt like he was being tossed and shaken like a rat snapped up by a dog. The force would surely tear the thing apart.

He had only one option. He killed all forward movement and put the ship into a sustained hover, relying on the peculiar lift the Locust generated to keep it aloft. The downside—and it was considerable—was that sitting motionless in the sky made him a sitting target for the arrowhead, should it follow him.

He just had to hope that his enemy would not dare to pursue him this far.

Alan rotated the Locust so he could look back the way he had come.

"Stay up there," he muttered to the unseen pilot. "You don't want to come down here into hostile airspace. You've chased me back to Dreamland. Job well done. Now go report back to whoever the hell sent you and leave me be."

His voice was soft and low, little more than a whisper. His eyes raked the pale blue high above the clouds.

Nothing happened.

Alan breathed: a slow, unsteady intake, a hold, and then a long relieved sigh as he blew it out. He smiled and breathed again.

And then he saw it.

Slicing through the sky, zeroed in on his position and still trailing the smoke of reentry, the arrowhead closed on him.

Alan cursed. He had seconds left, maybe less.

The old cliché, that your life flashes before your eyes in the moment of death, turned out to be true. Alan saw his missions. Flying. Aerial landscapes and heart-in-mouth strike sorties. Even a dogfight or two. No friends or lovers. No family. No great moments that didn't involve being zipped into a flight suit.

Even with the dread of certain death upon him, it struck him as sad.

And then his field of vision was alive with craft streaking in from below, Locusts like his own, at least six of them, several flashing weapons fire toward the lone arrowhead, which was already pivoting into a retreat.

"Go home, Phoenix," came the voice of flight control over the radio. "We'll take it from here."

THE LOCUST HAD HELD TOGETHER, DESPITE LOSING A HOST of operational systems, slewing out of its automated high-speed cruise home only minutes short of Groom Lake. Alan, peering through fire extinguisher smoke, his face smarting, took it the rest of the way manually. The night was dark by the time he made it back to base, the landing strip lit up with emergency vehicles. The craft had broadcast its condition as soon as it had reached friendly airspace.

Despite his protests, Alan was stretchered out, and the ground crew swarmed around the ship in protective gear, fire hoses snaking back to various tankers parked at the base of the cliff. Medical staff—whether from the base or flown in from elsewhere, Alan had no idea—poked and examined him, the ambulance racing him to a hospital in a wing of the base he'd never seen before. There were five beds. It looked like the room had never been used. Alan lay surrounded by white-coated men and women who checked his pulse and blood pressure while his minor burns were dressed. The laser had stabbed at one corner of the ship, doing minimal damage and not touching the cockpit, but causing an electrical overload, which had led to the cabin fire. He would, he was assured, make a full recovery with minimal scarring.

So that was good.

So why couldn't he shake off the fear he'd felt? He'd engaged three hostile aircraft, at least one of which had the same technological prowess as the Locust, and he'd come away with only minor cuts and second degree burns. He should be ecstatic. He should be chugging champagne and singing "Born to Run" at the top of his lungs.

But he wasn't. He was rattled. He'd gotten so used to the impossible Locust's extraordinary abilities that the prospect of being shot down by another craft had not seriously occurred to him. A pretty nurse—Latina, perhaps, or Native American—lifted his arm to check the dressing on his hand, and he was conscious of the way his fingers trembled in hers. She shot him a quick look and he clenched his fist, gritting his teeth against the pain.

"Relax your hand," she said. "You don't want to crack the skin. Let me put some more ointment on that burn. Does it hurt?"

Alan hesitated. Yes, it hurt. It hurt like hell, if she wanted to know the truth, like the worst sunburn he'd ever had, times a thousand, but he didn't want to say so. He felt more than wounded. He felt ashamed.

"A little," he said.

"That's actually good," said the nurse, smiling sympathetically. The smile was genuine but slightly crooked. It reminded him of Lacey. "Pain at this stage is good. Means there's no nerve damage."

"Okay," he said. "Great."

She gave him another look, apparently unsure if he was being sarcastic, so he thanked her and smiled.

"Get some rest," she said. "Your body needs to recover."

"Right," said Sgt. Barry Regis, who stood at the door. "This guy will do anything for attention. I hope you didn't promise him a sponge bath."

"Jackass," said Alan, giving an understanding nod to the nurse.

"Loser," said Regis, pulling up a chair beside his bed and grinning. "How you doing, Major?"

"Fine," said Alan. "A lot of fuss over nothing."

"Not exactly nothing," said another man in the doorway.

Hatcher.

He looked dour.

"Getting pretty crowded in here," said the nurse critically.

"We'll only keep him a few minutes," said Hatcher.

The nurse shot a last, rueful smile at Alan and left. Regis got up to follow her out, but Hatcher waved him back into his chair.

"No," he said. "Stay, Officer Regis."

Alan shifted. Something in the man's manner worried him.

Hatcher scanned his bandage as if he were a doctor.

"Quite the trip, Major," he said simply, sitting. He looked unlike his normal unflappable, privately-amused self. There was a heaviness to Hatcher that bothered Alan, alarmed him. He shot Regis a look and saw the same concern in the big man's face.

Alan slid his burned hand under the thin coverlet and tried to sit up.

"I didn't get the data uploaded," he said.

"Not all of it, no," said Hatcher. "But it wasn't an all or nothing deal. It's incomplete, but there's stuff we can use."

Alan nodded. It didn't make him feel better. A crushing weight was evident in Hatcher's aspect, his expression, the droop of his shoulders. A possibility occurred to Alan: there was more to this than his own wounded return.

Something had happened.

"I owe you an apology, Major," said Hatcher.

This was unexpected. Alan frowned, eyes narrowing.

"An apology?" he said, wary.

"We rushed you into action," said Hatcher. He was about to say more but Alan, panicking at the thought he was about to be fired, cut him off.

"I was fine," he said. "I was ready. I got away from the Flankers, no problem, but the other ship . . ."

"Am I authorized to hear this?" said Regis. "I can come back later . . ."

"The other ship is what I'm apologizing for," said Hatcher, ignoring him. "It's not that you weren't ready."

"Wait," said Alan, his mind catching up as he realized he wasn't being reprimanded. "The other ship. It was one of yours?"

"If by 'yours' you mean '*ours*,'" said Hatcher, heavily, "no."

"No?" said Alan. He was in freefall, like his engine had cut out and if he couldn't reignite it he would slam to the ground. Something was coming. Something that would change everything.

"No," Hatcher repeated. "It was Russian."

"Russian?"

"Or operated by Russians, on behalf of . . . someone else. Not us."

"I don't understand."

"Major Young, you have perhaps been under a misapprehension," said Hatcher carefully. "The technology we have, which you've been discovering over the last few weeks, these ships that seem to defy the very physics of conventional aviation—we aren't the only ones who have it. I suggested this to you before but I did not discuss with you the possibility of active engagement with craft matching the capabilities of our own because I did not think that would happen. This was an error on my part. You see, Major, you are being trained for a war. Not a war we anticipate in the future, but one we are fighting now. We should have told you this before."

"Ya think?" said Alan. "You sent me into a war zone without telling me the enemy had something that could engage me?"

"Your next training mission will cover full use of the Locust's munitions systems."

Alan laughed once, stopping only because he felt the burned skin of his face stretching. "A little late, wouldn't you say?"

"You have to bear in mind that our first priority is to maintain our covert stance," said Hatcher. "If pilots start loosing munitions over built-up areas . . ."

"People would probably ask questions if a Locust gets shot down in their backyard too, don't you think?" Alan snapped.

"That's why pilots are instructed to extricate themselves from combat situations, rather than engage the enemy," said Hatcher, his defensiveness wearing thin.

"It would help if your pilots knew there *was* an enemy."

"The others did," Hatcher shot back. Alan winced. "I'm sorry if this hurts your professional pride, but you are new to this, Major. We are a secret operation. Beyond black. You knew that. You must also have assumed we wouldn't announce to new recruits every element of what we do the moment they sign up. You were aware that we were running surveillance and counterintelligence missions over Russia. You must have assumed they would try to prevent you from completing your mission."

"Not with something that could take me down," muttered Alan, though his tone was grudging.

Regis watched each speaker in turn, like he was watching a tennis match. He looked both fascinated and desperate to be somewhere else.

"True," said Hatcher, conceding the point. "Though, for the record, they didn't take you down, did they? I've looked at the flight recorder. That was some fine flying, Major. It's because of flying like that that you are in the Locust program in the first place. I want you to know that in addition to my apology, you have my admiration, and your country's gratitude."

"My country doesn't know what happened," said Alan ruefully. Hatcher's words had mollified him some. Against his better judgment, he felt the old prickle of curiosity. And excitement at the prospect of flying in combat again.

"No," agreed Hatcher, "and I'm afraid we aim to keep it that way. Sometimes heroism goes unnoticed."

Alan did not know what to say to that, and for a moment there was an awkward silence between them.

"You did well, and you are going to need to remember that in a moment," said Hatcher, and now the heaviness was back, the sense of something coming. Something bad. "You too, Officer."

Alan braced himself but said nothing.

"The ship that pursued you," said Hatcher, his eyes down and focused on the bed, "was a decoy. They weren't just after you. They were after us, and they had more fire power waiting."

Alan's eyes widened with horror.

"The ships that went up to cover me?" he said.

Hatcher closed his eyes, then shook his head slowly.

Alan stared.

"All of them?" he managed.

"One got back, in even worse shape than yours," said Hatcher. "But the others . . ."

"The pilots?"

"All but the last one—Hastings—lost."

Lives flashing before his eyes . . . Other people's lives.

"Jesus," breathed Regis.

"Morat?" asked Alan, dreading the answer.

"He was not on base today," said Hatcher. "He's quite safe. Again, Alan, it wasn't your fault. And like I said, you have to remember that what you did was heroic . . ."

Alan shook his head but no words would come.

JENNIFER
Hapsel Ranch, Nevada

JENNIFER STARED AT THE BLACK SUV AS IT CAME TO A halt, doors opening.

"Eight minutes," said Hapsel, checking his watch approvingly. "Faster than usual."

In spite of her terror, Jennifer couldn't help looking at him. His smile was the same as before. When she moved towards the porch steps, the old man reached behind him and, with a swift, precise movement that defied his years, drew a heavy looking revolver from behind his back. He didn't point it at her. He didn't need to.

He set the gun on the table, next to the phone, but did not take his hand off it. It was a severe, purposeful weapon, designed without elegance or whimsy for a single purpose. Jennifer became very still, staring at it, dimly aware of the swift movement of four men pouring out of the SUV in trim black suits, white shirts with black ties, shiny black wing tips, and wrap-around sun glasses.

"Environmental Protection Agency," said the first, brandishing a wallet badge. "Step down from the porch, Miss Quinn."

Jennifer turned and stared at him. Though gripped by fear, she couldn't keep the incredulity out of her voice.

"You're EPA?"

"Step down off the porch, Miss," said a second officer.

She couldn't see if they were armed. No one was brandishing a firearm, but an air of professional menace was present in every thread of their outlandish attire, every studied movement of their athletic and no doubt highly-trained bodies. She opted for cordiality. If they could bluff—*EPA my arse*—so could she.

"Is there a problem, officers?" she asked, sweetly. "I wasn't aware I was trespassing. I was just having a refreshing glass of lemonade with my hosts here . . ."

"Step off the porch now, please," said the first officer.

"Fine," said Jennifer. "But for the record, I wasn't doing anything wrong. I violated no signs and was invited in for a drink . . ."

"Now, please," repeated the officer, "or we will remove you by force."

She didn't like the sound of that and took her first step down the steps, hands raised in mock surrender, head shaking in baffled amazement and indignation, as if it were all a silly misunderstanding that had gotten out of hand. She hoped they couldn't read the terror in her eyes.

The one who had shown the badge was still brandishing it, but she didn't even look at it. *Dan* had had a fake badge too. She stepped down to the dusty earth and forced a smile.

"Now, what can I do for you gentlemen?"

"Get in the vehicle, please Miss," said the first officer. He was very pale. They all were.

Jennifer's unease re-doubled.

"If you're moving me on, I can take my own car," she said, hurriedly. "It's parked right there . . ."

"Our vehicle, please, Miss," said the man in black.

There was a moment's stillness as she actually considered running. She felt their eyes on her, and she knew the moment was hers to control for just a second longer. She relived a dozen outrageous YouTube videos of US law enforcement officers assaulting suspects and traffic violators. She didn't want to get into their car, but if she gave them the excuse . . .

She shrugged with mock nonchalance, as if none of it mattered and she had nothing to hide, and said, "Okay," then walked to the car. The sun baked down on her and on the car with the black-suited men, one of whom went in front of her to open the rear driver's side door. She was sandwiched on the back seat by two of them, their shoulders firm as concrete against hers. The one who'd been doing the talking climbed into the driver's seat and waited for the man beside him to close his door, and then the central locking system clunked, and she was, finally and irrevocably, trapped.

No one spoke.

The SUV's air conditioning was on full blast. After a few seconds, the inside of the vehicle was positively frigid. All four men sat very still, looking directly ahead. It took less than thirty seconds for the strange and uneasy silence to get the better of Jennifer.

"Look, I'm sorry I was out here," she said. "I didn't know I had crossed any boundary or done anything wrong. I can't think why the Hapsels called you instead of just asking me to leave . . ."

Her voice trailed off, but no one spoke or moved. The AC roared, and the sun slanted through the heavily-tinted windows, but otherwise nothing happened. After a full minute of silence, Jennifer watched with something like alarm as the elderly couple went into the house without a backward look and closed the door behind them.

Still no one spoke.

"So what happens now?" she asked, not really wanting to know, but keen to break the uncanny silence.

There was no response. For a full minute they just sat there and then, without warning, the driver turned the engine on and the car rolled forward along the rutted road. They didn't slow down, driving as fast as the uneven surface would permit, not back towards the gate, she realized, but deeper into Hapsel's property.

"Where are we going?" she asked. They could surely hear the quaver in her voice.

As if in response, the man in the front passenger seat began to speak in a low, drab monotone, without turning around.

"The Ash Meadows Speckled Dace is a member of the Cyprinidae family, genus *Rhinichthyus*, species, *osculus*, subspecies, *nevadensis*. The fish is approximately eight centimeters long, and was originally included with the Amargosa Speckled Dace group occurring only in the Ash Meadows area of the Amargosa river basin in southern Nye County. Though it was formerly identified in ten springs, it has, as of 1985, become extinct in all but three. It prefers fast flowing water and feeds on a variety of emergent insects and larva, but is imperiled by invasive species such as largemouth bass and the bullfrog which, contrary to popular belief, are not in fact native to the area."

Jennifer gaped, but no one said a word. The car continued to rock its way across the baked ruts of the track, but the men all kept their eyes front, their faces impassive to the point of blankness.

"Okay," she said. "That's very interesting, but it doesn't really answer my question about where we . . ."

"The Southwestern Willow Flycatcher or *Empidonax traillii extimus*," said the man sitting beside her without turning around and speaking in the same drab monotone as his colleague up front, "is a small bird, less than six inches long, including the tail, and distinguished by light-colored wing bars. Unlike other *Empidonax* species, it lacks the pale eye-ring, and is brownish olive above, and gray-green below. The beak is proportionally quite large, but the clearest identifying mark is the flycatcher's song, which is a distinctive and liquid *Whit!*"

Jennifer stared at him.

"What are you doing?" she asked, wondering why she felt no urge to laugh. The situation was so bizarre that it felt dreamlike, though behind the biology lesson—deriving perhaps from its flat, drawled and disinterested delivery—she sensed menace. He did not respond to her question, and there was another long silence. Under the circumstances, she preferred it to the weird ecology lesson. As time passed, she found herself dreading that he would start up again. The tension built as they drove.

She felt the man on the other side of her take a breath before he began to speak, and—inexplicably—had to fight back a sob.

"Considered one of the rarest fish in the world," he began, his voice uncoiling from him like smoke, uninflected by emphasis of any kind, a droning, soulless sound that conveyed no thinking presence at all, "the Devils Hole pupfish, is a mere twenty-five millimeters long and feeds on diatoms . . ."

He went on, but Jennifer had her hands clasped to her ears and heard no more. For a while, they let her ride like that. When she thought she was seeing pieces of landscape they'd passed before—a lightning blasted tree, gaunt against the pink of the rock, and a tall cactus like something out of a John Wayne movie—she slowly dropped her hands.

They were swinging back around toward the highway. A moment later, she saw the Hapsel house sitting off in the distance, strange and solitary and offering none of the relief it had evoked when she first saw it. She twisted in her seat to watch it as they drove past, but there was no sign of life. No one in the SUV said anything as they slowed alongside her dust-streaked rental.

They parked, opened the doors and got out like some presidential security detail, silent and deliberate.

As Jennifer's feet touched the pale ground, she turned on them, trying to muster some defiance or outrage, but she took in their bizarre blankness, the sunglasses, which meant she could not see where they were looking, and could say nothing. Despite the heat of the sun, something of the car's chill had got into her bones and she wanted nothing more than to be gone.

"You may leave now, Miss Quinn," said the driver, nodding toward the road. "The airport is that way. I suggest you make good use of it. And should anyone ask about the land on this side of the highway, I'm confident that you will be able to present them with a wealth of fascinating insight into the region's wildlife. Any other disclosures are unlikely to be believed by sane, rational people, and could result in all manner of unpleasantness."

"Is that a threat?" she managed, though her voice was low.

He removed his sunglasses revealing eyes of an unnervingly piercing blue. He did not blink.

"By no means," he replied, still unsmiling. "But this is hard country and it is easy—as you have heard—for things to become endangered. Enjoy the rest of your trip."

He put his sunglasses back on, and Jennifer found herself relieved not to be looking into those strange, unblinking eyes.

Without another word, they climbed back into the car and barreled off, kicking dust and sand in their wake, so that Jennifer had to wipe her face clean before braving the heat of the rented Impala. Once inside, Jennifer sat very still, listening to the sound of her own labored breathing. As it slowed, she opened the windows, closing them again two minutes later as sanity finally registered and she started the car and turned on the AC. Her hands, which had been fluttery on the steering wheel, grew steady at last, though the strangeness of her encounter with the so-called EPA men lingered like the memory of a dream. She took a long, lung-filling, hand-steadying breath and came to a realization: she needed a drink.

There weren't a lot of options. She drove past a place with a hokey looking alien sign outside, but having driven several miles and seen nothing more promising, she turned back, parked and steeled herself for whatever strangeness awaited inside. She'd had a month's supply of weird.

Which was, she supposed, the point. All this *Men in Black* ridiculousness was designed to either make her question her own sanity or guarantee that anyone she told about her experience would do that questioning for her. It was, she decided, far more effective a strategy than the veiled threats with which her encounter had ended.

The Little A'le Inn turned out to be pleasant enough, and its intergalactic kitsch was refreshingly tongue in cheek. It was, in fact, just what she needed, and if her impulse to dissolve her worries in alcohol took too high a toll on her, they even had rooms.

"Perfect," she muttered, looking up into the face of a smiling waitress who took her order for a grilled cheese sandwich and a beer.

She regarded the diner—that was what Americans called such places, wasn't it? Or was it a bar? It was quiet, whatever it was, considering it was dinnertime. Perhaps it was more of a daytime place, providing lunches for tourists too savvy to be driving on these long, gas station-free Nevada highways at night. A stop off en-route to . . . wherever the hell people round here went, other than Vegas. She had no idea. There was a heavy-set, middle-aged couple in the corner who chatted to the waitress as if they had known her for years: locals or annual UFOlogist pilgrims? There certainly weren't a lot of other places around where people could socialize. Her dread returned when she imagined the Hapsels walking through the door . . .

But they didn't seem the types to frequent bars. Or diners.

But then she had no way of knowing what "types" they were because they'd simply kept her talking while waiting for the "EPA" to arrive, dodging her questions. Was it impossible to imagine them dropping their *Little House on the Prairie* routine and whipping out machine guns if they spotted her around the house again? Did they just receive checks and not ask questions, or were they involved and complicit in whatever was going on on their land? Assuming something was.

It wasn't all about the Ash Mountain Speckled Dace, she was bloody sure about that.

She almost called the waitress back with a question about the menu, realizing, in the instant, that she hadn't had a single conversation with anyone since her father died that wasn't loaded with danger, or strangeness, or secrecy. For a moment, she wanted only to pretend she was a tourist passing through, keen to chat, to "shoot the breeze" as the Americans said, with whomever strayed into her path.

As if on cue, a man came in, tall, good looking in a regular, corn-fed American kind of way, at least until he turned and revealed a dressing taped to one side of his face. His hand was bandaged too. His hair was short, and there was something about his posture—vertical and square, despite the weariness in his face—that said *military*.

Despite her desire for a little empty socializing, Jennifer tensed, watching him scan the room. If he were a soldier of some kind, he was apparently off duty. There was no reason to believe he was looking for her. He glanced her way, and their eyes met. His gaze lingered for a fraction of a second, and she looked down, staring at the menu. When she looked up, his eyes were on her again. There was a kindness but also a blankness in his eyes, an emptiness that seemed subdued or tired.

This was a man who needed a beer.

Maybe even, she thought wildly, *a little company*.

Not *that* kind of company, she scolded herself quickly. She wasn't that desperate. And she wouldn't be confiding in him or anyone else. But if a little light banter would take her mind off the bloody Ash Mountain Speckled Dace, so much the better.

He realized she was looking at him and nodded awkwardly.

"The burgers are good," he said.

"Thanks, but I already ordered," she said.

"Oh," he said. "I thought . . . Because you were looking at the menu . . .?"

"Yeah. No."

"Right. Well, enjoy your dinner."

"Thanks," she said. "I hope you're not the chef."

His brows creased in confusion and he hesitated. She gestured at the side of her face and nodded at the dressing on his.

"Sorry," she said. "Bad joke."

"Oh," he said, smiling a little bleakly. "No, not a kitchen injury."

"Sorry," she said again, meaning it this time, a little horrified by her clumsiness. "That was insensitive of me."

"Not at all," he said. "I'm fine."

"Buy you a beer to make up for it?"

The words were out of Jennifer's mouth before she had really considered them.

He seemed taken aback, and there was something else in his eyes, something dark and sad which flashed into sight and then was wrestled back down. It intrigued her. And she was sick of being alone.

"Sure," he said. "Thanks."

"Good. I've had quite the day."

As soon as she said it, she thought it sounded stupid in view of his dressings on what looked like to be burns. She'd had a weird day, a frustrating day. His had been genuinely bad.

"Yeah?" he said.

"Nothing," she said, waving it away. "Just, you know, stupid tourist stuff. I don't seem to be able to make sense of your maps."

"Ah," he said, hurriedly moving over and sitting opposite her. "I'm Alan, by the way."

"Jennifer," she replied, offering her hand. He shook it with his good hand.

"You're English," he remarked.

"I am?" said Jennifer with mock astonishment. "So *that's* why I talk so funny!"

He looked momentarily baffled by the joke, even a little stung.

"Sorry," she said quickly. "Not everyone gets my sense of humor."

"Right," he answered, nodding emphatically, as if that would counter the flicker of alarm in his eyes. Nice eyes, she decided. They were somewhere between blue and green and a little smoky, but they looked haunted, weary. "So what are you doing out here? Looking for UFOs?"

He laughed, but it didn't feel like a real laugh, and her answering laugh was about the same.

"Just passing through," she said, adding, as she processed that absurd western gunslinger cliché in her head, "to look at the scenery."

"Grand Canyon?" said the man, nodding, his bandaged hand rising self-consciously to the strapping on his face, then pulling away again.

"What?"

"Did you come to see the Grand Canyon?"

Jennifer had no idea where anything was. She had come to see a dodgy bit of land across the street from a classified airbase. She had no idea the Grand Canyon was anywhere close by.

"Right," she said. "Yes. The Grand Canyon. Hoping to get there soon."

"How long are you over?"

"Not sure yet," she said. "It's an open-ended trip."

"Must be nice."

Jennifer looked at him. Was there a hint of criticism there?

"I'm between projects," she said, immediately wishing she hadn't and determined to head him off before he could ask her *what kind of projects*, which she would have to answer with lies she wouldn't be able to keep track of. "What about you? You work locally?"

"At the moment," he said. "Yes."

Again for a second she saw the bleakness in his face, but he avoided her eyes.

"What do you do?"

He seemed to hesitate again, and there was that momentary sense that he was checking the room and lowering his voice.

"I was a pilot," he said. "Marines. But I'd rather not talk about it."

"Right," she said, mentally pushing herself away from the table.

"What?" he said.

"Nothing."

"You seem . . . I don't know. Did I say the wrong thing?"

"No. It's nothing."

"Doesn't seem like nothing," he said.

"Well it won't be if you keep pushing."

"Get you a beer or something, hon?" said the waitress materializing at his elbow.

"Sure."

"Bud, Bud Light, Miller . . .?"

"Bud's fine," he said, his eyes still on Jennifer.

"And something to eat?" asked the waitress.

"Haven't decided yet," he answered.

"You take your time," she said. "I'll be right back with that beer. You okay for now, hon?" she asked Jennifer.

"I'm fine, thanks," she answered, wishing the woman would leave.

"Another beer?" the waitress suggested.

"I said I'm fine. That means no."

She said it more crisply than she meant, and the waitress looked slightly taken aback as she bustled off.

"Guess you're not too keen on waitresses either," said the man called Alan. This time, the criticism was unmistakable.

"I just don't know why they can't leave people alone," Jennifer replied, trying to make light of it, but needled. "In England they serve you and you pay them. Here it's like they are trying to be your friends. I don't need that."

"Just trying to be nice, I guess," said Alan.

"I understand that but, as I said, I'm not looking to make friends."

"I'm getting that," he said. "Not too keen on soldiers either, huh?"

Jennifer sighed. She could play nice like ladies were supposed to, or she could speak her mind, and though she had been ready—even eager—to relax and have a beer with a stranger who didn't want to talk about secret finance schemes or endangered species, she was in no mood to play the demure school girl.

"You want to know the truth?" she said, sitting back.

"Sure," said Alan. "I don't think we could get off on a worse footing, so what the hell?"

"Fine," she said, bristling. "No, I don't automatically think it's wonderful when people sign away their capacity to think for themselves, or make their own moral choices, and rely instead on orders that come from other people with their own agendas, orders that involve killing other people."

"Those orders come from our democratically elected government leaders, who are protecting the freedoms of the American people."

"Bollocks," Jennifer spat. "How many wars has the US fought in the last hundred years that had anything to do with American freedoms? Invading Iraq didn't. In fact it made more enemies for America, more threats. Everyone can see that. The US military protects American business interests, not American freedom. And those interests rarely have anything to do with ordinary people. The US military is driven by corporations, by multinational companies whose sole purpose is maintaining whatever economic landscape will best maximize their profits. Do you know who you work for, Alan? Do you really?"

He was staring at her as the waitress arrived.

"Your beer, hon," she said.

"You know," he said, "I think I'll drink it at the bar."

As he walked away, Jennifer took a long swallow of her beer and muttered, "Nice to meet you too."

But she watched him for a moment, and he wasn't just angry or bitter at the way she'd spoken to him. He was miserable, and she had been too busy climbing on her high horse to see how deep that misery went. Her righteous indignation stalled, but she felt not so much pity as dread, as if he had seen things most people would never have to see, and that somehow chilled her even more than the Little A'le Inn's hyperactive air conditioning.

45

TIMIKA
Location Unknown

FOR A SECOND, SHE STARED, THE MUNDANE EXPLANATION somehow more surreal than the idea of an actual alien. She reached for the bulbous head, grasped its yielding softness in one fist and pulled. The whole head slid up and off, revealing a pale man with wild blue eyes and a sweaty mop of dark hair. Timika flung the mask away in disgust and punched the prone man hard in the cheek, a thoughtless, spontaneous blow driven by all her formidable anger.

It hurt her hand, but not as much as it hurt him. He'd been trying to get up, and the blow banged his head on the floor and he lay still.

"That's right," she muttered to herself. "Pull that *Scooby Doo*-mask shit on me . . ."

She took her foot off his back, and saw a vial of clear liquid roll out of his pocket. She'd been drugged. She kicked the fallen man's knee, but when he did not respond she stepped to the door, aware of the bustle of shadowy movement through the smoked-glass windows, and pushed on it. She could still see no handle and assumed she was now locked inside, but the panel yielded to her touch. For all its high-tech appearance, it was plasticky and thin. She shoved it harder and it moved aside, the force of her action dislodging it from some unseen rail so that it popped out and hung at an angle. The room beyond was cluttered and untidy, the desk behind the smoked windows scattered with soda cans and snack-food wrappers. What was sleek and spacey inside the hexagonal room was, seen from the other side, roughly nailed slats of wood and low tech controls, hung with wires and an old-fashioned microphone in a desk stand.

It was, she realized with a shock of both relief and outrage, a stage set.

The other two "aliens" scrambled away from her. One was tugging its clumsy head off. It was a woman, blond and scared looking. The anxious, uncertain look in the woman's blue eyes filled Timika with a kind of savage triumph. She raised the scalpel menacingly, and the woman huddled further away.

"Yeah," Timika snarled. "You'd better run."

The control room, such as it was, was not much larger than the cell itself, and there was a single exit door, closer to her than to the two terrified "aliens." Timika tried it, keeping her eye on the scared woman in the corner who, so far, had not said a word. It opened, admitting her to a long concrete corridor lit by a red light in a cage over the door: a warning light that their little show was in progress.

Not anymore.

Timika broke into a trot. The corridor was flanked by other doors with red lamps above them—all dark. It felt utilitarian, like the hallway of a multi-story car park, and it ended in a flight of steps. She went up and found a wider space, more internal doors, a locker room of sorts, and another with windows and desks and computers. It seemed deserted. She would have passed it by, but she glimpsed her own jacket hanging over the back of a chair.

She set her teeth, muttered to herself about people who stole her shit, and burst through the door. There was no sign of her laptop, but she caught up the jacket, feeling the weight of it: Jerzy Stern's journal was still nestled in the lining.

Good. They weren't having that at least, whoever they were.

She put a little pressure on her left breast and felt the little key digging into her skin. Despite the electrodes they'd positioned to monitor her life signs, they apparently hadn't searched her that thoroughly.

Also good.

She followed the corridor round and came to an elevator. She considered it. If her escape had been announced— and she was sure it would have been—using the elevator might leave her trapped between floors. She looked for stairs and found, instead, a narrow shaft with a ladder set into the concrete.

"I guess we go up," she muttered to herself, unenthusiastically.

The rungs were solid, smooth and rust free, but Timika didn't like heights. She took a long breath, glanced back along the empty hallway to see if she was being pursued, and started to climb.

She counted the rungs as she went, not looking down, trying to figure how high she was. At thirty rungs, she figured she'd gone at least two stories. The end was in sight. Forty-four rungs brought her to a small concrete chamber with a metal door.

It will be locked, she thought, desperately, *and I'll have to go back down . . .*

But it wasn't. The door was, she guessed, an emergency exit, and barred on the inside. She released the bar, turned the mechanism with difficulty, and dragged the heavy, squeaking door open.

She was greeted with a howl of cold and a dusting of snow that made no sense at all. It had been chilly in Pennsylvania, considering it was supposed to be spring, but this?

She was outside. But where?

As she stepped clear, she looked back. The iron hatch gave onto what looked like a concrete hut and nothing more. There was no sign of the complex she'd been in below ground. Above it were trees and a road, but these were not the trees or road of the Pennsylvania forest where she'd been abducted. The trees were closely packed hardwoods, silver-barked and heavy with snow, a wild and vast forest, traversed by a road quite unlike the one she'd been driving on.

That had been a narrow ribbon of blacktop with lane markings that wound leisurely through the woods in an undulating wave as the ground rose and fell. This was a dirt track, rutted but straight, shooting arrow-like through miles and miles of unbroken woodland. And the cold, the deep snow? It made no sense. She shrugged her way into her jacket and looked around.

Lose yourself in the woods, or follow the road, and if the latter, which way?

A hundred yards or so along the track was a signpost. She trudged through the softness of the freshly fallen snow, rounded the sign and peered up. It was yellow and battered so that the bare metal shone through and the words on it were . . .

Greek? Russian? Something like that. Three lines of unfamiliar letters and exclamation points. She stared at it.

Where the hell was she? And, more to the point, how was she going to get out?

The road showed no tire marks. If she set off walking, how far would she make it before she froze to death? She considered the long, straight road through the trees, and the answer floated back to her with a chill certainty.

Not far enough.

She thought furiously. Whatever the facility was, there were people here. That meant supplies and ways of getting them in and out. In other words, vehicles. Somewhere.

She'd come up the ladder shaft, but there had been an elevator too. Where did that come out?

She turned around and saw, just beyond the concrete shaft, where a second road, almost obliterated by the snow, cut back toward the underground facility. She took it, her pace quickening. She'd gone no more than forty yards when the trees to her left opened up and she saw, set back from the road and concealed behind a row of trees, a concrete bunker with a wide roll-up door and a collection of concrete buildings behind it. One sprouted a pair of radio masts and three oversized satellite dishes. Parked alongside it was a pair of pickup trucks, and a snowcat with skis at the front and caterpillar tracks in back.

Jackpot.

Of course, she'd need keys. It was too much to hope that her abductors had left the doors unlocked and the keys tucked behind the driver's vanity mirror. But if they hadn't . . . The prospect of going back inside the concrete bunkers with its alien-suited people made her flesh creep. Perhaps if she went back to the ladder . . .

"*Stop! Ne shevelis!*"

She turned to find a soldier in gray-and-white camo, legs shoulder width apart, some kind of automatic rifle with a banana clip shouldered and trained directly on her. He was young and pale, his face pink from the cold. He wore a fur hat instead of a helmet, but his camo was clearly a uniform, and the points of color on his shoulders and collar were insignia of some sort. She stood very still, her hands rising behind her head.

The soldier called out again, over his shoulder this time, and two more soldiers appeared, one with a pistol, the other armed like the first. The one with the pistol pulled a lapel radio close to his mouth and spoke hurriedly into it. Timika stood very still, dimly aware that it was snowing again, small, icy flakes that blew purposefully in the stiff breeze. She turned only fractionally as she heard the garage door at her back roll up. Two sets of feet. A man and . . .

Her. The woman who had been one of the "aliens" down below.

She was wearing ordinary clothes now, but the eyes were the same as before, cool, blue. Before they had been frightened. Now they were hard with anger. She muttered a few words to the man hurrying to catch her up—Russian? Timika thought so. She was in Russia. Probably Siberia, from the looks of it. The woman's eyes stayed locked on her prisoner. The wind blew her hair in her face and she whipped it aside, her gaze freezing hard as she strode closer. Timika watched the eyes, so she did not see the hand with the syringe before it was too late. The woman jabbed her once, a quick, precise and practiced gesture that found her neck a second before the man beside her took hold of Timika's hands so she could no longer resist.

The world went white.

JERZY
Parque Teyú Cuare, Argentina, October 1946

IN THE END, I OPTED TO GET AWAY FROM THE ABANDONED jungle compound and go back to Buenos Aires as soon as possible. Ignacio and I fashioned a stretcher from bedding we found in the stone complex and two lengths of pipe, and carried Belasco back to the car. We made him as comfortable as we could, aided, at the first village we came to, by the locals who gave him leaves to chew on that eased his pain and made him sleep, and then we drove as fast as we dared on the rutted forest road. We made good time, eating as we rode and stopping only for gas in a huddle of buildings grandly titled Urugaiana. It was almost dark by then, but the roads were better as we left the high woodlands behind and kept going. South of Salto, we pulled over for a couple of hours, but we did not pitch the tent, and most of the time I sat awake, monitoring Belasco and watching the skies. I saw nothing unusual in the heavens. At dawn we pressed on, reaching the city by lunchtime.

As we headed south, an anxiety that the *Kitchener* might have already sailed swelled in my gut. Having to slow for the traffic, after having the road to ourselves, was doubly frustrating. Turning one corner recklessly fast got us the attention of a military policeman on a motorcycle who sped up beside us and waved us over, but as soon as he saw our situation, he put his siren on and drove in front of the car, clearing the road. He led us not to the dock but to a hospital, where we unloaded Belasco into the care of some crisply dressed nurses. He was awake enough to wink at one of them, then give me a fractional nod of acknowledgment before I jumped back into the car and headed down to the quay.

Captain Jennings—alerted by the hospital—was waiting for us. He listened to my story in silence, showing not the slightest trace of emotion except when I told him about Hartsfeld, when his eyebrows arched and he turned away from me, his head bent in contemplation. The chart of Antarctica seemed not to surprise him at all.

"You knew," I said.

"No," he said. "But I had been warned that there was a possibility of this."

"'This' being?"

"A Nazi base," he said. "They went to Antarctica before the war. Claimed a portion of it, which they named Neu-Schwabenland. Supposedly, the mission was to look for places they could hunt whales. Whale oil is used in margarine and various other products, but they were really looking for somewhere to build a naval base. Planted little swastika flags in the ice and everything." He unrolled the chart on the tabletop and pinpointed a spot with his finger. "The Schirmacher Oasis," he said. "Named after the guy who spotted it during one of their aerial recon missions. An area above the ice shelf. Fairly temperate by Antarctic standards."

"You know a lot about it," I said, annoyed that so much had been kept from me.

"Mostly learned since you left," he said. "This is all top secret. Even if I had known before you went, I wouldn't have been allowed to tell you. And now you know, so it's water under the bridge."

"And Hartsfeld?" I demanded. "You knew about him too."

"Only suspicions, which I voiced to you. It could have been any number of people who were helping the Nazis slip through our nets."

"Sounds like they are doing more than escaping," I said.

"Yes," he conceded. "It does."

"There's something else," I said. I hadn't mentioned the strange end to the firefight in the jungle, the light in the sky, or the one I had seen the night before which Hartsfeld had said was a meteor. "Something took them away. Something that came at night, flying in silence. It hovered over the hideout, and then there was a light and I lost consciousness. When I woke up, they were all gone."

Captain Jennings eyes narrowed and he became very still, but said nothing for a long moment. At last he simply nodded, and said, "Anything else? Do you remember any other details?"

"No," I said. "What do you think it was?"

For a second he looked vague, his eyes not clearly focused on anything.

"Probably a helicopter," he said. "You've never seen one, I take it? Remarkable things."

I was about to respond when he turned sharply away and, with his back to me, said, "Thank you, Seaman. Good work. That will be all."

I had no right to be outraged, of course. I was about as junior as it was possible to be, and he was my commanding officer. I suppose he had also become a kind of parent to me, since I had no one else, but after what I'd gone through in the jungle, I felt he owed me more than this. I just stood there, not knowing what to say, what to think, and then he turned and put a hand on my shoulder. For a moment, I nearly shrank away, but then I nodded, saying nothing.

"You should go rest up," he said. "Take a couple of days. When the order comes, we'll need to sail quickly."

I looked at him. "There?" I said, indicating the map. The prospect of going back into combat, fighting a war the world thought was over, in the freezing waters of the Antarctic, was too exhausting to contemplate.

"I have to talk to Admiral Byrd," he said. "But that's my guess, yes."

REAR ADMIRAL RICHARD E. BYRD WAS AN EXPLORER WHO'D been to the Antarctic several times before. His first expedition in the twenties had involved a flight to the South Pole itself in a Ford Trimotor, during which he'd had to ditch supplies and fuel tanks to maintain altitude. Partly as a result, he was made an admiral at forty, the youngest in the history of the US Navy. During the war, he'd led recon missions in the South Pacific, scouting for land that might be used as airfields and forward command bases, and he had—it was said—been present at the surrender of the Japanese. A hero and a big shot, in other words, who was involved in important things, and he did nothing by halves.

Whatever Byrd had been planning, the operation had been in its preliminary stages long before the details of our experiences near the Paraguay border could be relayed to him and I never learned how much our findings shaped the mission to come. What was clear is that Captain Jennings' report gave the enterprise new focus and urgency, as did seasonal conditions. The window in which the Antarctic was accessible, before the Southern Hemisphere winter made any kind of exploration there impossible, was very narrow. We holed up in Buenos Aires for two more weeks before the *Kitchener* set sail to meet up with the rest of the fleet.

By the time Byrd's armada had been assembled, Task Force 68—approaching the Antarctic from both the west through the Marquesas Islands, where weather stations were set up, and the east, from an island called Peter I, off the western coast of the Antarctic peninsula—the armada consisted of over four thousand men in thirteen ships, with thirty-three aircraft at their disposal, most of them based on the aircraft carrier *USS Philippine Sea*. Given the battle-weary condition of the military, so soon after the war, and the growing anxiety about the standoff with the Bolsheviks in Europe, it was a massive deployment of Naval power for what must have seemed, to the outside world, to be a bewilderingly unimportant spot of the globe.

Everyone was in position a few days before Christmas. I say that the weather was warming up, but that was a relative concept. The Antarctic—as my winter reading had revealed—was covered by an ice sheet a mile thick year round. The South Pole proper never warms above minus ten degrees Fahrenheit. The Antarctic coasts weren't that cold, and the west, our targeted destination, was warmer than the more mountainous east. Summer temperatures still tended to be a below freezing. Much of the continent is also technically a desert, with little or no precipitation. The snow on the ground is ancient, gradually becoming part of the ice sheet. Though my Polish blood was keen to escape the sweltering weather of the tropics, the prospect of heading to the South Pole was daunting.

Belasco had made a complete recovery, and though he was still his crass, boorish self, quick to anger and contemptuous of anything he couldn't drink or bed, he had decided I was to be protected, as one might look after a fragile pet who could not forage for itself. He brought me chocolate when he had it, even books—a bizarrely random assortment of classics, westerns and smut, which was probably illegal—and he made it clear to the other bullies on board that I was to be unmolested. This raised eyebrows, and because we could not discuss what had happened to us in the jungle, some assumed that he had taken a particular kind of fancy to me, such as sometimes happens on ships. When a corn-fed Kansas boy made the mistake of suggesting as much to his face, Belasco beat him senseless with a chair. No one made the insinuation again. It was ironic, because I had my own suspicions about Belasco that ran contrary to his ostentatious womanizing, not that it mattered to me either way.

The cold of the Antarctic was impossible to prepare for, despite all my reading. It was bitter, bone chilling and constant. If it fluctuated much, you couldn't tell, as your senses could not distinguish variations so far beyond human tolerance. The only thing you could do was stay out of the wind. The cold wasn't the only environmental hazard. After a few weeks of twenty-four hour daylight, forcing your body to sleep on a schedule it refuses to recognize, going to bed with the sun in the sky and getting up with the same sun still in the same sky, it felt like you were going insane.

The mission went well at first. Byrd took the first flight himself, using the JATO rocket assist tubes to help get the plane airborne. Soon there was a steady stream of sorties, day after day, though it wasn't clear what they were doing. Mapping, we were told. But the flying boats went up with

P-51 escort fighters, despite the fact that the only things that lived down here at the bottom of the world were skuas, terns and penguins. There were indeed whales and seals in the frigid waters, but nothing and no one on land, or so we were told.

I saw Captain Jennings only a few times in those first days, and he kept his distance, which was fine by me. After what had happened in the jungle, I was content to be a regular seaman for once. The appeal of secrecy had worn off. Then things took a turn for the worse, and I was reminded why we were really here.

We lost one of the flying boats on the thirtieth of December. It was a Martin Mariner, what they called a PBM—patrol bomber—and it went down with its nine-man crew in heavy weather. Mariners are a rugged, versatile airframe, adaptable to all kinds of specialized roles from recon and air/sea rescue to antisubmarine assault, but we never knew what equipment the flying boats were carrying. What I knew, first hand, was that the Mariner that had gone down had been accompanied by a pair of P-51 Mustangs, and though they made it back to the *USS Philippine Sea*, they'd been pretty badly carved up. The official report said weather. Belasco said otherwise.

He had a buddy on one of the repair and refueling tenders who said the Mustangs had holes through their fuselage and wings, big, round holes, the kind made by serious cannon, twenty millimeter or larger. The fighters were lucky to have gotten back at all. The pilots had been sequestered for debriefing, and the planes had been sealed up below deck while they were repaired, off limits to all but top brass.

Meanwhile, a search-and-rescue operation was mounted for the Mariner's nine-man crew, an operation that required a ground team as well as air support, because the Mariner had gone down over land, possibly effecting a crash landing. Jennings volunteered me and Belasco.

I wasn't angry, and I knew why he had done it, but I needed to hear it from him. I was summoned to the Captain's quarters that evening, and didn't beat around the bush.

"Why me?" I said.

"Because you've already seen," said Jennings.

"Seen what?"

"The Nazi presence here. Nocturnal airlifts and charts of Antarctica."

"Airlifts?"

"How else did Hartsfeld and his Nazi cronies evacuate except by helicopter?"

We'd gone over this before. I hadn't seen helicopters in operation. The Nazis and the Allies both had a few in service during the war, but they'd been rare and specialist aircraft. I found it hard to believe that that was what I'd seen in the jungle that night during the firefight at the Nazi compound, but Jennings assured me it couldn't have been anything else.

"Is that the only reason?" I asked. "To keep the knowledge among those who already have some awareness of it?"

"That's a big part of it," he said. "But in your case . . . there's more."

"Like what?"

He drew a manila envelope from a drawer and slid out a series of large aerial photographs.

"These were taken on the mission, prior to the one when we lost the PBM," he said. "It was going back for a second look. We were mapping an area that's warmer than most of the region and accessible by inlets. Natural harbors, suitable for use as such, assuming they haven't already been claimed. But look here. Seen this before?"

He pointed to a ring, darker than the icy ground beneath it. It was perfectly symmetrical. Man made. And then, when he showed me the enlarged version of a different picture, one taken not from directly overhead but at a shallower angle, the awful familiarity of the thing was clear.

"We know the Nazis were working on an atomic weapon at the end of the war," he said. "Based on this, we think they still are."

I stared at the picture. It was what I had come to think of as a henge, a circle of pillars, probably concrete, connected at the top to a ring, run with cables and charged from beneath. I saw it all in my head, the peculiar underground chamber with the bell-like structure, the ladders up the side of the henge, the men, the gunfire . . .

Ishmael.

"Yes," I said. "I will go."

The weather was getting worse. The brief window of what we laughably referred to as the Antarctic summer seemed to be closing earlier than expected, and the sailors discussed the possibility that the mission would be abandoned sooner than had been scheduled. And of course, no one could survive out there for long. If a rescue of the surviving PBM crewmembers was to take place, it was going to have to be soon.

Jennings confided that the Mustangs had indeed taken fire, but the weather had been so bad that they couldn't be sure whether the guns had been mounted on the ground or had come from hostile aircraft. No definitive sign of a runway had been discovered so far. That meant that we did not dare go too close to the site where the Mariner had gone down, for fear of straying into the same AA fire. Belasco and I were to be ferried to the icebreaker USCGC *Northwind*, then fly on a Coast Guard helicopter to a drop point two miles from where the PBM came down, meet up with the rest of the team, and cover the rest of the ground on foot.

Again, I'd never so much as seen a helicopter up close, let alone ridden in one, and I will admit to being scared. Compared to planes, they felt slow and fragile, easy to shoot down, and we stayed terrifyingly low, so that it seemed a single gust of wind would flip us into the gray, freezing waves. I gripped my seat all the way and tried not to stare into Belasco's massive and malicious grin. He was cradling a Thompson submachine gun in his lap—for all I know, the same one "Hartsfeld" had tampered with when we were in the jungle. He seemed quite content, like it was all a bit of fun, not worried about what might be waiting for us on the ice.

Including me, there were eighteen men on the ground, led by a pair of Rangers, and two radiomen who'd been ashore already, and a dogsled team for the equipment. We were to move inland from the edge of the Ross Sea toward the Queen Alexandra Range. We wore scarves around our faces and fur-lined gloves and boots, so that we looked like lost Cossacks. No one talked much. Even the dogs went quiet once we started moving, and though it was slow and heavy going, the ground underfoot was hard, and the forced march generated as much warmth as I'd felt in weeks.

We'd been walking for a little over an hour when we heard fighters coming in with two more of the Mariner flying boats, the latter low and slow, scanning the ground, the Mustangs up high, circling, waiting. We slowed as we navigated an icy shelf that canted up toward the mountains, and paused on the top to see what we could see.

There was depression in the ice, a stretch of tundra that ran for a couple of miles to the mountains, then shot up in a steep impassable wall of rock. It was latticed by shining, icy ridges, any one of which might be cover for a base of some kind. One of the Mariners made a particularly low pass, and suddenly it was pulling up steeply.

"They've seen something," said Belasco.

"Or something has seen them," said someone else. There was a crackle of gunfire, and we all shrank instinctively. Then the radio was blaring, and the Mustangs were streaming in, and we were moving again, running now, down and up the next rise until I could see it, a huddle of nondescript buildings, and the great concrete henge in the center.

Out of its ring, rising slowly, was an impossible ship, disk-shaped but bulging in the center, which flashed with glass. It rose vertically, soundlessly, and two ports beneath the windows flared as its guns opened up.

The Mariner labored to get clear, and the disk craft gave chase, quickly hitting a rapid cruising speed so that it was on top of the flying boat in seconds. Only as it wheeled to fire did I see the swastika stenciled on the side.

TOMMY REZNIK
Malmstrom Air Force Base, Montana, March 16, 1967

OMMY REZNIK FIGURED HE'D LANDED THE CUSHIEST
job in the services, at a time when the alternatives
could have been a whole lot worse. According to the
paper, the House Appropriations Committee had just
approved another twelve billion dollars to satisfy President
Johnson's demands for security concerns. In other words,
for the war. That was on top of the sixty billion that had
already been assigned for the year.

Sixty billion to get them through the year had got
them as far as March, but now President Johnson's people
were saying there was no end in sight. Robert Kennedy,
Senator from New York and brother to the late President,

John F. Kennedy, was saying the US needed to pull out and go back to the conference table.

Tommy wasn't sure what he made of that. It sounded like defeat, but then, they had been fighting in the jungle for years already and it sounded to him like the mess was just getting worse. It had started quietly, when Tommy was a kid in Cleveland, so quietly he barely remembered it. Gradually, the word had started to echo from every radio, every TV set.

Vietnam.

It felt constant, like an itch that wouldn't go away. Except that it was more than an itch. It was a fire, and it was spreading, getting hotter. It was terrifying.

When Tommy enlisted in the Air Force, rather than letting himself get drafted into the Army, he thanked his lucky stars he was in Montana, under the big, open American sky, and not huddled in some soaking jungle trench, waiting for some guy in black pajamas to run a bayonet through his guts as he slept. He stared up at the sky to banish the image, the great velvety black canopy with its constellations scattered like glitter. The long night patrols around the base perimeter were tedious, but hell—there were worse places to be. He hugged his parka, stamped his bunny boots for warmth and hummed the opening bars of The Beach Boys' "Wouldn't it Be Nice."

It wasn't unusual to see shooting stars up there, and Tommy, born and raised a city boy from Cleveland, a place that always seemed shrouded in smog and street lamp glare, still marveled at them—but the one he saw now was something special. It had moved steadily across the sky from roughly east to west, but then it seemed to slow, changing direction quickly twice, executing a rough circle before coming to rest like the star of Bethlehem, right over head.

Tommy stared. It wasn't a star, shooting or otherwise. That much was obvious. But there was no sound in the still Montana night, and its initial approach had surely been too fast to be a helicopter. You could sometimes see satellites, like Echo. He remembered Sputnik, the satellite the Ruskies had sent up when Tommy was eight years old and had found his parents sitting by the radio, white faced, holding hands. But satellites didn't move like this. They didn't change directions and hover. There had been missions sending men into space, of course, again chasing the Ruskies who had beaten them to it, but after the Apollo disaster in January when all the astronauts had burned before takeoff, Tommy wasn't sure that would ever happen again.

Which meant that what he was seeing wasn't a US spacecraft, and that meant Soviet, because no one else could do it, and that was very bad news indeed. Tommy's private nightmares were all about the jungles of Vietnam, a place he couldn't find on a map and that lived in the whispered horror stories he heard among the men who had been out there and seen it. But the *nation's* nightmare was the Russian commies, an enemy they were fighting by proxy in 'Nam, but who were an altogether different brand of scary. The kind of scary that demanded bases like Malmstrom.

Tommy's patrols were routine, but they were also meticulous, like everything else at Strategic Air Command.

You had to be careful around nuclear missiles, and that was what was pointing skyward in the ten silos of Oscar Flight, only a few hundred yards from where he stood. Tommy was part of the Combat Support Group, located some thirty miles east of Lewiston, one of five launch control facilities in the area that formed the 490th missile squadron, each equipped with ten Minuteman I Nuclear armed Intercontinental Ballistic Missiles.

Tommy moved close to the perimeter fence and gazed upward, the Beach Boys' song momentarily forgotten as he unslung his AN/PRC-6 "banana" walkie-talkie and turned it to broadcast.

"Base, this is Airman Reznik, come in. Over."

There was a momentary silence, then a crackle and the radio came to life.

"Right here, Reznik. What's on your mind? Over."

"Got a weird light in the sky, just outside the north east perimeter fence. Over."

"What do you mean, 'weird?' Over."

"Moving erratically. Hovering. I don't know. Weird. Over."

"Er . . . Okay. Not sure what to do with that, Reznik. Let us know if it gets weirder, I guess. Over and out."

Tommy could hear the amusement in the squad leader's voice, and he hesitated before retrying.

"Airman Reznik again. I think you should come see this. Over," he said.

The silence was longer this time, and the voice, when it came, less amused.

"Be right there, Reznik. Make sure the site is secure. I will alert Command Post. Over and out."

Tommy bit his lip. He wasn't sure he was ready to start a panic down in the launch bunker, but it was protocol that the duty officers sitting in the launch capsule be made aware of any security concerns, however preliminary. Someone would have to come and give the okay before getting back on the phone and calling down to the officers sixty feet below ground. It would all be officially recorded and documented. Tommy chewed his lower lip nervously. His breath billowed clouds of steam into the cold night air. He had to keep his nose clean. He was a good airman, reliable, punctual, always in control of himself. He didn't need a mark on his record, saying he was some Ohio rube who imagined stuff or cried wolf. If he called the base quickly, told them he'd made a mistake, he might head off any call down to launch control, and it might not make it into his record.

But the light was still there, and as he watched, it moved, getting lower as it swept out toward the main gate of the launch facility. Canceling the alert was not an option.

Tommy broke into a jog in the direction of the light, talking into the walkie-talkie as he did so.

"Base, this is Reznik. Come in. Over."

"Still here, Reznik. What's up? Over."

"The light is coming your way. Over."

Another momentary hesitation.

"Say again. Over."

"It's coming down and heading for the main gate. Over," said Tommy, who was now running, his rifle bouncing on its shoulder strap.

The light was larger now, and had gone from cold white to a burning orange that shone on the eight-foot fence and lit the ground like a forest fire. It moved again, drifting closer and closer until, quite slowly, it moved over the gate. It was hard to tell how big it was. The light seemed to fluctuate and spread, so that Tommy wasn't sure of the outlines of the object inside the light. He had the impression of looking at something about the length of an El Camino or a Plymouth Barracuda, though it was circular, disk-shaped. He could see no jets, no rotors, no means of keeping the thing up. It remained eerily soundless.

It continued its steady slide through the air over the gate, no more than thirty or forty feet above the ground, he thought. Suddenly the air was torn by sirens as the Russian craft—if that were indeed what it was—started tripping sensors all over the base. Over from the far side of the road, he could see four or five other guards moving quickly, heads turned upward, weapons at the ready. As cold dread settled in the hollow of his gut, Tommy did the same, dropping to one knee as Sgt. Pinter—the NCOIC he'd been talking to on the walkie-talkie—came scuttling over to him, his eyes wide and scared.

Pinter outranked him, something Tommy had resented until about five seconds ago. Now he couldn't imagine anything worse than being the guy who had to decide what to do next.

"Get over to the comm station," said Pinter, trying to look sure of himself and not quite pulling it off. "Call security and tell 'em what's going on."

"Okay," said Tommy, though he hesitated just long enough to add, "What *is* going on?"

Pinter, whose eyes had not left the amber glow overhead, shook his head. "Damned if I know," he said.

Tommy ran clumsily, still looking up, unable to believe what he was seeing. When he reached the phone and snatched it off the hook, his hand was unsteady.

"What the hell is going on up there?" demanded Lieutenant Salas, the Intercept Control officer.

"Sir, we've got a glowing red object right over the gate. It's just . . . floating there. We're ready to engage but . . ."

"But what?"

"I'm not sure that would be . . . wise."

He wasn't sure why he said it. It was just a hunch.

"Well, you're gonna need to do something," said Salas. Tommy could hear another man's voice in the background, exclamations of astonishment and panic from down in the launch bunker.

"What's happening, sir?" asked Tommy.

"I don't have a clue," said Salas. "But whatever that thing is, it's shutting down our guidance systems. Every missile just went off-alert and no-go, one by one. This facility's capacity to launch a nuclear strike was just switched off."

OSCAR FLIGHT WASN'T THE ONLY FACILITY WHERE THE missiles went down that night. Fifty miles away, Tommy later discovered, the weapons of Echo Flight also shut down, one by one, despite the fact that each missile was separately controlled and powered by its own generator. Something similar had, it turned out, happened at Minot Base almost a year earlier. The missiles were taken off line and examined. All were deemed to be fully functional, and no explanation for their going down could be found.

No one died. No missiles launched. The glowing object simply left, and the base eventually went back to normal. Or at least its systems did. Its machines. The men did not. Though the morning came without the disasters the night had threatened, the guards were all haunted by what they had seen.

They were never debriefed, and though they had made formal reports, all investigations as to what had happened were abruptly terminated and everyone involved forced to sign nondisclosure documents. The guards were reassigned, split up, scattered into other parts of the service, which, for some, meant a change of nightmares. Tommy Reznik received his orders in April. By June he had deployed to Tan Son Nhut Air Base, Saigon, where he died when the base came under attack during the Tet Offensive of the following year. He never told a living soul what he had seen in the skies over Montana.

48

JENNIFER
Rachel, Nevada

SHE WAS STILL MAD ABOUT THE GUY IN THE BAR, OR
rather about the way she'd behaved. Or something.
Maybe she was just mad.

She'd sat eating her food, drinking her beer, watching
the sun go down through the plate glass windows, ignoring
the other few stragglers who came in to drink and chat, and
she was acutely aware of the bandaged man called Alan,
sitting at the bar by himself in his private cloud. When she
felt the urge to apologize getting the better of her, she left
without a word. She hadn't actually said anything she didn't
believe, but it had been unnecessarily confrontational of
her to say it.

She left to escape the bar, not because she had anywhere better to go. She sat in the rented Chevy with no idea what she was going to do next. She'd considered spending the night at the Little A'le Inn, but she couldn't face talking to the waitress who she'd snapped at and who, she worried, was also the owner.

She also knew that Alan might be able to see her rental car from where he sat inside the bar, so she drove off quickly. Wouldn't want to look indecisive.

That's so typical of you, she scolded herself. *Backing yourself into a corner, forcing your own hand, out of what? Defiance? Pride?*

"Fuck off," she muttered to herself.

It was surprisingly dark. The English spring days— being further north—lengthened gradually, so that by mid-summer, the evening unfolded over several hours. She'd been unprepared for how quickly day became night here. Now she was driving with her high beams on, wondering where the hell she was going. A sign to her left flashed white in the dark. Red letters shouted "Warning." She slowed to read the small print. Military Installation. Trespassing prohibited. Photography prohibited.

She sped away, her anger cresting once more as she felt the presence of the impervious monoliths she'd always fought against: authority, control, private interest, exploitation of the masses . . . It was all here. She could smell it on the night air, like blood.

Your temper will be the death of you, she thought, but she heard her father's voice. *So impulsive, so quick to fight . . .*

"I said, *fuck off!*" she shouted, stepping hard on the accelerator as if to emphasize the point.

But for all her bravado, the point was a good one. Her bullheadedness had got her where, exactly, since she'd run from Letrange in the fields outside Heathrow? Leads that didn't go anywhere and the death of a Senator, perhaps because he was seen talking to her. If she were going to take any more chances, pick any more fights, they had to lead somewhere. The men in black had let her go with a surreal lecture and a warning, but next time, they might not be so bizarrely forgiving. Letrange hadn't been. She was lucky to be alive, she reminded herself. She should be very sure of what she was doing before putting herself in that kind of danger again.

Specific risks, she thought. *Productive danger. That was what she needed if she wanted answers.*

She thought of the Hapsel's ranch, the single strand of barbed wire surrounding it, the way the "EPA" guys had driven her round in circles, never pushing more than a mile or so into the old couple's curiously well-funded acreage. Wandering around there after dark sounded like a pretty specific risk . . .

She drove along the road that ran around the edge of the Hapsel farm, looking for a place she might pull over where the car would not attract attention, and as she did, she thought about what Powers had said about unexplained aerial phenomena. It had sounded crazy then, and it still did, though out here where the world was so unfamiliar, it felt, perhaps, a little less crazy. The blackness of the night beyond her headlights was uncanny. In England, there would be hedges and trees flashing green like walls on either side of her, but this strange openness here, an emptiness so complete her headlights found nothing but the asphalt strip and the sky, was unnerving. Whatever might be out there was impossible to see.

Feels like a metaphor.

The road was an image of what her life had become, a stumbling, half-blind pursuit of God-knew-what, and the only thing she was certain of was that her headlights would not find the one thing she really wanted: her father, walking back to meet her.

But if she could find out what was going on, if she could connect the dots that led back to his death, maybe that would be something, even though the idea that chasing down some half-baked nonsense about UFOs would give any insight into her father's life seemed too preposterous to seriously consider.

Except.

Something had been pushing against her conscious mind, a half-memory, flexing against the dark membranes that kept it hidden. She'd been conscious of it for a few days now, but it hadn't registered as more than a kind of hunch, a pointer in the dark, a notion that there was something to see if she looked hard enough.

Now there was more, though she didn't know what had knocked the memory loose.

She'd been six years old, alone in her room and unable to get to sleep because the skeleton man had been over for dinner and had tousled her hair in a way that made her want to scream. Herman Saltzburg, her father's friend and a fellow board member at Maynard, had been their dinner guest, along with two other men whose names she did not recall. He'd sat there, grinning his skull grin, the skin of his hands painted on during the day, she'd decided, so no one would know what a monster of bones he was at night.

She'd lain in bed, rigid with fear, waiting for the sounds of the front door and the house settling into sleep, and then she'd gone out, looking for her father, who would put her to bed properly and drive the memory of the skeleton man from her head. She looked in the train room but hadn't found him, and had to stalk her way across the long corridor with the creaky floor to his office. She opened the door without knocking and stepped inside, finding him with his back to her, studying a chart on bluish paper pinned to the wall behind his desk.

This was the detail her mind had buried, but she saw it now quite clearly, freed by her turning and returning of Senator Powers' troubling phrase: unexplained aerial phenomena.

The chart showed a curious shape that six-year-old Jennifer had thought was a kind of airplane, its details labeled with little words and numbers that she couldn't read. There were two images. One from in front, which reduced the craft—if that was what it was—to a long, slender line that bulged in the middle. And one from above, which showed it as a slightly rounded triangle.

She remembered to this day, but not because the images had struck her as significant. She remembered because she'd started to speak and her father had whirled round, his face a mask of fury the likes of which she'd never seen. He snatched the chart from the wall, tearing it in the process and yelled at her to *Get out!* with such awful violence that it was like seeing a person she'd never met before.

She fled to her room and locked herself in.

The following morning, he apologized, but also said she must never enter his study without knocking again. She didn't feel like his apology was quite real. When he asked her what she'd seen on the chart above his desk, she'd lied and told him she didn't have chance to look at it.

But she remembered that strange triangle, even if it never meant anything to her except as a sign of her father's furious commitment to his work, which she preferred not to think about.

She was thinking about it now. Wonderingly. Amazed that the memory had taken so long to surface, like something that had been lying beneath muddy water.

There was a turnout and an outcropping of rock, screening the road. It wasn't perfect, and would only hide the car from traffic coming from the west, but was the best she'd seen. She made the decision and swerved hard so that the car slewed slightly on the russet gravel.

It was much cooler, now that it was dark, and reminded her of Africa, and though she wouldn't have to worry about hippos or leopards, it occurred to her that the desert south-west had a decent supply of venomous snakes. Rattlers and the like. Did they hunt at night? She had no idea. Cold blooded. Probably not.

Caution, regardless.

She took a small LED flashlight from the glove compartment, brought her purse, and climbed a crumbling dirt embankment. She swept the flashlight across the dry, tall grass and desert scrub, and saw the dull, rusty glow of the Hapsel fence. The wire was slack, and she could pull it low enough to climb over easily, shutting the light off so as not to attract attention. The moon was high and partial, but the sky positively blazed with stars and once more reminded her of Africa. She found there was just enough light to see by, as long as she stayed out of the trees.

She was about a mile south of the farmhouse. The Hapsel ranch was extensive, but the protected habitat was only a few square miles, bordered by a rocky ridge that ran, if she remembered the Google Earth map, about two miles to the west.

It took her an hour and a quarter, and though the night was a good deal cooler than the day, she was dripping with sweat by the time she mounted the wall-like escarpment with its clutter of EPA "Keep Out" signs. The fence was not—as far as she could see—electrified, or draped in razor wire, but it was purposeful, new and well maintained. She could get over it, but it was designed to make it clear that doing so constituted a serious violation of law. One sign said that the territory was both under continual electronic surveillance and subject to security patrols. For a long moment, she read and reread the signs, scanned the perimeter for the telltale red lights of cameras or motion sensors. The longer she hesitated in the dark, the more her determination flagged. She could, she told herself, just walk away. She should.

And then what? Fly back to England and spend the rest of her life on the lookout for Letrange, or someone similar who thought she knew more than she did?

That would be intolerable. And insulting. She gazed into the darkness beyond the fence and the same simple question floated back to her, with memories of her father's rage as he tore down the strange chart in his study . . .

Dad?

He wasn't out there, of course. Not really. But maybe if she could see what was out there, she would learn more about him, what he had done, and what he had tried to back away from or expose. And what had killed him. She set her teeth, pulled the cuffs of her shirt until she could wrap them around her fingers, and took hold of the wire.

No electrical current. No unseen sharp edges.

In seconds, she was over and running clumsily down the other side of the ridge, where the vegetation grew thicker and the starlight glittered on a series of streams emerging, she assumed, from an underground spring. Whether there really were Ash Mountain Speckled Dace, she had no way of knowing, but the water supply had at least made those claims plausible. It also made her own progress more difficult, since she now had to splash around the water's edge in the dark, looking for places to cross, though since she didn't have a set destination, that didn't matter too much.

But it was noisy moving around in the stream, and there was just enough reflected light off the water that she felt conspicuous. She headed deeper into the nature reserve and made for higher ground.

The land was slashed by gullies and long, stony shelves that rose like the ribs of some emaciated torso, so that Jennifer found herself climbing and then stumbling down through swollen succulents and stiff, prickly plants over and over. On the fourth ridge, and still with no sign of any kind of facility or habitation, she opted to swing east along one of the ridges, skulking low to the ground in case anyone might be watching from below. There was a stand of low, twisted trees at one end, their bark smooth, their dry leaves pale and papery. She paused under them for a moment to scan the desert floor. Something stirred below her, a dog-like form picking its way through the grass, fifty yards away.

Wolf? she wondered, momentarily anxious. The animal moved away from her in a light trot, its body rangy and low to the ground, its ears back.

Coyote, she decided, though the name meant little to her beyond roadrunner cartoons. Maybe they were here too. The idea pleased her, putting a lightness in her step that made her momentarily careless. The stone under her foot turned as she put her weight on it and she lost her balance, falling on the baked earth and landing with one arm and the side of her face in a thorny, gorse-like plant.

For a second, she lay still, eyes squeezed shut, her body shifting slightly to test how much damage she had done.

The pain in her face and hand shouted loudest, but she was sure the scratches were all superficial. The throb in her ankle was more worrying. She had rolled it, and it felt tender even as she lay on her back, looking at the sky. What would it be like when she got up and put some weight on it?

A point of light flicked into view overhead, fast as a shooting star, but then, quite suddenly, still. It stayed where it was, so that she began to be sure she had imagined its previous movement, but then it was swelling, and the light, at first singular and pinkish, divided into three lights, equally spaced.

A triangle.

Like the one on the chart in her father's study so many years before.

The triangle stayed where it was for a moment, then seemed to grow bigger, spreading evenly across the blackness behind it. Jennifer stared, her brain hurrying to catch up. It was coming down.

A pair of slim red needles of light lanced down from the craft and flickered over the land below like scribbling pens. They seemed to flit from point to point, as if they were searching for something, or mapping the contours of the ground, and Jennifer rolled to watch them, suppressing a gasp at the twinge in her ankle as she shifted onto her side.

The red lasers vanished as quickly as they'd come, and now the triangle was dropping steadily and silently toward the floor of the shallow valley. It was impossible to tell just how high it was until it was level with her and she saw that what she had assumed was very large indeed—the size of a football pitch, say—was in fact not much bigger than a double-decker bus on its side. There was a fractional hum, less a sound than a kind of sensible vibration in the air, and then the mechanical *thunk* of what might have been landing gear. It hung for another ten seconds before settling down soundlessly on the desert earth.

There was no cover to speak of, but Jennifer was well hidden in the tangle of weeds and struck by something too close to awe to move a muscle. The craft had come down as if it weighed no more than gossamer, as if the laws of physics themselves had been suspended. It was like watching a magic trick, studying the conjurer's hands for a telltale sign of the reality behind the illusion, but finding nothing. And this was no stunt designed for an audience. This was true. She knew it, and not just because her eyes told her so. Again, she thought of the chart on her father's wall and knew in her heart that the craft etched palely on that blue print had just landed on the Nevada dirt only fifty yards or so from where she lay.

The ship was dark now, because the lights she'd seen came from its underside and had dwindled to nothing as it had drifted lower than her vantage point, but as she watched, a new set of lights swelled around the triangle's edge, a soft, amber glow that seemed somehow alive. She heard a series of dull clicks in a broken and uneven stream, and then the desert was white and green, every stunted plant and water-starved bush casting long, hard-edged shadows. The blue-white glare came from beneath the craft itself and was so bright that, though she wanted to watch, Jennifer twisted her head away and shut her eyes.

When she looked back, the ship was gone. It took her a moment to see the triangulated lights, already getting small as the ship rose steadily into the night sky. The points of white pulsed once, and then it vanished, speeding away like a bolt of lightning, arcing across the sky, then taking an impossibly hard cut to the west and out of sight.

For at least a minute, Jennifer did not move, and when she got to her feet at last, it was reluctantly, like she was the last person to leave a movie theatre as the final credits rolled out and the house lights came up. Reluctant and uncertain. Those last few minutes had shaken her, challenging a lot of things she thought she knew about the world and her place in it. These thoughts would surely have swamped her, left her gazing up at the heavens until the sun rose, except that a sound from the valley below had caught her attention.

A breathy grunt, a groan, as of exertion . . .

Jennifer scoured the desert floor.

There, just where the impossible triangle had just taken off, getting unsteadily to her feet, was a woman.

49

ALAN
Rachel, Nevada

ALAN HAD BEEN NURSING THE SAME BEER FOR OVER AN hour, and as it warmed and turned flat, it had become, even by his undemanding standards, undrinkable. The waitress twice offered to get him another, but he'd shaken his head and tried to suggest—more kindly than the English woman had—that he wanted to be left alone. She seemed to get the message. He pushed the glass to the edge of the table where it sat beside the phone he had turned off.

He was not in the mood to talk to anyone.

It was amazing, given all that had happened, that the English woman—Jennifer, she'd called herself—was in his head at all. But then her little speech, her accusation that he wasn't serving American freedoms, had gotten under his skin. On a night like this, when calls would be made to the parents and wives of soldiers who'd been lost on a classified mission somewhere, it needled him to think their sacrifices might be called into question.

But it was worse than that. He'd heard such rants before and had always been able to dismiss them, but this time, in this place, he was less sure.

What if she was right?

What exactly was he doing here? Who was he fighting, and on whose orders? He had never had a problem with the secrecy of a mission before. It made sense to him that military strategies and objectives should be kept from the public, lest the enemy learn of them and use that information to better their position. But the Locust program was a different kind of secrecy, in which everything—equipment, methodology, purpose, hell, even the nature of the enemy—was unknown, not just to the press and the general public, but to ninety-nine percent of the military, including top brass. He was used to covert ops as part of a larger and officially-sanctioned war, but this was different there too. He didn't know what he was doing, how he was doing it, or who was calling the shots.

Possum Plant, Hatcher had called the R&D division, because when people look too closely, everybody plays dead.

And maybe that was how things had to be. But it didn't feel right.

He'd always had questions, but he'd always been able to take the answers to those questions on faith, as he'd been trained to. Now there were five dead pilots, lying in some secret morgue, and they hadn't known what they'd been doing any more than he did. What if they hadn't been serving US freedoms? What if they had been lied to from the outset, used, exploited?

That would be more than insulting to their memories. It would be a violation of everything Alan had always believed his country stood for.

Another hour slid by, and it was the only thing he could see. Twenty minutes later a car pulled up outside and Barry Regis came in. He ordered a beer and then nodded to the door.

"Feel like getting a little air, Major?" he said.

Alan frowned but he went with him, out of the diner and along the empty desert road. For a moment, neither of them said anything, and then, when they were a good couple of hundred yards from the bar and surrounded by the emptiness of the desert, the FAC man gave voice to an idea at least as dreadful as those haunting Alan.

"We were set up," he said.

Alan stared at him.

"You were a lure," said Regis. "They kept their distance and waited for the rest of the squadron. That means it was a trap."

Alan said nothing.

"Someone on the inside," said Regis. "Has to be."

"Yes," said Alan at last. His voice was flat, and as dead as he felt, but it made sense.

"A leak?" Regis mused. "Or a rat?"

Alan scowled into the settling night. Neither option was good, and he feared the worse of the two was more likely.

"This isn't just giving information away," he said. "This is active sabotage."

"A rat, then," Regis agreed. "Who do you trust?"

There was a long silence while Alan thought, his eyes fixed on the middle distance.

"You," he said at last.

"And?" Regis prompted.

Alan bowed his head, eyes closing for a moment.

"You," he said again.

Regis turned to look at him, a long, searching gaze ending in a nod.

"Then we are, as they say, of one mind," he said.

"I wish we weren't," said Alan.

"No shit," said Regis. "So, next question. If we were set up, if the enemy wanted to punch out our air strike capacity, you've gotta think something is coming. What?"

"Damned if I know," said Alan.

Something in his voice caught the other man's attention, and his eyes narrowed.

"Someone meant it to happen, and we need to find out who. And why."

"Doesn't seem like I know much of anything anymore," said Alan.

Regis just shook his head.

"Gotta be someone high up," he said. "I don't know. This wasn't spur of the moment. That don't feel right. Feels to me like this was planned a long time ago. Has to be someone who's been pulling strings all along."

"Hatcher?" said Alan, turning to face him.

"Think about it," said Regis. "We wouldn't be here if it wasn't for him. He came in, overruling every branch of the military we'd ever heard of. I don't know. He gave you the Moscow mission?"

"Sure," said Alan, shrugging. "He gave me every mission I've flown since I got here. Maybe he was fed bad data."

"Maybe."

"Did he ever say why he brought you here?" asked Alan.

"Some say I'm good at my job," said Regis with a crooked smile.

"Yeah, and I'm not bad at mine," said Alan, "but the CIA only got interested in me when I saw something they couldn't explain away, and they opted to bring me on the inside. But you were in the bunker when that ship appeared in Afghanistan. You didn't see it. So why did they bring you?"

"He never really said," answered Regis. "But he implied it was partly to—what were his words?—*ease* your transition. I wasn't feeling too kindly disposed to you at the time, if you recall . . ."

"I recall," Alan inserted. "Vividly."

"So I wasn't too keen on being your babysitter, but then he showed me what you were flying and . . . Well, that changes a lot of things, doesn't it?" said Regis, with a touch of wonder in his voice.

"You can say that again," said Alan, flatly. "Do you ever wonder what we're doing? Why it's all so secret? Who we're fighting and who we're obeying?"

Regis kicked some of the dust off his boots. Alan knew he was stalling.

"Sometimes," he said at last, avoiding Alan's eyes. "I guess."

"I mean," said Alan, fumbling for the words, "I don't mind risk. I don't mind sacrifice. So long as it's worth something."

"You don't think it is?"

"I don't know. Not for sure. Do you? I go up there in those impossible airplanes and zip around, spying on people, running from people when they shoot at me, shooting back, without ever knowing who any of those people are, or what happens to the information I gather, or what war we're fighting. I mean, I can handle the fact that the newspapers don't know what we're doing. But who does? The Pentagon? The government? I swear to God, Barry, I have no clue."

"You told anyone else you feel this way?"

"No," said Alan. "And I wouldn't. Like I said, I trust you. And no, whatever uncertainty I'm feeling now would not make me change sides or put anyone on our side at risk. I hope I don't have to say that."

"You don't," said Regis. "Major, it's what happened to those other pilots. You feel responsible and it's playing on your mind. That's to be expected. It's normal. Hell, I'd worry about you if you didn't go through it. But you and me? We're the rookies here. There's a lot we're not told."

"Maybe that should change," said Alan, with sudden certainty.

"Maybe it should," Regis agreed. "And maybe tomorrow we'll set up a meet with Hatcher . . ."

"Hatcher," said Alan, frowning.

"You really don't trust him?"

"I don't know," said Alan, honestly. "But like you said, if I was set up—if those other pilots were sent out to get killed, their machines shot to pieces—that takes some serious access."

"And some stone cold son of a bitch," said Regis. "You think Hatcher has that in him?"

"If I were honest, no, but I also know he has, every step of the way, shown me what he wants me to see, a bit at a time. Enough to keep me interested and compliant, not enough for me to glimpse anything like the whole picture. If he turns out not to be the man he says he is, I can't say I'll be totally surprised."

"The problem is that by the time we find out for sure . . ." Regis began.

"It will be too late," Alan concluded for him.

"So what do we do? The clock is ticking. I don't even know how to go up the chain of command here. It's a fiefdom. Or at least it feels like one. We could go to Langley, or even to National Intelligence, but if we're wrong and we bypass the chain of command . . ."

"That would be bad."

"No kidding," said Regis. "And maybe it is all above board, but when you have this degree of secrecy, your best case scenario is that no one knows what the fuck is going on."

"And the worst case?"

"Then it's like you said. We don't work for the people we thought we worked for. We're screwing our own country. We're accidental traitors."

"Jesus," breathed Alan.

"I think I need that beer now," said Regis. "You?"

"Not sure I feel like drinking but I'll sit with you."

They walked back toward the bar. When they got there Regis' beer was waiting for him, and the waitress had replaced Alan's.

"That one was looking a bit old," she said.

He nodded his thanks. They had barely taken their seats when the door opened and Morat came in.

"Figured I'd find you here," he said.

Regis gave him a nod, but he met Alan's eyes first, and there was a change in the atmosphere, as if a kind of veil had been pulled across the FAC's face.

"Any news?" asked Alan.

"Nothing good," said Morat leaning forward and speaking in a whisper. "Outside."

Regis set his beer down and frowned at Alan.

"Didn't we just do this dance?" he muttered, as they followed Morat outside.

This time they went only far enough from the bar that they wouldn't be overheard, loitering in the thickening shadow of the pickup truck with the model flying saucer hanging from its mini-crane.

"Well?" said Regis, looking over his shoulder.

"LOTS OF SHOUTING," SAID MORAT. "TOP BRASS WANTING to know what the hell is going on. Eyewitnesses on the news talking about lights in the sky all over the country. Civil liberties types moaning about confiscation of cameras by a recovery team north of Reno. Questions being asked in DC." He frowned and his tone lowered in register, no hint of further flippancy. "The casualty list hasn't changed. Five dead. One critically injured. The surviving triangle is going to be in the shop for weeks, maybe months."

"Leaving us with how many?" asked Alan.

Morat gave Regis a wary look.

"He's head of base security," Alan snapped. "I'm pretty sure he knows what he's guarding."

"Three operational Locusts," said Morat grudgingly. "One more in dry dock which needs a few days' work. Couple of weeks on one more."

"And the prototype," said Regis. "The sport model."

The other two just looked at him, Alan remembering the glimpse he had got of the silvery disk-like craft in the hangar he'd glimpsed before being forced to look away.

"You know what I'm talking about," said Regis. "This isn't the time to pretend you don't."

"I've only seen it once," Alan said. "Never been in it. Certainly never flown it."

"No one has," said Morat. "The engineers are still working on it. So if whoever hit us comes back . . ."

"We're fucked," said Alan.

"There's more," said Morat. "Still bad."

"What?" Regis prompted.

"I said we had three Locusts operational. There should have been four," said Morat. "There were an hour ago. Now one of them's gone. So is Hatcher."

"What?"

"That's why I came for you," said Morat. "I called but . . ." he eyed Alan's phone critically. "We need you back on base and ready to go. Command structure is being revised. It looks calm because everyone is doing their jobs right now, but if anything happens . . . it will be chaos."

"You think something's going to happen?" asked Alan.

Morat gave him a level look and said, "Don't you?"

"Anything else?" asked Alan.

Morat managed a bleak smile. "Not enough for you? Okay, well there was a chemical spill in locker room C2, so you'll have to stay out of there, but I don't think that's a massive priority right now, do you?"

Regis blew out a long breath, then nodded.

"Okay," he said. "Let me pay for the beer I never got to drink and we'll go."

50

TIMIKA
Central Nevada

IT WAS WARM. HOT, COMPARED TO WHEREVER SHE'D BEEN before. She couldn't remember where that had been or how she'd gotten here. In fact, she realized as she struggled to make sense of things, she couldn't remember much of anything.

Drugged?

The idea touched a chord, like there was something she should remember, but it wouldn't come. But she sure as hell hadn't been . . . wherever she was now, that much was certain.

She was outside in what looked like a desert. It was night, but she could feel the dryness all around her, under her shoes, in the air. She shrugged out of her coat and

535

instinctively felt for something at the back, something that wasn't there, though the lining of the stylish black coat had been slit open.

She felt a swell of failure and sadness, but could not recall why. She had lost something, but she didn't know what. Her fingers spread open over the indentation in the back of the coat where the fabric had stretched slightly.

A book.

That was what was gone. Old. Handwritten.

Memories moved like animals in the dark: just enough to show they were hidden.

She had come from . . .

She looked up, but saw only the vast emptiness of the desert sky, pin pricked with a thousand stars. The action made her woozy, and she sat heavily on a fire blackened tree stump, her posture sloppy, as if she had been drinking heavily. She waited for her head to stop swimming. She was suddenly parched with thirst. She should, she supposed, be frightened, but none of it felt quite real. She had the drunk's sense of invulnerability, even if she knew it was an illusion.

Shit.

She kept very still and focused on her breathing, trying to process the landscape she saw in the darkness. She wasn't in New York, which was, she recalled, where she lived. Her name was Timika Mars, and she lived in New York. She ran a website.

This was good. It was coming back. Though the memory of the website brought a rush of despair which, for a second, she could not explain. Then it came to her.

Debunktion. Ruined, she thought, along with her professional reputation. *Marvin's missing . . .*

"Oh yeah," she said aloud to the night. "This remembering stuff is just awesome."

She looked up, conscious of some presence that had not been there before, and there was a white woman, about her own age, cute in a no nonsense kind of way, but covered in dust and muck, about twenty yards off but walking toward her, her eyes full of uncertainty.

"Who the hell are you?" said Timika, lowering her eyes again when the strain of looking up became too much. "No," she added. "Strike that. I don't really care. Where am I?"

The white woman's uncertainty seemed to increase.

"Nevada," she said. Her voice was weird. Fancy.

"Nevada?" Timika shot back. Her voice sounded slurred. "What the hell am I doing in Nevada?"

"I was going to ask you the same question," said the woman who Timika realized was English.

"Why? Is this your property?"

"No."

"Huh," said Timika. "You got something to drink? My head . . ."

"Sorry," said the woman, shaking her head. She had long chestnut hair gathered into a ponytail. "But I can take you somewhere you can get something."

"Yeah?" Timika said, looking up again. The woman was cautious, and watchful, but the offer seemed genuine.

"Can you walk?" asked the woman. "I don't think we should stay here. But my car is a couple of miles away."

"A couple of miles?" Timika echoed. "Damn, lady—you need to work on your rescuing."

"Is that what I'm doing?"

"Hell if I know," said Timika, getting laboriously to her feet. She waited for a second to steady herself, then said, "Okay. Which way?"

"Do you know what just happened to you?" asked the woman. "I mean, how you came here?"

"Not sure," said Timika, hedging. "You got any theories?"

The woman seemed to hesitate, as if coming to a decision, then said, "I saw it."

Timika met her eyes and saw the truth and the concern in them. And the questions. That was okay. Timika had questions too. She held out her hand.

"Timika Mars," she said. "I've spent my life saying a bunch of stuff isn't real, and it has come back to bite me in the ass. You?"

"Jennifer Quinn," said the woman. "I seem to have stumbled onto a financial conspiracy that involved my murdered father, centering on the development of what the late Senator Tom Powers called 'unexplained aerial phenomena.' And as a result, some very powerful people want me dead."

"Yeah?" said Timika, more memories snapping into place. "Me too. I had a book. A journal, written by an old man, but . . . I lost it. Or it was taken."

Once more the stab of failure and sadness. Timika would have said more, but the other woman—Jennifer—had become very still, gazing off along the valley floor.

"Do you hear that?" she asked.

Distantly, but getting louder by the second, was the unmistakable rumble of a car coming over difficult ground. Two cars.

"Yeah," said Timika, who still felt a little dazed. "Not good?"

"I'm thinking that whoever is coming is supposed to be your welcoming committee," said Jennifer, threading a supportive arm round Timika's shoulders.

"So why don't I feel like they'll be all that welcoming?"

"Because you're smart," said Jennifer. She looked towards the crest of a long, rocky ridge. "That way. We need to get out of sight. Quick as you can."

They crossed the rock-strewn desert in a loping, ungainly trot, and were soon scrambling up the ridge, sometimes using their hands to pull themselves up. Jennifer urged Timika over the top and down the other side, pausing just long enough to look back to where headlights splashed the desert sands. Memories of her pursuit through the streets of New York, her encounter with soldiers in what she believed had been Russia, eased back into focus, as if the peril were sharpening her mind as part of some ancient survival instinct. By the time they surmounted the third ridge, she was dusty and her legs were trembling from the exertion, but she felt like herself again.

They clambered over a fence, and then the land was flat and open, so they ran as best they could, in case the cars should come barreling up behind them, painting them with their high beams. Timika wasn't in as good shape as Jennifer, and she was starting to gasp and wheeze as she jogged along, conscious that she was holding the other woman back, but she was damned if she was going to stop. She didn't know who was in those cars, but she had had enough of being pushed around.

For an awful moment, as they cleared the last fence, a single strand of barbed wire snagged on her pants, and Timika thought Jennifer was lost. She saw the panic rising in the woman's face, the desperate way she looked left and right as she walked, but then they reached an empty road and, thirty yards from where they had rejoined it, sat a dusty Chevy Impala, half obscured by a rocky outcrop. She got in and the car pulled silently away, moving slowly, headlights off until they had gone a half mile or so.

"I need a drink," said Timika. "And I mean a *drink* drink."

"I know a place," said Jennifer. "Let's hope they're still open."

Timika said nothing, sitting back and waiting for her heart rate and breathing to return to something like normal.

Normal.

She didn't know what the word meant anymore, not here with this strange woman in this even stranger place, after everything that had happened. She considered the English woman as she drove. It had not occurred to her to distrust her. She'd been cautious at first, as had Jennifer, but as they drove, united in strangeness, she could feel the barriers between them lowering. She was not surprised when the Englishwoman slowly broke down the details of her own experience in a matter-of-fact tone. When she was finished, Timika did the same, as much as she could remember, with edited highlights but nothing deliberately kept back.

The mutual trust between them was as strange as everything else and grew, Timika suspected, out of a mutual desperation born of weary anxiety. Neither of them had spoken to another person, face to face like this, for what felt like a long time. Both had spent the previous days skulking, prying, teasing at problems, and running for their lives. Their backgrounds could hardly be more different, but being out here after all that had happened was common ground.

They drove through the night, seeing little until the roadside bar hove into view. Timika took in the alien on the sign outside and gave Jennifer a look.

"Seriously?"

"Not a big bar scene in Rachel, Nevada," said the Englishwoman.

"I'm getting that."

The strangeness they both felt slipped for a second, became absurdity, and suddenly they were both laughing with relief. It took a good thirty seconds to stop, and Timika had to wipe her eyes before she got out of the car.

"Lord," she exclaimed. "I needed that almost as much as I need a drink."

"Me too," said Jennifer, grinning at her as if she had known her for years. "The laugh and the drink. And water won't do."

"Give me a minute to rehydrate," said Timika, "and I'll be right there with you." They were still sitting in the car, the engine off. Timika considered the Little A'le Inn. "You think this place is safe? Whoever was in those cars were looking for me. Expecting me, maybe. You think it was those bogus EPA guys?"

Jennifer nodded solemnly. "That would be my guess," she said. "Unless the guys who came after you in New York are here too."

"Two different groups trying to kill us, you mean?" said Timika. "Awesome."

"I don't know," said Jennifer. "The men in black made no attempt to harm me. Just freaked me out. So either their strategy has changed since Letrange—or whatever his name is—tried to finish me off, or they're two different groups."

"One of them government?"

"Maybe. But whoever was looking for you in the desert never saw us," said Jennifer. "I'm pretty sure of that. Did you get a look at the types of cars?"

"Not really," said Timika. "Not military and I don't think they had roof lights, so probably not law enforcement either. Sedans, I think. One paler than the other. Maybe white."

Jennifer shrugged, looking impressed.

"None of these, anyway," said Timika, nodding at the cars parked alongside the Little A'le Inn. "Let's get that drink," she said, opening her door.

She was walking to the bar's entrance when she realized that Jennifer was hanging back. Timika turned, mouth open to ask what the problem was, but stopped at the terror etched into Jennifer's face. She was staring through the window into the well-lit interior of the diner where three men stood at the bar, apparently paying their tab, one white, one black, and one who might have been Spanish or even middle eastern.

"It's him," Jennifer gasped. "Letrange. He's here."

MORAT
Safid Kuh, September 2014

JEAN-CHRISTOPHE MORAT LOOKED UP AT THE SOUND of feet coming down the hallway to his cell. The tunnels were long and narrow—part concrete, part rock—and sound carried a long way, so he always knew when they were coming. They usually came in pairs, one with a food tray, the other to watch over him, AK-47 at the ready. Sometimes they came with questions, but he had not been tortured, which was unexpected, and he had been well treated.

Which was worrying.

The whole situation felt off, somehow. His captors were Afghans. He was certain of that, but there were others among them who weren't: pale men, their skin easily pinked by the sun, men who kept to themselves and spoke only in whispers. Russians, he was fairly sure, though what they were doing here, he couldn't begin to guess. They'd stayed away from him, which was also strange. He detected no sign of his Afghan captors doing or saying anything to suggest Moscow was pulling the strings.

He'd been here a week, though it felt longer. He still wasn't sure how they had found him in the first place. Morat knew this country as well as he did his own, and was expert at blending into it. He spoke flawless Pashto and Dari, the latter with an immaculate Tajik accent, and could tell you the history of his village going back three generations, though he could also pass as Uzbek if needed. Most of the guards seemed to think he was local, an informant, perhaps, though it was far from clear who they thought the enemy was. If it weren't for Dubchek, Morat felt there would have been a decent chance that he could talk his way out of this prison.

Dubchek was the fly in the yogurt. Or rather the spider.

He'd appeared on the third day, accompanied by other men Morat took to be Russian. It was immediately clear that the local mountain men deferred to him, though he did not swagger or threaten. He was quiet, soft-spoken and mild-mannered to the point of an old world politeness that was both dignified and ominous, as if it masked a great and dangerous passion. His ethnicity was unreadable. He was dark skinned—though that might have been the sun—and black eyed, with black hair to match. He wore it swept back and shoulder length, and might have passed for a sultan or a tsar, and he had a dense beard without a wisp of gray. Though Morat had heard him speak a few words of Russian—making a casual joke suggesting deep knowledge of the language—he didn't think the man came from Russia, in spite of his name. He spoke Pashto as well as Morat, but instead talked to his prisoner—Morat was under no doubt that he had somehow become *his* prisoner—in immaculate English. Morat spent almost an hour with him on the third day, trying to detect any regional accent, but it was curiously neutral, and when he did show flashes of something—an Irish lilt, or a flat American Midwestern vowel—the man would then say something that gave a completely different impression.

Learned, then. Studied. It was his feet Morat heard echoing in the hallway. Morat had grown used to the sound, the precision of those well-made boots—and not a mountain man's boots either. These were built not just for tarmac and concrete but also for the polished wood floors of formal dining rooms, where people sipped champagne under crystal chandeliers. Morat listened. One pair of feet only.

He rose from the wooden cot where he'd been sleeping and licked his lips. If Dubchek were alone, that meant . . . what? He would come clean, share how he was going to get Morat out? Or something else?

Morat thought of Dubchek's strange, impenetrable smile, the twinkle in his dark eyes as he spoke, the chill amusement underlying his affable and urbane composure, and estimated he was no ally, poised to spring him to freedom.

Dubchek didn't bother to test the little window before unlocking the door, even though he was alone. He was confident that, should Morat try to force his way out, he was more than up to the challenge of stopping him. Morat sat again on the edge of the bed and sipped from the glass of apple tea the guard had left him. Dubchek wasn't the only one who could show composure.

The heavy door creaked open and Dubchek came in, slim mouth smiling, eyes watchful as a cat's. Morat started to rise—persisting in the social niceties that had become part of their game—but Dubchek waved him down and drew up the room's only chair. He had not closed the cell door. Morat felt a tension in his body, like a sprinter in the blocks, waiting for the starter's pistol.

But unsure which way he would run.

The idea amused him, but did not make him smile.

"Mr. Dubchek," he said. "This is an unexpected visit."

"Your rescuers, I'm sorry to say," said Dubchek, pleasantly, "have made it necessary."

"My rescuers?"

"The Americans are coming. Like the cavalry in those Westerns films you people love so much. Always in the nick of time."

"I was never much of a movie fan," said Morat.

"No?" said Dubchek, taking a cut-throat razor from his pocket and unfolding it. "Then you missed out. The world in films can be extraordinary. Beautiful, and passionate, and thrilling, full of good and evil, right and wrong. People making big moral choices. John Wayne. Wonderful stuff."

He said it almost sadly, and the shrug at the end struck Morat with a special poignancy. The man had come to kill him. He didn't particularly want to do it, might even feel bad about it, but he was going to do it anyway. There was no doubt about that.

"Well," said Morat, rallying, "that's good. About my rescue, I mean. I don't know why you are sorry to say it."

"Yes, you do," said Dubchek simply. He looked at the stone floor like a man who had just stubbed out a cigarette, and Morat felt the cold of the cell settle into his bones.

He started to say something but his voice cracked and he had to clear his throat before proceeding. "You could let them take me," he managed, eying the razor.

Dubchek nodded thoughtfully and smiled a wan, distant smile. "Unfortunately, not," he said, "but I wanted to tell you how much I have enjoyed our little chats over the last few days. I meet so few interesting and cultured people in my line of work."

He moved the razor to his own throat and absently began cutting away chunks of beard. Morat watched, mesmerized.

"I don't think you ever told me what that line of work actually was," said Morat. He was stalling now.

"No," said Dubchek. "And I must keep the specifics to myself still, I'm afraid, though I'm sure you have the general picture already. I'm in the same line of work as you.

And I know the costs, the losses such work entails. I am sorry that it must come to this. Ordinary people have other things to give their lives meaning. Money. Love. Respect. Not for the likes of us. You've been in this country so long, I don't suppose most of your commanders even know what you look like anymore. That is very sad, I think, though it will make my job easier. Have you never noticed how alike we are? We did. Months before we captured you."

He smiled as Morat's puzzlement turned to horror.

"That's right," said Dubchek, waggling the razor tellingly. "We have been planning this moment for a long time."

He couldn't be serious.

"Switching places?" he said. "Taking my identity? You'd never get away with it."

"Not for long, probably," said Dubchek. "But I won't need long, and I am surprisingly well-prepared."

Morat stared at him. The man's composure was astonishing. How could he consider such a thing so calmly when it must end in failure and death? Morat had had his share of dangerous missions, but accepting something so obviously suicidal was beyond him. Even here, in what were probably his final minutes, the thought made him angry.

"If the US has sent a rescue team, they won't come short-handed," Morat said, defiant. "They'll send a crack team. And air support. You won't be able to fight them off. Surrender and I'll put a good word in for you."

Dubchek shook his head slowly.

"I won't be able to fight them off, no," he said. "Nor will our Afghan friends. But I have other allies who will more than level the playing field."

He smiled at that last phrase, as if he had been hoping to be able to use it.

"They'll never get here in time," Morat tried, his final bluff.

"Time," said Dubchek, standing, and drawing the Strike One pistol from the waist band in the small of his back, "as you well know, is not something they need in large amounts."

Morat did not move. He took a breath. Perhaps if he lunged for the gun at just the right moment . . .

Dubchek fired twice, then added a third shot to be sure. He waited for a few minutes, then said a blessing over the man he had killed and moved into the next room to dress and finish shaving. The disguise would not need to be especially good, not given what was about to happen and the chaos it would lead to, but if something was worth doing, he thought, giving one last look at the body of Morat, it was worth doing well.

52

JERZY
Ross Ice Shelf, Antarctica, January 1947

I HAD NEVER SEEN ANYTHING AIRBORNE MOVE WITH THE agility of the Nazi disk. It rolled and pivoted over the Antarctic mountains, leaping forward and stopping abruptly in mid-air as if gravity had no power over it and aerodynamics were irrelevant. It spun, firing cannon shells, and the Mustangs fell on it like dogs on a bear.

On the ground, we could only watch, dumbfounded, and then, at the urging of the rangers, make a double-time run down the ridge toward the base and the henge at its heart. We ran clumsily, eyes on the sky, as the saucer-like craft dodged and wove with improbable grace and speed as the Mustangs pelted it with .50 caliber machine gun fire. It had abandoned the lumbering Mariner, which was lightly armed and therefore the least of its worries, but the Mustangs were quick and deft, hard to see against the pale sky, and too scattered to target. For all its speed and maneuverability, the saucer was losing. As it turned to fire on one plane, two more swooped in from behind, riddling it with gunfire, and soon it began to smoke.

Whoever was piloting it made the decision to run, which is probably what it should have done to begin with, and the whole thing began to pulse with an amber light as it sought to leap into some new uncatchable velocity. But the act of powering up had forced it to hang in place, its guns silent, and in that moment, it was pummeled by the Mustangs. There was a brilliant flash as it surged into an upward acceleration of dazzling speed, but the damage was done. As it streaked away from our planes, climbing ever higher, the plume of smoke it left behind thickened and darkened, until there was something sickly about it. Moments later the disk exploded in a fireball that could be seen for miles.

THE NAZIS HAD FINISHED IN ANTARCTICA WHAT THEY'D been unable to complete at the Wenceslas mine, but it had absorbed all their resources. The ground fight was surprisingly, mercifully desultory. Once the disk exploded, the defenders were quick to lay down their arms, and they emerged looking drawn, weather-beaten and defeated. Many had lost fingers and toes to frostbite, and walked like badly constructed marionettes, hobbling, unable to carry their own gear. When we made our way into the buildings to round up the survivors, we found men emaciated from hunger and dysentery, as well as a stack of bodies that resembled the piles of corpses I'd seen in photographs from the concentration camps. I cannot pretend to have been sorry about it.

Their rations were largely gone, their generators failing, and half of the men had frozen to death. There were a few concrete bunkers cased in ice, but the great Nazi war machine had not survived the journey to this bleak place. Any member of the Third Reich who believed this was the ground upon which they would rebuild was delusional.

But then that was hardly news.

Under the henge, we found the bell chamber, though the soldiers in our ground party were quickly herded out once it had been secured. The subsequent airlift of parts and wreckage was designated a matter of the tightest classification and it was only my special orders from Captain Jennings that allowed me to see anything at all. What was clear—to me at least—was that this was no atomic weapons factory. I had seen the way that disk moved, the way it hovered in the air, and though it had been too poorly armed to engage a squadron of fighters, it clearly represented a colossal technological leap forward.

The henge, it seemed clear, was part of an anti-gravity system, or its development.

It did not survive our arrival. Moments after getting everyone clear, the Nazis blew up the entire structure with a series of demolition charges causing the whole thing to collapse under a great feathering of concrete dust and ice shards that rained down on us like hail. Amazingly, no one was seriously hurt, and it took no great time to find the men who had ordered soldiers to set the explosives. There were two. One was the man Captain Jennings had pointed out as a high-ranking SS officer and engineer called Hans Kammler. When cornered, his last shot was for himself.

The other man did not feel the same suicidal urge, a blond officer in the uniform of an SS *Hauptsturmführer* with the domino insignia of three pips and two bars on his collar: Ungerleider.

I knew him at once, though his face was blank when I stood before him. I felt at my back for the trenching tool that was part of my kit. It was a one handed, folding pick used for breaking up ground.

Or someone's skull.

I drew it out and snapped it open as I walked toward him.

Then Belasco barreled into me, dragging me aside and pulling me back, his great coat drawn tight about him, his scarf wound tight around his face.

I was no match for Belasco. He told me to calm down, that it wasn't worth it, and then he handed the trench tool back to me, promising that justice would be done, and telling me to find shelter while we waited for the helicopter. There was no point ending my career to do what a war crime tribunal would do just as well.

Within an hour, I convinced myself that he was right, that it was good that I had not killed Ungerleider.

A month later, I was less sure. And two months after that, I was positive that I should have killed him when I had the chance.

There is one more thing. The Nazis had eaten everything they could, whether it was technically food or not, and they had burned anything that would take a flame, including crates of paintings that had made their way from the Fatherland in one of those stray U-boats. But there was one thing they had not touched, something squirreled away into Kammler's private quarters, where it was kept under lock and key.

It was a box, metallic, possibly lead because it was very heavy, about a yard long and stamped with a German eagle. Jennings and I opened it, back onboard the *Kitchener.*

I will not say here what it was or why our superiors thought it unworthy of their attention, but I will say where it may still be found, and I will say that of all the things that came out of Operation High Jump (for so the mission was called), nothing was more important, even if we did not see its importance at the time. Its implications are so far reaching that they will one day redefine world history.

I saw the significance right away, though I think that of all the people there, only Jennings understood why it subsequently became my obsession. But I was not the first person to be drawn to the strange metal box. Kammler had been. So was the blond officer who had done his bidding.

Ungerleider, like the other Germans, was arrested, disarmed, and put in confinement back on one of the ships. But while most of the soldiers were shipped back to Germany—some to face trial— he was not.

He was special. He knew things. He was the last best hope to rebuild the bell and the henge above it, and the flying disk it had enabled. He was given a new name, a new job, and a government ID, then he was deployed to a test facility in Nevada.

The metal box went with him. Captain Jennings reported it gone from stores the day after Ungerleider left. HQ confirmed that he had claimed it as personal property, and since none of our superiors on hand had thought it worth special attention, while the Nazi apparently was, he had been allowed to take it.

After everything we had gone through, the injustice of this—the sense that a monster like Ungerleider would not only escape punishment but would be rewarded for what he had done—burned into me like the frigid wind whipping the decks off the Ross Sea. It cut its way inside me and lodged there, hard and cold, leaving me no choice as to what I would do next.

Ungerleider had taken his knowledge, his talent, and his secret treasure to Nevada, and I would go after him.

53

JENNIFER
Rachel, Nevada

"PULL OVER!" SAID TIMIKA. THEY WERE DRIVING FAST, too fast, and not driving *to* anywhere. Just away. "Damn it, Jennifer, pull over!" She grabbed Jennifer's arm, so that the Chevy veered to the right. Jennifer shook her loose.

"Can't," said Jennifer.

"We've got to find somewhere to talk," Timika insisted.

"We've got to get away from here."

Letrange, standing outside the bar with the military guy, Alan, who she'd argued with only a couple of hours before. It was mad. And terrifying.

"Hey," Timika snapped. "I just got dropped off by a goddamned flying saucer, so if anyone has the right to freak the fuck out . . ."

"Triangle."

"What?"

"It wasn't a flying saucer," said Jennifer. "Not in shape, anyway. It was a triangle."

"Oh," said Timika, her voice heavy with sarcasm. "Well that's just fine, because—as everyone knows—when it comes to being abducted by guys in rubber alien suits, it's the shape that matters . . ."

Jennifer stepped hard on the brakes and the Impala slid to a keening halt, pitching both women forward in their seat belts.

"You want to talk?" snapped Jennifer. "Fine. What do you want to talk about? The guy who tracked me across the fucking Atlantic, so he could put a bullet in my brain? Part of the team who engineered the fake suicide of a US Senator, and my father too, for God's sake! Let's talk about that. Maybe we should get tea so we can chat it out properly, have a good old-fashioned chinwag, full of wit and repartee, while he finds us and puts us both in the fucking ground. That *does* sound like a plan."

Timika waited to respond. "And I thought New Yorkers were the masters of sarcasm."

"What?" Jennifer, shot back, still lost in her own fire.

"What the hell is a chinwag? Jesus. *Chinwag*. If you put as much energy into figuring out what we should do as you do into making up words . . ."

"It's a not a made-up word," said Jennifer, distracted out of her fear.

"Sounds made up to me. Chinwag. Jesus."

"It's a perfectly normal phrase, where I come from."

"Which ain't here," said Timika with finality. "Now. Where are we going?"

Jennifer's head was swimming. The shock of seeing Letrange had driven everything else from her thoughts. She knew it wasn't fair to Timika, but she couldn't help that. She'd let her guard down with Letrange once, and it nearly cost her everything. She would not make the same mistake twice.

"I don't know," she said at last. "Home. England."

"You think you'd be safe there?" asked Timika. "That's where he tried to kill you."

"Maybe if he doesn't think I'm a threat anymore . . ." she tried, but she didn't believe it, and neither did Timika. "You have a better idea?"

"Take the fight to them," said Timika. "Sometimes the best defense . . ."

"In football, maybe. In life, when you are two unarmed women up against the hired hit men of a clandestine multinational corporation . . ."

"And the government," said Timika. "They run this place, right?"

"Maybe," said Jennifer. "I'm not sure. Suddenly, I'm not sure of much, except that I don't want to be here."

"I hear the Caribbean is nice this time of year," said Timika. "Maybe you're right. It's not like there's anything we can do here in . . . where did you say we were?"

"Area 51, or close to it."

"Of course," said Timika. "Post a bogus UFO story on my site and drop me off outside the crazy capital of the world. It's genius in a depressing kind of way. I've been debunktioned."

"You've been what?"

"Wait," Timika gasped, her eyes suddenly wide.

"What?" asked Jennifer.

"Nevada!"

"As I told you an hour ago. What are you doing?"

"Please be there . . ." the other woman was muttering as she unbuttoned her shirt, and reached into her ample cleavage. She plucked a tightly folded piece of paper and held it up with a look of triumph.

"Yes," she hissed.

Reading Jennifer's look, she buttoned up again.

"What's that?" asked Jennifer.

"It's from the book I told you about. Jerzy Stern's journal. This was at the back."

She unfolded it. The paper had numbers on it. Coordinates. The words printed carefully above it said "Airfield. Groom Lake, Nevada." The sheet had been wrapped tight around a brass key.

"Where does this lead?" asked Jennifer, considering the paper.

"Here, or hereabouts," said Timika. "Stern was stationed in Nevada in the fifties, on an airbase and test range. See? Groom Lake. He put something here. Something important. And he obviously assumes it's still here."

"I'm not wandering the desert digging for buried treasure. We'll die."

"Not many caves need a key," said Timika. "This is a building."

"But Groom Lake is Area 51," said Jennifer. "And I'm pretty damn sure it's where those guys in the diner were going. There's no way we can walk into the most secret government facility in the country on a scavenger hunt."

"And I'm telling you that this," said Timika, tapping the key insistently, "will blow the whole thing wide open. Jerzy obviously thought so, and the bad guys—whoever they are—think he's right. Find this and we're safe. The truth will set us free, right?"

"But we won't get anywhere near it!" said Jennifer. "We get caught by the government and packed off or imprisoned, or—assuming the *bad guys* are not working with them—we disappear."

"There's always a way in," said Timika. "I don't care how secure a place is."

"Not this one," said Jennifer. She thought of her experience at the Hapsel ranch. "They can see you coming miles away. And there are signs that say deadly force is authorized. And that's the government! If they admit they'll shoot you for looking, you don't want to know what else they're prepared to do."

"I thought you said it wasn't government," said Timika. "That it was private money in support of corporate interests?"

Jennifer sighed heavily. "I don't know, Timika, okay? The more I think about it, the less I seem to know."

"Well," said the other woman ruefully, "that makes two of us. So why not let Jerzy point us the right way?"

"How? We can't get in!"

"Let's ring the front doorbell and see."

"What?"

"We drive up to the entrance," said Timika, reasonably. "If, as you say, they intercept us before we get there, we talk our way in. I can be very persuasive."

"You're insane," said Jennifer.

"Maybe," said Timika as if she were seriously considering the possibility. "But I've been driven from my home, shot at, abducted and taken to goddamned *Siberia*, for Christ's sake. I'm done. I want to know what's going on."

"We won't find out what's going on. We'll be arrested or killed or . . ."

"Or something," Timika agreed. "But you know what? If we run. They'll come after us. And they won't stop until they find us. I've been living like that for too long and I'm not about to spend the rest of my life like this. Turn the car around and we'll find the entrance."

"To Area 51," said Jennifer.

Timika held up the little brass key.

"To Jerzy Stern's last secret," she said.

54

ALAN
Dreamland, Nevada

THE THREE MEN DROVE SEPARATE CARS BACK TO THE base, then climbed aboard the blacked-out bus. If Hatcher had taken a Locust Alan figured he needed to be on hand and ready to fly at a moment's notice, so while Regis went to his office and Morat went to check on repairs at the hangar, he took the bus to the flight facility and suited up.

It was Hatcher who had brought him into this world— and that was no idle metaphor. Dreamland was like a window on a new universe. It was Hatcher's faith that a rattled Harrier pilot could ride out his panic at the strangeness of this new universe and become a useful member of the team charged to protect it that had, he now saw, saved his sanity. Maybe even his life. That Hatcher was a rat was devastating. A personal betrayal. Another set of truths he had not questioned had turned out to be lies, and Alan was—again—in free fall.

He went to see if Morat was still in the hangar, but there was no sign of him and he felt in the way. The techs had a hurried, anxious air as they busied themselves around the remaining Locusts. They'd also left the door open to the sleek, silver disk, where two men in hazmat suits examined the aircraft as if unsure what to do next. It occurred to Alan that, with the fleet depleted, it was possible that they might consider rushing the new aircraft into service before it had been fully tested. He didn't like the idea.

"Can we help you, Major?" said the red-haired man Alan recognized as Riordan.

"No," he answered. "Anything I can do?"

"Not here."

The tension in the man's voice was palpable. He was holding a tablet computer and looked keen to get back to work, but something in his manner made Alan's irritation spike. He knew it was his feeling of powerlessness along with his confused rage over Hatcher's treachery, but he suddenly felt the urge to punch Riordan squarely in the face.

He turned on his heel and blundered down the hallway with its wash of white noise, desperate for somewhere he could be alone. He wanted to shout, to hit something, to release all the frustration of Dreamland's constant secrecy.

His hand was on the locker room door before he registered the stripe of yellow tape across the latch.

C2, he recalled. *Chemical spill.*

"Fuck that," he spat.

He twisted the latch and shouldered the door open, tearing the tape from the jamb in the process. He stepped inside, sniffing the air and, when he smelled nothing, flipped the light on.

The changing room was complete with toilets and shower stalls, as well as the equipment lockers and racks of hanging flight suits. As the door closed behind him he slammed his fists onto the counter and bellowed a stream of curses into the mirror. He did it again, and again, and then he stopped, and the room fell silent.

Or almost silent. In fact, the sound of Alan's labored breathing bounced off the hard white tile. Distant noises from elsewhere in the building echoed vaguely through the ventilation shafts. He considered his reflection. He looked gaunt, haggard. The hairs on the back of his neck had started to rise. His rage gone, he felt strangely ill at ease.

In the mirror he saw that one of the shower curtains had been pulled closed. It felt . . . off.

Alan took a step towards it.

"Hello," he said, wishing base security permitted the carrying of sidearms. "Anyone in there?"

There was no response, no sound of any kind beyond his own breathing. He reached out, hesitated, then seized the curtain and pulled.

Nothing.

He released the breath he had been holding and chuckled at his own nervousness, then turned to see a dark stain on the linoleum floor, a pool of blood seeping from one of the toilet stalls. He pushed open the nearest stall door and recoiled.

Sitting on the toilet, fully clothed, his suit drenched in blood from the savage slash across his throat, was Special Agent Martin Hatcher.

Alan staggered back.

ADMIRAL RICHARD E. BYRD
Santiago, Chile, March 1947

Extract from Chilean newspaper *El Mercurio*, March 5, 1947:

[EXT]Admiral Richard E. Byrd warned today that the United States should adopt measures of protection against the possibility of an invasion of the country by hostile planes coming from the Polar regions. The admiral explained that he was not trying to scare anyone, but that the cruel reality was that in case of a new war, the United States could be attacked by planes flying over one or both poles at incredible speed. This statement was made as part of a recapitulation of his own polar experience, in an exclusive interview with International News Service. Talking about the recently completed expedition, Byrd said that the most important result of his observations and discoveries is the potential effect that they have in relation to the security of the United States. The fantastic speed with which the world is shrinking—recalled the admiral—is one of the most important lessons learned during his recent Antarctic exploration. 'I have to warn my compatriots that the time has ended when we were able to take refuge in our isolation and rely on the certainty that the distances, the oceans, and the poles are a guarantee of safety.'

JERZY
Newport News, Virginia, March 1947

I TOLD CAPTAIN JENNINGS THAT HIGH JUMP WAS MY LAST mission for the Navy, and that I wanted other assignments ashore. I told him I wanted to be at the forefront of research and development in the exciting new field of aviation and rocketry. I told him that if scum like *Hauptsturmführer* Ungerleider could come to America and stay on a government salary, then so could the people whose lives he had destroyed.

Jennings said there was nothing he could do. Ungerleider had been added to a list of scientists, engineers and technicians who the US deemed valuable in the anti-Soviet efforts that would dominate the decades to come. Operation

Paperclip, it was called. Some Nazi scientists would be dragged back to Germany, in spite of the US, to face war crimes trials, but that was difficult and required hard evidence, and lots of it. Ungerleider had spent most of the war quite literally underground, and most of the people who'd seen him up close were dead. Now he was a valued member of the United States, a man who might help them build faster, better aircraft or rockets to the moon . . .

I thanked Captain Jennings for all he had done for me, shook his hand, and resigned my commission. I disembarked from the *USS Kitchener* and stood for a moment, giving the destroyer a long look, but from that day to this, I have not set foot on a ship of any kind ever again.

I went to Nevada, following what I had heard about his deployment, where I got a job at an airstrip near Groom Lake, partly on Jennings' reference. I had been there a year and a half before I heard anything more about Ungerleider, though I often drove around the areas where I'd heard he might be, looking for him. Then one day I opened the local paper, and there he was, smiling at the camera with a group of other scientists, standing in front of some engine or other. His name had been changed, but I would have known him anywhere.

He was not the only one, of course, and many would go on to become famous and wealthy. Walter Dornberger, who had once been Werner von Braun's commander, went to Bell Aerospace. Rudi Beichel to Aerojet. Magnus von Braun (Werner's brother) got a job at Chrysler, Alexander Lippisch at Collin Radio Company, Hans Multhopp at

Martin Marietta and Heinz Schlicke at Allen-Bradley. There were many more and I could not keep track of them all, let alone punish them. They were successful men who had spent a portion of their lives trying, in various ways as suited their talents, to destroy the allies and eliminate people like me.

But Ungerleider became, in my mind, their representative, and as such, with the memory of Ishmael burned into my heart—I had no choice but to act.

One day in 1952, I followed Ungerleider home from work. He lived in a large, ranch-style house almost a mile from the closest neighbor. A nice house. It was a typically hot Nevada day, and I found him in his kitchen, taking a beer from the refrigerator. He was not married, I was relieved to find, and lived alone. He was not particularly surprised to see me, though he had no idea that he had actually met me several times before. He thought he vaguely recalled me from the Antarctic mission, but had no recollection of forcing me to work the henge at Wenceslas, or the specifics of gunning down my brother.

"It was war," he said with a shrug. "It was not personal."

It was neither apology nor explanation, but I nodded in agreement before I shot him.

The metal box with the German eagle was in his closet. He had kept it all this time. Perhaps he had convinced the authorities that it was vital to his work. Perhaps no one had ever shown any interest in it. I had no way of knowing. The key was in a pouch of his wallet. It looked like it hadn't been touched for years.

There was another beer in the fridge, so I took it and drank it, sitting opposite him as he died, thinking of Jennings and Ishmael and my parents, while I waited for the police to come. After twenty minutes, it was clear that the shot had gone unheard, so I had to telephone them.

They did not seem to understand what I was saying, and it took a long time for them to realize that I was not merely raving. Though I was no longer active military, they opted to hand my case over to the Navy. I was briefly held in a facility in New Mexico, until the government decided what to do with me. All the while, the metal box that I had claimed from Ungerleider's home had been stashed away and I said nothing about it, until it was clear what the powers that be determined to do with me. They wanted no scandal, no awkward questions about the past, no reopening of old wounds. I was squirreled away and looked after, with others who had seen or done things that could prove embarrassing.

The box I left in Nevada, locked away in a facility I knew was to be abandoned, where it would wait to be found by the right person.

It gives me some measure of peace, after all these years, to hope that I may have found such a person.

57

JENNIFER
Nevada

THEY DROVE BACK TOWARD RACHEL, TOWARD THE BAR, but ultimately toward Area 51. Jennifer wasn't sure she'd really changed her mind, but something of Timika's fire had got into her head. She was tired. She wanted it to be over, and if necessary, she would go down fighting. That was what she did. It was who she was, and there was no way she was going to change that now.

She didn't hate governments. She hated the greed of people who worked for them, manipulated them in the name of profit. Whether they hid behind flags or shareholders didn't much matter to her. She had been fighting it all her adult life. Today was no different.

From time to time, the two women got glimpses of sensors with antennae and, perhaps, cameras, sprouting out of the ground up on the rocky escarpments on the side of the road, which stretched back towards the base, where increasingly strident signs warned against trespass and photography. They chose the road to the main gate, feeling the tension rise with each passing mile.

At first, the landscape didn't change, but gradually all signs of civilization, already few and far between since fleeing Rachel, fell away entirely and they were alone in the desert. Once a night bird, some kind of owl or nightjar, flashed across the road ahead, and on one rise, they caught the silhouette of something Timika pronounced a mule deer, and on another a jackrabbit that reminded Jennifer of Mrs. Winterburn. Otherwise, the night was utterly still.

They were perhaps two miles from the main gate when they saw the pale pickup truck, parked on the bluff above the road. The Impala's high beams splashed the truck with light for a second. Two men stood beside it, both in desert camo, with binoculars around their necks. The momentary glimpse left Jennifer with the impression that their faces were covered by masks. It was unsettling.

The lights and sirens came up behind them less than five minutes later. Jennifer looked at Timika.

"This is as far as we go," she said.

"Maybe," said Timika. "Let's see how they play it."

"You think this could have been one of the cars we saw in the desert?"

Timika tipped her head doubtfully, then shook it. "Would have seen the lights on top even if they weren't on," she said.

The man in the car was a sheriff's deputy—local law enforcement rather than military, or anything more sinister, like the bizarre men in black, who Jennifer had come to dread. He got out of the car, flashlight at shoulder height, and approached the driver's window with a slow swagger, muttering into his lapel radio. He was perhaps forty-five, white, with arms that suggested off-duty time in the gym but a belly that suggested he spent an equal amount of time at McDonalds. He looked slightly bored, but officious, and he considered the two women with something close to contempt.

"You ladies blind?" he drawled. "This is a restricted area. License and registration."

Jennifer produced the Alamo paperwork and her international driving license. The deputy took it and considered it skeptically, holding it by one corner as if afraid to soil his fingers.

"And you, Miss?" he said. "See some ID."

"I don't have any," Timika said. "My purse was stolen."

"That right?" said the deputy, not troubling to conceal his disbelief. "Wait here please."

He stepped away from the car and spoke into his radio. Jennifer caught "foreign national," and, "local but undocumented," and risked a glance at Timika, who was sitting very still.

"What will they do?" she whispered.

"Turn us around and send us on our way, probably," said Timika. "That's what normally happens. I've read a hundred accounts of crazies sneaking around Area 51. Worst case scenario—if they insist on driving to the base to stop the little green men from monitoring their thoughts or whatever—they wind up in the lock-up for the night, with a big fine to deter them from doing it again when they get released. Right now, I really don't need a big fine."

"I'll cover the fine," Jennifer said.

"Yay for that," Timika said.

She sounded nonchalant, but Jennifer wasn't buying it. The deputy was back.

"Turn the car around and drive away," he said. "Watch the signs. If you cross back into the restricted area, you'll be placed under arrest."

Jennifer nodded, mouth dry.

"We need to keep going," said Timika.

Jenifer gaped at her.

"No, you don't," said the deputy with a short patience that said he wasn't going to warn her again.

"We really do," said Timika. "We need to get inside the base. It's important."

The deputy turned away for a second, sighed at the way he was being inconvenienced, and said, "Step out of the vehicle please, Miss."

"What?" said Jennifer, unsure who she was talking to. "She didn't mean . . . It's just a misunderstanding. We can turn around . . ."

"You too, please, Miss," he said. "Hands on the roof of the vehicle where I can see them. Yeah," he added into his radio. "I'm going to need back up. Two for the lock-up."

"I said we needed to get in," Timika said. "Tell him, Jennifer."

"I don't think he wants to hear about Jerzy's lost journal . . ."

"No," Timika shot back. "Tell him about the threat to the base."

For a moment the desert was quiet.

"What did you say?" said the deputy. One hand strayed to the pistol holster on his hip. Ready.

"We believe the base has been penetrated by a hostile agent," said Timika. "Tell him, Jennifer."

The deputy turned to look at her, and she felt his disbelief, edged with a wariness that frightened her. She wanted to leave. To get back in the car and drive to Vegas and a plane to . . . anywhere. Again. But this bloody woman had dropped her even further in it, and that didn't seem possible.

"I saw a man earlier," she confessed. "He was talking to a pilot from the base and another man. He is very dangerous. You need to alert their security."

"We can identify him," Timika chimed in.

The deputy shot her a disdainful look. Whatever else happened, that last demand would not be met.

"You realize that making this kind of allegation is tantamount to making a terrorist threat?" he said. He was giving them one last chance, one final opportunity to let him keep his evening hassle free.

"It's true," said Jennifer.

His jaw flexed, his eyes held hers for one exasperated second, and then he was stepping backwards and speaking into his radio again.

"We have a threat on the base," he said. "Repeat: we have a threat on the base. Request back up and full security notification."

"Well," said Timika, giving Jennifer a rueful smile across the roof of the Impala. "We have their attention."

"Yeah," said Jennifer, her tone hollow. "Great."

The deputy spoke into his radio for a full two minutes, his eyes never leaving them, then stepped in closer, hand still close to his gun.

"I hope this isn't your idea of a joke," he said. "Because if it is, things are going to get real expensive for you ladies."

She wasn't sure how long they waited, saying nothing, breathing the dry desert night, wondering who would arrive first, the men in black with their EPA badges, the camo guys in their pickup, or someone else, someone perhaps who would—as they said in the movies—shoot first and ask questions afterwards. The deputy seemed to have redis-covered his bored exasperation, and though he checked his watch from time to time, and spoke a few monosyllables into his radio, he just watched them in silence.

To her surprise, the vehicle to arrive first was a helicop-ter, but it thrummed overhead without descending. The next was an open-sided military vehicle, half-Jeep, half-pickup. A Humvee, she remembered. It was sand yellow and came, not from the road behind them, but from the base ahead. It had a bank of four spotlights on the front, so that as it roared to a halt in a billowing cloud of dust, she and Timika had to take their hands off the hot metal of the car to shield their eyes.

The deputy stepped up to the vehicle as three men got out, all in military gear. The two in the back had automatic rifles. But it was the man in the front that scared her. He was broad shouldered, black, and his head was shaved, a phone jammed against the side of his head, his square jaw set. A man unaccustomed to being messed with.

He was also the man who'd been chatting with Letrange and the pilot in the bar, less than an hour before.

58

ALAN
Dreamland, Nevada

ALAN WASHED HIS FACE AND DRANK STRAIGHT FROM the tap to soothe his burning throat before calling Regis.

The security man had to shout over the engine of his vehicle.

"Hatcher's dead," said Alan over the phone. "Found him in the locker on B corridor."

Regis' hesitation was momentary. Alan could almost hear the big man locking away all his feelings as the implication slid home.

"How?"

"Throat cut," said Alan through gritted teeth.

"So Morat's our rat," he said.

"Looks like," said Alan. "You think he's a defector?"

"Unless he was never ours."

"That would mean that the whole mission at Safid Kuh was a set up, that he always wanted to be here. How's that possible?"

"Not sure," said Regis. "I'll look into it."

"Find out where he is," Alan said. "And lock the base down."

He'd barely spoken when the alarm sounded.

For a second, Alan thought it was Regis, sealing the facility so Hatcher's murder could be investigated, but then he heard the words between the wail of the siren.

"All pilots report to stations at once. This is not a drill."

"We're being scrambled," he said into the phone.

"I heard," said Regis. "Okay. Do what you have to. I'll watch things on the ground. And Major?"

"Yeah?"

"Keep an eye out for Morat. He may be up there. And he knows you."

Alan nodded and hung up. Regis was right. There was nothing worse than being hunted by someone who'd trained you.

Alan moved to the equipment racks and suited up, grabbing a helmet as he left, and made for the hangar, where what had been confusion was turning to chaos. The men knew their jobs, but did not know who was in command.

"Where's Agent Hatcher?" asked Riordan as Alan strode in. He looked scared.

"He won't be here," said Alan. The other man waited for a split second and, when Alan merely held his eyes, the color drained from his face.

"Status?" Alan asked, forcing the man back on track.

"Sir, radar picked up seven incoming hostiles, moving supersonically," said Riordan. "Seven of them. They are taking up positions close to the Wyoming nuclear missile fields. Reports suggest they're tampering with the missiles' launch sequences."

"What?" Alan exclaimed. "How can they do that?"

Riordan looked uncomfortable. "There is," he said, picking his words carefully, "historical precedent."

"Meaning what? This has happened before?"

"Not on this scale, but yes. A long time ago."

"I never heard about it."

"You weren't supposed to," said Riordan, closing the subject. He said it simply, but the terror in his eyes gave away just how bad he thought the situation was.

"Seven?" said Alan.

Riordan nodded. "Nonconventional aircraft by their flight signatures," he said.

"Matching the ones we engaged two days ago?"

"Not certain," said Riordan. He glimpsed Alan's impatience. "Probably, sir."

"And we have . . . what? Four?" He'd realized, when he found Hatcher's body that Morat had lied about Hatcher stealing the fourth Locust.

"Three, sir," said Riordan. "Agent Morat took the fourth on patrol."

I'll bet he did, thought Alan.

"Pilots?"

"Rodriguez, Jackson, and Hastings," said Riordan. "And you."

"And what about that one?" said Alan, nodding towards the forgotten silver disk.

"Still undergoing tests, sir," said Riordan, his eyes wide.

"Is it armed and fueled up?"

"Well, sir, yes, but . . ."

"What?" Alan demanded.

"It's a completely different operations system," said Riordan. "None of the surviving pilots have any experience in it at all."

Alan considered the strange saucer across the hangar.

"I'll take it," he said.

"I don't think I can authorize . . ."

"It's on me, Lieutenant Riordan," said Alan. "We're under attack."

"Yes, sir. But . . ."

"How does the disk perform compared to the Locusts?"

Riordan hesitated, his eyes flashing from side to side as if looking for someone with the authority to take the matter from him.

"Lieutenant!" Alan barked. "We don't have time for this."

"Well, sir, it's what you might call next generation tech," he said.

"Faster?"

"Faster, more maneuverable, better armed . . ."

"Get it out," said Alan.

"We don't know for sure how . . ." Riordan exclaimed. "We're still discovering how it . . ." He hesitated.

"What?"

"How it performs," said Riordan, but there was something evasive in his manner. Even now, the sky threatening to fall in on them, Alan thought bitterly, he was being lied to.

"Just get it out," he said.

Flying was all he knew how to do. He lived and breathed it. Always had. If this was how it would end for him, so be it. What else was there?

His phone rang.

Regis.

"What?" Alan barked.

"Talked to the recovery team who went in at Safid Kuh to get Morat," said Regis.

"And?"

"Among the kills was a man in US-made boots and underwear," said Regis. "But he'd been shot at close range. None of my guys did it. He was wearing an Afghan coat, but his shirt was buttoned up wrong and his fly was unfastened. They figured he'd been caught napping, but they also thought he had had less sun than the others."

"You're thinking this was the real Morat? That his killer put his clothes on and took his identity?"

"Sounds that way," said Regis, his voice heavy with frustration.

"Jesus," said Alan, striding across the hangar to where Riordan was presiding over preflighting the saucer craft. "So now what?"

"Time to get out of the pocket."

"Okay," said Alan. "No one seems to know what's going on. With Hatcher dead and Morat defected, I'm taking over. Till someone steps up who outranks us, we're calling the shots. Me in the air, you on the ground. Get communications command in touch with the Air Force, but make sure they know what we're up against. I don't want conventional fighters taking on those arrowheads. And put the word out about Morat."

"Will do," said Regis. "And if you see him up there," he added grimly, "take him down."

Alan hung up.

"I have to caution you against this," said Riordan. "It's a very different ship from the Locust. There's still a lot . . ."

Again the hesitation, the evasion.

"What?" Alan demanded. "I'm taking it up. That's how it is. So if you know something that might help keep me alive while I'm in it, now's the time to tell me."

Riordan's internal struggle lasted only a second. The constant looping wail of the siren and its various warnings seemed to be getting to him.

"It's a captured ship, sir," he said. "The tech is unfamiliar because we didn't build it."

"Russian?"

Riordan's eyes flashed away.

"That's what I heard, sir," he said.

"You're not sure? How is that possible?"

"We're just the engineers, sir," said Riordan with a touch of hauteur. "Our job here is to figure out how stuff works.

In this case, we're still learning. We've had men working on it day and night for weeks, and we still don't know . . ."

"It will fly?"

"Yes, sir, but we've only brought it to a controlled hover in the hangar. It's never really gone up. The controls are minimal, keyed to the user."

Alan stared at him.

"Telepathically," said Riordan, looking more than uncomfortable. He was frightened of what he was saying, and Alan couldn't blame him. It was staggering. "You hold on to the controller inside," said Riordan, his voice low, "and it . . . *reacts*. To your thoughts. To be honest, sir, we haven't dared take it more than a few feet off the ground. We just don't know what it will do."

Alan nodded, feeling a strange calm come over him as if he were already in the pilot's seat.

"Maybe that's the point," said Alan. "You need to really want it to fly."

Riordan stared at him. Alan took one last look around the scrambling hangar, watching the three remaining Locusts pulling out into the open, and nodded.

"Okay," he said, turning back to the strange, saucer-like craft in front of him. "Let's see what it can do."

TIMIKA
Area 51, Nevada

TIMIKA SAW THE WAY JENNIFER STIFFENED.

"Him?" she asked, staring as the African-American security officer hung up the phone, spoke earnestly first to one of the soldiers, then to the deputy, and finally came striding towards them, head lowered, bullish.

Jennifer shook her head.

"His friend from the bar," she said, her voice low.

The officer was in no mood for politeness. She could see it in the way he walked, the look in his face. His eyes flashed, and she thought she could hear, the sound riding the wind coming from the base, the distant keening wail of a siren.

Something was going on.

"You alleged an attack on the base?" he spat. "Details. Now."

"We have rights you know," Timika ventured.

The anger in the soldier's face was terrible. He moved in close, and she could see how much he was sweating. His eyes were wide and his teeth clenched. For a second, she thought he was going to hit her.

"I don't have time for civil liberties, lady," he said. "Talk quickly."

He didn't need to threaten what would happen if they didn't. Jennifer looked too scared to speak.

"The man you were with before," said Timika. "He's a killer."

The security officer, whose nametag said Regis, blinked and stared at her, but something in his face changed.

"Which man?" he said, and already, some of his fire was gone.

"The man in the bar," she said.

Jennifer, feeling the change too, nodded.

"Not Alan," she said, pushing through the quaver in her voice. "The other one. He called himself Letrange, but he has other names."

"Morat," said Regis, almost to himself.

The two women checked each other.

"I've never heard him called that," said Jennifer. "Olive skin. Black hair. Good looking."

She said that last grudgingly and Timika gave her a sharp look, wondering just what had passed between the Englishwoman and the man she said had tried to kill her.

Regis nodded thoughtfully.

"How do you know Major Young?" he asked.

"I don't," said Jennifer. "We just met."

"Okay," he said, and he was quiet now. "Okay. And you just came to tell us about this Letrange guy?"

Jennifer nodded.

"Wish you'd gotten here an hour ago," said Regis. There was a bitterness there, but it wasn't directed at them.

"There's something else," said Timika, fishing the folded page from Jerzy Stern's journal from her pocket and thrusting it into Regis' face. "We need to go here. It's important."

"What?" asked Regis, stepping back and focusing on the hand-written words, his face screwed up in disbelief. "You can't come on the base. This is a military installation. I'm grateful for the warning, but there are things I need to do. The deputy here will escort you back to the main road."

"This attack," said Timika, "whatever this Morat guy is trying to do—it's about this place. We need to go there."

"You're not listening to me . . ." said Regis, something of the frustration coming back into his face.

"No," said Timika. "You're not listening to me. Something is going on at the base, right? Something bad. It's about this. We need to go there. Now."

Regis stared at her, stalled by her determination, then he took the fold of paper and barked at one of the soldiers behind him.

"Put these coordinates into the GPS," he said, reading them off. "37°16′35″ North. 115°45′19″ West."

The Humvee had a bracket in front of the passenger-side dash. It held what looked like a tablet computer and other equipment. Timika walked towards the vehicle as the soldier climbed in and entered the coordinates. Regis seemed to consider stopping her, but didn't. Jennifer sidled up alongside her as Regis read the numbers back again.

"There's nothing there, sir," said the soldier. "It's not Groom Lake. It's further east. Restricted territory, but not the base itself."

He had pulled up a Google map. The little red exclamation point that marked the spot was alone on a blank white screen. As Timika watched, Regis leaned over and zoomed out until a complex of roads appeared, a few miles from the coordinates they'd input. Regis frowned.

"The man's right," he said. "There's nothing there."

"Switch to earth view," said Jennifer.

The soldier did so. The screen filled in with tan-colored earth. The complex of roads marked the Groom Lake facility in the pale area of the dry lake bed, a distinctive pattern of crossing lines indicating runways, but the red exclamation point to the east tagged an otherwise unmarked landscape of desert scrub.

"Zoom in," said Timika, fighting back a pang of despair. They'd come all this way. For nothing?

"There's nothing there," protested the soldier.

"Just do it," she shot back.

When no counter order came from Regis, the soldier did so.

"What's that?" asked Jennifer, leaning in. "There's something there. Faint lines. You see that?"

Regis stared at the screen. She was right.

The red exclamation point now sat in the middle of a pale circle at the intersection of two broad lines forming a T. Though faded and apparently unserved by any current road, their resemblance to the Groom Lake base a few miles west was undeniable. Yet while the modern, secret installation sat clear and bright in the pale hollow of the lake bed, the location on the right of the screen looked faded with age, disappearing back into the landscape. But there was no doubt that they were looking at airstrips.

"What the hell is that?" muttered Regis.

"How old is the Groom Lake base?" asked Timika.

"Damned if I know," said Regis, his eyes still on the screen. "Sixties, I guess. Why?"

"There was a facility here before that," said Timika. "In the early fifties. That's where we need to go."

Regis turned to consider her, but before he could say anything, the soldier at the data terminal spoke up.

"She's right, sir," he said, scanning the page he had just pulled up for data. "Indian Springs Auxiliary field number 1. Administratively part of Creech Airbase, close to Vegas, but separate. Looks like it hasn't been used since the fifties."

"We need to go there," Timika said again.

She could feel the tension and strangeness in the air. Regis looked unsure, and she had the distinct impression that he was unused to feeling unsure.

"What's there?" he said. "What do you need to see?"

"I don't know," she said, opting for honesty. "Something someone put there a long time ago. By someone I trust. But it's vital. And I think your Morat and his friends want to get there too. You said it's not near the modern base, right? So we wouldn't be seeing anything we weren't supposed to see."

Regis snorted derisively. "Lady, we're all seeing stuff we're not supposed to tonight."

He wasn't agreeing, but she pretended he was.

"So let's go," she said. "You need us to help understand what you find there. And if there's nothing, we'll go quietly."

She saw the way he looked down, trying to decide what to do. And then he looked up, his face full of decision.

"Get in," he said.

ALAN
Dreamland, Nevada

"**C**AN YOU HEAR ME, PHOENIX?" ASKED RIORDAN AS soon as the hatch closed. He sounded nervous, which, under the circumstances, wasn't surprising. Alan wasn't nervous. He was scared shitless.

The disk was just large enough to stand up in. There was a single chair that might have been ripped out of an F-16, mounted in the center, with a railing, its surface flattened into a semicircular console ten-inches high, ringing the command seat, save where the exterior hatch opened. The metal—if it was metal—was curiously violet and blue, like fine tempered steel, except that the color seemed somehow integral to the material. It was marked with symbols, some like letters, others like tiny pictograms. One—a kind of curl like a backwards C or the flourish of a treble clef—might have been a stylized wave. One resembled a pair of arrows. Another, a sun.

None of them meant anything to Alan.

There were no windows or viewer screens of any kind. No buttons, toggles or joysticks.

It was absurd. Of course it was. Even if such a thing could fly—which seemed unlikely—there was no way he could possibly learn how to control it. In any other situation it would have been comic, a gag set up by the tech crew to see just how gullible their pilots might be.

But there was nothing funny about it. The three remaining Locusts were already up, trying to make a difference in a fight that would almost certainly cost them their lives and perhaps a whole lot more. They needed Alan up there, which meant that if this thing really could fly, he needed it to do so immediately.

"This is Standpipe," said Riordan's voice. "You there, Phoenix?" The sound came from speakers in what Alan decided to call the canopy above the chair. It was, like the rest of the craft, a low-glare, silver color, the cockpit an odd combination of ultra-high tech and jerry-rigged improvisations patched together by the hangar crew.

"I'm here, Standpipe," said Alan. "For what that's worth."

"You in the chair?"

"Yeah. Belted in, right?"

He heard Riordan hesitate. "Sure," he said, like he had any idea one way or the other.

Alan swallowed and checked the seat harness.

"Now put your hands on the command panel, palms down," said Riordan.

"I can't see out," said Alan, his heart racing. "If this thing starts moving, I won't know where it's going or . . ."

"Just put your hands on the console."

"Where?" he asked, studying the symbols etched into the odd metal.

"It doesn't matter."

Alan spread his fingers and lowered them to the console surface, half-expecting it to be hot. It wasn't. It was cool and smooth, like stainless steel or brushed nickel, but as soon as his hands were in place, he felt the ship wake up.

That was the phrase in his head. It was bizarre, but that was what it felt like, as if the disk had been slumbering, but now it was alert and ready. The console bar seemed to ripple, a wave of bluish light pulsing softly through it, around the chair, and somehow into the entire disk. The metal glowed for a second—closer to gold than bronze—and Alan felt it move. It rose, he was sure of it, and settled into a steady hover a few inches from the ground, with the faintest hum of energy.

"That's it," said Riordan into the radio. "Looking good. Now push out of the hangar and into the open air."

"How?" asked Alan.

"Just . . . think it."

"What?"

"Focus on what you want and don't take your hands off the console."

"This is nuts," said Alan, who was started to sweat. He was making light of it, but he was scared. "Even if I could move it, I wouldn't do it blind like this."

"Swipe your hand along the surface away from you."

"Which hand?"

"Doesn't matter. Just do it."

Alan did so. And suddenly he was in the hangar with Riordan and three other techs watching warily. He was still sitting in the chair, but the metal disk around him was gone. It was like the dreams he'd had when he was a boy.

"What the hell?" he muttered. "What happened?"

"What do you mean?" asked Riordan.

Alan turned to him and made a face.

"What does it goddamned look like?" he said.

"Same as before," said Riordan, not looking at him. "Can you see us?"

"Of course I can see you. The goddamned ship is gone."

"No, Major, it's not. You're just seeing through it."

Alan swallowed back his disbelief. It wasn't like the disk was now glass. The outer shell of the disk was just gone. But when he reached out and touched it, he felt the same density and texture as before, though the hull was now invisible.

"Now try moving it forward," said Riordan.

Alan brought his eyes front and considered the open hangar door and the night air beyond. He wasn't ready, but there was no time to waste.

Mentally, he pressed forward, like he was giving his car a little gas with his right foot. The image helped. The disk moved out, slow and steady, gliding through the air perhaps a foot off the ground. It was like a fairground ride, exposed to the air on all sides, though he felt no breeze through the globe's transparent walls, and he was moving it with his mind.

"Whoa," he said.

"Controls are all mental," said Riordan, stepping up to the disk and looking it over critically. "The different symbols bring different systems online, but we just don't know much about them. You'll have to experiment and use your instinct. But you seem to have a gift for it."

"Meaning what?"

"The disk has already done more for you than it has for anyone during our tests."

In other circumstances that might have been a satisfying feeling. Right now it just meant that no one on the ground would be able to offer meaningful guidance once he was up.

"Weapons?" he asked.

"The one that looks like a curvy X, we think."

"Think?"

"Never tested," said Riordan. "I'm sorry, Phoenix. We're way out of our depth here."

"So even if I can find the bogeys, I might not be able to do anything about them?" said Alan. He didn't wait for Riordan to answer. "Okay. I get it. I just needed to say it. I guess we'll see."

"I'm sorry, Phoenix," said Riordan. "I wish there was more I could tell you."

"Don't apologize, Standpipe," said Alan, feeling some of his own dread drain away, as if the technology was siphoning it right out of him. "I'm sure I'll be fine."

And then, in the instant that he imagined it, he was soaring skyward, rocketing up into the black Nevada night without a sound, the heavens all around him, and only the seat and the floor it was welded could break the illusion that he was flying under his own power.

"Navigation," he said to himself. "Radar. Need to find where they are."

And then there was a kind of map, curved as if rolled out on a screen that matched the interior of the disk, and there were small lights moving around on the map. Ships. He stared at them and felt the saucer shift direction, streaking through the thin layer of cloud and out, still climbing, to where the remaining Locusts were engaging the arrowheads and Morat.

That seemed unavoidable. The man who had pretended to be his friend would be out there, looking to shoot him down.

"Well," Alan mused aloud, his heart slowing as if by force of his own determination. "Let's see how they handle . . . whatever the hell this is."

JENNIFER
37° 16′ 35″N and 115° 45′ 19″W, Nevada

JENNIFER AND TIMIKA SCRUNCHED TOGETHER IN THE back of the open-topped Humvee. On her left, a young soldier in desert camo utilities watched her unashamedly, his automatic held so that its muzzle pointed out into the darkness, but ready, she thought, to turn on them if they posed any kind of threat. Timika said nothing. They were both cautious of the soldiers with their guns, but Jennifer thought her new friend seemed wary to the point of hostility.

For their part, the soldiers seemed unsure of what they were doing. The man called Regis was clearly in charge, but Jennifer had seen the two younger men exchange a quick glance when Regis had permitted this jaunt into the desert, east of the main base. After a few minutes driving on an overgrown track that hadn't been a real road for years, the driver turned to Regis and said, "You think this is right, sir?"

It could have been a check on directions, phrased to avoid any hint of insubordination, but it seemed more than that.

Regis did not speak for a moment. Finally he said, "Yes, Airman, I do," without looking at the driver, who gave him a tiny nod and then focused on the road ahead.

There was no warning that they were approaching their destination. One moment they were barreling through the rocky desert, and the next, they stopped on Regis' orders, but there was no change in the landscape, which was flat and featureless in the dark. Regis climbed out, his sidearm drawn, a powerful flashlight in his free hand. Its light bounced and flashed dizzyingly along the pink rock and gravel, but there were no trees, no shrubs or cacti more than a couple of feet high, and no buildings. The difference between the road and the surrounding ground was negligible. If she hadn't seen the lines on the Google Earth view from far overhead, she might not have known there was a road there at all.

Regis scowled at the ground, then shot a look back at the Humvee where the rest of them sat patiently.

"Get out and look," he shouted. "Corporal Simmons, there are spare flashlights in the tool bin."

Moments later, the corporal had slapped a heavy 500 Lumen Surefire into Jennifer's open hand and, when she met his eyes, she saw his fractional shrug.

Your party, not mine.

She switched the light on and turned it down to the red earth. Straw-colored weeds poked improbably up from the baked dirt, but the longer she walked, the less there was to see. Maybe Timika had it wrong. Or the journal, in which she put so much store, was just a clever hoax. Or maybe it was real, but the information in it was badly out of date. That seemed likely. Whatever had once been on this spot, it had long since been turned over to the coyotes and rattlesnakes, assuming even they found value in so desolate a place.

"Here!"

It was Timika. She was standing fifty yards to Jennifer's right, shining her light on what looked like a concrete rim, rising a few inches above the desert floor. Jogging to her, Jennifer saw that the rust-stained concrete framed a single manhole cover, like what one might find on a storm drain, rusted now to match the orange and red of the desert dust. There was a central handle, folded down, but there were also four large and ancient bolts close to the rim.

"Get the toolbox," said Regis. The soldier who'd given her the flashlight hustled back to the Humvee and returned a moment later with a set of socket wrenches. He squatted down and fitted a couple before deciding which to use on the old iron bolts.

The first came off quickly, but the second needed the encouragement of an impact driver before it budged. It took five minutes to get the last two out, Regis checking his watch and his radio irritably at the delay, occasionally gazing up at the sky over the base with what Jennifer took to be apprehension. It took two men to lift the manhole cover free. They set it on its rim, then let it drop flat on the earth. It landed with the soft, deep chime of a large bell, and for a moment everyone waited, as if something ceremonial were happening.

The hole was a concrete shaft, with rungs set in the wall all the way down. The rungs were dull with age, but showed no sign of rust, and apart from a single crack that spider-webbed through the concrete, the great tube looked almost new. Jennifer leaned over and shone her flashlight down to the concrete floor, perhaps twenty feet below. There was a passage that moved away from the ladder, but from where she stood, she couldn't see how far back it went or what sort of shape it was in.

"I'll go," said Timika, dropping to her hands and knees to step to the topmost rung.

"I'll go first, Miss . . . Mars," said Regis. "This is still a military facility."

"One you didn't know was here," Timika shot back. She had already got one foot onto the ladder.

"That's not relevant," said Regis.

"Officer Regis?"

Regis turned. It was the corporal.

"What?"

"Did you call for back up?"

"No. Why?" said Regis, tense again.

"Two vehicles coming in from the southeast," said the corporal, handing him a pair of night vision binoculars.

Jennifer could hear them, could even see them, two vehicles driving without their headlights on. She'd bet good money they were the same vehicles that had been looking to pick up Timika in the desert.

"Miss Mars," said Sgt. Regis, still looking through the NVGs, tracking the incoming cars. "Go down the ladder and stay there until I come get you. You too, Miss Quinn."

The change which came over the two other soldiers was electric. They went from merely present to alert and hostile in the blink of an eye. Both readied their rifles, one dropping to his knees, the other running over to the cover of the Humvee. Timika dropped out of sight, and Jennifer, momentarily paralyzed with a new sense of dread, could do nothing but watch the approaching vehicles as they emerged from the darkness.

62

ALAN
US airspace over Nevada

THE SILVER DISK SPED FASTER, PUNCHING THROUGH THE cloud deck at 20,000 feet and into the clear night sky above. Alan felt like he was perched on the top of a skyscraper, all his attention focused on absolute control of the craft. Every wobble, every deviation or hesitation in its flight plan depended on his mind and his unflickering concentration.

It was exhausting.

No matter how he turned or angled the ship, his body experienced no sense of motion or torque, and the chair remained level and still, as if he were at the center of some great gyroscope, but in his head, he saw each shift in trajectory and acceleration, as if he were a living computer, consciously, deliberately firing neurons, steering the unearthly vehicle as if it had merged with his own muscle and bone.

"Uploading attack locations," said Riordan's voice. "The first is at F.E. Warren Air Force Base near Cheyenne, Wyoming. Silos are spread over to Colorado and Nebraska too, so we'll have to take them one at a time, beginning with the main base. See it?"

Alan's eyes picked up the blinking symbol in the air to his right. Mentally, he clicked it, and it opened, scattering maps and data across his field of view.

"Too much," he snapped as the disk kicked and shifted in his head.

"Sorry. It takes some getting used to."

"Except that we don't have time for that," said Alan, fighting down his anxiety and irritation. His feelings were impacting the disk's performance. He could sense it. He took a deep breath and waited as the ship gradually settled into steady, level flight heading northeast. Only then did he relax enough to squeeze his eyes closed for a second, blinking the sweat away, and taking a long, steadying breath. He wasn't sure how long he could keep this up.

He had no idea how fast he was moving. It felt fast—very fast—though how he knew that, he couldn't say. His body was utterly still, hands still spread over the console, arms and torso rigid with concentration. But he felt the ship's speed in his head. Mach five? Six? More? He could feel the calculations at the edge of his perception, waiting for him to demand they be made and relayed to him, but he couldn't take any more information in. It was, as he had told Riordan, already too much.

And suddenly he was there, forcing the disk to slow its approach as he tried to take in what he was seeing.

Feeling, more like.

Yes. He wasn't actually looking at the silos on the ground or plotting the way Jackson's Locust was playing hit and run with the three arrowhead craft that had stationed themselves above the missile silos, and he certainly wasn't seeing the curious pulses of energy they were using to disrupt the missiles' arming systems, but he felt it, all of it, like waves of data in his head. Whatever sensor array the disk used, it was feeding directly into his mind, and he read it all intuitively, like identifying texture or heat with his fingers. It was overwhelming. He closed his eyes to shut out the merely visual distractions of the sky and the earth below as he sent the disk tearing through its intercept cycle onto the unsuspecting ships.

The ground below him was dark as the sky, but he saw Jackson's Locust immediately as it arced and wove a rapid spiral away from two of the silvery arrowheads. One of them gave chase, matching the Locust for pace and agility, but Jackson executed a deft spin move and caught his pursuer in a stream of laser fire that lit up the night with stabbing lines of red. The arrowhead corkscrewed away, but one great delta wing was carved by the laser, and it dropped heavily, smoking.

Alan felt a wave of elation pulse from him into the craft, as if he were supercharging its engines, and he pulled up so he could survey the scene. The other two arrowheads had left the missile silo below and were sweeping towards Jackson with deadly speed. Uncertainly, Alan inched one hand toward the symbol for his weapons systems and braced himself for another tsunami of information.

As his head swam in the impressions of data—weapon types, targeting systems, range, lead time, recharge rates— he sent the disk into a steep dive, like a peregrine dropping on pigeons. One of them saw him and broke left. The information in Alan's head scrambled briefly and he was left momentarily confused.

Too much, he thought, forcing himself to focus, to bring his thoughts into line, when what he wanted to do was let go and float away.

He sighted on the left arrowhead, realizing, as he was about to fire, that the other had locked onto Jackson's flight. He saw the Locust feint right, then enter a steep climb, but the arrowhead wasn't fooled. It banked and rolled and fired.

There was a stream of colored flashes, yellow and green iridescent light slashing up and through the Locust. It bobbed like a cork on wave, and then it was all light and fire, bright as the heart of a star, as it came apart.

Alan felt Jackson die, and his horror and sudden, vengeful grief lit up his weapon systems in a surge of energy that streamed out at both arrowheads and vaporized them in less than a second.

TIMIKA
Indian Springs Auxiliary field number 1 (closed), Nevada

THE SHAFT WAS UNCANNILY SIMILAR TO THE ONE SHE had emerged from in what she had decided was Siberia, though this culvert was not so deep, and it did not end in the maze of passages. In fact, the ladder led to nothing more than a recess, a concrete alcove just high enough to stand in, where she found three heavy metal doors, each only four feet high, one on each concrete wall. They looked like safes, and had apparently been sealed into the concrete rather than fastened with bolts like the manhole cover above.

Each one had a keyhole and a steel latch handle.

Timika worked her fingers into her pocket and wriggled out the single small key. She pushed it into the lock on the left hand wall. It slid in easily, but would not turn, and when she tried the heavy latch, it didn't move.

She tried the door in the facing wall with the same results, and some of the exasperated anxiety she had felt as they had hunted for the shaft cover returned. She could hear the drone of engines above her and the roar and snap of gravel under wheels, and then silence.

She paused in the act of slotting the key into the final lock, listening. Hearing nothing, she turned the key, her heart rising into her throat.

Come on, Jerzy. Don't let me down now.

It turned and she heard the latch disengage. Grasping the handle, flashlight unsteady, she twisted it much harder than she needed to. It thunked home easily and she felt the sudden heaviness of the steel door as it swung toward her.

She looked in.

There was a sliding metal palette, like the drawers used to hold corpses in the morgue, but this held no body. She pulled the slide toward her. On it was a box, heavy looking, perhaps ten-inches tall, three-feet long and half that wide. A rigid eagle, wings spread, was molded into the metal.

She felt for seams or hinges and found a pair of clasps like the catches on an attaché case.

She hesitated, conscious of both the enormity of what she was doing, and—like an animal sensing something dangerous close by—felt a change in the atmosphere above her.

She froze, listening.

Dully, from the bottom of the concrete tube, she heard the murmur of conversation and then, quite suddenly, a shot. It rang in the shaft, making her wince, knees buckling slightly as she instinctively tried to shrink away and make herself small.

There was a shout, and then another shot—different this time—and then another, and another, until the world above became a blanket of noise, the booming echoing around the concrete walls with the terrible urgency of pain and death.

64

JENNIFER
Indian Springs Auxiliary field number 1 (closed), Nevada

THERE WERE TWO CARS, ONE WHITE, ONE GRAY, TWO men in each. At first, they idled, twenty yards off, but when the corporal who'd driven Jennifer and the others to the abandoned airfield moved to challenge them, rifle at the ready, the men in the first car got out. They were young. Uniformed, though Jennifer couldn't make out what the uniform was in the erratic light of the flashlights. Blue, she thought. Not military.

They exchanged a few words, formalities, she had supposed, so the first shot was a complete surprise. The corporal dropped where he stood. The man who'd shot him turned his pistol on her.

"Get down!" Regis shouted, throwing himself on the ground and firing multiple rounds as she ran for the Humvee. The young soldier there, Simmons, who'd sat next to her in the back, was firing from one knee over the mudguard of the front wheel.

Jennifer made for him, half-crouching, the air thrumming with bullets and alive with panic. She half-tripped, half-threw herself to the ground behind Simmons, who'd paused to reload. Beyond them, she saw the second car moving, flanking them. In the passenger side was a white man in his sixties. His face looked familiar though it took a moment to pull his name from her memory of the Maynard board meeting: Manning. When she saw the flash of his pistol, she ducked back behind the Humvee as the bullet careened off metal and into the night. Their cover wouldn't last much longer.

She looked desperately into the Humvee for something she could use as a weapon: a spare pistol, a flare, even a tire iron. There was nothing. As another shot came from the gray car, she ducked down again in terror.

"They are coming around us," she managed to say to Simmons.

He nodded, white faced but calm, and squeezed off another round toward the white car. She saw the way the bullet punched through the open car door like it was paper. Surely, it was only a matter of time before one of Simmons' bullets found a target.

But time was something they did not have. The gray car was coming around behind them now, and she could see the driver, his thin, skull face leering out at her like one of her childhood nightmares.

Herman Saltzburg.

Of course it was. A part of her had known he would be here at the end.

ALAN
Colorado airspace

THE DISK SLID SOUTH INTO THE AIRSPACE OVER THE Colorado missile facility in under a minute, Alan's emotions still running hot. Riordan told him Hastings had been hit and gone down, safe but out of action. Below him, Rodriguez's Locust was in a high, fast cruise, cut off from the arrowhead parked directly over the silo by four other enemy craft and one Locust. And that meant . . .

Morat.

It had to be.

Once more the stream of data he was trying to process was disrupted by the red spike of Alan's outrage, and once again he felt the ship buckle and swerve as he momentarily lost control.

Fight it, he told himself, sweat running down his face. *Focus. Breathe.*

It was his confusion, the sense of being overwhelmed by distraction, that had delayed his rescue of Jackson, and that had meant the pilot's death. He had to get it together.

"Riordan," he said, dimly aware of how they'd abandoned protocol as the two of them cobbled together the mission like amateurs, "I have a rogue Locust in view. I need to ID it so I don't confuse it with Rodriguez."

He spoke in a clenched voice barely above a whisper, mind riveted to what was going on below.

"A rogue Locust?" said Riordan. He sounded wary.

"It's Morat's ship," said Alan. "He is flying for . . . the enemy."

He didn't know what else to call them.

"Agent Morat?" said Riordan. "That can't be right. Let me check with Special Agent Hatcher . . ."

"Hatcher is dead," said Alan, feeling the disk dip and stall again as his feelings got away from him. "Morat killed him. I don't have time to discuss it. I need a way to tell the two Locusts apart. Can you help?"

The mental strain was making it hard to speak. Finding each word was like fumbling in the dark, pulling them from a sack and trying to arrange them in an order that made sense while doing a dozen unrelated things. Even so, he registered the long silence before Riordan spoke. He sounded anxious, but resigned.

"Each Locust has a different energy signature. I'm sending you the data now."

Alan braced himself for yet more information, tensing his whole body as if anticipating a punch to the gut.

"Got it," he managed.

"I can't authorize any action against Agent Morat without higher authority," Riordan said. "The data I've sent is strictly precautionary. I hope it helps keep you safe, Major."

Alan grinned bitterly. Riordan was covering his ass. Again the disk shimmied and shifted its trajectory, and had to be wrestled back to readiness.

"Okay," Alan said. "Going in."

And with that thought, the disk plummeted toward the swarm below, targeting systems lighting up in Alan's head and locking on. There would be no hesitation this time.

He felt his thoughts move toward Jackson, and before he could pull them back, he'd fired, though what the weapon was that he'd trained on the arrowheads chasing Rodriguez, he couldn't say. He felt the blast leave the ship but only a disturbance in the air, a bolt of something with no more substance than steam. Whatever it was tore through the group of arrowheads and burst like ripples on the surface of a pond where a stone has dropped as Rodriguez shot clear. The spreading pulse caught all three arrowheads and threw them from the heart of the blast, so that they turned in the air, out of control and coming apart. For a microsecond, the three arrowheads seemed to have gaseous tails before the ships blossomed in spectacular explosions of light and wreckage.

Alan corrected the disk's course and came barreling in on the arrowhead hovering over the missile silo, but it broke and ran. He dropped in behind it, matching its speed easily, and as it turned to face him, stabbing at him with laser fire, he unleashed a stream of energy that stripped the ship to burning fragments.

As the disk streaked through the falling remnants of the ship, Alan turned, scanning the sky for Morat's Locust.

"Major Young?" came the voice of Rodriguez. "I don't know what the hell you're flying, but thanks!"

Alan tried to say something in response, but the words would not come. Then he spotted Morat's Locust. It was making a hard, steep climb out of the atmosphere.

Okay, he thought. *We can do that.*

And with that moment of clarity, words came back to him.

"No sweat, Rodriguez," he said. "Riordan will take care of you. There's one more hostile I have to deal with."

And then he was in pursuit, pushing the disk harder and faster than ever as Morat made for the emptiness of space.

TIMIKA
Indian Springs Auxiliary field number 1 (closed), Nevada

Timika did not like guns. In fact, she used to joke, she didn't mind guns, per se—it was the bullets she didn't like. Particularly when they were coming at her. Always got a big laugh.

She didn't feel like laughing now. Her hands were clammy on the rungs of the ladder. The world above had turned into a kind of hell, but there was no point staying down in the bunker. They would find her eventually. Maybe, just maybe, she could do something to help. She didn't know Jennifer, and they'd only been together a couple of hours, but the Englishwoman had bailed her out, and looked after her when she needed it, and Timika always paid her debts.

She crawled up the ladder and peered cautiously over the concrete rim of the shaft, her flashlight stuffed into her pocket. She felt it heavy against her thigh. Might prove useful as a club if the moment arose.

It was hard to make out what was happening at first. Someone had turned on the Humvee's floodlights, but they shone only on open desert. She caught the silhouettes of two people next to the Humvee, sheltering from the fight, and saw the muzzle flash as someone returned fire with an M16. To her right, Regis lay prone behind the toolbox. She wasn't sure if he was still alive. Another soldier was on his back over by the white car. He didn't look good.

The gray car was in reverse, creeping behind the Humvee, a man in a suit leaning out of the passenger window with a pistol. She couldn't see who was driving. A shot rang out from behind the white car, aimed at Regis but slamming into the ground. She glimpsed a young man. When he moved to get a better shot, she saw the uniform.

Cop.

No, she reminded herself. *Fake cop*.

For a second she was back in New York, running from someone who'd called himself Cook. This was the other one, the one who had been rifling through her office. Her outrage grew as she inched up the ladder, throwing one arm over the rim, about to pull herself up and out . . .

That was when she felt the cold muzzle of the pistol, jammed into the nape of her neck.

"Get up," said the voice behind her.

She did so slowly

"Hands on your head."

Again, she did as she was told.

The fighting stopped. The gunman at her back shouted for everyone to hear.

"Drop your weapons and step into the light or I blow her head off."

He moved around her, watching as first Jennifer, then Simmons, and then reluctantly Regis complied. The driver was dead. Timika saw the man who had his pistol trained on her and knew him immediately.

"Get around, don't you, Miss Mars?" said Cook.

The man who'd hunted her on the streets of Manhattan, the man she had evaded with a quick change of clothes and a lot of nerve. Neither option was available to her now.

JENNIFER
Indian Springs Auxiliary field number 1 (closed), Nevada

ENNIFER KNEW THEY WERE —WHAT WAS THE PHRASE?—
dead men walking. Timika knew it too. She could see
it in her eyes as they were huddled together facing
the muzzles of the Maynard Consortium's hired guns as
directed by Saltzburg and Manning.

She wondered now if Letrange—or Morat, as Regis
knew him—had been assigned to kill her the day of the
disastrous Maynard board meeting, as he'd almost certainly
killed her father. He'd underscored the aerospace item on
her agenda, leaving her a clue to follow, to see what she
already knew, what breadcrumbs her father might have
left for her, and the extent to which he was betraying the

Consortium. She had been set up, decoyed into thinking she was making progress, when in fact she was just being used to test the Consortium's security. As soon as it appeared she had indeed unearthed some damaging truths, she had to be eliminated.

But here she was. Not dead yet. Not quite.

"Herman Saltzburg," she snarled as he came in close, his death's-head leer plastered across his loathsome face. "I always hated you."

"Amazingly enough," said Saltzburg, pleasantly, "I surmised as much. You will be disappointed to know your feelings did not upset me. Quite the contrary, in fact."

"I'll bet," she said.

She was still scared, but the imminence of her own death had given her a kind of clarity. The blind, trembling terror she had felt during the firefight was gone. The fear was there, but it had been surpassed by the rage she felt, and the revulsion, seeing Saltzburg's sepulchral face.

"I will spare you the villain's self-explanations," he said. "You have something I want. Give it to me."

"I don't know what you're talking about," said Jennifer.

"An item you've been directed to by a Polish Jew," said Saltzburg with disgust. "It was not his to give away."

"I don't have it," said Jennifer. "And if I did, I wouldn't give it to the man who arranged the death of my father."

"Arranged?" said Saltzburg, amused.

"I assume it was you who set Letrange, or whatever his real name is, on my father."

"Oh no," said Saltzburg, his skeletal grin stretching wider than ever. "Letrange was otherwise occupied at the time. I took care of that little matter myself."

Jennifer took a breath, fighting back the tears.

"Now," he said, pleased by her response. "The object the plucky Miss Mars has been pursuing, please."

"I told you," she managed. "I don't have it."

Saltzburg's expression did not change and his eyes never left her face as he raised his voice fractionally.

"Mr. Cook," he said. "Kill Miss Mars, please."

Cook pointed his gun squarely at Timika's chest.

68

ALAN
Low Earth Orbit

I F THE DISK'S APPARENT TRANSPARENCY HAD BEEN STRANGE in the lower reaches of the atmosphere, it was positively surreal in low earth orbit. As Alan left the world behind him and emerged in the silent blackness of space, just a man in a chair—or so it seemed—moving without support or protection, he had to fight the impulse to hold his breath.

He'd been apprehensive about taking the disk this high, something Morat had surely guessed, because he had no idea how—or if—it would perform in the near vacuum that was home only to satellites and potentially lethal debris.

Crossing from the lower atmosphere momentarily obscured his sensors as he realized, with a heart-stopping shudder that rippled through the disk's trajectory, that he'd lost Morat's Locust. He wheeled around, using his eyes as much as the ship's sensory array, and saw only blackness and the asymmetrical hulks of satellites. He rotated the disk in every direction, feeling the ship's various scanning devices gradually turning back on as the craft adjusted to its new environment.

Something lit up. A spot above Alan's right shoulder. He pivoted the disk to see, but there was only an ungainly satellite that looked like something from a junkyard bolted together and sprouting a single bluish solar panel, rimmed with gold. He adjusted the disk, scanning a patch of space that seemed smeared by a cloud-like patch of tiny fragments. He slowly spun the disk towards it and set it in motion, making a cautious approach just a little faster than the speed at which the debris was orbiting the planet below.

He didn't see Morat's ship emerge from behind the satellite where it had been hidden until it was out and shooting.

The disk shot to the right, entering an upward, diagonal spiral followed by a deep dive and a slanting, lateral slide. It was barely conscious. The saucer was reacting to Alan's instincts rather than his thoughts, as if man and ship had fused together. The movement was all speed and evasion without caution, and it was only by chance that it didn't hit any of the space trash floating about. It was the spatial effect of panic, and when Alan drew the disk back into conscious control, he realized he had no idea how far he'd moved.

Morat was gone again. The residual energy signature of his Locust indicated he'd shot back down toward the lower atmosphere.

"What's his trajectory?" Alan said aloud, fighting with his flagging concentration. "Where is he headed?"

The ship's computer—not entirely separate from Alan's own overworked brain—sorted through the data and projected a flight path in front of him

Alan blinked. That couldn't be right.

"He's returning to Dreamland?" he said. "Why would he do that?"

He paused.

"Are there other ships with him? Other arrowheads, bogeys?"

The invisible screen in front of him became a radar map, and on it glowed the little sparks representing hostile craft. Dozens of them, converging on Nevada.

"Major?" came Riordan's voice. He sounded brighter, but confused. "The enemy's broken off their attack. They're leaving the silos. Not sure what you guys did up there, but I guess we won."

Alan did not relax. He stared at the pattern of markers streaking across his viewer.

No, he thought. *We haven't won. We've been duped. Again.*

They didn't want the silos. They never wanted to set off the missiles. They needed something to draw us into the air, to engage us, pick us off one by one.

Because what they really want, what they always wanted . . .

The thought froze him cold.

"Riordan!" he shouted, taking one hand off the console to wipe the sweat from his face and eyebrows, then slamming it down and heading for earth as fast as the ship would go. "Riordan! You have incoming. The hostiles are targeting Dreamland. They want the goddamned base!"

TIMIKA
Indian Springs Auxiliary field number 1 (closed), Nevada

I T WAS ABSURD. SHE WAS GOING TO GET HERSELF KILLED. But then, she was going to be killed anyway, so it didn't matter.

Timika had her hands raised. Cook took a step toward her, pistol at chest height, and she smiled. It was a playful, flirty smile, the smile you shoot to someone over the rim of your mojito at a party, before you lead them to the bedroom. Cook's eyes narrowed with confusion, and in that infinitesimal moment of hesitation, she clapped her hands together on either side of the gun, pushing it up and away.

It went off with a blast like a cannon, but the muzzle was well clear by then, and her knee was already in his groin. Cook doubled over, and Timika stamped one heel hard on his foot. In the same moment she gripped the warm barrel of the gun and twisted it up, tugging until it rotated clean out of his grip.

She was dimly aware of Regis' forehead rocketing hard into the face of the other fake cop, but she heard the man's nose break before he fell. The man Jennifer had called Saltzburg fell back in alarm as Timika came around with the gun. Cook, who'd not gone down entirely, gave her a look of pure hatred and came at her.

She fired once.

But she heard two shots, not one. For a moment, the night was full of bitter smoke. Cook crumpled, bleeding from his chest, and then Timika saw the other gun, in the hand of Saltzburg, the old guy who looked like the Grim Reaper. As if in a dream, she processed the fact that it was still pointed at her.

And then she felt the pain.

70

JENNIFER
Indian Springs Auxiliary field number 1 (closed), Nevada

J ENNIFER SWOOPED AT TIMIKA WHO WAS FOLDING AT the knees, blood spilling from the bullet hole in her chest. She caught her before she hit the ground, staring desperately into Timika's vacant, rolling eyes. She heard a scramble at her back, a flurry of movement that ended with another snap of gunfire. Three, maybe four shots in rapid succession, like peels of thunder.

She held Timika to her, tense, braced for the stab of agony that would mean she'd been hit, but nothing came, and she finally turned.

Regis was on one knee, sighting down the pistol he'd taken from the cop he'd head-butted, and Manning was motionless on the ground. Saltzburg, who'd been at her back only moments before, had loped away in the confusion, shooting as he made for the gray car.

"Stop him!" yelled Jennifer.

Regis fired twice, but if he hit the banker, it did not slow him down. They heard the car engine turn over and the squeal of tires as Saltzburg pulled away.

Regis stooped to Timika, snatching up a flashlight and shining it on her wound. It was higher than Jennifer had feared, closer to the shoulder.

"Simmons!" he said. "Get the med kit out of Humvee. Can you look after her?" he added to Jennifer.

"Me?" she answered. "I have no medical training."

Regis frowned, but didn't hesitate, sweeping the flashlight over the other bodies. Manning and the man they had called Cook were both dead, so was the army corporal. The fake cop with the broken nose was unconscious and bloody, but breathing. Regis rolled him onto his belly and used cuffs to secure the man's hands behind his back.

"Stay with her," he said to the soldier with a nod at Timika. "Clean and dress the wound, then keep pressure on it until the bleeding stops. Give her painkillers and keep her awake until help arrives."

"What about me?" asked Jennifer.

"You're driving," said Regis, throwing her the keys to the Humvee and picking up the corporal's fallen rifle. He didn't wait for her response, instead barking into his radio, calling for back up, for a medical team, and for eyes on the road to the disused airfield.

"And put me in touch with Major Young," he roared. "Now."

ALAN
Nevada airspace

ALAN DIDN'T KNOW HOW FAST HE WAS GOING. HE WAS driving the disk to its limit, hurtling through the sky, his vision briefly a fiery red as he re-entered the lower atmosphere, fighting to order his thoughts and prepare for the onslaught that would come. He still had no clear sense of the ship's defensive capacity, whether it had some form of shield or cloaking technology, and though he'd fired its weapons several times now, each one had been subtly different, and he didn't known why, as if the ship were making choices for him, choices he did not understand and could not process in the split second it took to select a target, prime, and fire. His nerves were ragged, the sweat on his face might have been mixed with tears if only because he dare not blink for fear of what he might miss, his heart and lungs working at maximum load.

But this was minimal, compared to the strain on his mind. It was collapsing under the weight of that constant, calculating focus, the mental sifting and arrangement of countless streams of information. He was at the limits of functionality. He had only moments before he would collapse, black out.

But there was no one else. Jackson was dead. Rodriguez had gone hunting at the other silos and wouldn't be back until it was too late.

It was on him.

And suddenly he was there, high above the pale crater of Groom Lake, and before he had had time to think, he was in combat range. His viewer was a swarm of arrowheads and—buried in their midst—a single Locust. Morat. Once more, the peeling, shrieking peregrine dive, and once more, the enemy ships scattering like minnows evading a pike, and once more, the flash of laser fire and other, stranger weapons. The disk shuddered as it was hit again and again, and suddenly Alan was no longer a chair in space, but a man sealed inside a metal saucer. Whatever allowed him to see through the hull of the ship had shut down or been destroyed, and he was, momentarily blinded.

He instinctively pulled the disk into a complex evasive climb, zigzagging up and out of the swarm, rotating as he went and scattering weapons fire in his wake. He was back to the screen viewer now, limiting what he could see in his periphery, but he saw the glare and puff of at least two arrowheads exploding.

Triumph, defiance and blood lust swam red through his mind as he wheeled the ship, pinioning, ratcheting, leaping back into the fray, targeting one ship, then another, firing as fast as he could think, and with each desperate shot, he felt himself grow weaker, less in control, as if he were firing bolts of his own life force.

But then he saw Morat's Locust and swept into pursuit, firing half blind with rage and exhaustion. Whether he was traitor or imposter didn't matter any more. Morat was a killer, an enemy combatant. Alan strained to hold on, angling, adjusting, jinking the saucer left and right as Morat tried to shake him. Alan could feel the other ships tearing toward him at the edge of consciousness but his anger gave him focus till he could see nothing but Morat's ship. He twisted, dove, rotated . . .

And fired.

The moment he got the shot away Alan gasped with relief, but now the rest were on him, pummeling the disk so that it shuddered and slid first one way and then another, and he could feel the lasers carving into the metal. His craft slewed into a ragged climb and he lost sight of Morat's Locust, all of his attention scanning for the other ships. He must have hit Morat. Surely . . .

Then there was something else, two pale streaks, like missiles but not clearly solid, coming right at him. He dropped the disk a thousand feet in under a second, and one of the streaks shot over head. The other, somehow, adjusted, dipped, swerved, and hit him.

The disk did not come apart, but it began to roll in the air, such that Alan turned over and over, systems failing, and he was holding on by the edges of his mind as he lost sense of what was happening.

Dimly he remembered the weapon he'd used before when he'd saved Rodriguez—his one achievement for the day—the thing which had sought out the center of their attack and then burst like a firework, tumbling the enemy to nothing. Perhaps if he could find that, or something like it, something bigger.

The thought was dreamy and unspecific. Alan felt himself sliding into something like sleep, and for a second, he thought he was hallucinating the new ship.

It was not an arrowhead, and not a Locust, and not a silver disk like the craft he was flying. It was something different, spherical and glowing with a steady orange glow that reminded him of the craft he had seen over the Afghan mountains so very long ago. He didn't know where it had come from or what it was going to do, but he saw the light at its heart focus, and knew some kind of terrible weapon was coming.

With the last of his strength, he muttered, "Fire."

And as the blast radius spread towards the tumbling arrowheads, coursing through them, and blowing many of them away like leaves, he careened at full speed into the sphere.

TIMIKA
Indian Springs Auxiliary field number 1 (closed), Nevada

TIMIKA OPENED HER EYES AND TRIED TO SIT UP.

"Keep still." It was the soldier who had been in the back of the Humvee with them. Simmons.

"How long was I out?" she asked as memory rushed in.

"Couple of minutes. Maybe five," said Simmons.

"Which is it?"

"Which is what?"

"A couple—which is two," said Timika, "or five, which is—you know—longer."

"Five," said Simmons, irritated. "How do you feel?"

"Well, I seem to have this fucking hole in my shoulder. So, you know, been better."

"Apart from the pain?" said Simmons, his patience peeling away like sunburned skin.

"Apart from the pain, I feel like I could run a marathon. I couldn't, of course, because I'd die," said Timika. "On account of the pain."

"Right," said Simmons. "But your breathing's okay? You don't feel nauseated or like you might pass out again?"

"No," said Timika, taking pity on the boy. "I'm okay. Thanks."

She looked around. "Where's Jennifer and the officer?"

"Took the Humvee to go after that . . . guy."

"Skeletor?"

"That's the one," said Simmons, grinning in spite of himself. "There's a medical team en route. There's a lot going on at the base, but they'll be here soon."

"Good," said Timika. "Wait. No. Not good. There's something I have to do."

She tried to get to her feet.

"I told you to keep still," said Simmons.

"You gonna shoot me?" she asked.

"No ma'am," said Simmons, chastened.

"Then help me up," she said.

Simmons sighed but knew that there was no point arguing. He let her use him to get upright and then escorted her to the manhole.

"You can't manage that ladder," he said.

"I won't use my right hand," said Timika. It was a concession, but one she knew she had to make. Her shoulder throbbed, and she couldn't raise her arm without excruciating pain.

"I gotta stay here with him," said Simmons, nodding at the cuffed and unconscious man in the police uniform.

"It's okay. If I need you, I'll holler."

She maneuvered herself awkwardly into the shaft and descended, one rung at a time, relying on her left hand, until she reached the bottom. She reached around with her good arm and plucked the flashlight from her right pocket, then approached the open door with the drawer and the box.

She considered the metal lid, molded with the square wings of a German eagle. She fumbled with her left hand until the clasps popped and she opened it to reveal the treasure she'd been chasing for so very long, even now wondering what Jerzy Stern could have thought was so important.

She gasped.

Inside the box was a slab of stone, covered with deeply scored carvings in some language she did not know. It reeked of antiquity. It was, she thought, Old Testament old.

Around the rim was set a band of bluish metal, which pulsed and glowed as she moved her hands over it. It was the same material Katarina Lundergrass had shown her, though her piece had been a mere fragment of something her father had picked up long ago at the world's most famous crash site.

"You got something?" called Simmons.

"Yeah," she breathed. "I got something."

73

IT WAS LIKE DRIVING ON THE RUTTED BACK ROADS OF Africa, as if they were rushing to glimpse some nocturnal lion kill or to outrun a territorial hippo. The four-wheel-drive Humvee sped along the road and handled those moments when, as they tried to stay close to the gray car, they sometimes left the road entirely. Saltzburg, by contrast, was weaving erratically.

"You think he's hit?" Jennifer shouted, shifting down a gear.

"Not sure," said Regis. He had braced himself into a precarious kneeling crouch in the rooftop gun port, his head and shoulder exposed, the rifle aimed forward as he tried to get a shot. When she asked if he thought that was safe, he shrugged. "So long as you don't flip the vehicle and cut my damn head off," he said.

"Where the hell is he going?" Jennifer muttered.

The car's taillights showed where Saltzburg left the road, pulling hard up a ridge not unlike those she'd hiked on Hapsel's land earlier in the evening. It would be hard going for a low, two-wheel drive vehicle, and she wasn't surprised when the car stopped to redirect, pulling hard up the ridge. In the delay, the Humvee closed the distance between them until they were almost alongside him. It was in that instant that Saltzburg risked a shot from the driving seat.

Jennifer saw the flash of the pistol but didn't hear it over the Humvee's engine, and then Regis was returning fire above her, shell casings raining down into the cab and spinning under her feet. Saltzburg smashed his way through the desert brush of the ridgeline, but he was on level ground, whereas the Humvee canted dangerously as they ran beside him. One false move and they really might roll. She risked a glance at Regis as he fired again, and this time he hit.

The flank of the gray sedan, already scuffed and buckled from the drive, was punctured in several places close to the front wheels. Then the tire blew and the car slewed dangerously, first down their side, then back up and over the ridge, where it bucked against a boulder, careened on two wheels, and finally flipped, rolling down the slope on the other side.

Jennifer slowed the Humvee and angled its nose over the ridgeline and down again, until its lights fell on the mangled wreckage of the other car. She was out and running before Regis could stop her, before she even knew what she would do when she reached the man who'd killed her father, if he had survived the accident.

He hadn't. That was instantly apparent. She felt a savage triumph, chased by more complex feelings that she could not put into words. At last, conscious that those strange emotions had settled into a kind of profound relief, and closure, she trudged back up to the Humvee where Regis was shouting into the radio, one hand pressed hard against his ear as if to wring whatever sound there was from the headset.

"I can barely hear you," he was saying. "What? Yes. We're on the ground. I think we can get there. Hold on, Alan."

And then they were driving again.

ALAN
Nevada airspace

THE DISK WAS GOING DOWN. HARD. SO WAS THE sphere. He'd hurtled into it, all weapons blazing, and now his barely conscious mind was telling him that that had been a mistake.

He'd targeted the craft because he'd assumed it was part of the hostile fleet, but its weapons had not been locked onto him. He didn't know how he knew that, but he had felt it at the moment of impact, the shrill cry of alarm and surprise that he'd sensed through the metal of the battered disk, until a single awful thought registered, even as he slammed into the sphere's hull.

It hadn't come from nowhere. It had come from the base. It was one of ours.

Alan fought to track its fall, guiding the saucer as best he could as it lurched haphazardly into its final descent, but his mind was darkening, as if he were sliding into the water in some subterranean cave.

"Coming down," he murmured, barely awake. "Sphere. Get to that ship."

He wasn't sure if Riordan could hear him, or Regis, or anybody. He was really only talking to himself.

He watched the sphere struggle, fight to regain its momentum, and fall. As he finally slipped into the dream, his hands slid lifeless from the console, and the disk tumbled from the sky.

75

"C OMING DOWN," SAID THE SPECTRAL VOICE ON THE radio, a voice of inexpressible weariness, quite unlike the man Jennifer had bickered with in the bar not so very long ago. "Sphere," the voice said. "Get to that ship."

"Major!" called Regis into the radio. "Alan! Can you read?"

But the pilot did not reply. Suddenly there was a steady thrumming in the air, rising in pitch and volume, and when she looked up, Jennifer could see the light coming down in a hard, straight line.

A ship. Not landing but crashing to earth.

"Follow it!" bellowed Regis.

Jennifer turned the key in the ignition and set the Humvee lurching down the ridge toward the road.

She saw the burst of light, heard the deep, resonant thud of the crash, the echoes trembling in the air over the noise of the Humvee's engine, and then they were speeding along an old, forgotten highway, their eyes fixed on the fiery glow that rose up from behind a ragged line of barren hills.

They made for it, though what they would find when they got there, Jennifer could not imagine.

TIMIKA
Indian Springs Auxiliary field number 1 (closed), Nevada

THE BOX WAS TOO HEAVY TO MOVE, ESPECIALLY WITH HER right arm crossed painful and useless against her chest, so Timika fumbled in her pocket, drew out her cellphone, turned on the flash and took three pictures of the stone tablet in its curious metal frame. Then she slid the drawer closed, locked the door to the safe, secured the key and clambered awkwardly back up to the desert and the bodies.

She was halfway up the ladder when she heard the distant boom and emerged to find Simmons gazing off to where the sky was lightened by an amber, uneven glow.

"Something crashed," he said, awestruck, barely aware of her. "I saw it come down, right there."

As he pointed, the second craft descended. It wasn't lit up, but the whole thing seemed to glow softly, like a ball at the end of a long punt, accelerating as it fell.

The impact sounded different, shorter, less booming, but there was still something jarring about it. It shook her from her watchful reverie and sent her running to the white sedan the fake cops had been driving.

"Hey," said Simmons. "You can't take that. You've got to stay here until the med team arrives."

"You keep your eye on him," Timika shot back, pointing to the handcuffed man on the ground and climbing into the driver's seat.

The keys were in the ignition.

She had to see.

ALAN
Nevada

SLEEP. IT FELT LIKE SLEEP, BUT IT WASN'T. NOT QUITE. It was a drowsiness that closed his fluttering eyelids and shut down his senses, but his mind still worked. Just. Thoughts reached out, thin and wavering. It felt like trying to move an oak tree by pulling on its outermost branches, his mind straining. Alan, who was no longer Alan but the broken disk, flexed and dragged, and then the branch was sliding through his fingers and he was holding nothing, forgetting the metaphor of the tree, of the saucer, just drifting through the blackness of space.

The disk struck the earth. It did not bounce, instead blasting a crater that it excavated as it slewed, plowing up rock and dirt and carving its way across the desert floor, glowing hot, so that the dry bushes it touched flared with sudden fire and were gone, but slowing,

Slowing,

Stopping.

All noise ceasing, as if all sound had been sucked out of the night.

78

JENNIFER
Nevada

THEY REACHED THE FRACTURED DISK FIRST. REGIS sprang from the vehicle, picking his way along the trench the ship had made when it hit the ground before Jennifer had shut the engine off. She jumped down from the Humvee, slipping where the sandy earth had turned into hard, crystalline glass from the heat of the impact.

A curved panel that might have been a door had popped off the disk. She directed her flashlight inside, where Regis was unstrapping the man in the chair. Alan. He was unconscious but, amazingly, was not dead. His body was intact, despite the crash. She stepped back to examine it. The saucer appeared to be largely intact, if battered and bent out of shape. It ticked as it cooled.

A handprint—Regis'—had burned onto the side by the hatch. It smoked still.

Jennifer approached, feeling the heat of the thing shrinking her hair as she got close. She could smell it smoldering.

Careful not to touch the strange metal, she reached into the hatch and helped guide Regis out, taking as much of the pilot's weight as she could manage. Regis' bare arm brushed the edge of the hatchway and she heard the flesh sear, but he only grimaced and kept working.

Once they had him out, they moved him away from the ship and laid him on the ground, where Regis pressed his ear to the pilot's chest.

"Is he alive?"

Regis hesitated. "I think so, but his pulse is very faint. He's breathing."

As Regis barked into the radio again, Jennifer got back in the Humvee. There was another ship to see.

79

TIMIKA
Nevada

THE WHITE SEDAN STRUGGLED WITH THE TERRAIN THE moment she left the road. Timika drove as fast as she dared. When the big man stepped into her headlights, waving his arms frantically, she swerved to go around him before she realized who it was.

The officer called Regis.

She skidded into a sliding halt, then reversed when she realized what he wanted. He had a man with him. The man lay slumped on the ground, his head tipped back in an alarming manner. He was wearing a tan flight suit, and for a moment, Timika thought he was dead.

"Help me get him in the back," said Regis.

Timika shone her flashlight to where something sparkled and smoked at the end of a deep, black trench.

"He was in that?" she gasped. "I'm not sure we should be moving him."

"Sphere," said the pilot, his eyes cracking open a fraction. "Take me to the sphere."

"You heard the Major," said Regis.

"What if he has . . . I don't know. Broken bones, or internal bleeding?" said Timika.

"I'm fine," breathed the pilot. "Just . . . tired."

Timika gaped at him.

Tired?

"The craft wasn't breached," said Regis. "He's shaken up, but he's okay. If he says it's important to get to the other ship, that's what we should do. Okay?"

Timika bit her lip, then nodded and pulled open the back door.

To her surprise, Regis didn't need her help. The pilot—whose name badge read A. Young, presumably the Alan Jennifer had mentioned—was recovering rapidly, though he still seemed strangely shell shocked. His eyes were vague and unfocused, but once Regis had him on his feet, he seemed able to stand by himself.

Even so, he labored clumsily into the back seat and slouched there, breathing hard as Timika got into the driver's seat and pulled away.

"Over there," said Regis.

The underside of the white sedan whined in protest as the car picked its way among the stones and scrub brush.

If she wasn't careful, she thought, eying a particularly nasty looking rock, she'd peel open the gas tank like a sardine can.

"Faster," said Regis. "They'll be here soon."

"Who's they?" she shot back, irritably.

If he knew the answer, he didn't say, turning over his shoulder to consider Alan, sprawled on the back seat.

It wasn't hard to see where the second ship had come down. There was a wide, blackened track, part of which still smoked in her high beams, and a few small brush fires.

Timika nosed the car up the side of a ridge, grimacing at the scraping of the underside and feeling the wheels spin as they tried to get enough purchase on the sand and gravel to haul the vehicle to the top, and then they were tipping over the crest and the headlights fell on the scene below them.

It looked like the sphere had clipped the ridge, then bounced over the downslope before slamming into the next rocky outcrop. There were more scattered fires up here, and a wider swathe of scorched undergrowth. Though it had been badly distorted by the impact, the ship had not exploded. It was smaller than the disk and sat in the blasted ground like the egg of a dragon, sparkling with strange energy. A portion of the outside had been torn away—the source, presumably, of the debris they had been following—and it provided a dark opening into the heart of the craft, as if the egg were hatching.

Jennifer was sitting on the ground beside it, the Humvee abandoned halfway down the ridge, its lights blazing. She stared into space, her face creased into a stunned bewilderment that was unnerving to look at.

"You okay?" Timika demanded, getting out of the car.

The other woman didn't answer. She looked dazed. Drugged.

Timika rushed over to her.

"Jennifer?" she said. "What is it?"

The Englishwoman seemed to grow slowly aware of her, looking up and focusing. There was dirt and something like oil smeared across her face but she seemed unaware of . . . anything.

"Jennifer!" Timika said again. "What's wrong?"

Jennifer licked her lips and said simply, "Look."

ALAN
Nevada

ALAN SLITHERED OUT OF THE BACK SEAT, FORCING HIS legs to work. His body was intact, he was pretty sure, but his mind was still sluggish and his limbs felt heavy when he moved. He got his feet on the ground, but as he stood up, the world swam and he had to steady himself against the car.

The sphere was there, a great rupture in one quadrant, though whether he had done that or if it had been split open by the crash, he didn't know. A surge of nausea rose up in him as he considered the awful probability.

Friendly fire.

The craft had risen to protect him, and he had taken it down because he hadn't been able to keep his mind focused any longer. He had done this. But he had to be sure.

Regis was already scrambling up the ridge toward the sphere, flashlight held out in front of him. Alan saw two women, sitting together. Then one of them followed Regis, peering over his shoulder. He needed to know what they saw.

There would be insignia, surely? Badges. Identifying marks so they would know for sure which side they were on. And maybe, just maybe, the crew wasn't dead.

He took a cautious step, then another, still clumsy, and then dropped to his hands and knees to make the climb up to the ship.

But then Regis was pulling him up and whispering into his face.

"Come on, Major. We gotta go. We can't be here."

"What?" Alan muttered. "No, I have to see . . ."

"You don't," said Regis. "You've seen too much already. We all have."

Alan shrugged out of his grip and nearly over-balanced, but he spoke with determination. "No," he said. "I have to know. Was it ours?"

Regis stared at him, his face contorted with emotion. Then he shook his head.

Thank God.

"Theirs," said Alan. "Hostile."

Regis dropped his eyes, then shook his head again.

Alan stared at him, trying to understand.

"What do you mean?" he said.

"Not ours, Major," said Regis. "Not theirs. Different."

"Different how?" Alan pressed.

"These craft you're flying," said Regis. "Where did we get them?"

"What do you mean?" he said. The two women were staring at them.

"Where did these ships come from?" Regis demanded, his voice raised. "Who built them? *What* built them?"

Alan opened his mouth to speak, but no words came, and suddenly the night was full of a familiar and steady droning sound. He saw lights in the sky over the base.

Helicopters. Coming in fast.

Alan took a step towards the downed sphere.

"You don't want to look in there," said Regis, pulling him back. "We need to be elsewhere. Now."

Alan fought back, but in his present state, he was no match for the big man.

"Get back in the car, Major," said Regis. "We gotta go."

But Alan had to see, and with his last ounce of strength he worked out of Regis' grasp and stumbled toward the fractured sphere.

He looked.

He saw.

And dimly, inadequately, he understood, even if what he saw merely confirmed that all he thought he knew before that moment was wrong.

THEY TOOK THE HUMVEE, ALL FOUR OF THEM PILING IN and sitting in silence as Jennifer drove it back toward the road. The helicopters arrived before they made it. Soldiers spilled out, rifles raised, so they stopped and got out, hands on their heads, watching as a pair of dark SUVs came speeding along the road toward them. The men who got out wore black suits and sunglasses.

JENNIFER
Indian Springs Auxiliary field number 1 (closed), Nevada

THEY RETURNED TO THE ABANDONED AIRSTRIP, WHERE Timika, in spite of her arm, insisted on being the one to lead the soldiers down the ladder to the three tiny vaults. They looked the same as before, she said. When they came back up, the drawer that had contained the box with the stone tablet held only a laminated information sheet detailing the identifying marks and habitat of a rare breed of fish.

"What the hell is an Ash Meadows Speckled Dace?" she said.

It was almost funny, Jennifer thought, wiping the dust and filth from her face, thinking about her father and the men who had killed him, about all she had learned, and all the new questions she still had to answer. Almost funny.

The soldiers, the medics and the so-called EPA men, had decided to give them some space. They had a lot to explain, they had been told, but criminal proceedings seemed unlikely.

Which actually *was* kind of funny.

While the various representatives of officialdom filed reports and documented the scene and did God-knew-what else to spirit it all away in the trucks and choppers, Jennifer asked a question.

"What do you think they're talking about?" she said, giving the men in the distance a look.

"Cover stories," said Regis. "The Roswell protocol. My money's on marsh gas."

"Weather balloon," said Alan with a bleak smile. "Definitely weather balloon."

For a moment, they all turned to watch as men in hazmat suits climbed down from yet another helicopter. The patch of desolate ground, empty of people no more than a couple of hours ago, and for the last fifty years, was starting to look like Piccadilly Circus at rush hour. For a minute or more, the four of them watched.

"So now what?" said Timika.

Regis shrugged.

"They'll take statements," he said, "get us to sign declarations . . ."

"No," said Timika. "I mean what do we do next? After we leave here. I mean, I had a life, I thought, but it doesn't seem to make much sense now. I think there's stuff I need to do, questions I gotta ask, you know?"

"Yeah," said Jennifer. "I know. I'll be right there with you."

The two women caught each other's eyes and grinned.

"You could probably use a pilot," said Alan.

"Easy there, Captain America," said Timika. "I'm not sure you're on our side."

"Well," said Alan, "to be honest, neither am I. But I think maybe I am."

Jennifer stared at him. "Are you serious?" she said.

He seemed to consider this, then nodded. "I think so," he said. "I've spent a long time doing what I was told. I've got some questions of my own. What about you, Barry?"

"Barry?" said Timika. "Who the hell is Barry?"

"Me," said Regis.

"I thought your name was Regis. Like *Regis and Kelly* or some shit."

"My name's Barry Regis," said the big man, scowling. "And yeah, I guess I got some questions."

"Well all right then," said Timika. There was a long silence as a strange and unexpected harmony settled within the group.

Off to the east, Jennifer saw a long slash across the horizon that was slowly turning the sky pink.

"Hey, whadyaknow?" said Timika thoughtfully. "Sunrise."

And so it was, though what the new day would bring, Jennifer could not begin to imagine. But, she thought vaguely, at least the night was over.

TIMIKA
Indian Springs Auxiliary field number 1 (closed), Nevada

ANOTHER HELICOPTER ARRIVED, THEN A TRUCK, AND another couple of Humvees. Last, with a dragging roar that anticipated its arrival by over a minute, came a cement mixer. Timika had no idea where they got a cement mixer at this time of night, but she had a pretty good idea what they were going to do with it. The vaults at the foot of the concrete shaft had, after all, been emptied already.

She took a minute to upload the pictures she had taken to a private drop box. It was too much to hope that she'd be allowed to walk away from this with her phone. As to what *this* was . . .

"This way, please, Miss Mars," said one of the newly arrived soldiers, gesturing toward his Humvee. He was not wearing a name badge.

"I think I'd rather stay with my friends," she answered, wondering a little about the ease with which she had said that last word. It wasn't a term she used much, and certainly not to describe people she'd only just met.

"I'm afraid that won't be possible," said the soldier. "Interrogation will be separate."

"Interrogation?" Timika shot back. "About what? We should be getting the damn Medal of Honor or some shit."

"You have violated numerous security protocols, you've trespassed on government property and leaked classified information. And your friends," he continued, nodding at Alan and Barry Regis, "have questions to answer about the death of a special agent."

"What?" Timika exclaimed. "They didn't kill anybody. You need to find that Letrange guy. Or Morat, or whatever his name is."

She spoke with a certainty which—like her use of "friends" a second ago—made little objective sense but felt absolutely right.

"Mr. Morat is missing and presumed lost," said the soldier. "Now if you would get into the vehicle, please. I am authorized to use force if you do not comply."

There wasn't much you could say to that, and before she could frame any kind of quip, Timika's phone rang. She snatched it up before the soldier could stop her.

"Timika? It's Marvin."

"Thank God," she said. "Where the hell have you been?"

"One of those bogus cops showed up at my place so I took off. I went to—"

"You can tell me later," she replied. "Right now I need you to get in touch with my lawyer. I'm being held at Area 51 in goddamned Nevada, if you can believe that."

"Dude!" said Marvin. "No way."

"Way," said Timika, as the soldier reached for her phone.

"You need to hang up, ma'am," he said.

"Later, Marvin," she said. "We'll be in touch. And Marvin?"

"Yeah?"

"I'm glad you're okay."

She hung up pointedly, staring down the soldier who, unsure of his authority, looked away.

Timika scanned the surreal landscape, the pink desert sand strobed by the brights of half a dozen vehicles, the waiting helicopter kicking up dust in a wide arc as its rotors thrummed steadily. Her gaze found Jennifer and for a moment the two women's eyes locked and Timika nodded.

That was all she needed to do for the Englishwoman to get the message: they'd reconnect, they'd find each other, and they'd make sure the men weren't tagged with some bogus murder charge. This wasn't over. They were just getting started.

ALAN
Secure Facility, Nevada

ALAN WAS STILL GROGGY FROM THE CRASH AND FROM whatever medication he'd been given to stabilize him, and he was pretty sure he had slept through most of the helicopter ride. Even if he had been awake, there would have been no way he could have gauged how far they'd traveled in the blacked-out helo. When they landed, he was immediately blindfolded.

He protested, proclaimed his innocence of Hatcher's murder, expressed his drug-fogged outrage that a man of his rank and service record should be treated like this by his own government, but he got no response at all. He was bundled into an open-topped vehicle, driven for a few minutes, then forced out. He was marched inside a cool, air-conditioned building that hummed with the white noise speakers he knew from Dreamland.

But it didn't feel like he was in Dreamland. He wasn't sure why he thought that. A smell, perhaps? It just felt different, and though he could merely have been taken to some part of the extensive facility he'd never visited before, he didn't think so.

He thought there were three men with him, possibly four. One of them left after they rode an elevator, which smelled of new, institutional carpet. The elevator was smooth. Alan estimated they descended at least five stories, and when they came to a stop, the sound echoed, as if he were in a cave or tunnel, though the surface he walked on was level and hard: concrete, almost certainly.

A dull whir rose in pitch and volume, wound down, and then they were getting onto some kind of train.

"We going to see Blofeld?" Alan quipped woozily.

No response. Maybe not the time for James Bond jokes.

They spent maybe five minutes on the monorail—or whatever it was—got off, walked for maybe three minutes, took two left turns, then waited as a door was unlocked and he was pushed inside. The door closed and his blind-fold was removed.

There were two guards on the door and a man in a suit sitting at a table with a battered book in front of him. He looked up and nodded Alan into the chair opposite him.

"You can't do this," Alan muttered, trying to sound defiant but conscious of the way his voice sounded ragged and woolly. He tried to sit up straight, but his body was sagging into a weary slouch in spite of his best efforts. His mind, too. He wanted to sleep for a week.

"Yes, Major Young," said the man at the desk. "We can."

He was small, balding, mid-forties, with watery blue eyes. Nondescript. A man you would pass on the street without noticing. A forgettable man, except that Alan had met him before.

"Agent Harvey Kenyon," said Alan. "We met on the plane from Kuwait."

The bald man smiled. "You have a good memory, Major," he said. "Though names are . . ."

He gestured vaguely with his hands: *unreliable*.

"I saw inside the sphere," Alan said. He felt a strange exhilaration that was overriding his natural caution. "I saw the pilot. You guys have been experimenting, or genetically engineering some kind of . . ." his voice tailed off. He couldn't find the words or the conviction. "Why are you so damned secretive about everything? Why don't we just tell the world what we have, what we can do? You don't even tell your own people. I work for you. I have clearance."

The small man sat back, smiling cryptically, as if he were both puzzled and amused.

"You think this is about clearance?" he said. "Not at all. Or not in the sense that you mean it."

"So why am I here?" Alan said, managing to dredge up a little defiance. "You know I didn't kill Hatcher."

The man whom he knew as Kenyon nodded thoughtfully, his eyes falling on the book on the table. It was bound with black leather or something like it, worn and cracked, and when he flipped it open, its pages were thin as tissue and marked with a slim gold ribbon.

"Tell me, Major," he said absently. "Are you religious?"

Alan blinked and tried to focus. Maybe he was already dreaming.

"Not really," he said at last. "Why? What does any of this have to do with religion?"

"Oh," said the bald man, looking up and smiling, a cat-like grin that did not reach his eyes. He pushed the book across the table to where Alan could read the two words on its spine. "Absolutely everything," said the man, tapping the book with his index finger. The lettering on its spine said *The Odyssey*, by Homer. "Though perhaps *myth* is a better term than *religion*. Less loaded. Major Young, did you ever wonder how the Apollo space program got its name?"

Alan blinked. "Apollo was the god of the sun, right?" he said.

"And crossed the sky daily in a glittering chariot," Kenyon agreed.

"So?"

"So let's consider the possibility that that chariot was more than metaphorical."

"Let me get this straight," said Alan. "You're saying that the craft we're flying were brought here by aliens which humans took to be the gods of ancient Greece, but they left and now we have their stuff?"

In response to Alan's contemptuous tone, Kenyon smiled but, for a moment so long it became uncomfortable he said nothing, just staring unblinkingly at Alan—that odd, knowing smile fixed on his nondescript face. At last he opened his mouth, but the next eight words came out so low that Alan had to strain to hear them.

"What makes you think that they ever left?"

TO BE CONTINUED . . .

AFTERWORD

There is no doubt fiction makes a better job of the truth.
—Doris Lessing

What you hold in your hands is a piece of a very large puzzle. It represents the first installment in one of the most ambitious projects ever undertaken in this or any other field. It is a project that involves science and history, politics and religion; fiction and non-fiction. All of these elements are woven together in an effort to express a singular truth. While they each can be appreciated in a stand-alone way—and who, after reading this thrilling novel, could disagree?—taken together they reveal an aspect of reality that is so astonishing that it only can be understood intuitively, as well as rationally.

It was Tom DeLonge who conceived of this revolutionary, multi-disciplinary approach that includes books, art, music, and film: all as individual facets of a single polished gemstone of revelation. Some truths—as Nobel Laureate (and science fiction author) Doris Lessing reminds us—can best be expressed in fiction, and this is what A. J. Hartley has accomplished, spectacularly, in this novel. What has been missing in most published accounts of the Phenomenon at the heart of human experience is the narration. There are many books on the subject that are vast accumulations of facts, dates, interviews, personal accounts, and declassified documents. They are necessary, but they cannot convey the whole truth. They cannot convey the emotional impact of the Experience which is, after all, its essential characteristic. That is because we have no vocabulary to define it, categorize it, measure it, box it in. All attempts at doing so swing wildly from the dry statistics of a government report to the wide-eyed fanaticism of mystical revelation. The only solution to this problem is a conscious, deliberate juxtaposition of fact and fiction to arrive at a truth that transcends both, a solution represented by what you have just read.

I won't say too much more about this project. Where's the fun in that? You will have to see it for yourself. Watch it unfold. Gradually, as you read both the fiction and the non-fiction, you will find the facts meshing with the narrative; you will see how the one influences the other and how they both reveal the warm secrets buried beneath the cold snow of official memoranda. Then the art, the music, and the film will expand on the theme and show it from many different angles. In this we are going back to the original form of story-telling, what the anthropologists and the archaeologists and the philosophers have told us is myth and fantasy—with their associated arts, music, and drama—but which we understand to be the honest efforts by honest people to leave an account of the miraculous and the numinous in the only terminology available to them. Oddly, we moderns have not done much better.

It is time we stopped thinking of the people of the past as ignorant, as superstitious, as stoned temple priests high on alkaloid fumes and druggie daydreams. They fought wars; they built monuments; they left behind their art and their literature and, yes, their science. Their math and their physics, astronomy and medicine, were populated by gods and demons, by angels and jinn, and yet they still were able to build the pyramids and the henges using this crazy calculus of consciousness and desire. We can learn from them. In fact, we must.

Evil people as well as good have attempted—since time immemorial—to exploit this knowledge, and you have read some of this here already. There *was* an Operation Paperclip. There *were* secret weapons under development at the slave labor labs of Nazi Germany. And there was more. Much more. The facts are as astonishing (and as entertaining!) as any fabrication, and we promise to tell all as this Project continues to unfold.

When you start to read the non-fiction version of these events—which represents my own contribution to this Project—you will remember aspects of this novel and you will begin to realize what we are doing, what an enormous undertaking this represents. You will also sense a challenge in these accumulated pages, a charge to confront this subject in a new way, an active way, an approach that combines scientific inquiry with artistic sensitivity such that it never has been contemplated before (at least, not since the Renaissance).

More than anything else, though, you will feel the passion and the excitement that we feel. It's contagious, to be sure. You will start to see what we see, maybe even feel what we feel, and you will never be the same.

—Peter Levenda, 2016

ABOUT THE AUTHORS

Tom DeLonge

is an award-winning American musician, producer, and director best known as the lead vocalist, guitarist, and songwriter for the platinum-selling rock bands Blink-182 and Angels & Airwaves. His home is San Diego, California, where he focuses on creating entertainment properties that cross music, books, and film with his company To The Stars... Check out his other multi-media projects at ToTheStars.Media.

▼   ▼   ▼

A.J. Hartley

is an international bestselling novelist whose work includes archaeological thrillers, the *Darwen Arkwright* children's series, the Will Hawthorne fantasy adventures, novels based on *Macbeth* and *Hamlet*, and two upcoming young adult series, *Steeplejack* and *Cathedrals of Glass*. He is also the Robinson Distinguished Professor of Shakespeare at UNC Charlotte. His website is www.ajhartley.net.